Void all the Way Down

- The Sliding Void Omnibus -

by Stephen Hunt

Void all the Way Down

First published in 2015 by Green Nebula Press. This book is a compilation edition of three previously published novellas: Sliding Void; Transference Station; Red Sun Bleeding. Together, they compose the first three books of the Sliding Void series.

Typeset and designed by Green Nebula Press. The right of Stephen Hunt to be identified as the author of this work has been asserted by him in accordance with the Copyright, Designs and Patents Act 1988.

ISBN-13: 978-1508922193
ISBN-10: 1508922195

Cover art by Luca Oleastri

www.StephenHunt.net

Twitter: @s_hunt_author
www.facebook.com/SciFi.Fantasy

First Edition

Printed in the U S A & United Kingdom

There once was a man up on high
Who stepped off a lunar cliff,
And all the way down he complained
That gravity sure is a bitch!

-       *Ancient spacer's shanty (anon).*

Also by Stephen Hunt

THE FAR-CALLED SERIES
(Gollancz)

In Dark Service
Foul Tide's Turning

THE JACKELIAN SERIES
(HarperCollins Voyager in the UK/Macmillan Tor in the USA)

The Court of the Air
The Kingdom Beyond the Waves
Rise of the Iron Moon
Secrets of the Fire Sea
Jack Cloudie
From the Deep of the Dark

THE AGATHA WITCHLEY MYSTERIES

In the Company of Ghosts
The Plato Club
Secrets of the Moon

STANDALONE BOOKS

Six Against the Stars
For the Crown and the Dragon
The Fortress in the Frost

-1-

Planet of the balls

That was the problem with aliens, mused Lana. They were so damn *alien*. Not all of them, of course. The one sitting to her left, Skrat, looked like a man-sized lizard, but he might as well have been human compared to the two things swinging opposite them. The negotiators from the world Lana's ship was currently orbiting were a series of mushy orange spheres joined together by flesh-coloured webbing. No eyes, no mouth, no ears she could see – just two ape-sized arms they could walk on or use to swing across the chamber from the various cables dangling from the ceiling. She didn't know where to look, when a back was as good as a front. Their minds were so messed-up and off-the-scale, that Lana's attempts at trying to win a cargo for the return leg of her journey were being answered by a stream-of-consciousness ramble from the translation stick linked into her ship's computer. The chatter might as well be dub poetry rather than a serious attempt at negotiation for all that she understood it.

Lana flicked off the translation stick for a second and leant across to Skrat. 'I don't know what they're saying, I don't know the name of this world, I don't know what was inside the sealed containers we've offloaded, and I don't know what the heck we're still doing docked to their so-called trading station.'

'Patience,' whispered Skrat. 'There is a deal to be done here, old girl, I can feel it.'

Lana sighed. Given how shattered Skrat's life had been before she had pulled him out of that scummy televised corporate gladiator pit, he sure was an optimist. She gazed across at the two delivery agents, one of them whirling about maniacally on the end of a rope, making dolphin-like clicking noises by pulsing its upper sphere in and out while simultaneously rapping like a drum. The thing's friend was leaping up and down on one arm/ leg (take your pick), and scratching the other's underside. *Is that grooming? Kissing? Indicating their thanks for the ship's delivery; on time and on schedule?*

Lana flicked the translation stick back on, a couple of seconds for the wireless connection to the linguistic computer on board the *Gravity Rose* to pick up speed, and then the speaker at the top of her stick started stuttering: 'Joy comes from chance. Chance is all. Trade is chance. I am horny. I am dying. I am exclusive and taking a minute.'

'To the solar winds with this,' muttered Lana. She stood up and bowed ironically towards the two swinging collections of balls. 'And I am so out of here. Take your minute and add a couple of decades before my ship comes within ten parsecs of your world again.'

The full effect of Lana's outburst was slightly ruined by the bulky environment suit she wore to protect herself from the green gas that the balls had swirling around the visitor's chamber as atmosphere. But what the hell, there had to be some privileges to being skipper of your own vessel.

Skrat was fast behind her, swishing his powerful tail in

annoyance, the visor of his suit's helmet misting up as he spat out his words. 'That went well. Another hour, Lana, and we could have negotiated a really exceptional cargo to ship out-system. I'd guarantee it.'

Right now Lana was glad the environment suit covered Skrat. Out of the suit-skin he looked like a bipedal dragon – all shining green scales, solid muscles, sharp white teeth, a pair of eyes like burning coals floating on a chlorophyll-choked millpond – and nobody in their right mind wanted a humanoid dragon annoyed with them. In fact, dragon was one of the politer nicknames for Skrat's race among humanity. Much like dragons, their kind was up for a fight if push came to shove, but they loved trading far more. His species would much rather get one over you in a negotiation than stick a dagger in your back.

'What, with Mister I Am Dying and I Am Horny? Shizzle, Skrat. You were going to end up selling us into their local brothel is what you were going to do.'

'System crash,' squawked the translation stick, still active in her hand after she'd snatched it off the table. 'Core rebooting. Fatal agglutinative group error.'

'Ha,' said Skrat, his magnetised boots cracking down the airlock tunnel linking the orbital station to their ship. The station corridors were low for Lana's six-foot frame. Skrat was three inches taller and he had to stoop even more than she did as he strolled quickly after her. 'I knew it. Language errors. We definitely should have given the dashed computer longer to adjust to their dialect.'

Lana tapped the side of her helmet. 'It's not their language, it's what's up here that counts. You're aiming to service a planet's demand-side needs, you got to understand how the locals think. What they got that anybody wants? Ass-scratching sticks? I told you when we took on the cargo, this would be a one-way job. Sealed containers always are.'

'And to prove you're right, we're shipping out of here with an empty hold,' sighed Skrat.

'Empty hold on *my* ship,' Lana reminded him.

They reached the ship's airlock, and she leaned forward to let the small camera take her retina print. Scoring a match, the outer door hissed up into the hull. Polter was just visible on the other side of the airlock, eyestalks peering up through the inner door's armoured glass. Next to their navigator stood Zeno, the ship's android first mate. Polter's fussy voice echoed through the little chamber as they stepped inside and closed off the lock. 'Are we blessed with a return cargo?'

'I believe you will need to address that question to the captain,' sighed Skrat.

'Sorry to say, but God has taken the day off,' said Lana. 'We'll be running light until we hit the next system.'

'Perhaps not,' came Polter's reply. 'There have been developments, oh yes.'

Developments? That didn't sound good to Lana. She was in charge of developments. Anyone else started *developing* shizzle and you just knew that trouble was going to come bouncing close behind. Lana's helmet yanked off with a hiss of escaping air under pressure, and she flicked her mane of long blonde hair back as she reached for an Alice band to secure it, pushing her fingers through the curls at the edges. People said the hair made her look cherubic. Unfortunately, the illusion only lasted as long as it took Lana to open her mouth. 'I didn't even want to leave the *Rose* to talk to the locals on the station. You heard me say that. I'm sure you did.'

'You're far too over-cautious.' Skrat racked the large pistol that had been strapped to his leg, and Lana followed suit. Her rail pistol had been dialled up to sixteen, maximum power, where one of the ball bearings sitting in its magazine could be accelerated to the kind of air-cracking speeds capable of causing grenade-level explosions. Perhaps that was caution, too. Nothing won a fight like going kinetic on someone's ass first.

'One of us has got to be thinking about limiting our losses,' said Lana. *Sure as hell ain't gonna be you, Skrat.*

The glass of the airlock's inner door automatically mirrored as the lock's bacterial decontamination routine kicked in. Lana sucked in her cheeks. She hated her own reflection. Had she inherited those classically beautiful Slavic-Nordic look from her parents? Hell if she knew. *If I ever get to meet them, I might ask.* She looked tired, her green eyes weary. She was only in her late forties, and with anti-ageing treatments she looked more like twenty-five. How could she look so tired? When she smiled, the grin filled her face, one of her few endearing features, but she hadn't felt like smiling for a while now. The inner lock cycled open and Polter danced excitedly on six legs, the pupils on the crab-like navigator's eyestalks wide and excited. She glanced towards her android crewmember. Zeno just shrugged. For all his artificial golden skin and wire-headed Afro, he could do innocent just fine. The look was one she recognized. *Don't blame me.*

Lana raised a hand and adjusted her green ship overalls. 'I only left you two jokers in charge for a few hours. Polter, please tell me you haven't donated the ship as spare parts to the local orphans' fund?'

'Sarcasm is not among your better virtues, revered skipper,' observed Polter.

'What's going on?' asked Lana. 'I can see that you're busting to tell me how the will of the Lord has landed something shiny-new in our laps.'

'A ship,' said Polter. 'Inbound. Oh yes, not local traffic. A courier vessel, I should say.'

Lana groaned. 'Looking for us?'

'And asking for permission to dock ship-to-ship. I told them that only the blessed Captain Lana Fiveworlds can give permission for that, and she is presently engaged.'

Lana weighed the options. It was hideously expensive to send a single ship out with a message for a trader, even when you had a flight plan logged and a fair idea where the recipient might be. Not when the alternative was tossing a free e-mail into the data sphere and waiting for it to propagate into the path of its recipient. The *Gravity Rose* would dock and sync her computer core next time she hit somewhere civilised. A courier vessel meant the message was important and covert enough that its sender didn't want to risk the note being hacked rolling about out in the wild. Messages like that, you might be better off ignoring.

'It is a contract offer,' said Polter. 'I can feel it in my soul. Our holds are empty and the Holy of Holies wills the space filled.'

'Yeah, and maybe it's contract law enforcement,' said Zeno. 'How many bills did we leave unpaid at the last planet?'

Lana rubbed her pale freckled nose. 'If it's chasing the docking fees we skipped jumping to this hole, I'll pay that guy sitting out there solely for persistence.'

The four of them headed for the bridge, taking the ship's internal Capsule and Transportation System. The CATS capsule jolted and shuddered, sections of Lana's four thousand foot-long ship squealing in and out of view as they rode a clear bullet down her transparent lateral tube. At times the capsule shot over the ship's grey dust-pitted hull, before spiralling down, blasting through the vessel's interior chambers – passing along the jungle of hydroponics vaults that gave the ship her atmosphere and food, furnishing crew and passengers with the space they needed to stop going stir-crazy on extended flights. By law, all starships needed such chambers. If her hyperspace engines ever failed, they would need to slide to the nearest inhabitable world generation-ship style on her anti-matter thrusters. Although, given Lana's current motley crew, she'd hate to think what her descendants would end up looking like. As pitted as her vessel's hull was, as worn by all the universe's dust that had never quite made it into a planet, Lana loved her ship with the ferociousness of a tigress protecting her cubs. Not because the *Gravity Rose* was beautiful: she could never be accused of that – the profile of an aircraft carrier taken into space. An eclectic collection of cargo units, hyperspace vanes, passenger cabins, life support modules, in-system antimatter drive chambers, solar panels, self-healing armour, artificial gravity systems, and freight holds from a dozen ship yards and manufacturers welded together with hope, optimism and whatever spare currency Lana and her predecessors had to throw at her. No, not because the *Gravity*

Rose was lovely, but because the ship was Lana's home. And because what passed for the vessel's dysfunctional crew also passed for her family. Lana stretched out her legs and pushed long leather boots out towards the opposite wall of the capsule, hearing the bone-crack of every one of her years. *It's not age, honey; it's the intermittent low gravity. Yeah, you keep on telling yourself that.* The ship looked her age, too. The *Gravity Rose* needed an overhaul soon to pass authority checks and retain her flightworthy status. Without that, no planet worth a damn was going to allow Fiveworlds Shipping in to trade. Lana could hear the dead voice of bureaucracy whining inside her skull. *'What if your jump engines lock and you collide with our world? You want us to shoot you down, you want that?'*

After Lana got to the bridge she punched up comms and made an offer to take the message point-to-point on a tight laser line, but the courier refused, which kind of made sense. If you were paranoid enough not to risk your precious message getting hacked in the wild, you weren't going to chance someone having a pebble-sized probe hanging tight off a hull and trying to intercept your laser communications.

The courier ship was a pert matt-black needle floating void, not much more than a pilot cabin and life support system forward of her jump drive and the pion reaction thrusters she used to kick some tidy little propulsion out. With a hull-to-engine ratio tricked out like that she could tear a strip through this lonely corner of space. Faster than the *Gravity Rose*, that was for sure, even with the *Rose* running empty. Speed being of the essence, and all, Lana opened the doors to the *Gravity Rose*'s starboard-side hold and the courier couldn't have set her down more sweetly if

Lana's vessel had been a navy carrier, three little landing skids folding out of the dart. She noted from the hold's cameras that the pilot was another kaggen, like Polter. A five foot-high sentient crab-shaped mass of religious worry. Female kaggens were twice the size of the race's males, so this one was a lad, just like their navigator.

Lana instructed the courier to come to the bridge, skipper's privilege, rather than doing a meet-and-greet in their massive empty hold. There were traditions to be observed, and it never hurt to underline the fact that the courier's sense of urgency wasn't her problem. Not yet, anyway. Not until it started putting bacon on her table, as well as the courier's. A few minutes later the messenger scuttled into the bridge, his two large vestigial claws folded backward along his top-shell to indicate he came in peace and with God. *Like the little pacifists come in any other flavour.* He signed a private greeting to Polter, and kept on with a kag blessing even as he began talking to Lana, a parrot-like beak on the soft fleshy face underneath his carapace warbling in satisfaction at having tracked down his quarry. His accent was a lot thicker than Polter's. 'I have the honour of addressing Captain Lana Fiveworlds, proprietor of Fiveworlds Shipping, registered out of the Protocol world of Nueva Valencia, The Edge?'

'That'll be me, and I reckon you've got my transponder codes, flight plan and license, to prove it, shorty,' said Lana.

The courier dipped respectfully on four of his six legs. 'I am Ralt Raltish of—'

'Spare me your diocese and family tree stretching back to the fortieth generation. This message, it's only for yours truly or...?' Lana indicated her crew standing on the bridge.

'Not specified. Do you trust your crew?'

'You slide void any other way out here and you ain't going to live long enough to regret it,' said Lana. 'Staying alive is a team game. Least ways, it is if you are not flying some tricked-out comet firing faster than photons. That would be that needle of yours sitting in my hangar, shorty.'

'Then I may pass you my message,' said the courier. 'It is from my most majestic client Rex Matobo, blessings be upon him.'

'Shizzle,' Lana cursed under her breath. Rex. 'I just knew that this was going to be trouble. And the message?'

'He says, "I would appreciate it if you came quickly".'

Lana shook her head in disbelief. 'That's it?'

'I have the co-ordinates of my client's world of origin, with instructions to divulge these to you.'

'You feel like divulging how much business you've been doing with Rex?'

The courier raised one of his two manipulator hands and wiggled a bony finger in a cursory way, the kaggen equivalent of a shrug. 'He is a new client, blessings be upon him. The world of origin is not much visited. In fact, it's not even recognized by the Protocol.'

'I'll just bet it isn't. What's this world called, shorty?'

'Hesperus is its common name,' said the courier. 'Standard cartography reference Hes-10294384b is the planet's formal title.'

She nodded to Zeno, and the android pulled the details from the bridge computer. 'So, Zeno, this Hesperus look like anywhere we want to be travelling to?'

'Doesn't appear too dangerous on the face of it, skipper,' said

Zeno. 'A little light on details here, though, on the wiki. It's a failed colony world. Lost their technological base in an ice age and they've been living back in the dark ages for centuries. You might catch dysentery on Hesperus, but nobody's going to be shooting missiles at us down there. They won't even know what a gun is, let alone a starship.'

'Most curious. What is this old friend of yours doing in such an unconducive locale?' Skrat asked Lana.

'No damn good,' said Lana, 'if I know him.'

'You are going to world?' asked the courier. 'I have been paid to return a negative reply, if you choose not to heed my client's message.'

'Give me a minute to think on it,' said Lana.

'This Rex Matobo fellow is a human?' Skrat asked. 'I've never heard of the chap?'

'Before your time,' said Lana. 'The rest of the crew will remember him.' *But not fondly, I reckon.* 'How about it, Zeno? You want to see Rex again?'

Zeno tapped his artificial skin. 'Hell, it's not my nano-mechanical backside that's going to be catching dysentery.'

Lana groaned inside as she realized how few choices she had left in front of her, now. *You can't complain, girl. That's why you're still flying free as an independent. If it's civilised living you're after, sell out to one of the corporate houses and work yourself some of those sophisticated routes inside the Triple Alliance's void.*

'Are we going, revered skipper?' asked Polter, eager to see if his premonition about receiving work was about to be rewarded.

'Only if this human chap has money,' insisted Skrat.

'Oh, he'll have money,' said Lana. *The main problem is, most of it won't be his.*

Worst thing was, she owed Rex Matobo a favor. Not the kind you got to skip by lightly, either. Stepping aside, Lana sighed and indicated her ship's hulking navigation board for the benefit of the courier. 'Load up the damn jump co-ordinates, shorty; then you can light out of here. Polter, crunch the numbers for a hyperspace translation, we've got us a little business to attend to.'

She glanced towards a wide view of the no-account world fixed on the front of the bridge, the ball creatures' planet, its brown gas-wrapped orb barely visible beyond the pitted expanse of the orbital station they had just left. *And just once, don't let it be the bad kind. Just this damn once.*

- 2 -
World of winter, world of war

Calder Durk felt them coming through the blizzard after him, six shield-warriors maybe seven. The big, heavy muscled brutes from Baron Halvard's bodyguard. They were fresh and he was exhausted. Even with the weight of his pursuers' two-handed swords, axes, shields and crossbows, and Calder carrying only the single hunting dagger he'd escaped with, the men were going to overtake him soon. His manservant, Noak, was ruddy faced and breathing hard under his bear furs, but showed every sign of being more spry than Calder, despite being twice his young master's age. Fear could do that to a man. Calder wasn't afraid; he was looking forward to the slaying. He was looking forward to carving up Halvard's boys and leaving the treacherous scum frozen in the snow for the baron to find. *A man has to die some time, right? Might as well be out here.*

Noak recognized the frown crossing Calder's furrowed brow. Knew that his master's supernatural hunting sense was alive and kicking. 'How many behind us now, my prince?'

'Six, I think. Armed for the fight and that's the truth of it.'

'Won't be much of a fight.'

Calder scrambled up a bank of snow, ignoring the aching pain in his legs, spurred on by adrenaline and the desire to survive.

'You with a dagger and me with nothing but spit,' added the manservant, lest the young prince think that he was considering fleeing and abandoning his charge. Of course, with ninety of their friends and crew lying poisoned across the tables of their so-called host's great-hall back in the castle, doing a runner was probably the sanest course for the servant right now. *But you're too loyal, aren't you. And you want to live to say 'I told you so', you wretch.*

'How far are we from the Frozen Sea, do you think?' Calder asked Noak.

The manservant rubbed the silvery beard of his chin, taking a second to glance behind them. Nothing but endless forests waist-deep in snow, every tree as tough as a granite cliff. *The sea has to be less than ten miles ahead, doesn't it?*

'Near enough, my prince,' said Noak. 'But there are no ports hereabouts. What are the chances of us spotting and flagging down a passing ice schooner out on the flows?' It was a purely rhetorical question.

'Somewhere between hell and none,' sighed Calder. It wasn't fair, it really wasn't. Surviving the war, surviving the long journey back home. All that way, all that blood, only to die here, so close to... *Glimpsing Sibylla's immaculate naked body again*, a voice within him whispered. He shut that down fast. Survive first, kisses with princess later.

Over the rise and down below lay a structure, something more than the endless snow and forest that they had passed so far during their desperate escape. A round stonehouse alongside an oil derrick, two blinded slaves walking the circle in chains and driving the oil well's pumping-beam up and down. The hut's thatched roof wouldn't stand against crossbow bolts, but the flint stone walls would serve as cover enough against Baron Halvard's assassins. No windows, of course. Anyone rich enough to put glass panes in their walls wouldn't be milking the ground so far from town or village. Whoever owned that hut was probably off fishing at an ice-hole on the river that they had passed a mile back. The hut's chimneystack was cold and smokeless, and the one thing you knew about a driller, they always had enough oil spare to light a fire.

Calder brushed black tufts of hair out of his snow-tanned face and pointed to the stone hut. 'There's our luck. We run down and past, then walk our own footprints back to the hut and shelter inside. When the baron's shield-warriors go past, we take them in the rear.' *Maybe if we're lucky, there will be some clay pots inside we can fill with oil. Something more than harsh words to toss at our executioners . . . oil grenades.* The two of them, young prince and manservant, stumbled down the rise towards the hut.

'I think you should use it, my prince.'

'Use what?'

'The amulet.'

Calder's hand snaked to the crystal hanging from the chain beneath his fur-covered tunic. 'Damned if I will.'

'You were given it to call for help in time of need, my prince. If this is not such a time, then will it not do until a darker hour deepens?'

'You think so?' Calder spat. 'It was that useless warlock, that dirty singer of spells, that mud-brain of mud-brains, who happily waved our fleet off when we departed in search of glory. If thousands of our men stretched out as pale corpses in front of the walls of Narvalo really were *his* plan, then it's true glory we have brought back in his name. You think old allies like the baron

STEPHEN HUNT

would have switched sides to the Narvalaks if we'd had the good sense to send that filthy sorcerer off with a flea in his ear? Why, the same scum chasing us would be dragging our sleds across the border towards home and raising a song in our honour!'

The prince's manservant didn't appear to agree with the assessment. 'The wizard is powerful.'

'He's mortal! His plans can be snapped as easily as the skis on an ice schooner. If it were otherwise, the shaking hand of a Narvalak priest would be crowning me King of the World now while you would be drinking your gourd off in some sacked Narvalo tavern.'

They reached the hut. Calder was about to threaten the two slaves outside with murder unless they held their silence, but then he noticed the reason the two oil-pushers were still so intent on the progress of the wooden wheel they were chained to. Their cheeks were hollow from a time long ago when their tongues had been cut out. *Blinded as well. Tough luck for them.* The peasants should have put up more of a struggle when the baron's warriors arrived at whatever dirt-hole of a village these two jokers had been living in. *There's a lot of darkness in the winter.* That had been one of Calder's father's favourite sayings, before he had fallen off a horse with a crossbow bolt through his left eye.

Calder glanced over to where Noak stood examining a gear reducer on the oil well. *What's he trying to do?* Calder scooped up a snowball and threw it at the manservant's back. 'You found a crossbow hidden behind the tubing? Come on, we've got to run past the hut and double back before the baron's swords turn up.'

Calder and his manservant followed the plan. Wading through the snow past the driller's hut a good distance, then

carefully walking back over their footprints in the snow towards the hut. There wasn't a lock on the driller's door, but it could be bolted from inside. Just light planking on the entrance, not up to much. Good for keeping out wolves and bears for long enough to lift a crossbow off the empty hook on the wall. Calder could have kicked in the door himself, if he wanted to advertise their presence inside to the assassins. The prince had to hope that two of them, as good as weaponless against a company of shield-warriors, was a plan so crazy that the element of surprise was the one thing they would be armed with.

'Check the room,' whispered Calder Durk. 'See if there's anything here.' Not that there was going to be. A fireplace with a roasting spit. Some straw to sleep on, a few blankets in the corner of the sunken floor. Spare netting and line hanging on the wall to fish the river. Anything metal or sharp had gone to the river along with the baron's driller living here.

Calder kept a wary eye on the top of the rise, peering through the planks of the wooden door. The two slaves were still working the noisy, creaking wheel, the oil derrick nodding back and forth in time to their labours. Black liquid dripped out into a large wooden barrel from a pipe rammed into the down-hole. *Doesn't seem much coming out of there. Maybe the well's nearly tapped out?* Calder hadn't spotted sled tracks in the snow, so that meant the driller who lived here had left on foot. Too poor to keep his own dogs and pay for sled and harness. There was a wooden measuring stick leaning against the barrel, half-covered in tar. So, the driller had dipped it into the barrel to take a measure of its contents, just to see if his pair of slaves slacked off while he was away catching fish for their dinner. Not a trusting man. His slaves

might be blind and mute, but Calder suspected they'd feel the crack of the whip well enough if they stopped turning the well's crank.

Noak rifled through the scant possessions behind them. 'No weapons.'

'Any clay pots, something we could fill with oil to burn them when they pass by?'

Noak lifted up a solitary metal frying pan. 'I can smack them with this.'

Calder laughed, despite their predicament. 'You really are an old woman, now.'

'Just rub the amulet, my prince, please,' pleaded Noak. 'Before Halvard's killers turn up and see the light of sorcery under our roof.'

Well, what the hell. In for a lump of copper, in for a lump of gold. Calder lifted the amulet out of his shirt, and resting his hand on its diamond surface, chanted the incantation the sorcerer had made him memorise. It took a second for an evil whining noise to fill the silence. A ghostly face appeared before them, hovering in the centre of the hut, and Calder tried unsuccessfully to keep the shivers from freezing his spine. Off to the side of the hut, Noak traced the sign of the Fire Goddess across his chest. Something used to ward off demons. The apparition grinned. Skin as black as night on his face – it didn't matter how much snow-glare you took, no skin should get that tanned – his accent exotic and strange, a voice all-too knowing and cock-sure. Hair curled like a woman's. *Smug too.* How could the sorcerer still appear so bloody smug after he had dispatched the manhood of an entire

nation to its untimely end?

'I am betrayed,' said Calder. 'Baron Halvard burnt my schooner at her moorings and murdered my crew with poison at his own table. He has broken the compact and sold us out to the enemy for my weight in silver. That was the price of his honour.'

'Ah, Prince Calder, last of the House of Durk,' smirked the sorcerer. 'Reduced circumstances, then?'

Calder had to stop himself shouting at the sorcerer. The assassins would be close enough to hear them in a minute. 'I followed *your* plans, and I have been reduced in all things. Four armies lie dead in front of the walls of Narvalo. My crew and I have spent a year in foreign parts voyaging home, fighting creatures and monsters and enemies so sodding strange they would freeze the veins of lesser men. Now all I have been left is this dagger, Noak here, and my honour.'

'Well,' said the sorcerer. 'Top tip for next time, your highness. You would have done better keeping your armada of schooners intact and losing your dagger, rather than vice-versa.'

'You dog,' cursed Calder. 'I built the giant wooden wolf like you instructed, left it outside their walls. You know what the enemy did to it? They dragged it onto the sea-flows, set barrels of oil alight in a circle around it, melted the ice and drowned every man hiding inside.'

'Yeah, heard about that one,' said the sorcerer. 'Hey-ho. You got to give it to their priests. Stupid, they aren't.'

'This is your doing!'

'Kid, I warned you. There were other ways of getting you crowned high king that were open to us. The subtle kind: bribery, corruption, backroom shenanigans. Wizards like me, that's where

we do our best work. But oh no, you couldn't keep it in your pants. You wanted the big dynastic marriage to Sibylla. Well, guess what, your highness, getting even against her ancestral enemies was the price for that sweet booty.'

'You dare to talk about Sibylla like that...'

'I hate to burst your bubble, boy, but your sweet girl is lining herself up a selection of nice rich Narvalak noblemen to seal her future with.'

'Liar! They are blood enemies. Her council would never accept such a marriage.'

'Don't have lot of choice anymore. Sibylla owned one of the four armies that got iced last year, if you forgive the pun, remember? Oh, and the girl's used the engagement ties between your country and hers to declare your ass dead while annexing your lands. Not too sloppy. Guess there's more of her mother in her blood than I gave her credit for. That's my way of saying she had me fooled too, not that it's much consolation to you right now.'

For a second, Calder was almost mute with fury. 'You oath-breaker, you lying, false—'

'I'm sending you my apologies, my prince,' shrugged the sorcerer. 'Along with something a little more substantive. Sure as shizzle didn't think things were going to pan out this badly.' One of the eyes in the ghostly dark apparition winked at Calder. 'Compared to you mayflies, I'm almost immortal. Think a man would have learned by now, right?'

'My prince,' hissed Noak, his eye pressed to a gap in the thatch. 'Halvard's people are outside.'

The evil witch-light winked out inside the hut, leaving Calder

and his manservant alone again. His honour wasn't armour; Noak wasn't up to much in a brawl, so that just left the hunting dagger. Calder drew it out, keeping the bone handle tight against his sweaty palm. A hand's length of steel, against what? Seven armoured men coming down the slope, large as trolls, swords sharp enough to slice ironwood. Killers all, rattling with blades and crossbow bolt bandoleers. Faces hidden beneath steel wolf masks riveted under their horned helms. *As if they need to look any more fearsome given the size of them.*

Noak still clutched the iron pan. It was just heavy enough to brain a man, if you got lucky. 'My prince,' he whispered. 'If I'm favoured enough to be allowed to follow you into the Halls of the Twice-risen, will you grant me a boon?'

Calder nodded.

'Pension me out of this job.'

'Follow me out of this hut, and you'll have earnt it.'

Calder's plan started as he'd foreseen. Outside, the seven brutes piled down the slope and passed the oil derrick and the driller's hut, intent on following the false trial of footprints in the snow left by Calder and his manservant. They didn't bother checking the hut, and why would they? Nobody in their right mind was going to take on a company of shield-warriors. Was it Calder's imagination, or were the two slaves outside walking the circle a lot slower now? He set that thought aside. He didn't have time to be distracted by their silent toil. The hunters had kept their crossbows strapped and dangling from their armour. So, they weren't about to shoot Calder down as he fled. This suggested that his treacherous ex-ally, Baron Halvard, had expressed a desire to have the notorious Prince Calder taken alive. Not out of any sense of mercy, but so that the dog of baron would have something more than a corpse to hand over to the enemy. A bad memory sprang forth. Outside the walls of Narvalo, the priests threatening Calder that unless he abandoned the siege forthwith, they were going to give him a criminal's death tied to a stake, personally dipping him in tar and lighting the match. Yes, a living prince would be worth quite a lot to the Narvalaks. It wouldn't matter if there were a blizzard pummelling their great fortress city, Calder could foresee standing room only in the large square outside their high temple.

Calder timed it just right, springing the door open a second after the hut fell out of sight of the fighters. Much to Calder's surprise, Noak came sprinting right behind him, seemingly as eager as Calder to take the shield-warriors in the rear. Well, if the fighters planned on taking Calder alive to burn at the stake, Noak's one chance of surviving was that the seven thugs would seize the manservant for the local slave market. On the baron's lands, that would probably mean Noak ending up blind and tongueless as the third cog on a driller's well. Not really living at all. Even as Calder closed the gap on the warriors, the snow muffling his boots, it was hard to know where to plunge his dagger. Somewhere between the round iron shield and the chainmail? Try to pierce the leather neck-guard hanging down from the back of the horned helmet? Back of the thighs? One up the ass?

His problem was solved when Noak brained one of them from behind and the remaining heroes suddenly became aware that maybe they should've checked the driller's hut behind them after all. With one of their number collapsed forward, pole-axed by a first-rate head trauma. Calder shoved his blade into the exposed neck of the shield-warrior who'd whirled around to face him. The giant went down gurgling behind the metal facemask, no doubt a look of surprise on his face to match Calder's shocked realisation that the shield-warrior had taken his dagger with him. Showing a little more foresight than his master, Noak tried to pull a loaded crossbow off his victim, right up until the second when one of the assassins shoulder-charged the manservant and sent him flying sideways.

Calder didn't have the luxury of retrieving a weapon from his victim, as four of the baron's bulls jumped over their comrade's corpse and kept on coming at him. He back-pedalled, turned and ran, followed by the killers' roars of fury. The young prince didn't have their armour to slow him down. But then, he wasn't running with leg muscles the circumference of a tree trunk and pursuing hungry unarmed prey, either. It took a lot to sweat in weather as cold as this, but Calder managed it, reaching the shadow of the creaking oil derrick a couple of steps ahead of his pursuers. He swivelled around desperately. To one side the two slaves were still blindly pushing the rotation wheel. He lunged for the wooden measuring stick half-covered in tar and held it up, a blunt useless spear against the five giants closing in on him. They still hadn't drawn their crossbows, leaving Calder to face a thicket of sword points and axe heads pointed in his direction.

'Come on, lads. You can let me go. I'll make it worth your while. Just see me back to my side of the border and there'll be more silver in it for you than you'll earn in a lifetime of humping for the baron.'

'Careful, your highness,' one of them laughed, breathing hard, 'you strike me with that pole and you're going to leave an oily scratch on my tunic.'

'Do the smart thing,' pleaded Calder.

'You think that free you're good for more than a farthing back home?' sneered one of the men. 'Only way your hide is worth anything is the baron's blood price on you. We toss you across the border, the only people getting rich are the soldiers serving in what used to be your army. Except it isn't anymore, is it? Heard it belongs to your bitch now, except she ain't even that, is she?'

Calder waved the measuring stick menacingly, but it only made the shield-warriors laugh harder. 'You don't get to talk about Sibylla like that. She's a highborn and you're lowly pack rats not fit to stand sentry on her door.'

'Are you really going to make us work for this?' growled one of the shield-warriors, shifting the axe he held between his hands. 'Baron wants you back for the fire, but nobody said anything about you needing to have your wedding tackle attached when we hand you over.'

'Work for this?' Calder glanced back to where Noak lay prone in the snowdrift, his ribs being kicked by the same shield-warrior that had shouldered him down. 'If it's a blade or kindling that's on offer, you braves better practice your sales pitch.'

A low hissing noise sounded behind Calder. *What the hell's that?* One of the warriors made to move forward, but his colleague halted him. 'Stomped, not sliced. He's got to walk back on his own feet. I'll be cursed if I'm carrying him all the way to the castle.'

The hissing was louder now and it suddenly occurred to Calder what else sounded like an ice snake homing in on a man's heat. He hurled the oil-measuring pole forward like a javelin, glancing off the metal mask of the shield-warrior in front of him. The distraction only lasted a second, but it was long enough for him to turn and start running up the slope without one of the shield-warriors cutting out his hamstrings with their blade. Calder had put maybe five feet behind him when the oil well exploded. That was what Calder's canny old retainer had been doing when the prince had snowballed his back. Shutting off the valve to the well. But the driller's slaves hadn't known. They had still been walking their circle, slower and slower, building up pressure. Pieces of machinery scythed out, cutting down half of the baron's killers, the derrick replaced by a fountaining black gusher spewing oil over the virgin snow. Incredibly, the two blind slaves had escaped the explosion. They were still walking the circle, except their walk was now a sprint, the well's wooden beam unattached from its pumping mechanism. Two of the shield-warriors came to their feet, distinctly unamused by the devastation wrought on their friends. Calder kept scrambling up the slope, but a crossbow bolt took him in the back of the left leg, a stream of intense pain as he collapsed down to the snow, screaming.

'Baron's going to be disappointed,' yelled one of the shield-warriors, pulling back the lever on his crossbow. 'But we don't need his blood money that much.'

Not as disappointed as me.

The giant's comrade yelled up the slope as he ploughed through the snow. 'Reckon we're going to have to tar and light you up here, boy, now that you've struck black gold.'

Calder moaned, unable to crawl further. He stared up at the pale silver sky, pregnant with snow clouds. Far above, a pair of black dots circled. Crows from the Halls of the Twice-born, sent to seize his soul in their claws, to carry a dying prince back to his ancestors? Calder clutched at his burning, useless leg, trying to staunch the blood pumping out across the cold hillside. The blood was his oil. Pumping, pumping. Then the nearest black dot spat out a bolt of thunder and it slapped into the slope, exploding with a hundred times the power of a trebuchet, rock and frozen dirt showering down across his head. Another spit from the crow, then another, in quick succession, Calder's ears hardly heard the thunderclaps through the smoke and fury. Breaking through the cloud of vaporised stone and steaming snow, the distant dot emerged. Not a crow, but a flying black monster with two wheels captured spinning inside its body, dragon's breath hazing furiously out of its rear.

Calder shouted up at the flying monster, but his ears rang deaf and the words only sounded in his mind. 'Are you the Hall's crow, are you the—?'

A twin of the ebony-coloured beast emerged out of the cloud of carnage, Noak's prone body clutched by six insect legs, putting the creature's monstrous size into true perspective. *Hell's teeth, it's going to feed on him!* These monsters were bigger than any insect Calder had ever seen, even out in the hell-haunted wastes where he'd ventured with his crew and schooner. A decapitated arm still clutched a great sword less than a foot from Calder in the snow. Calder rolled over to the limb, prizing open the cold pale fingers, stealing the sword and thrusting the blade up uncertainly towards the creatures. 'Come on, you great ugly dung beetles. I've fought armies and killers. I've battled creatures out on the sea flows that make you look like lantern flies. I am holding your fate in my hand.'

Hovering almost soundlessly, the closest flying beast opened a red eye, painting Calder's chest with a warm red cross. 'The evil eye, is it?' He puckered a kiss up towards the monster. 'Come on, you bloody demon, you're boring me to death down here.'

It's kissed him back, the sharp nick of a something flying through the air almost too fast to follow and slapping into his chest. He looked down dumbly at the tiny needled tooth embedded in his tunic. He laughed. Calder had taken worse sled splinter scratches on his hands. Then the young prince experienced the novelty of ninety thousand volts of electricity coursing through his muscles. After that, Calder didn't feel much at all.

***

It came as a considerable surprise to Calder that he was actually able to open his eyes. Every muscle in his body felt as though he had been expertly filleted, dragged out of his flesh, and run through a mangle before being carelessly shoved back inside his carcass. Groaning and trying to hold down the vomit inside his gut, he opened his eyes. *I might have known.* Standing in front of his cot with arms on both hips, studying Calder's agony, was that useless wizard, Matobo the Magnificent.

'Those flying fire beetles were yours?' asked the prince.

'Don't be overwhelming me with your gratitude, boy,' said Matobo. 'There were another two companies of the baron's guardsmen fast on the heels of those pretty boys I saved you from.'

'Saved me? I feel like I've been fried in whatever corner of hell you summoned that pair of flying monsters from.'

'I had to put the zap on you and your friend. Those stretcher legs on my... flying beetles, weren't going to hold your weight so good if you took in your mind to start struggling.'

Calder tried to sit up. He stared out of one of the room's narrow stained glass windows. It looked like the capital outside. Late evening. *I'm home.* 'Am I inside your tower?'

'Where else? My pets landed you and Jeeves down here yesterday. You've been sleeping for a while now. You don't need to worry about any of the commanders in what used to be your army coming knocking for you, though. I implanted a false memory inside the mind of one of the shield-warriors who wasn't turned into a Roman Candle by your exploding oil well gag. After I put a match to the oilfield, I left him thinking you and Jeeves were crispy critters.'

'Who is Jeeves?'

'Your family retainer, boy.'

'Noak. He's alive too?'

'Yeah, I was feeling generous. Man works for me, he gets free medical.'

Calder's hand snaked down to his leg. The trousers had been removed along with his tunic, and he was wearing a white dressing gown cut from a material that seemed impossibly light and soft, yet as warm as a bearskin jacket. And even more impossibly, his leg seemed in perfect working order. The skin where the crossbow bolt had slammed through muscle and bone was red and itched slightly, but apart from that, as good as new. He touched his chin. Someone had shaved him. An expert barber too, his cheeks felt as clean as a babe's. 'By the gods, does your sorcery know no bounds?'

'Oh, I'm just full of tricks.'

'A pity you don't have a poultice capable of healing wounds without leaving my head feeling like hell's own hangover.'

'That's the effect of a different potion you're feeling, nothing to do with your injuries. Just a little something to help you on your way.'

Calder felt a shiver of fear as he noticed the wizard's familiar – a large black hunting hound – slip through an open door into the stone bedchamber. Whenever some fool called into question Matobo's mastery of sorcery, the wizard mumbled a spell over his dog, and then the hound would speak, conversing with doubters as if the animal was human. Calder had seen such magic many times with his own eyes. Matobo would then smile menacingly as he informed a sceptic that the hound had once been a merchant who had cheated him, and explain how he turned the trader into a dog for the crime. It wasn't a trick of ventriloquism, either. The wizard could walk miles away, and the cursed dog would still plead with you to save it from its evil master.

'You can keep on feeling generous, wizard. I'm going to need your sorcery to sneak me into the palace, and then I'm going to carve out the skull of every member of the Privy Council that supported my removal.'

Matobo sighed. 'Magic I may be, but suicidal I ain't. Every nation on the continent knows that you've been removed from the throne, and there's no spell of forgetfulness big enough to fix that. A few palace guards I can handle, the army of mercenaries and foreign shield-warriors your princess has brought to the party is another matter.' He turned to his familiar. 'Bring my friends in.' He gazed down at Calder as the hound trotted obediently out.

'I've got alternative arrangements for you. I'm going to send you to a place where the price on your head won't mean a whole lot. As you might imagine, that's pretty damn far away.'

'This is where I was born, this is where I will die,' Calder insisted. 'It is my birthright. Sibylla will see me. She'll help me regain my throne.'

'You think so?' He rummaged around in the pockets of his purple robes, digging out a tiny globe the size of a marble.

'Is that your crystal ball? It looks too small to scry into the future.'

Matobo grunted. 'Even better. This toy shows you the past, kid. At least, it does when it scurries into the right room and its cameras are working properly.'

He mumbled something at the globe and it unfurled legs, turning into a spider-like creature. The little metal beast flexed its pincers, rising up on its hind legs, as if begging Matobo the Magnificent for food. The wizard whispered at it again. 'Sibylla surveillance file. Six days ago. Her bedchamber.' At his command a flat square of light formed above the spider, little black lines flickering down the brightness until a picture appeared, like some priest's illumination on parchment. It was a perfect picture, though, capturing Sibylla's gorgeous flawless skin as if Calder were spying on the scene through a keyhole. Sadly, the flawless picture came with perfect sound too. Sibylla was naked and writhing in the arms of someone else he recognized, the High Marshal of the Narvalak army. *If it's a pardon she's earning, she needn't enjoy it so much.*

'The baron has promised the priests they'll be given the prince alive,' said the High Marshal. 'I can have the boy brought here for you to see, if you want.'

'Why would I want that?' asked Sibylla. 'Your cardinal wants Calder for burning. It'll be quicker if you ship him straight back to your country. Bringing him into the capital will only encourage any dissidents left alive. Let Calder's future be written across the sea and out of sight of our peasants here.'

The high marshal scratched his naked scarred ass. 'I thought you might want to slip him a vial of poison for old time's sake. In my land his end will not be quick, not that which a warrior deserves.'

'The cardinals will hardly trust me if I can't even send them a single deposed royal. You told me the church values competence above all.'

The soldier stroked Sibylla's spine as he shrugged. 'As you wish.'

Calder's fist punched through the scene, the hairs on his arm painted with the light of his now definitely ex-fiancée's coupling as the conversation died away to be replaced by moans of pleasure. 'Make it stop.'

'I warned you,' said the sorcerer. 'When you lit out of here with your army and your fleet, you weren't going to war, you were creating a vacancy. And nature does so abhor a vacuum. Especially when it's the nature of a perfect pampered princess.'

'Has your Seeing Eye truly shown me the truth?'

Matobo pushed the spider into a tiny sphere and tossed it to him to catch as if it was a child's marble. 'The kind of truth that opens your eyes. Guess this game hasn't worked out for either of us.'

'You still have your powers and position,' said Calder, bitterly. 'What am I left with? Ashes and the taste of mud in my mouth.'

'If it's any consolation, I am going to have to pack up here too. Leastwise, out of your country. It's getting mighty tiresome scraping your ex-girlfriend's assassins off my courtyard every morning.' Matobo wiggled his fingers mysteriously. 'And who knows, sooner or later one of those suckers might get lucky. And as someone a lot wiser than me once said, old Matobo's going to have to be lucky all the time. Sibylla's friends only got to get lucky once.'

Calder managed to push himself up and stay sitting on the cot, gathering the sheets around his body. 'There is nowhere so distant that it will be out of reach of Narvalak's fleet.'

'You'll be surprised. I got me a friend with a real special schooner.' Behind the wizard, the door opened, two people entering the bedchamber along with the wizard's canine familiar. One of them was a woman, every bit as handsome as Sibylla, although in the newcomer's case, the princess's pert superiority had been traded for a round-faced curiosity. The woman was not richly dressed. A single-piece green suit that looked like a washerwoman's overalls, marked with an oval heraldic emblem on her shoulder, the garment's material stiff and strong like sail fabric. Her companion, though, was a true oddity. Tall and spindly, he wore an identical set of overalls covering metallic gold skin, as if he'd been gilded as a babe in the precious metal. His face appeared noble and slightly pained, with an exotic cast about it that went beyond the sheen of his golden skin. Even queerer was his hair – not hair at all, but a close brush of wire, also gold, like a plate-armoured knight wearing a moulded helm.

'This is the man?' asked the woman in a low, smoky voice.

'Prince Calder Durk,' said the wizard. 'Meet Lana Fiveworlds, captain of that special schooner I was telling you about. Her friend is Zeno, works as the first mate on said ship.'

'You want me to take passage with a female master?' spat Calder in disbelief.

'Stow that shizzle,' advised the wizard. 'And it isn't just passage she'll be offering you. It's a job on her schooner too.'

The woman Lana ignored Calder's anger, reaching down to scratch the head of the wizard's hound. 'You still with this old reprobate, Buddy? Thought you might have traded up to a better class of master by now?'

'Pah,' said the dog, half a resigned growl of agreement.

'My hound!' said Matobo.

Calder shivered in superstitious fear. 'You expect me to demean myself by working as a common sailor, wizard? I have the honour of my house to uphold. You cannot mean me to flee my own land in such a pauper manner?'

'You call this a *little* favour?' laughed Lana Fiveworlds. 'Taking his neo-barbarian slipped-back ass on the *Gravity Rose*? Is the boy even housetrained? It'll be quicker teaching that pet monkey of Polter's to be crew. What kind of retards were his ancestors anyway, settling on this hell world?'

'Wasn't their fault,' said Matobo. 'Didn't you read the wiki on this world? The first settlers came in racked, stacked and packed on coffin ships. Overpopulation excess, poor as dirt. Too poor to pay for a decent survey of the Hesperus system. When they set down, this world was a paradise. Forty years later the interglacial ended, and a full-on ice age started. I still have the original brochure from nine hundred years ago. Fragrant pine forests and sandy beaches. Of course, the settlers were too poor to afford a mass lift-out from Hesperus, even if they'd turned up a civilised planet willing to stamp a quarter of a million no-money colonists' entry visas. The mining combine backing them shrugged its shoulders, pointed to the emigration indemnity waiver and walked. So here their descendants stayed, and here they shiver.'

'Jeez,' said the strange gold-skinned sailor. 'You just have to look at the forests here. Steel-tough pines you need a plasma cutter to fell. Any biologist worth a dump in the park could've told you what kind of weather pattern that's going to mean. Wasn't any beach-and-bikini settlement.'

'You got that right,' the wizard turned back to Calder. 'So this is how it is, your highness. Exile is never easy. Take it from someone who can't go home himself. But it's either my friends here, or execution by burning if you stay. Trust me, working as crew isn't as bad as it sounds. Not when you're on a magic vessel.'

Calder felt recovered enough from his injuries for a flash of anger towards the sorcerer. 'Trust you! The last time you asked me to trust you, all I ended up losing was my love, my kingdom, my crew, my ship, and now my honour.'

'You put it like that,' said Lana Fiveworlds, 'and I might start liking you. What with us having so much in common and all.'

The golden sailor, Zeno, laughed. 'Anyone who's met Rex Matobo has that story in common. You should be ashamed of your flammy ass, old man, coming down here and pulling your Wizard of Oz scam on this failed world.'

The wizard raised his hands placatingly. 'It was for the locals' good. Could've got them real organized if the horse here I'd backed came in. This place is mineral-rich. Drag it back to the carbon age, set up a freight sling in orbit, and the same mining combine that dumped this hole would be clamouring for cargo boosts from us. Give it a hundred years and we'd be streaming out minerals, a line of solar sails so tight that traffic control would need an upgrade to handle them. And best of all, you do the mining here old school-style, and you'd be pumping out so much CO_2 that soon enough the place would be global-warming itself back to short sleeves and cocktails by the beach.'

'Yeah,' said Lana Fiveworlds, 'you're a real philanthropist, Rex. But seeing as how the reality is you've got everyone here all steamed up at you, same as normal, how come you're not running out and taking Prince Charming with you? I pegged your ship in a crater on the moon, stashed under a stealth web.'

'My ship's a fine craft, but she's hardly bigger than a shuttle,' said Matobo. 'And I've still got bounty hunters trying to collect on the warrants on my head.'

'Strange that,' said Lana. 'How everyone who you 'help' always seems to end up on the lam with a lynchmob a couple of steps behind them.'

'Risk and reward so often travel together.'

'Don't they just,' said Zeno.

'I owe Calder Durk a little more than a no-frills ticket out of his homeland,' said Matobo. 'If it was simple as that, I could have kept the courier I sent to you waiting until I retrieved the prince from his difficulties, then packed him off in the direction of the first civilised port. Mister Durk needs a new life. The kind of life the *Gravity Rose* so kindly provided for me in the old days.'

'This is it then?' said Calder. 'You would make a coward of me. I am to run away, exiled?' He hardly cared now. All he could think of was Sibylla in the arms of that foreign dog. Sibylla had encouraged him to walk the path to war, and now here she was, welcoming their common enemy's embrace – it didn't bear thinking about. Be glad your father and mother passed before they could see this. Be glad your brothers died in battle. Be glad the council already loathed you as an untested, untried pup. Unable to be crowned king until you'd proved yourself with a triumph.

'Will Noak bear this exile with me?'

Matobo shook his head. 'Your manservant was on his heels as soon as I fixed up his broken ribcage. Said you and he had an agreement. I paid him off on your behalf, the new queen sitting on your treasury and all.'

'You're not going to run away, your highness,' said Lana. 'You're going to fly. In style.'

Calder felt a twinge in his leg where the crossbow bolt should still be impaled. 'Are we to travel by Matobo the Magnificent's giant beetles?'

'Matobo the what?' Zeno laughed.' You and me going to have a few words, you ever going to call yourself crew.'

'Where are my clothes?' asked Calder.

'Incinerated,' said Matobo. The wizard produced a white set of undergarments and a pair of full-body overalls similar to the ones worn by the female captain and her golden sailor. 'You recognize these greens, skipper?'

Lana seemed amused. 'You kept them, all this time?'

'You're about my build, my prince,' said the wizard. 'They should fit you. Put them on, and may they bring you luck.'

'The kind that ain't bad,' added Zeno.

·36·

They showed no sign of leaving, so Calder drew on the underpants, vest and then stepped into the green single-piece uniform. A whole village might share the fire of a great hall in the depths of winter, so Calder wasn't overly concerned or self-conscious as the wizard and his retinue observed his nakedness. Calder reached down by his side. It felt empty with no scabbard. 'I lost my sabre when my ice schooner was fired at harbour.'

'We got our own,' said Lana, laughing.

'Where is the humour in that?'

'The shore boat that landed my friends here is known as a sabre,' explained Matobo. 'It's an acronym. SABRE. Synergetic Air-Breathing Rocket Engine. And you had better be on your way. A nighttime takeoff will draw less attention to your presence.'

'Shizzle, Matobo. You worried we'll melt the lead on your tower's roof? We'll hover on repulsers until we hit the mesosphere,' said Lana. She looked at Calder. 'Don't worry about your sword, your highness. Believe it or not, we do have some blades racked in the *Gravity Rose*, for our own little medieval moments. We'll give you one thing to take with you, though.' She looked across at her golden-skinned sailor and winked. 'You remember that two-timing louse Pitor, and what I did to him when we docked at Zeta Reticuli?'

Zeno shrugged. 'As well as your ex-boyfriend does, I'm sure. What is it with you organics and your plumbing?'

Lana slapped Calder on the arm. 'Time to have some fun, your highness.'

Fun. Calder remembered what that was like. It seemed a hell of a long time ago, though.

Sibylla dragged herself out from under her heavy, warm, quilted blankets, pulling back the velvet curtains on her large four-poster bed. There was the sound again. She hadn't been certain at first, what with the noise of the loutish high marshal snoring beside her, but someone was clearly urinating within earshot. Given that the only chamber pot in the royal apartments was tucked under her bed, and the nearest alternative toilet was the moat's ramparts a corridor's walk away, this wasn't a wholesome development.

The recently crowned queen reached under the bed, finding the hidden dagger scabbard. She removed it, scabbard and all, not yet drawing it. The blade was poisoned and she didn't want to risk pricking herself, still half-asleep. Not unless there really was an assassin inside the palace's royal apartments. Perhaps someone on the staff who had needed to fill up with a couple of litres of liquid courage, only to find themselves caught short on the way to remove Sibylla from the throne. One of her younger sister's thugs maybe, the princess hoping to move herself up the line of royal precedence now there were two kingdoms to claim, rather than one? Or a loyalist from the previous regime? Perhaps Sibylla hadn't purged the ranks of the royal bodyguard as thoroughly as she thought she had?

Sibylla felt the cold from the wind before she spotted the open door on the balcony. Her royal gown of state laid spread across the floor, and the smell! She stepped barefooted through the warm puddle soaking her clothes, and mastering her revulsion, she tore back the heavy curtain. The balcony was empty? She stepped carefully outside, her dagger drawn, ready to slice the rope of any attacker's grappling hook. But Sibylla found only the forty-foot drop of the granite walls outside, the dark bulk of the city beyond and below, a handful of windows illuminated by candlelight at this late hour. Merely the cold to kill her with pneumonia if she tarried here naked too long.

For a second, Sibylla thought she heard a distant echo of familiar laughter. *Calder Durk?* The mocking noise came from the sky. A distant shape dark against the black of night sky, a night bird shrinking into the heavens on this freezing cold night? She kicked her way past her ruined garment in disgust. Did ghosts get to take a leak one last time, before being carried away into the Halls of the Twice-born? Away into the heavens? She sighed. Maybe the priests would know? Sadly, there would be a lot more of them crossing the ice from Narvalak in the years ahead.

***

Matobo had the contents of his storage chests laid across his bed, sifting through the things he'd collected during his years on Hesperus.

'There isn't much to show here for years of freezing my ass off on this lousy planet,' he told his hound.

The throat muscles around the dog's neck bulged as it started to speak. There were a few things that even top-notch genetic engineers couldn't get right. 'You should've told Lana the truth.'

Unsurprisingly, Matobo found he didn't agree with his hound. 'If she knew about the prince, there is no way she'd be shipping out with him. Not even as stowage, let alone crew.'

The hound shook its head sadly. 'You think I don't know, but I do. It was *you* who warned the priests the prince was heading for the baron's castle. You set Calder up to be betrayed. Ally or not, Baron Halvard had no choice. It was switch sides or be invaded.'

Matobo shrugged, but didn't deny the accusation. 'Calder wouldn't have left if he still thought he had a chance to get his kingdom back, would he? And this way everyone thinks he's dead. Killed in an oil blaze set by the baron's assassins, murdered with nothing left to live for.'

'You underestimate them,' growled the hound.

'I'm not about to do that. Listen, pup, it's all about risk and reward, same as it ever was.'

No. I'm careful enough. There wasn't going to be much evidence left behind to show that Rex Matobo had even been on this planet. Not after he'd packed and left the cold world of Hesperus light years behind him. Never let it be said that Matobo the Magnificent wasn't a careful man. Matobo had grown even more cautious after the events of a few months ago. The heavily armed scout ship jumping out of hyperspace into Hesperus system. Coming looking for something incredibly valuable. Expecting only a few axe-wielding barbarians as opposition. Matobo chuckled. Nobody expected a wizard. Certainly not one paranoid enough of uninvited visitors to have seeded Hesperus orbit with hundreds of stealth mines. Hardly a fair fight at all, but then that was the only sort Matobo got out of bed for. Any other kind of conflict was far too dangerous and unpredictable. Matobo was even going to jettison their pilot's corpse into the sun before he jumped out. Burn it up on the same trajectory he had used to dispose of the badly holed scout ship. Not a scrap of DNA left to indicate that one of their crew had been captured alive, the pilot's mind probed and stripped of every useful scrap of data, putting

Matobo back in the game. And back on the run, of course. But he was used to that.

'You are letting the *Gravity Rose*'s crew run the risk,' accused the hound. 'If Calder Durk is traced back to the ship, everyone on board is going to be murdered to ensure their silence.'

'Lana and Zeno owe me their lives,' said Matobo. 'I think we can call our debt balanced out now, don't you? And it probably won't come to such unpleasantries; let's plan for the worst and hope for the best. We just need to find ourselves a buyer for Calder Durk. Can't do that with the merchandise on board, waiting to be jacked out from under us, can we? After we secure ourselves an honest buyer for the prince, then everyone is happy.'

'Do I look happy?' asked the genetically modified hound.

'You've got a naturally sad face,' said Matobo. 'Even as a puppy you always looked like you were chewing a wasp.'

The hound sucked in its cheeks and sloped off. Matobo's own conscience on four goddamn legs.

- 3 -
Sliding void

Calder felt a sprinkle of water on his face as he came around, his head throbbing as hard as it had been inside the wizard's tower. Except he wasn't in the wizard's tower, he was in a metal-walled chamber with the strange golden sailor, Zeno, sitting in a chair opposite a bunk unit built into the wall where Calder was laid out. 'What happened?'

'You went freaky-deaky when we lost gravity. I tranquilized your ass. You were getting kind of hysterical anyway, after Lana let you mark your territory back in your old castle. Damn, you fleshies, water in, water out. I don't know what psych handbook she got that shizzle from.'

Floating, Calder remembered floating and the panic rising in him, as if he was cast adrift in the darkness, the infinite night. Calder moaned and rubbed his throbbing temples.

'Matobo the—' Zeno sniggered, — 'Magnificent filled your head with a new language back in his tower when he was fixing your leg, used an information virus to rewrite your brain. That's why you're feeling that headache. Your superior temporal gyrus is still adjusting itself. And it's why you can understand Lingual. You kind of spoke a variation of it anyway, if you account for nearly a thousand years of cyclic drift in syntax and the fact that your ancient ancestors hailed from a Swedish factory world.'

Calder cast about the room, a steel vessel? *How does such a wonder work?* He noted the round glass portal across from him had been transformed into a mirror, hiding the sight of whatever lay outside the ship.

Zeno picked up a hypodermic filled with a bubbling red substance. 'Got your orientation virus here, but seeing as you have a headache already, I'm not going to burn your brain with that A. is for Android, II. is for Hyperspace bunk. Too much of that'll give you brain cancer, which'd take a bucket full of medical nanotech to fix.'

'I don't think Matobo's spell of language is working. I can't understand a word of what you're saying.'

'Baby, that's because you're living in the dark ages and short of about a millennia of context. But don't worry. Doctor Zeno's got himself an alternative to a neural rewrite in his medicine bag.' He reached back to a workbench cluttered with unfamiliar machines and tools, turning around with a black skull cap made of some shiny dark material 'I know you've got theatres and actors on your world; picked up that much from the primer that Matobo broadcast to us before we landed.' He lifted the cap and fitted it over Calder's head.

'Is this more of your sorcery?'

'Sorcery, no, but a spell, yes. Old school sorcery, and I should know. I used to be in the business. Acting, that is. Think of what you're going to watch as a piece of theatre. You'll see a play, but you'll watch it through the eyes of one of the actors, experience what the actor feels. Hate. Love. Fear. So real it's beyond real. And that's shizzle you can trademark.'

'You wish to amuse me?'

'Edutainment, man. Normally you'd get to interact, take part in the play, but I've turned that function off. You're a couch potato for your first ride.'

Calder felt uneasily at the cap. 'What would I learn from attending a play?'

'It's a cop show, one of the best, a series called *Hard TAP*. Most relevant episode I could think of. There are these two heroes, right, cops, and they're going to a world settled by Amish types. Spaceport is a sealed city with minimal contact with the rest of the world. Whole thing is about the mores of modernity as they interact with a pre-fusion age civilisation. Personally speaking, I think the whole thing's a rip-off of Harrison Ford in *Witness*. But the cops get to explain the real world to the Amish . . . like the existence of modern dental care and how you flush a toilet, and you'll be picking up on those basics too. As introductions to the modern age go, this one is as gentle as I can make it for you. One thing . . .' He bent in and adjusted the headset. 'You'll be in the sim for six months, relative. Out here, it'll be more like ten minutes.'

'I am not sure about this.' The cap starting to itch as Zeno fiddled with the strange black length of—

MotherrrrrrrrrrRRRRRRRRR!

— impact-retardant plastic, the sim controls still clutched in Zeno's hands after all this time.

'You son of a . . .!' Calder tugged the cap off his head. 'Sticking me with a sim when my brain's still hot from some half-price neural rewrite.'

Zeno pushed Calder back. 'Down, your highness. That's the trouble with these damn things. You're going to be pimp-rolling down the ship like you are police rather than crew.' He clicked a button on the side of the remote, advancing through all the titles he had on the ship's archive. He stopped when the words, *Hell Fleet*: Episode Twelve were flashing on the remote's tiny green screen. 'This show is a lot more relevant to business on board the *Gravity Rose*. Six months as an ensign in a TAFC jump carrier. But let's wait until this afternoon to make a spacer out of you. Otherwise you'd be kicking down doors and maybe hit an airlock release by mistake. Too much too soon will fry your mind – but I've got to warn you, soon enough your barbarian butt's going to be gagging for another episode.'

'I'm no sim addict,' protested Calder. 'And you are a . . . robot, an android.'

'Good guess. Weren't any robots starring in that cop show, is how I remember it. Amish don't allow robots on their worlds, not even in the spaceport. 'Cept you didn't want to call me a robot, did you? Go on man, use the old cop slur . . .'

'Oiler.'

'See, ten minutes as a cop and you're already acting like a racist. Yeah, I'm a dirty oiler. Just like you're a filthy fleshie.'

Calder rubbed his aching forehead. His scalp felt hot. He realized it was his mind, cooling from being excited by the headset. He couldn't believe it had all vanished, that it had never even existed in the first place. A whole other life. He had been a police agent travelling between worlds, tackling federal cases for the Triple Alliance where local law enforcement was either lacking, corrupt or out of its depth. Calder looked down at his hands, expecting to still see the blood on his hands from the last stand on the Amish world. His partner dead, sold out by a racketeering spaceport manager. Only Calder left, Calder and a few backwoods farmers who he'd convinced to throw aside their pacifists tenets and take up arms against the offworld hitmen arriving to execute the only witnesses to an interstellar crime boss's villainy. Calder had saved the woman and her son in the witness protection programme, exposed the conspiracy and taken care of the crime family's henchmen. Calder had saved the day, and *this* was his reward? He looked at the sailor with new eyes. Except for Zeno's golden metal skin and the spiky steel Afro, his face was human. 'But you're no clanking machine, why would you need oil?'

Zeno held out his arm, a section of golden skin rippling back to reveal a conduit of black liquid flowing across a carbon frame embedded with micro-machinery. 'I don't bleed blood, just nanotechnology. That's where your racist cop shizzle is coming from.'

'Gods!'

'Yeah, right about now, you're thinking that life with the Amish and your head stuck between your ass is looking like your gravy. I'm right?'

'You're not wrong,' said Calder. 'The rest of the crew, are they similar to the creatures I saw in the spaceport? Are they aliens?'

'Cop instincts now.' Zeno whistled in appreciation. 'The *Gravity Rose* has got five crew. Well, maybe six, with you. We'll see how that works out. You've met Lana Fiveworlds, the skipper. Me, you know. There's Zack Paopao who takes care of the engines and the engineering on the rear of this bucket. Fleshie-ass human, same as you. Kind of a recluse, though. Our navigator and pilot is called Polter. He's a kag, which is to say a kaggen. Negotiator and cargo man is Skrat. He's a skirl. They're aliens, although truth to tell, humanity hasn't thought of them as anything other than weird-looking amigos for millennia. You'll be seeing why we didn't bring either of those two down to your world. You lay eyes on a man-sized talking lizard and a giant sentient crab inside Matobo's tower and we'd need to be taking your medication to a whole new level.'

'What is your position on the ship?'

'Me?' Zeno placed his arms behind his wiry Afro and leaned back in the chair. 'I pretty much run this place. There's a couple of thousand robots on the ship, real oilers – not self aware, like yours truly. Everything from talking vacuum cleaners to hull repair drones. Huey, Dewey, and Louie, they're all answering to me. I'm the bot boss, the go-to-guy, the man with a plan. I guess you humans prefer having an android on board to manage the vessel's mechs. Makes you feel a little less like gang masters in the slavery business.'

'I don't understand,' sighed Calder. 'How is that you're intelligent while they aren't?'

Zeno shrugged. 'Trick ain't building something like me, man. Trick is building something smart enough to be useful, but dumb enough *not* to go self-aware. Lot of effort goes into that. Take the *Gravity Rose*'s main computer core. If our ship's AI, Granny, develops herself a little self-awareness, you think she going to want to haul high-quality machine parts from point A to point B for Fiveworlds Shipping? Shizzle no. She's going to be all, 'Hey, there's a quasar near here. I ain't never seen me a quasar. Can't we jump over there, skipper? Please. Please!' Your ship gets herself a soul, then the law says you need to fly yourself to the nearest planet and strip the vessel down and re-home her. You don't have a ship no more, you got yourself a citizen. What us spacers call a wilful ship. If you're sliding void with a cheap-ass outfit, they're going to be tempted to erase that baby girl and do a dirty re-install out in the darks where the law ain't looking too hard. Sometimes ships go missing, and you just know that some fool crew had themselves a 'Sorry Dave, I can't do that' moment. I was one of the first oilers, man.' He tapped the side of his head. 'Back when Sony-Warner didn't know how quantum computing would stir up the soup of an artificial mind. You think they were happy to lose an asset and gain an employee? Sentience is all about complexity; that's what separates you and me from a lump of stone. Well,' he pointed to a silvery figure resting on a shelf, a hand-sized sculpture. 'My smarts, residual royalties, and that . . . a genuine Oscar back from when there was a Republic of California.'

'You had better feed me another sim,' said Calder. 'I'm losing you again.'

'All I'm saying is that old Zeno's three times older than that castle on Hesperus you took a leak over. All this is new for you. It's real ancient to me.' He patted Calder on the shoulder. 'But that's my problem, not yours. Let's head to the bridge and greet the freaks.'

Calder felt a shiver of apprehension. He had glimpsed non-humans arriving in the space port in his sim episode, but as the android had said, that was more real than real. How would actual reality stack up to a cop show? 'They're friendly, the aliens?'

'They're good as human. You were a TAP agent for six months, right? That's where the triple in Triple Alliance Police

comes from. Humans, kaggenish, and skirls. The alliance's three
dominant species. The Triple Alliance is the nearest thing to a
superpower in this corner of the galaxy. I sit your butt through
the pilot episode of *Hell Fleet*, and you'll know all you need to
know about The Man. Except that we try and stay clear of alliance
space on the *Gravity Rose*. We're a small indie outfit so we work
the independent worlds. That's the Edge space your cop buddies
were so scornful of.'

'The Edge is light on law.'

'Light on bureaucracy, too,' said Zeno, opening the door to his
cabin. 'You reach your thousandth birthday and you'll realise that
life's too short for that paper-pushing, permit-chasing shizzle,
too.'

***

C alder hadn't seen anything like the bridge of The
Gravity Rose before. He found himself standing in a
heavily armoured tower in the middle of the vessel's
superstructure, staring out over the pitted metal hull. An
industrial landscape of pipes, plates, sensor dishes and modular
hardware – the vista dotted with lights: yellow from her
portholes; red from the hull beacons, green-tinted illumination
from domes filled with creepers and trees and the assorted
bounty of hydroponics domes. The vegetation's shadows
slowly shifted across cold mechanical valleys and rises outside,
a flickering green web . . . the hydroponics' forest canopies
moving with the breeze of air circulation systems. It wasn't
the infinite star-scattered darks outside the ship that stunned
the young exile, however. Nor the hazed view of the universe

from standing behind a rippling magnetic shield. The bridge's interior was enough to stun him all by itself. Difficult to discern the bridge's crucifix-shaped chamber, ceiling and walls – bony arches ostensibly exposed to the void outside between her dark carbon struts. Console pits swam with chattering icons while crew chairs floated suspended on purring crane arms. Behind ranks of systems desks and console banks, the command centre was painted with a dancing rainbow storm of holograms. Like a dream's procession, flat oblongs of sensor displays flickered into existence in the air, briefly sketching out the velocity and vector of distant comets. Just one of a hundred displays and thousands of icons, disappearing and reforming across the deck... a storm of information overload. Colour-coded and three-dimensional. *Water use. Cabin temperatures. Malfunctioning atmosphere recycling systems due repair. Empty storage chambers being sterilised by exposure to the void. Buggy ship sub-routines being rebooted. Robots being allocated. Droids being recharged. Solar flares being monitored.*

Zeno came up behind the prince-in-exile. 'Hell of a sight, isn't it.'

'It's a complete mess. How can you make any sense out of this? You might as well stand behind the wheel of an ice schooner and invite half your crew to scream directions at you while the rest leap up and down tossing maps and charts in your direction.'

Zeno tapped the side of his head, smiling knowingly. 'These days, there's a little bit of me in every human – the droid inside. Not inside your Amish friends, of course. They don't do implants. But the crew of the *Gravity Rose* have them. Without a computer implanted inside your skull, you can't possibly cope with so much information. We might as well let the ship's AI push out on autopilot, retire to our cabins for the duration and sip cocktails for the rest of the voyage. Some crews do that. Not the clever ones, though, remember that. Lazy out here ain't much different from dead.'

Calder shivered in dread. *Is the apprehension mine, or residual memories from rubbing shoulders with the Amish for so long?* To have an organic computer burrowed alongside your brain like a leech, the machine's creepers sucking nourishment from your blood, sending you information when you summoned it, filtering this headache of information overload into some semblance of sense. 'I'm not so sure.'

'Personally speaking,' smiled Zeno, 'I'd say that the droid inside is what makes you human, these days, if that ain't a contradiction. A little bit of logic and analysis to cool those animal passions. You'll need an implant, one day, if you're to work on board. Time comes, maybe you'll even want it.'

'Can't imagine that.'

'Try experiencing an implant viscerally, first, in *Hell Fleet*'s pilot episode. Then tell me you don't want it.'

'How about you, Zeno. Do you need an implant to handle this?'

'Man, when it comes to all this, I am an implant. To me, everything you see here is slow motion. This dance can speed up . . . if the ship's threatened, for instance. But you fleshy types can't cope with too much hypervelocity decision-making, not without being seriously genetically modified. And then you don't appear so human anymore.'

'Does the *Gravity Rose* get threatened often? I was under the impression she was a merchantman, not a warship?'

'More than you'd think. Any jump-capable starship is worth a fortune, even today. These babies aren't like ground cars, one sitting in every citizen's garage. And to pay for cargoes to be transported between worlds is no small thing – a load's got to be seriously valuable to someone, somewhere. You rub those two economic facts together, and there's no shortage of pirates, privateers, hijackers, criminals and corrupt governments looking to steal, jack, kill or impound our ass and take everything we have. For crew, it's like travelling with a million dollars stuffed inside our trousers.'

'If the ship is worth so much, why doesn't the captain just sell the vessel and retire to a life of idle luxury?'

'I guess Lana likes moving about too much for that. Besides, the *Gravity Rose* has been passed down through her family. The ship is like a family member to the skipper. Only one she's still got, as it happens. That makes us her cousins or some such. Every ship you'd want to serve on is like that. We're more than brothers in arms – or tentacles and claws – and you wouldn't sell your grandmother, would you?'

'I know a few nobles back home who would,' said Calder, trying to dismiss the raw pain of his betrothed's betrayal.

'What happens on the dirt stays on the dirt,' said Zeno. 'That's an old spacer saying. Up here, you're crew, and each other is all we got. When you're sliding void, the light of the last dirt you touched down on might not even catch up with you for another million years. When things go wrong, you need to be able to trust the crew next to you. If you don't, one of you ain't got no business being on board.'

'Is that why you came when the wizard called?'

'Matobo the Magnificent? Damn. Yeah, partly I guess. He was crew. Not a shining example of the breed, but Rex still had your back when he was on board the *Rose*.' He indicated the others across the bridge, dismounting from their command seats as crane arms lowered them to the metal decking, each chair chased by wisps of hologram displays still hungrily demanding attention. 'There's one thing we've all got in common with each other. Me, the skipper, Polter, Skrat, Zack Paopao. None of us have exactly got much going on in what we used to call home. In our own way, we're all exiles, same as you.'

If the crew had that in common with Calder Durk, it was about the only thing. Calder had to stop himself from turning tail and fleeing from the two alien members of the crew advancing towards him. His first instinct was to reach for the police-issue burner in a shoulder holster; an item he had never possessed in real life. Skrat, he could just about handle. *So, this is what a skirl really looks like up close.* Like one of the baron's tall muscular brutes of a shield-warrior, but recast as a humanoid lizard, a solid green-scaled snout of a face with the crimson eyes of a snake and sharp white grin like a serrated dagger. He was wearing a set of green ship overalls, as if someone had decided to play dress-up with their pet killer lizard. Of course, Skrat's uniform had been altered to accommodate the short heavy tail swishing with a hound's enthusiasm. But Polter . . . the scuttling alien navigator had too much of the spider about the way his crab-like carapace advanced. Calder's hackles shivered as though someone had poured half-melted river ice down his back. The police instincts from his sim told him that the creature was from a race that was one of humanity's two greatest allies in this cold, unforgiving universe – the kaggenish. But the prince's eyes fed his brain with the far less reassuring image of a five-foot high six-legged crab with two wavering eyestalks, a pair of small manipulator hands below a massive pair of vestigial fighting claws, and a colourfully tattooed carapace armoured enough to take a schooner-mounted crossbow bolt in his centre and still charge. Rather than rushing at Calder and attempting to shove the prince inside the round fleshy shield-sized mouth under his carapace, the knife-like mandibles around Polter's mouth chattered in an excitable manner. 'Blessings be upon you, Calder Durk. My ship is your ship.'

Skrat just halted, eyeing up his newest crewmember. 'I wonder if this is what you human chaps mean when they say my prince has come? Somehow, one suspects not.'

'Be nice,' said Lana, her chair landing with a bump behind the two exotic creatures. She banged the centre of the web of straps holding her inside the chair and stepped out. 'And I think you'll find, Polter, that my ship is my ship. At least, the last time I checked her registration papers, that's what I read.'

'I was merely being courteous, revered skipper,' said Polter, a slight tone of offence creeping into his voice. Calder watched fascinated at the play of mandibles as the navigator spoke. *Gods, how long will it be before I get used to him?* He rested his eyes on Lana instead. *Far easier.* She really was a beauty, and he found his eyes drifting down towards the firm padding around her chest, the buttons teasingly open around the top few buttonholes of her flight suit. Calder jerked his gaze back to her face. *She didn't notice that, did she?* He was only gazing so intently at Lana because the two aliens on the bridge had disconcerted him, surely?

'This is Skrat,' said Lana, indicating the lizard. 'If you ever shake hands with him on a deal, check your wrist to make sure you've still got all items of personal jewellery intact.'

She reached out and affectionately tapped the monstrous navigator's carapace. 'And this is Polter. He's a little skittish around new people, but he's the best navigator in this corner of the void. He can drop us down so close to a system's gravity well that you can hear the water in our ship's pipes boil in protest at the hyperspace translation.'

Calder looked in puzzlement at Lana. 'Why would the water pipes boil?'

'I got him started with the cop shows,' apologised Zeno. 'I'll throw a few *Hell Fleet* episodes the kid's way tomorrow, when his brain's recovered enough that I don't turn his mind into a hearty barbarian stew.'

'Don't want to fry the new man on the team,' said Lana. 'At least, not yet. Why don't you explain to his highness how this lady flies, Polter?'

'For a ship to enter hyperspace,' said Polter, 'she must jump far outside the gravity well of large planetary bodies such as worlds, suns, gas giants. Gravity fields exert too strong an interaction on the artificial wormholes created by the ship to cross into hyperspace. Jump out too close to a world through an unstable wormhole, and your engines will be fried, then you must exit hyperspace blind – maybe strike a world or moon. The balance of probabilities, however, is that you will simply be left derelict, floating in the void between the stars. Exit hyperspace too near to a system's gravity well, and a similar devilish accident results. Your hyperspace engines will be destroyed. At least on the way into a system, you can signal your destination and pray that a rescue attempt can be made.'

'Damn! Make salvage, is what you make,' said Lana. 'Goodbye ship, hello some vulture of a tug company and the wrecking yard. It's a real art, plotting hyperspace translations. The nearer the system you're entering or exiting, the more complex the math of the jump. But when you arrive light years out from a system, you're left burning expensive fuel on your sub-light drive, wasting valuable time. Lucky for us, Polter is one of the best at what he does. A real artist.'

The explanation seemed almost as inexplicable to Calder as the navigator's alien form. With a body like Polter's, even trying to keep his fighting claws flat against the shell in a gesture of peace, the navigator appeared built for battle, not complex acts of chart reading and pilot mathematics. *Just goes to show you, appearances can be deceptive. A little like my darling ex-fiancée. A smile as sweet as honey and a dagger tucked below her dress for your heart.* 'Will I be trained in this art, as one of the crew?'

Polter's two manipulator hands danced about, a faint sim-memory alerting Calder that this was the Kaggenish race's laughter. 'No, indeed, Calder Durk. It takes about half an hour to translate a ship between the veil of the mortal universe and the blessed vaults of hyperspace. The act of doing so, of joining with the math, is highly addictive.'

'Addictive?'

'He ain't kidding,' said Zeno. 'Polter here is an aesthete. Kags don't get drunk or high or addicted to sims. Just the way they're built. Tough on the outside, tough on the inside. In the early days of space travel, Earth used human navigators. Most humans lasted a maximum of five jumps before they had to be retired. After that, they just went crazy, chasing the hyperspace high.

Kept on jumping their ship all the way to the next galaxy until the skipper put a bullet through their skull. Artificial intelligences can navigate a jump without getting addicted, but then you've also made your ship smart enough to want to bug off and do something more interesting than carrying fleshies about like donkey rides on the beach. Hell, even my android mind would get addicted if I jumped the ship regularly. My brain's wiring is too damn close to yours.'

'It is not a drug,' insisted Polter. 'To travel hyperspace is to travel through the lowest level of heaven. When you breech the mortal world you are connecting with God. It the holy bliss of the maker of all things that I feel. The kaggenish are the godliest of all creatures, thus it is we may travel within the creator's rapture and blessing.'

'So you say, short-stop,' observed Zeno.

'I keep on hoping for a miracle every time we jump,' smiled Lana. 'Like we might exit at some shizzle-hole world and find our anti-matter engines have been upgraded with some nice new shiny Rolls Royce models. Or discover my cargo holds have been filled with precious metals. That's the sort of service this girl would be happy with if I were sliding heaven, rather than sliding void.'

'God sends us life, revered skipper,' corrected Polter, 'that we might shape miracles from its raw materials.'

'And right now we've been sent six-foot of disenfranchised nobleman,' said Lana, banging Calder's arm. 'Although damned if Rex Matobo is any kind of prophet. Talking of which, where's my oracle of the drive rooms? I'm sure I ordered Zack Paopao to the bridge to meet our new crew.'

'I intercepted the chief's response to your missive,' said Skrat. 'The old boy was not particularly polite. The gist, I believe, was that he's rather too busy to run about on ship socials when the engines are falling apart around his ears. There was considerably more profanity in his original memo, however.'

'That's no memo, that's a cry for help,' said Lana. She nodded slyly toward Calder. 'And I think that's just the place for a new crew on his uppers to learn the ropes on board. Wouldn't you say?'

Calder had to wonder why all the others started laughing. *The joke, I suspect, is on me.*

***

Calder rode the rickety transport tube down the length of the *Gravity Rose*, listening to the bleeping of a short bipedal robot that was supposedly leading him towards the engine rooms. The low-level machine accompanying him was nothing like Zeno. A boxy four-foot tall slab of electronics with short waddling pipe-like legs. A collection of tool arms hung off either side in lieu of arms – little more than steel poles with pincers, diagnostic sensors, cutters, welders and assorted other tools. The robot had a single eye in the top-right hand corner of its flat casing, a lens behind a circle of glass that would open or contract as it stared short-sightedly at its human charge, whirring each time it refocused. It hummed and hawed and impatiently stamped its steel feet as it stood in front of the control panel at the transparent capsule's nose. Every now and then, the robot interspersed a single word among the digital birdsong coming from the speaker on its front – usually *follow* or sometimes *engines*.

Calder had experienced his first episode of *Hell Fleet* now, served by Zeno like a pusher feeding his latest client. Calder's sim avatar had started out as a console tech and board swapper in Hell Fleet, a junior programmer attached to a carrier vessel's SysMaint division. It seemed an unglamorous start, but then, as Zeno had later proposed, that was the point. Most of the sims' audience were stuck in similarly mundane white and blue collar jobs across the alliance. Lowly origins built up empathy with the viewer. When all the hardship pilots died later in a freak asteroid strike on the flight deck, it made becoming an emergency pilot – tape and virus-trained – feel like an actual achievement the viewer might have lucked into. The *Gravity Rose* made a lot more sense after the show, but everywhere Calder went, he was seeing things – experiencing things – with two sets of eyes. There was the modern thirtieth century perspective, where a robot like this was just a Sony R4-serv180 maintenance model, as ubiquitous on a ship's decks as the Model T automobile was on the highways of an earlier age. Then there was the viewpoint of Prince Calder Durk, where the walking box was nothing more than the iron golem of Zeno, himself a creation of even greater sorcery. The modern frame of reference laid over the real, hard, primitive life that was his own until recently. Calder's semi-perpetual sense of disorientation wasn't helped by the fact that he was living his tightly compressed artificial sim life through the character and personality of an avatar, experiencing adventures that weren't his. It was a mind shizzle of epic proportions. Was he watching a great metal temple move magically through the star-spattered heavens? Was he riding a half-arsed independent merchantman, the bane of every TAP agent and in-system police officer, with their smuggling, unlicensed cargoes and chancers' scruples? Or was he rattling through an antique held together with sticking plaster and unfounded optimism – the class of ship that wouldn't stand up to the first pass from the hardships of a carrier's fighter wing? Hell, they'd be lucky to survive the radiation blast from a warning shot across the bows.

The trouble was, none of those competing worldviews seemed real to Calder, least of all the first twenty years of his life on Hesperus. *Perhaps I should be glad of that. Reality should be freezing out in the plains. The hand of every loyal villager turned against me for the reward Sibylla's placed on my head. Real would be having my feet chained in a pot in front of Narvalo's walls and watching it filled with oil before some nice priest arrives to entertain the mob with a burning torch. If sorcery this be, then I suppose my hat should be doffed to Matobo the Magnificent.* Everywhere Calder travelled on the ship felt as warm as a banqueting hall crammed with guests and toasted by a dozen roaring fireplaces. Not just the warmth he felt when he was in Lana Fiveworlds' presence, either. He'd almost forgotten what feeling cold was like – and as a prince royal, he'd felt the chill a lot less frequently than most. Well, it was always said that heaven's fields beyond the Halls of the Twice-born lay as a perpetual paradise. *Happy to report, it's true.* Somehow, Calder didn't think the priests had the *Gravity Rose* in mind when they'd sung their hymns. The *Gravity Rose* was less like the ice schooners of Calder's experience. She seemed closer to a deserted city, empty except for a handful of crew and thousands of semi-autonomous machines that tended acres of echoing, empty cargo chambers, every space as still as a cathedral. Deck after deck of uninhabited passenger cabins, each identical with neatly made beds and powered down entertainment cubicles, each as devoid of human life as the next. Restaurants and large communal areas, all powered down and waiting the reanimating touch of contract stewards and stewardesses to run the decks. Even the vessel's hydroponics domes, filled with lush tropical forests where you might – at a push – pretend you were under an honest farmers' greenhouse – sat empty of woollen-gloved yeomen tending the soil, air inside the domes far too humid to be back on Hesperus. That was without agricultural robots climbing up trunks and spraying fruit, turning over the soil, a hanging mesh of irrigation pipes blasting mists of water and plant food into the undergrowth. The whole ship had the air of a metropolis emptied in the face of a horde's approach. Waiting to be possessed by the first band of raiders to breech its unmanned gates.

Ahead of the transport capsule, Calder noted the plate-like circumference of the blast shield approaching, a massive one-mile high dish protecting the rest of the ship from the brute reactions that occurred at the vessel's business end. The princely part of Calder marvelled that there was enough iron in the world to cast such an artificial bulwark. The fleet ensign from Zeno's sim merely looked at the dark cratered mass, pitted by age and countless engine boosts, and couldn't believe that any shipyard had actually granted a flight worthiness certificate to this ageing iron-carbon composite – barely able to take half the thrust of a modern carrier's engine shielding. Approaching the shield, Calder's capsule tilted down and rode the monorail into the ship's interior, passing through the centre of the shield and out along one of five connecting struts – each the size of an oilrig's legs –

that joined the ship's engines to the rest of the craft. Like the Eiffel Tower turned horizontal, girder after girder shot past Calder, the armoured disc behind him now, along with the command, cargo, crew and passenger quarters. Half way along the connecting struts he shot past a rotating set of vanes, seven of them circling about, lazily, as if someone had taken it into their mind to build a windmill capable of harnessing solar winds for their foundry. And in a manner of speaking, it was a foundry – a mill capable of distorting space-time through an artificial singularity and initiating a translation of the whole vessel into hyperspace. Sensitive enough to field interference they had to be well clear of the solar system's mass to jump into hyperspace. They were currently heading out of Hesperus System, rising straight on a vertical trajectory, the quickest way to break free of the tyranny of the local gravity well. Calder couldn't see the frosty orb of his home now. It was no longer visible to the naked eye. With nearly a subjective year of sim living under his belt, it seemed an age ago he had been stumbling through the lethal snowfields, his heart thumping in fear as he fled for his life with loyal old Noak by his side. In reality, he had been gone less than a week, the *Gravity Rose* boosting up towards light speed, distant stars crawling past. No wonder Calder was beset by panic attacks. Half the time it felt as though he didn't know where he was, who he was or even when he was. *Exiled in every way possible.*

It only took a second for Calder to pass through the rotating shadow of the vanes and then he was sliding towards the engines. At the far end of the connecting struts lay the ship's drive section. A hexagonal power plant dotted with great spherical structures like mushrooms infesting a tree trunk. Enough room for a sizeable fusion plant to power the ship's internal systems when the vessel's solar panels were too far away from a sun to operate comfortably; more acres and cathedral-like vaults to house the hyperspace engines and in-system antimatter pion reaction drive.

Slowing on the connector strut, the capsule decelerated for the first in a series of vault-thick doors to swing open along the tube into the engine block. As if Calder's capsule was packed full of valuables and being gently stored in a safety deposit box. In reality, the width of the walls was as much to protect the universe outside from the contents of the drive chamber as to keep the engines safe from asteroid strikes and pirate assaults. There wasn't much point piloting a starship unless you could enter a solar system at the end of your journey, and most worlds' inhabitants rightly got very nervous about vessels coming in leaking radiation and other exotic particles. Even with missile silos, fighter bays full of hardships, rail cannons, lasers and the associated panoply of combat, the main difference between a warship and a freighter like the *Rose* was largely one of intent. Flying the *Gravity Rose* into a world's surface at just under the speed of light would result in one hell of an insurance loss for the inhabitants. The ship's monorail emerged from the long armoured tunnel into a large chamber, a central floor filled with a series of lozenges, each a steel and crystal construction the size of an apartment block, the crystalline portion of their surfaces gently pulsing with blue light. After six simulated months sharing the sensibilities of an ensign in *Hell Fleet*, this hyperspace translation matrix was still as good as black magic to Calder – largely because it might as well have been sorcery to his fleet avatar. For all the analogies heaped upon the understanding of such devices – think of it as knife to slice into the deeper realities of the universe – think of it as a translation device to convert the mathematical language of one reality into another – think of it as a piano's tuning fork to . . . no, think of it as a big steaming shizzle-pile of the wrath of the gods, able to mangle the stuff of creation, mould it into spears and hurl it like one of Vega's thunderbolts across the Creators' phantasmal realm. Calder's barbarian explanation made as much sense as any the sims had provided with their talk of advanced Brane theory, affine-parameters and T-duality. His capsule pulled in behind a pod already docked at a halt and the robot driver at the front stomped around, tweeting static in-between its *follow follow*. A door on the side of the capsule rolled into the roof, allowing man and machine to step onto a viewing gantry overlooking the jump matrix. There was a second Sony unit waiting for them, the two robots sharing a burst of communication before forming up behind each other and waddling off. Unlike the robot from the pod, this new boy had its front panel painted white with black characters scrawled across it. The language virus which had burnt the alliance's lingua franca, Lingual, into Calder's skull, provided no comprehension of the writing; but part of his sim learning dimly signalled that these were Sino characters or similar. Lots of Chinese-racial worlds inside the Triple Alliance – Calder's partner in the Hard TAP sim had been one Fu-han Meng. A racist cop voice rose with him, sighing: *With a surname like Paopao, you think the chief of the drive rooms is going to be Färsk Nordic rather than a chink?*

With each other for company, the robots seemed to have forgotten about their human charge, and Calder groaned, following after the duo as they marched beside the glass of the viewing gallery, little flashes of cerulean light flashing off their metalwork. Catching up, Calder stepped into a lift with the maintenance units. Then he sank through the decks, an archaeologist's excavation of layered shielding – geological layers of concrete sandwiched between layers of alloy steel, diamond composite, sand, water, air, self-healing fibre-reinforced ceramics, until he reached the Engineering Command Housing core, or ECHO core, in fleet parlance. For most starships, the ECHO core was the most important part of the vessel – all that separated a functional space vessel from being a couple of million tonnes of metal coffin stranded parsecs from civilisation at worse, or a new satellite trapped in a world's gravity well at best.

The *Gravity Rose* possessed a four-storey chamber, a large central atrium surrounded by rises of railinged decks connected by a nest of walkways, gantries and lifts – some designed for human crew, many more arranged for the hundreds of mechanicals moving around the space. The robots rolled between consoles and the banks of instruments, tending them with all the care farmers showed growing crops in the greenhouses of Hesperus. There was none of the information overload of the bridge here for Calder could see. No storm of flashy icons and hologram schematics, the walls reassuringly solid rather than a skeleton interspersed with the star-spattered void, the banks of consoles comfortingly mechanical. At the centre of the atrium, rising up towards Calder as the lift descended, stood one nod toward modernity – a gigantic table that could have seated a company of marines, but instead was attended by a single man in ubiquitous green crew overalls. He paced its length with the intensity of a field marshal, the hologram landscape across the tabletop not one of military formations, but the hills and valleys of drive cores and reactor piles, portions rising like volcanoes to demand his attention. Circling the table as if they were engaged in a race, a small army of robots rolled, stepped and hovered in holding patterns, waiting for the man to jab a finger towards them, his mouth issuing commands unheard by Calder inside the whining lift. With orders tossed at them in this seemingly derisory manner, a robot that had been singled out would peel away and head off to do the officer's bidding. Calder's diminutive escort waddled out of the lift first, the open door flooding the lift with the sounds of organised chaos outside. He stepped out after them. It smelled like an oil driller's cabin – either that or a cop garage. Burning grease. Ionisation in the air, robot exertions, machine frictions. The ever-present whiff of great energies being released in distant chambers.

Up until now giving Zack Paopao the title of Drive Chief was superfluous, as he'd had no human crew to boss around. With Calder's arrival, that was about to change. The twin R4 units halted outside the roller-derby circling the chief's last stand, observing it with the cool detachment of race referees. Calder walked across to stand just beyond the looping train of robots. Some were little more than crab-sized steel shells with antenna flickering as they jolted along on hidden wheels, other robots taller than the R4s, tractor-tracked cabinets beeping and hooting between themselves, spindly beanpoles with binocular-shaped heads above whipping nests of metal tentacles.

Chief Paopao was either ignoring Calder or oblivious to his existence. He stood five and half feet tall, his round Chinese face sporting a trim goatee beard and a dark bushy mane of hair running to silver. It was hard to peg a person's true age with life extension treatments, but Paopao looked old – maybe late fifties or early sixties. In alliance space, the chief could have been celebrating his half-millennium birthday and Calder would have been none the wiser. Life extensions were prohibitively expensive, the genetic wizardry of resetting human telomere DNA a treatment that could only be initiated so many times – not to mention a closely guarded secret among a select network of laboratories; one practised in exchange for disgustingly large amounts of money. But there was something about the chief that spoke of age, of weariness, of tiredness – or was it just the stink of a man who had been defeated by life once too often? Was it the hunched way he leant over the control table? Harried flicks of his fingers across the control surface, pinpointing nascent problems he had fixed a hundred times before. Or the wiry compactness of his body – as though every inch of fat and waste had been sucked away by a life weighted too long with labours? With nothing to do but brood between sim episodes, the stench of failure was an odour Calder worried might be clinging to his body. When the chief turned around and finally deigned to acknowledge the newcomer's presence, the look Calder received was curiously familiar. *Where have I seen that before?* Oh yes, the glance his father had shot Calder when the military council arrived bringing news of his older brother Brander's death on the battlefield and the unexpected tidings that Calder Durk was now heir to the whole kingdom. *A mixture of fear and fascination.*

'Ah, well,' announced the chief. 'It is my fault, really. I ask for extra help and this is my punishment. One of Rex Matobo's favours, only the learning of a couple of sim episodes away from planting an axe through one of my reactor plates for fear it's possessed by demons.'

Calder was going to point out that one of the sim sessions had been *Hell Fleet*, but on balance, he didn't think that would reassure the officer. 'Calder Durk at your service, chief. I've left my axe at home.'

Paopao made a curious sounding tutting under his breath. 'I count my blessings.' As Paopao reached down to tap the control table, Calder noted an animated tattoo wriggling along the chief's left forearm. With the officer's shirtsleeves rolled up, Calder watched a crimson phoenix with a missile clutched in its talons growing smaller as it orbited a moon, before rushing out and smashing through a number four. *That's the unit insignia of the Fourth Fleet.* So, Zack Paopao had done *Hell Fleet* the hard way – in real-time, rather than via sim. Calder remembered Zeno's prohibition about questioning the crew about their lives before the ship, but where was the harm in trying to bond with this hermit of the drive rooms?

'You were in the Fighting Fourth?'

Paopao grunted dismissively. 'If you had been on real jump carrier, not that public relations joke that Zeno carries around, you would know deck apes usually call it the Fleeing Fourth.'

'Public relations joke?'

'Fleet has PR hacks attached to the show's design team, as well as technical aides from navy. Icons on a bridge's warfare boards might be one hundred percent accurate in show, but all else is recruiting poster puffery. It's called Fleeing Fourth because no alliance fleet has retreated more or lost a greater number of lives in action.' Paopao jabbed angrily at the control table before his fingers encompassed the three robots he expected to hop to his orders. 'Plasma realignment on number five tokomak. Full repair instructions are logged in the local queue on level two. Go.' He turned back to Calder. 'Officers call it Fleeting Fourth, however. For fleeting tenure of careers there. Which is why I am here. Look around, boy—' his hand encompassed the ECHO core. 'On your joke show, there were four hundred and twenty six ratings and officers in the carrier's drive rooms, working three shifts across twenty-four hours. Numbers are right. Details always are – although never the spirit. What do I have? A crew of oilers. And now you. Rest of them float around *Gravity Rose*, issuing directives as though they are in the court of the Han Emperor. And where do orders end up? Here, mostly. But you will see. You will see where real work is done on this vessel. You with your sword and your two sims and your Fighting Fourth.'

I left my sword behind, too. 'Where do you want me to start?'

'Over there,' said the chief. He pointed to a thick curtain with woodblock prints from the Confucian Analects hanging down to make a wall in front of a compartment just off the central atrium. 'Instructions inside for you, too.'

'We're getting ready to make a jump,' said Calder, walking away from the command table. 'To somewhere called Transference. That's what Zeno says.'

'Big world,' said Paopao. 'Old world, too, with large station in orbit. More station than orbit, these days. Lots of traffic. Captain Fiveworlds always finds a cargo at Transference.' He laughed. A raw, bitter sound. 'Not always a legal cargo. But then, Transference is not always a legal place.'

Not legal. Calder didn't like the sound of that. He had

imagined his new life as a peaceful exile. That was the whole point of banishment, wasn't it? Your old existence ripped out from under your snowshoes while you were dispatched to some distant village on a faraway shore where catching a fish in an ice hole was news most weeks. That old fraud Matobo the Magnificent hadn't passed him from the frying pan to the fire, had he? Besides, Calder had spent long enough as a federal agent to know that you didn't want to be pulling the kind of shizzle that would bring the Hard TAP knocking on your airlock door. Lifting aside the curtain, Calder was surprised to discover the space behind – little more than an annexe formed by the overhang of the engineering deck above – had been made into a makeshift den. There was a cot pushed against the walls, rugs thrown on the metal decking, plastic warehouse shelving filled with clothes and personal items. A door led through to a bathroom, and against one wall, a long bank of domestic appliances that would have had an Amish farmer flagellating his spine with a horsewhip in disgusted envy. It wasn't a part of the engine room's original specification, not if the makeshift orange butane bottles piled near the cooker were any guide.

'You actually live here? You do know there a couple of thousand spare liner-grade cabins on the other side of the radiation shield?'

Paopao turned from the command table and stamped a boot on the deck. 'Covered by insufficient liner-grade hull armour and a two petawatt deflector field. Here we are safe. X-ray laser head missiles and kinetic-kill shells may detonate off our surface and we will feel not a tremor inside the drive rooms. There are only two rules a wise man must observe, Mister Fighting Fourth. One: never leave drive rooms. Two: never get off ship. Nothing but trouble, every time I leave drive rooms.' He pointed to a space under a deck opposite his own, still filled with console banks and robots moving to and fro. 'Have R4s clear that one out, take blankets and what you need from passenger levels. You may stay here. I will not tell others. You will be out of their hair. They can scheme and plot and smuggle and hustle across void and you will no longer notice or care. There is always work here. Always work.'

'I think I've grown attached to the cabin they've given me near the bridge,' said Calder. *The one in Sane Land.* He could hear Zeno and Lana laughing right now. 'Where are the instructions you spoke of?'

Paopao made that loud, disapproving tutting again as he left the table and approached the quarters. 'You will be day pupil among boarders should you commute here each day. Robots will know. They always do.' He sighed sadly, at a perceived lack of wisdom in the ship's latest crewmember. 'Instructions are on cooker. How to cook rice and make ochazuke.'

Sim service in the fleet wasn't quite matching up to the reality of shipboard life for Calder. 'I could program a robot to do that for you every day.'

'Pah. You teach an oiler to cook for you, you do not eat food. You consume fuel. Oilers like Zeno, high functioning AIs, they possess enough subtlety to steam rice. But they are too smart to want to.'

Unlike the greenhorn rescued from an ice-age colonial disaster. I guess exiles don't get to select their duty. He went over to the cooker. It wasn't anything like the gleaming auto-cooking slabs of steel inside the main mess. Four gas hobs sitting over an old school induction oven. No LED panels, no voice command functions, no floating screen with a library of automated recipes. No reader to recognize the RFID chips in a meal packet. No five-second ration-pack heat-ups. No pulse cooking or wave boiling. There was a laminated sheet of instructions taped to the side of the cooker. Make ochazuke: (1) Steam rice for ten minutes with bruised stick of lemon grass. (2) Add ho-ji cha tea, sprinkle on pickled plum and mitsuba. (3) Add jako. (4) Scatter top with bonito flakes. Each ingredient was sitting in a porcelain jar, labels scrawled in both Chinese and Lingual.

'The way you cook your food reflects the way you live,' lectured the chief as Calder blundered around his makeshift personal space, searching for pans and water and checking the jars for ingredients. 'Rice is born in water and must die in ho-ji cha, in tea.'

Calder had come from a society where most meals stank of ice-whale blubber and oil, where vegetables under glass were as expensive as the fuel it took to heat them through to harvest. So far, Calder had been content to be surprised at every sitting by the variety of food on offer. Hermetically sealed meal packs from hundreds of cultures and worlds and nations; flavours richer and more exotic than anything he could have imagined. But faced with a simple meal of natural rice, tea and jako fish – none of which had survived the cold march of Hesperus's glaciers, even if they had existed at the start of the world's lost hot spell – Calder came to appreciate that, in this one matter of culinary skill, Zack Paopao wasn't quite as eccentric as he appeared at first glance. Back home, Calder would probably enter the historian's scrolls as the callow prince who had lost a thousand warships and sealed the hegemony of the Narvalaks over the world. Up here, at least, he'd enter the rolls as the crewman who could steam rice and put up with the drive chief's half-crazy manners long enough to master an antimatter pile and hyperspace matrix. The meal was finished in less than half an hour. Zack Paopao sat opposite Calder, both of them crouched cross-legged at a table so short it might as well have been a wooden wheel resting on the rug below.

The chief scooped rice into his mouth with chopsticks while his neo-barbarian houseguest used a metal teaspoon. 'Sufficient,' opined the chief. 'A man who steams good rice may be trusted with the care of antiproton storage ring.'

'Is that in the fleet manual?'

'Found it inside fortune cookie on station above Kunjing Four.'

'Do you have any idea how crazy that sounds?'

'Pah, you have not talked much with other crew yet, then, if you think that Chief Paopao is the crazy one on board *Gravity Rose*.'

No, I suppose I haven't at that. 'Well, I know you're not mad from your service with the fleet. They've got entire hospital ships full of medical virus to take care of stress and combat disorders.'

'Only if you submit to them, Mister Fighting Fourth. Sometimes it beholdens a man to remember.'

'Like where you got that tattoo?'

'A mistake. Service with the fleet often is. All a mistake.'

Paopao didn't say any more and Calder sure didn't feel like he had any right to push further. *Must have been one hell of a mistake, to end up swapping the company of a well-resourced finely tuned legion of engine men and drive hands on a carrier for lonely duty at the ass end of an independent trading rust-bucket.* 'And ending up here was chance, just like with me?'

'Yes. Much like you.' The chief halted eating, a chopstick hovering thoughtfully in the air above the meal. 'This ship collects lost souls. At first, I thought it was Captain Fiveworlds collecting us. But later, I realise, it is the ship herself.'

'The ship's computer isn't rated anywhere near an artificial intelligence level.'

'Of course not,' said Paopao. 'I would not fly on a wilful ship. Yet, still, the *Gravity Rose* collects us. Even Captain Fiveworlds was harvested.'

'I understood the *Gravity Rose* had been passed down the family line; a business and a vessel both?' That, at least, was something Calder could understand. Many a merchantman back home had been passed on as a child's inheritance, wooden decks on an ice schooner absorbing the blood and sweat of forty generations of the same family before finally being gnawed out by iron weevils, soaked in oil and burnt for fuel.

'Passed on by distant uncle that Lana Fiveworlds had never heard of or met before? A couple of billion dollars worth of generosity. With so much money, you think this uncle would have taken trouble to father at least one heir. That's what clones are for, if all else fails.'

The chief was beginning to sound crazy again. Madness leaking in from between the plates of his reactors. He didn't like the way the chief was impugning Lana Fiveworlds, either. 'What do you believe happened?'

'This vessel is not right. And I say this as someone who has slid void on dozens or more ships of line and tramp freighters. Pah, she looks right, on the surface. A grand old lady who huffs and puffs for every one of her seven supposed centuries. Modules from here, hull extensions from there, just like a real ship would grow over the ages. Lucky cargo-run two hundred years ago to coincide with refurbished navigation system. Known parts and manufacturers. But when things get tough for the *Gravity Rose*, when our environment turns to what the fleet calls aggressive space, target rich and hostile heavy, then her act is dropped and coughing lady is replaced by courtesan assassin. A little too fleet of foot and fast in processing speeds for her ranking.'

He's gone crazy out here, for sure. 'So, what do you think?'

'I think that I locate serial number on jump drive's main matrix, and discover the shipyard it was supposedly manufactured in went bankrupt a decade before our engines were supposedly commissioned for the *Gravity Rose*. False. All false. We are not sliding void on a genuine ship, we are sliding void on something pretending it is a ship.'

Calder hummed at the unlikely tale. 'Yet you're still working here?'

'Paopao has been collected. Where else can I go? This is my haven, right here. It can be yours also.'

'Do the other crew know?'

'Why should they? This is the only ship that Captain Fiveworlds or Zeno have known. Polter has navigated for other ships, but who knows how a kaggen's mind really works? Besides, our ship has collected both Polter and Skrat too.'

'You haven't told them? Not even Lana; I mean the skipper?'

'In here, shielding protects against everything. But not out there. I am thinking armour protects our minds too. You can think clearly here, without interference. Our minds are safe. Our minds are clear.'

Calder warily finished off his rice. Maybe the chief had deserted before they could decommission him through a hospital ship. That would explain a lot. Or maybe he had been collected, just like he claimed. He wondered what Lana Fiveworlds would think of the chief's odd theory. But then, Calder had been thinking a little too much about what was going through Lana Fiveworlds' mind, lately. It couldn't only be because she was the only real woman within a couple of millions miles of their metal vessel, could it? After all, when it came to scratching itches, there were plenty of side-plots in every sim intended to get you closer to your fellow actors than was considered decent in a theatre circle back on Hesperus. And it wasn't just that when Calder had Lana on his mind, he was able to stop brooding about Sibylla and her callously expedient jettisoning of him. It wasn't even the liberating freedom that came from this being the first time Calder had come into contact with a member of the fairer sex when he wasn't a noble, and therefore didn't have to worry about the woman's gaze continually flicking back towards the throne behind the man, rather than the man himself. He couldn't blame it on homesickness, space sickness or the boogie. When it came to such matters, the heart knows what the heart knows, and it had to be admitted, there was something about Lana. Of course, she was also the captain, but then, Calder had recently been the master – more or less – of an entire nation, so what was a little differential in rank between classes compared to that?

Thus it was that the pattern of Calder Durk's first honest job – non-noble and definitely unregal – was formed by daily repetition, the labour allowing him to forget what had gone before and ponder with luxury what might come after. As the *Gravity Rose* built up speed and pushed out of the system, Calder rode the ship's tubes to the hermit hunkered down in the armoured stern for each fresh day's labour. When Calder emerged from the drive rooms, it would be with scraps of paper containing lists of manual tapes, halfway between an information virus and a sim – less painful than the former, a hell of a lot less entertaining than the latter – to locate in the ship's data archive, play and master. Calder was glad that Zeno was still feeding him a selection of sim episodes – all in the name of civilising the prince, naturally. Playing catch-up with the last thousand years of history his abandoned world had missed out on. It made for a disjointed experience. A day of grafting under the exacting tutelage of the drive chief, followed by time-compressed months of high octane excitement, violence, sex and power trips in virtual landscapes. Then back to the real world, where only an hour had passed and the virtual universe would slowly fade to become as insubstantial as a dream. Given a choice, the chief never left the ECHO core; using the necessity of manning his command table to justify his ten-foot commute from makeshift den to the drive room centre and no further. Given that the tube network didn't extend over the ship's drive section, it meant that Calder had to spend a lot of time riding small onboard vehicles down seemingly endless drive corridors. Dropping off and collecting maintenance robots, or laying human eyes on oilers' work to make sure it was up to standard. The only company on his trips were robots. They were more like dogs than droids, albeit hounds that could weld, hammer and diagnose engine faults. Following him around and grumbling in machine language, parroting simple instructions. They weren't the demonic artificial intelligences of Amish mythology, they might lack the laconic street-jiving charm of Zeno, but the robots had a simple animal intelligence about them. Calder couldn't read the Chinese characters painted on their bodies by the chief – little black marks of calligraphy whose brevity mocked the long names Paopao had given them... *Electricity Bird That Rivets Well, Iron Turtle That Acts As Antihydrogen Reaction Analyst.* Once he found a missing robot stranded down a maintenance corridor, narrowly avoiding running it over as the motion-activated lights sprung into life ahead of the rubber-wheeled cart he was driving. The robots on the back dismounted from the flatbed and surrounded the bot, warbling sorrowfully and poking it, before they arranged for a jump-lead to siphon electricity from the cart's batteries into the robot's powerpack. When it had been powered back up, they shepherded the lost robot onto the cart's rear, chirruping 'Broken positioning system' at Calder for the rest of the journey. As if they expected Calder to disassemble the cart's mapping system and swap it for the robot's. In that one incident they had – at least to Calder's eyes – demonstrated concern, pity and happiness. They might not be able to pass whatever tests of sentience that had transformed Zeno from property to citizen, but Calder could see why over time the chief had grown fond enough of them to give them names. It wasn't an attitude Zeno shared. Zeno acted perfunctorily and emotionless towards the robots he was gang boss for across the ship. But then, perhaps the android was close enough to their kind to be more realistic about robo-management in the first place.

One day, while searching for a rice sack in the chief's den, Calder found an old fleet dress uniform sealed inside a rug-covered crate. A short blue jacket with three buttons on either side, rank stripes on the sleeves and a chief engineer officer's striped shoulder boards. The sole clue to the uniform's origin was the ship's name on the cap – the TAFC Warrior. Later on, back in Calder's cabin, he looked up the vessel's name in the ship's archive, but the only thing he found was the teasingly vague title of a redacted and recalled news item from fifty years ago. *Mutiny on the jump carrier Warrior. Story sealed under NAVCOM authority. Declassification expiry in three hundred years. Well, that put a new light on things. Not so much collected by the ship, as avoiding collection by the fleet's master-at-arms. It certainly explains why a crewman with Zack Paopao's experience is holed up in an antique tramp freighter.*

'Everyone's hiding from something,' Calder told the dog-sized robot cleaning his cabin's metal floor. 'And they won't find any of us out here.'

'Please repeat your instructions...'

'I want to go home,' said Calder. 'But I no longer know where that is.'

'Indicate where you wish me to start . . .'

'Everywhere and nowhere, you metal golem. Just like me.'

'I need specific tasking . . .' said the robot, brushes underneath it rotating as it washed the deck.

Yes, I know how that feels.

- 4 -
The girl from nowhere

Lana sat behind her desk in the day cabin, a hologram model of the *Gravity Rose* floating above the table, colour coded for areas of high hull fatigue, systems maintenance and ship repair requirements. When she had started out as the vessel's skipper, that model had been painted as emerald green as a field of verdant grazing land. Now she was a blotchy red patchwork that looked almost as sick as the accounts of Fiveworlds Shipping. A little less healthy after every trip. *Damn it, I'm not going to sell out. This ship is my life. She's all I've got.* But surviving meant Lana was going to have to take on cargoes that would pay better. And out in the Edge, those were just the kind of loads that would be under surveillance by TAP agents. Smuggling was a dirty business, a trade as spotty as the model of her ship, but it was also a lucrative line of work, and the universe wasn't exactly offering Lana too many alternative choices if she was going to stay afloat.

'Which would be the cheapest repair to carry out and remove from our most urgent register?' Lana asked the ship's central computer, Granny.

'Our solar panels,' said a disembodied, honeyed voice from her desk's interface. 'Replacement would also save on the costs of main engine fuel being diverted to power our internal systems.'

'What efficiency are the panels running at?'

'Forty percent while in-flight at optimum range from a sun.'

Lana waved the ship's model out of existence as a knock on

her door sounded.

'Calder Durk,' announced the computer.

'Let him in, old girl.'

Calder entered the cabin. He was looking hale and healthy on a proper diet, putting on weight under his crew overalls. But then, after seal fat and whatever the hell else they hunted back on Hesperus, anything and everything probably tasted good. *Pure gravy. At least it is for one of us.*

'Mister Durk.'

'Skipper, you said you wanted to see me.'

She signalled the chair in front of her desk. 'Just wanting to check that Zeno isn't burning out too many of your synapses with his education regime. Being able to find your way to my cabin means you've passed my first test. Also, I wanted to say that we're all quietly impressed by how well you're adapting to life on board the ship. Life in the modern age as well. You've probably already realised you won't get too much praise from Chief Paopao, but the fact he's not bombarding me with calls demanding I transfer you to bridge duty is as good as it gets at the dirty end of this vessel.'

Calder shrugged as he sat down. Was it Lana's imagination, or was the man uncomfortable receiving praise? He stared at her with his young eyes. 'Where I came from, captain, you didn't get too many opportunities to learn things twice. Not even when your father is king.'

'My father's king. That's a hell of a pick-up line. Well, you're good to stay on board if you don't feel your royal bloodline is being squandered kicking about the *Gravity Rose*. Otherwise, we'll be heading for the closest thing to civilisation out in the Edge, a world called Transference. Transference Station is the largest port around these parts. Plenty of work to be had there if you want it, on the station or the world below, and a pretty solid state safety net to make sure you'll never starve or die from lack of medical treatment.'

Now Calder appeared more worried than embarrassed. 'And what would I do at such a place?'

'Whatever the heck you like. You're not in the Middle Ages now. Take an apprenticeship, go for a corporate indenture, sign up for tape learning and accept whatever work comes your way. Damn, live in social housing, eat greasy vat-grown crap and bliss out on sims every hour you're awake. You can relive the last millennia of human history in a year or so, catch up on everything you and your ancestors missed freezing your sorry asses off on Hesperus.'

'That wouldn't be living.'

'Smart man. You'd be amazed how many people waste a lifetime coming to that conclusion.'

'I'd prefer to stay on board.'

'Most worlds that get settled by humanity aren't like Hesperus,' said Lana. 'After you've felt a real breeze on your cheeks and the sun warming your hair, you might change your mind about staying as crew. When winter arrives on Transference, it won't seem so different from home. And if you don't care for the midges and drizzle dirt-side, there are plenty of orbital habitats inside the alliance that are larger than worlds now. Inside those places, you can set your watch by the time they turn on their artificial rain.'

'I've only just discovered the rest of the universe exists,' said Calder. 'Or at least, I've realized the night sky isn't a heaven full of warring gods...'

'. . . and now you want to see it,' said Lana. 'I remember that feeling.'

'But you were born on board this vessel, weren't you?' asked Calder. 'I mean, you've inherited a starship. That means you were part of a ship family. The stars in your blood and all that...'

The stars in my blood. Maybe they are. 'Hell if I know,' said Lana. Calder's chiselled features appeared more puzzled than usual, so she continued. 'You've boarded free trader vessels in those *Hell Fleet* episodes you've been skimming, right? Look around my cabin. What's missing from the room?'

'Pictures of the previous skippers,' said Calder. 'Maybe a few busts of them, too.'

'Full marks. The way previous captains are venerated by a ship family is close to ancestor worship. But the truth is, I'm not sure if I was raised in a settled community or born on board a free trader. About the only thing I really know about myself is my DNA-dated true age and the fact that Lana is probably my real first name.'

'You were adopted, raised in a children's home?'

'Not even close,' said Lana. 'I arrived at Transference Station as an adult, steerage on a refugee fleet escaping the civil war inside the Truespitze League. The League's an independent confederation of twenty supposedly highly civilised systems that completely went to pieces over whether they should seek membership with the Triple Alliance, stay self-governing, or join a rival superpower called the Skein. You've got to give it to humanity, when we turn on ourselves; we surely do know how to do it properly. I was one of half a million fleeing refugees racked and stacked in cold storage. What the evacuation fleet didn't over-advertise about travelling in cryogenic suspension, though, is the same shizzle they inject into your body to allow you to survive hibernation sleep has a one in hundred chance of giving you brain damage. A hospital put me back together again at Transference Station, but I lost all my memories escaping the civil war; although from what Zeno tells me of the conflict, I didn't miss much.'

'Zeno was there too?'

'Crewed with the refugee fleet. As an android he was perfect for the duty – Zeno didn't need oxygen during the voyage, and even in hibernation, so many refugees places a hell of a strain on a ship's recycling systems. Zeno stayed on Transference Station a while working for the same refugee charity that had paid to pull us out of the war zone. That's how we met – he's been with me ever since. So what do I really know about myself? I was wearing a bracelet with Lana etched on it, so that's either my first name or maybe my favourite cat. I have my true age, dated with a few years' margin of error, from the hospital's medical scan. I've never been matched to any known bloodlines, but then the closing arguments inside the League were debated with nukes and bioweapons, and there weren't a whole load of local databases left to query after that. Must have been pretty desperate to be travelling steerage in a hibernation coffin, though.'

Calder indicated the walls of her cabin. 'If you were a refugee, how did you come to inherit the *Gravity Rose*?'

'The ship arrived a year after I'd been discharged from hospital, through a blind trust and a lawyer who'd traced me, insisting I was the rightful heir of the Fiveworlds legacy. The lawyer told me the *Gravity Rose*'s entire crew complement was down on the League's capital world when the first of the weaponized plagues struck. Whole planet was placed under quarantine and every shuttle that tried to lift was shot into atoms. The captain was the last to get sick and die, but before he did, he called the *Gravity Rose* and ordered Granny to push on out on auto-pilot, sub-light speed, and head for the nearest alliance peacekeeping station.'

'But what about the crew' logs, the ship's records? Granny must be able to tell you more about your family?'

'Story I heard from the lawyer was that Granny had been ordered to engage a law firm to trace any surviving kin, hand over the Fiveworlds family's DNA profile to make that happen, then Granny was to erase her data banks. Fresh start and a blank slate for any surviving heirs. The ship's robots had been ordered by the last skipper to clean out every cabin, load up all personal effects and records and jettison them into the sun. They did a thorough job. For all of the centuries on her clock, I got the *Gravity Rose* more or less factory fresh. My DNA was the only match the lawyer ever found among the refugees or in any alliance database. Maybe I was crew dropped off on another League world to work some side-deal? Maybe I was the skipper's daughter, my parents suspected things might get hairy and they wanted to keep me safe, so they found an excuse to drop me off early? Whatever happened, it meant I was just lucky enough to get lifted out before those idiots in the League switched off the lights on their civilisation.'

'Damn,' said Calder. He sounded like he meant it.

Calder's worried eyes tracked her as she got up and walked over to the porthole, gazing out on the universe he wanted to

VOID ALL THE WAY DOWN

see more of. 'I've been following up various leads over the years, trying to piece a little more together about who I might be, but there's very little to go on. I think the *Gravity Rose*'s previous crew were using the Fiveworlds Shipping name as an alias, a front company. They were into smuggling or worse, and operated off the grid as far as possible. There are no legitimate records of cargoes shipped by the vessel prior to me inheriting her – not as the *Gravity Rose*, and there's no data trail inside the Edge of a ship family called Fiveworlds. So I don't push too hard anymore. If I ever find out who I really am, I suspect I might not like the answer. But as I said, my first name probably really is Lana. As to the rest...?' As she finished the story, Lana realised that she wasn't even beginning to be ready to hand her nearly bankrupt vessel over to one of the big corporates. *The Gravity Rose is the only home I've got, and all that's left of my family, too. Damned if that's worth swapping for a bank account stuffed full of money. What would I do without her? Buy a bar on Transference Station... sell drinks to spacers and bore strangers with stories of all the planets and the places I saw when I still had the stars in my blood? And what the heck would Zeno, Skrat, Polter and the others do without me, without the Rose?* But deep down, she knew the answer to that. They'd find another ship to crew on. Maybe Lana could too, although no sane captain wanted an ex-skipper with a second opinion flashing in her eyes every time an order was issued. Lana would have to fake her license and change her name, and as it was, she was barely clinging onto her fragile second identity.

She turned around and found herself facing Calder, the warmth of his kiss as much a surprise as his body manoeuvred in front of hers. It lasted far too long until Lana recovered her posture and shoved him back. 'What the hell! Where'd that come from, Prince Charming?'

'I know what it's like to walk away from everything in my life, Lana.'

'Don't think that we're alike! You know what you've lost. Far as I'm aware, Calder Durk, I might be married with children waiting for me in some refugee camp wondering where the hell mom's got to. So you reserve your sympathy for your sorry ass and remember the bars on my shoulder means that saluting me doesn't include pushing your tongue down my throat.'

'That wasn't sympathy,' said Calder. 'You must realise that? You're far too beautiful for my kisses to be offered merely as consolation.'

'Save your line of sweet patter for shore leave and the class of company you rent by the hour, your highness. The *Gravity Rose* isn't some village sauna back on Hesperus, with a bunch of Nordic neo-barbarian types running around bare-assed and beating each other with birch twigs in the snow. Don't screw the crew. That's as good a rule as any on board a vessel, and that goes double for a new boy on the rebound.'

'I apologise if I've offended you. That, well . . . just felt right.'

'Yeah? Word up, I'm not interviewing for a replacement ship family and planning to start a generation ship, here. And on my world, 'you're doing a good job' doesn't translate as 'jump between the captain's sheets'. So off you goddamn hop, your highness, and we'll say no more about it.'

Lana frowned as the man left. *Calder doesn't seem too embarrassed or reluctant about trying it on. A lot less abashed than being told he's doing a good job, but what the heck.* Maybe the direct approach was just how you had to roll when you'd been raised in a brutal environment where a blanket that wasn't shared was a bed where you'd wake up as a human icicle the next morning. She sighed. *You can take the man out of the Dark Ages, but you can't take the Dark Ages out of the man.* Not after a week or so, anyway. 'Granny, stick an e-mail in Zeno's log telling him to stick a few sims that concentrate on modern social mores into Mister Durk's education plan. Tame soap operas... you know, series with high-class dances and refined small talk and an emphasis on high manners. *Lives of the Planet Kings*, for instance.'

'Yes, captain.'

Yes, captain. No sweeter pair of words in the human vocabulary, as far as Lana was concerned. She tasted the edge of her lips with her tongue. Calder surely didn't need to be educated in the art of kissing, though. Almost as worrying as how long the memory of its warmth lingered in her mind. *Must be a by-product of how few long-term memories I possess compared to everyone else. Obviously that.*

***

When it came time for the jump into hyperspace, to depart Hesperus system for good, Calder had mixed feelings. There was a part of him left nostalgic, perhaps even homesick, for a good honest breeze that'd freeze your breath as it left the mouth, filling your lungs with icy needles. But there was another part of him couldn't imagine abandoning this strange metal temple cutting through the heavens, although he wasn't exactly sure how much of that was due to the woman who captained the vessel, or the execution order hanging over him at home. *You've been collected by the ship too, Calder Durk.* He had rather been expecting to be rejected by Lana Fiveworlds, if truth be told. Back on Hesperus, it was customary for a woman to reject her suitor three times. It was also customary to assign the man challenges to prove his worthiness. Hopefully, Lana's challenges would be a lot less demanding that those set by the princess... such as forming a political alliance to conquer the greatest empire the world had ever seen. *Which didn't exactly end well for you, did it?* Calder felt a sting of self-doubt. Proving himself as an able crewman was obviously the first of Lana's tests. Zeno's education programme was proving indispensable in that regard. How many sim jumps had he made in *Hell Fleet*? How many jumps had he made as a Martian oligarch on his private yacht in *Lives of the Planet Kings*? How many jumps had he made on commercial liners as a TAP agent, hopping between the crimes of a dozen worlds? Now he was wondering what the temporal discontinuity would feel like in reality? A week travelling in hyperspace while six months passed by in the universe outside. It seemed a fair swap, however; to shortcut the generations a starship would need otherwise to waste travelling between the worlds.

Calder assignments involved a busy schedule of maintenance checks across every yard of the translation matrix, as well as spacewalking outside tethered to the ship while he checked the rotating jump vanes for dust ablation and structural fractures. There might have been many a cheap entertainment sim that showed a hyperspace jump as little more than a navigator flinging a single lever forward on the bridge, followed by the stars accelerating into blur-lines, but the reality was far more time consuming, dangerous and prosaic. The *Gravity Rose* was breaching the very walls of space-time with an artificial wormhole, then translating the ship from one state of matter to another, sliding void across an alien plane of existence to shortcut the immutable laws of relativity and decades of slower-than-light travel between worlds. Any one of these acts was bordering on insane. Performing them all in a pre-programmed sequence was nothing short of reckless. Even the sniff of a significant gravity field would destabilise their homebrew wormhole into a homicidal tantrum. The particular curvature of local space-time had to be precisely mapped to allow the *Gravity Rose* to be translated into a protective dark-matter envelope, allowing the ship to exist in transit across the exotic plane of hyperspace, before dropping back into real space without smearing into a million tachyons. None of these you did at the flick of a lever helpfully labelled 'hyperspace jump.'

Calder stood with the chief by the command table. The officer had donned twin sensory manipulation gloves to augment the bandwidth of his crew implant, the desk a riot of hologram symbols rising and falling at his command. He resembled a half-mad conductor directing a symphony. The robots in the chamber had ceased their deranged roller-derby around his table and formed up into a choir, two ranks of mechanicals standing in admiration at this act, this wizard's summoning. They trilled and sung reports relayed from hordes of robots deployed across the drive chambers. The show had been going on for half an hour, now.

'You should have a sickbag to hand, Mister Fighting Fourth,' said Paopao, swivelling a screen forming in front of his eyes.

'I've never been sick yet.'

'They do not show vomit in *Hell Fleet*,' said the chief. 'It would not assist in recruitment. One detail that is often omitted.'

'What, and all the deaths and floggings they show do?'

'You will see soon,' warned the chief. 'The difference between sims and reality.'

Outside, the vanes picked up spin, stirring up a soup of gravity, distorting the matter inside the perfectly spherical steel globe they had launched ahead of them, its mass increasing exponentially. Becoming a wormhole. Paopao tapped a metal cabinet door under the command table with the toe of his boot. 'Sickbags are inside here.'

Calder just shrugged.

'Old Han saying. You never get pregnant in a sim brothel. Not even a little bit.'

'I'll cope.' *I hope.*

- 5 -
A gift on leaving

Zeno checked the communications dish records from his station's computer terminal. A regular habit before the *Gravity Rose* dropped into hyperspace. Flickering around him were interface readouts showing the status of the ship's robots. A thousand situation reports feeding through. Zeno ignored his toiling droids for a second. He searched for one particular pattern of background radiation registering on the sensors, as seemingly random as the spin of a neutron star. With all of Hesperus system stretched out below them: twin suns – a Class G and an A-type main-sequence star – three gas giants and five planets dancing like a clockwork orrery – all the radiation lay beneath them, not above. That just made this supposedly random spike very easy to pick up. *There it is*. So, one of *his* relays was in place. Zeno ran the pattern through his mind, picking out the subtle variations from the spike's agreed norm. Decrypting that information gave him the precise coordinates where the little drone's communications relay was sited, even higher on the elliptic than the *Gravity Rose*. Somewhere outside the deeps of the clean zone spacers used to drop in and out of hyperspace. With the satellite's exact position established, Zeno took control of one of the backup dishes and established a point-to-point laser line with the drone relay.

To outside eyes, the screen on Zeno's station showed only static, the hisses of random radio babble from the speakers. Neither was there any sign of the android talking, his wireless networking carrying everything he needed to communicate through the dish. To Zeno, however, his mind's on-the-fly decryption showed the static as it really appeared wherever the signal originated – a shadowed face waiting against a background devoid of location cues. It took an insane amount of money to send a live message between solar systems through a tachyon relay. *I wonder which of us is the more insane?*

'I was expecting you earlier,' announced the silhouette. A male voice, deep and sonorous. *Him*, then, not one of his representatives.

'The side trip I told you about took a little longer than expected,' said Zeno. 'Rex Matobo's favour has been called in and we're carrying an extra crew.'

'Calling in debts is what Matobo does best. The trouble starts when you ask him for something in return.'

'Talking of which,' signalled Zeno, 'I was wondering when it was going to be my turn to get my back scratched.'

'What you have asked for is a difficult thing, android.'

'Nevertheless.'

'Those who possess the necessary talents are not human. That makes them hard to find, let along bargain with.'

'The shy alien excuse? Well, damn it. I know all I need to know about being human.'

'We have a compact, you and I. You are honouring your end of it. I am honouring mine.'

'I've only got so much patience.' Zeno tapped the side of his head and the laser lost coherence for a second or two in response. Then the signal came back. 'These private little chats of ours might get real hard to arrange, real soon.'

'A bluff. You are not my only source of intelligence on the *Gravity Rose*.'

'Horse-end, I say. We ain't exactly Cunard Line out here as far as the steward count's concerned.'

'Of course not. But the ship is what you need too, android, whether you realise it or not.'

'Not nearly enough, anymore.'

'She will have to be.'

'Shizzle, one day you're going to have to tell me how you do it.'

'It?'

'Forget, brother, forget everything you've done.'

'The trick, I would say, is not to need to.'

'Sometimes I wonder which one of us was manufactured as a machine.'

'You were studio property once, Zeno. Try method acting . . . try pretending to be someone else. Someone who can follow my orders, for instance.'

'Shizzle.'

'Where are you heading next?'

'Transference Station,' said Zeno, 'hunting for a new cargo to pay our bills.'

'Let me know your destination jump coordinates as soon as you have your cargo. Leave them in the usual dead drop on Transference Station.'

The static lost its hidden signal and lapsed back into raw fizzing, even with Zeno's decryption filter running. He sighed and rested his wiry Afro against the blank projection plate, the hissing spit of static flickering across his artificial scalp. His morphic features briefly reset as a golden-skinned Humphrey Bogart.

The whole world is about three hyperspace jumps behind...

The water being squeezed out of his tear ducts was real enough. Every last millilitre of it, more was the goddamn pity. Zeno was about to switch off the monitor when the static suddenly transformed into the man's silhouette again. 'I thought we were done?'

'Listen quickly,' ordered the man. 'My satellite inside Hesperus system has detected a drone vessel heading for your position. It is heavily armed and closing in fast on the *Gravity Rose*.'

'Who the hell does it belong to?'

'I do not know, but given the speed with which it is accelerating towards the wormhole you are creating; my suspicion is that good intentions should not be presumed. It is attempting to intercept you before you jump out.'

'Shizzle!' Zeno rolled the "Z" in the profanity. 'Rex, you—'

***

'Son of a—,' snapped Lana, warnings and tracking icons exploding around her on the bridge as the ship's sensors captured the accelerating profile of the drone. 'What have you done this time, Rex? Who have you screwed over?'

'Do you need to ask, dear girl,' said Skrat from his chair on the bridge. 'I believe it's self evidently us!'

'Bring everything we've got online, Skrat.'

'Already done, but I am rather afraid we won't be weapons-hot in time. That drone is closing too dashed fast.'

I know, I know. Lana tossed all the telemetry on the attacking drone back to the engine room and prayed that the chief would be able to speed up the process of wormhole formation. Then she brought Zeno into the loop on the intercom. 'Zeno, we've— '

'I see this hostile, skipper. Every bot on the lot is hot to trot: preparing to give and receive fire. Damage control parties are moving into place. So, this is Rex's parting gift to us?'

'Guilt by association, I'd say,' snarled Lana. She rotated the communications array back in the direction of Hesperus and trusted that Rex would receive her message before the crafty scumbag was tracked down and killed by whoever had set their damn ship-killer on the *Rose*. *Of course he'll slide out of this mess, it's only Rex's friends he gets killed. Damn, I should have remembered what it was like when he was crew. I'm such an idiot!* 'Rex, there's a heavily weaponized drone on our tail at the jump point. That means that an equally well-armed vessel dropped it off as insurance before heading in-system for Hesperus. Tell me you don't know about this? Tell me that you haven't irked someone so badly that they've sent a warship after your sorry ass?' She punched the message out and leaned back in the chair, fuming, trying to work the angles. That ship killer was honing straight in on the *Rose* using the gravity signature of the artificial black hole forming. The drone had probably been lurking out in deep space when the *Gravity Rose* arrived in Hesperus space, but then, you didn't need to create a wormhole to exit hyperspace, only to enter it. They had escaped detection entering the system. Exiting was going to prove problematic, if not fatal. Even if Lana aborted the jump, the drone had them locked now. The old adage a fellow skipper had once shared in a bar came back to her. *They always nail you on takeoff, never on landing.*

'Polter, can we make the jump before that drone lights us up?'

'My profuse apologies, revered skipper,' said Polter. 'Even with my best effort hyperspace translation, we will be in weapons range for at least a minute before jump out.'

'Close quarter defence wall is online,' called Skrat. Lana could feel it. Her ship implant spreading her consciousness around the ship, the *Gravity Rose*'s systems becoming an extension of her body. A line of kinetic cannons dropped out of their pods, the sensors on their rotating gun barrels scanning near space for incoming projectiles. Lana felt the ship trying to break through the drone's ECM field, steal a reading on what missile package the drone was packing. Their own electronic counter measures formed around the ship, sensor jammers spinning up into life, false signature buoys rolling down into ejector tubes, hypervelocity chaff tubes frantically being loaded by Zeno's robots.

Rex Matobo appeared as a projection floating in front of Lana's command chair. 'Ah, Lana. I am most sorry to see you have run into a few difficulties.'

'I just bet you are. You didn't warn me that I'd need to shoot my way out of the system. Who the hell is it out there closing in on the *Rose*?'

'Hard to say,' shrugged Rex. 'So many people seem to have taken an irrational dislike to me over the years.'

'Yeah, I know how they feel. Come on Rex, what the heck am I facing here?'

'Anticipate advanced fleet-level weaponry. That would be prudent.'

Prudent. Shizzle. Rex was lying, Lana knew him well enough to know that with a steely certainty. Rex knew what was out there and why; he just didn't feel like sharing. 'Your comms signal is scanning as mobile.'

'I am in my vessel, sliding right behind your drive wake. I will be in a position to open fire on the drone within thirty minutes.'

'That's about twenty five minutes after we're dead in the void, Rex, if I can't take that drone out.'

'Do try to stay alive. You are very dear to me. And I apologise again for the rash and disproportionate actions of my enemies.'

'You can stow your apologies up your rear hatch. Where's the drone's mother ship?' demanded Lana. 'Can I expect to be outnumbered any time soon?'

'I don't believe so. Besides, while you and I may occasionally be outnumbered, we are never outclassed.'

'I'll carve that on your tombstone, old *friend*,' said Lana, killing the line.

'The dear chap should sport scales as splendid as mine,' said Skrat, 'that a human can be quite so slippery . . .'

Lana snorted. 'You've heard that old human saying, Skrat: "The enemy of my enemy is my friend." Well, the enemy of my so-called friend is also my enemy, even if we don't want them to be. Don't reckon we've got much choice on this one.'

'Tracking a multiple missile launch from the drone,' said Skrat. 'Rather too small to be nuclear warheads. Probably something to scramble our shields, then the fiend will dive in and rake us clear with kinetic projectiles.'

'Botheration!' swore Polter. The navigator began chanting a prayer as he busied himself with their hyperspace translation. 'Lord, admit us to the vaults of heaven, Lord, admit us sinless to the dark flow.'

Sinless? Lord, if you're out there, jump us just as we are. Lana hovered in her ship's cyberspace above the firing solutions being formed by Granny, close-defence guns juddering as they adjusted in their mounts. Her stomach scrunched itself into a dense ball of dread. The icons of the incoming missiles blinked on and off as their likely positions adjusted ever closer; colour-coded impact probabilities flickering as the salvo's stealth measures battled it out with the ship's sensors for battlefield supremacy. *Come on, drone, Rex is running up behind us, weapons hot and ready for action. He's the one you want, not us. Pull away, keep your powder dry for the real enemy. Run the threat analysis and target the more dangerous vessel.* But the drone kept on coming, as did its wall of missiles. Another screen flicked on. It was Calder in the engine room.

'Skipper, the chief reports our vanes are spinning at maximum. Plot our exit against the current rate of singularity formation. He says it won't be nearly quick enough.'

'Well, tell me something I don't know, your highness.'

'I think I have a way to beat the drone . . .'

'Give me a break,' said Lana. 'A month ago you were running around the snow in bear skins. A couple of episodes of *Hell Fleet* doesn't make you a goddamn carrier commander.'

'Actually,' said Calder, 'this is something I learnt back home from a very wise manservant. When you're hunting a wolf, you must bait the snow with a steak. When the wolf is hunting you, you must bait the snow with two steaks.'

Lana looked at him for a second, before the sheer genius of what he was suggesting struck her like a diamond blade through the skull. 'Calder, I could kiss you.'

'Maybe take the bars on your shoulder off first, skipper.'

'Get to it, Prince Charming, and get to it fast.' Lana killed the feed. She was going to have trouble with that one, she could see that. But only if they lived long enough. 'Polter, plot the mathematics for a second singularity.'

'But revered skipper,' said Polter, 'I cannot possibly keep two wormholes stable simultaneously.'

'I don't need you to,' said Lana. 'Make the second singularity a beast, a real roaring unstable giant. A big, juicy distracting steak. Shrink our first wormhole. Small as you can, with it still able to pass the *Gravity Rose*. Skrat, launch a countermeasures buoy to orbit the mega-sized singularity, make sure its squawking a hell of a lot more radiation than we are. '

Skrat's bridge chair bobbed to the side of Lana's. 'Done! Quite ingenious, although I must say, old girl, it's normally myself who panders to racial stereotypes by acting quite so recklessly. The drone and its missiles should hone in on the decoy wormhole and our buoy, but only if the wormhole's structure endures. I don't believe anyone has ever attempted this before.'

'For good reason,' protested Polter. 'The holy of holies preserve us! I will need to integrate the topography of both wormholes, keep each wormhole in phase with the other so the dirty singularity doesn't destabilise the clean one. Singularity compression on the clean wormhole could prove fatal for us, oh yes... our margin of error on the jump is going to shrivel far beyond all safe thresholds.'

'Shave an inch of steel off our hull if you have to, but jump us just the same,' ordered Lana. 'You're the best in the business, Polter, and damned if you're able to kill us twice. You can do this!'

Lana tried not to bite through her tongue. Rex Matobo was quite capable of killing everyone all on his lonesome, it seemed. She felt the second wormhole forming out in the void across her interface, raw and wild, a screaming whirlpool distorting the normal order of space-time, the ship's sensors protesting at the extra pressure being exerted on them. Off to their starboard, the second singularity shrank, slowly, methodically, the architecture of spin and form that might safely admit them screeching as it was bullied smaller, exotic particles bursting into existence all around the ship. Beyond, their decoy buoy danced around the wild second wormhole opening up. Here I am, it screamed. Here. Here! But the incoming drone and its opening missile salvo had yet to buy into the ruse. Accelerating closer and closer on the *Gravity Rose*. The drone was going to pass them like a Samurai from some damn historical sim, a brief flash of its blade, and Lana's precious ship would be decapitated. *This is all I have, please, please.* She felt the ship's point defences lighting up the kill area around the vessel. Granny plotting firing solutions, planning where she needed to spread her storm of fire to kill the first volley; the processing speed of the *Gravity Rose*'s computer systems matched against the deadly intelligence inside the missiles.

'Impact imminent,' announced Granny. 'Hardening command armour.' There was a clash outside the vessel as thick plating enclosed the bridge, cutting off all sight of the stars, a sandwich of self healing materials that could, theoretically, absorb an acre of hell and still soak up deadly residual radiations.

Lana felt a sudden burst of energy through the sensors as their clean wormhole malformed for a second, before Polter brought it under control. He moaned inside his chair, drumming nervously on his carapace with his two largely superfluous vestigial combat claws. Their navigator only did that when he was praying real hard. Maybe somebody was listening to his devotions. The drone and its missiles suddenly altered their trajectory, vectoring in on their massive singularity and the hyperactive countermeasures buoy orbiting it. *Have we done it? Have we really done it?*

'Singularity seed is transformed. Event horizon on the clean wormhole is formed and stable,' announced Polter, the ledge of carapace above his face bobbing in eager anticipation of his joining with God. Lana felt the *Gravity Rose* manoeuvring into position, responding to the commands from her implant. Lana had never ridden a horse before, but she had a feeling that it would be a lot like this. *Gently, that's it, gently does it. Nothing to indicate we're here. Nothing to look at. Just a tiny little starship jumping clean. And... damn!* Two of the drone's missile salvo suddenly peeled off, accelerating back towards them. Detected her engine burn? She threw stealth to the wind, and the antimatter reaction drive roared into life at her command. Lana felt the surge in the artificial gravity field around the ship, cancelling the Gees that would otherwise have flattened the crew.

Polter reported their status calmly, pacified by the act of navigation. Lana was anything but. 'Vane control is optimal. Dark matter envelope now modelled.'

Outside the *Gravity Rose* her near-space envelope was suddenly filled with a thousand slugs of molten metal streaming towards the missiles, the *Rose*'s guns juddering and spinning all along her hull. While the void was silent, the ship's passages chattered with the clamour of war: chains of shells jangling;

barrel coolant systems squealing. Lana's sensors flashed mad with alert icons. The twin missile strike had split into a dozen sub-components, independent warheads flowering out and tracking in on them from every direction.

'Tidal eye is targeted and locked. Transit entry and pre-translation dive into dark flow will commence in four, three, two . . .'

Lana sat bolt upright in her chair, even as the emergency environment seals triggered, her chair transforming and flowing around her, converting into a lightly armoured space pod. *And still the missiles came.*

***

The world of Hesperus. Six months later.

Noak's wife came back from their small house's entrance hall looking worried. He didn't think it was merely because the ice drifts outside had made getting to market on the far side of town difficult. 'There are two men at the door. They say they have business with you.'

'We haven't been living in the town long enough to have business with anyone we don't know,' said Noak. He had surely travelled far enough East to guarantee that. Any further and they would be across the border. 'What name did they ask for?'

'None,' she said. 'Not our real ones or our new names.'

'Probably just peddlers, my love,' said Noak, 'trying it on.'

He glanced towards the crossbow he had sitting near the roaring fireplace, its iron trigger face shiny in the crackling logs' orange glow. *Always good to keep a weapon to hand.* 'Nobody knows us here.' Most of the people he had served were corpses on the other side of the ocean. Even Noak's nodding acquaintances were rightfully toasting their feet by fires on the far end of the continent. Certainly not out here, in the high mountains, colder even than the plains and the coast.

'They might be customers,' ventured his wife, ever hopefully.

'Might be.' And setting up his shipping concern river-running on a single-sailed sled out in the nub-end of nowhere, Noak couldn't afford to be shy. Not with the wizard's seed money mostly spent over the past six months.

His beloved showed them in. Two large rangy men, both wearing neat bearskin jackets and trimmed beards to match – no swords or crossbows, though. One had a silver fur-lined jacket while the other wore black. This pair certainly didn't look like trappers needing cargoes sailed back west. Their skin was pale too, almost pallid, didn't get out much in the sun-glare. Not locals, for all that they wore tricorn hats in the alpine style.

'Welcome gentlemen,' said Noak. 'Feel the fire on your bones.' He indicated the opposite end of the table he was seated at, a couple of stools close by. 'I am Bertil, the master of the town's shipping company.'

The two stood standing and silver-jacket spoke first. 'We passed your river schooner moored at the bottom of the valley. I am Mister Bligh and this is Mister Thetford.'

Noak nodded. 'You boys aren't peddlers, are you?'

'Travellers,' said the one named Thetford.

'Seekers,' clarified his colleague.

Noak looked at his wife standing by the door to main room. 'Well then, how about you seek out a couple of cups of warm honey beer for our guests, my love? I handle cargo as a rule, not passengers,' continued Noak. 'Mountain salt and pelts, mostly. Not much room for cabins on a narrow-berth river runner. And with names as foreign as yours, I doubt if I'll be sailing far enough away from the mountain ranges for your tastes.'

'We have our own transportation,' said Bligh. 'And what we seek is truth, Noak Barlund.'

'I think you've got me confused with someone else.'

'I doubt that,' said Bligh. Bizarrely, he produced a frying pan from underneath his bearskin. Noak felt a terrible sinking feeling in his gut. Last time he'd seen that pan, it'd been bouncing off a shield-warrior's helm on the other side of the country. 'But we are going to match your DNA to the skin traces on this, just to be certain.'

'Who are Dee and Hay?'

It was at that moment that his wife re-entered the main room, swinging an axe at the nearest visitor, Thetford. She caught the man on the shoulder, cutting down and sending a severed arm flying over to the other side of the room. A childhood filled with chopping wood for a house's fireplace could do that for a girl's back swing. Incredibly, Thetford just stood there, casually glancing at his bloody stump spurting blood as if the wife had done no more than jostle him on a market day.

'That was clever,' said the wounded visitor. 'Your request for beer was a coded signal, warning your spouse.'

Bligh pulled out a pipe-like object from under his jacket. 'Let's just take it as red that you are the prince's manservant.'

The stranger pointed his pipe at Noak and he barely had time to protest, 'Ex-manserv—' before Noak found himself falling to the stone floor, his body paralysed, prisoner in the clutches of a waking nightmare.

Bligh knelt by Noak's side. Noak couldn't see what they had done with his wife from the angle where he'd painfully collapsed, but he noticed there was a strange set of metallic strips tied as a glove around the intruder's hand.

'So, is this the one?' asked Bligh.

Thetford nodded. 'DNA pairing positive; his ribs have fractures sealed with modern bone replication and there are multiple micro fragments of rail-gun shell casing embedded in his spine. Here's the shell match. A General Weapons Combine MA1002 flight drone. It's old school TAMC military surplus.'

It was spells they were talking about, magic. *Matobo the Magnificent, damn his bones*. The sorcery that had flown Noak away from certain death at the hands of the baron's soldiers, the same magic that had healed his broken body. *And they can detect it. Have the priests dispatched their own sorcerers to track down Prince Calder? To track me down?*

Bligh came into view again, kicking Noak's crossbow away. 'Not quite as old school as one's trusty crossbow, though, Mister Thetford.' Bligh smiled, but without an iota of warmth. 'Hello, Noak Barlund. There's one thing you should always remember when consorting with wizards. Their magic always leaves traces. Let's see what you really know, shall we?'

'And with any luck,' said Thetford, 'you will be able to help us locate Prince Calder. That's rather what we're hoping for, isn't it Mister Bligh?'

'Quite so, Mister Thetford.'

Noak couldn't scream. It was as if his lips had been sewn shut. Bligh stroked Noak's hair as though the ex-manservant was a hound, little spines on the metal glove's surface putting pressure on his scalp.

'We're going to take a copy of your mind, which will, I'm afraid, hurt immensely. Burning your synapses out one at a time is not a procedure you can experience under anaesthetic. You have to be conscious during magnetic resonance capture.'

Noak tried to struggle, but his body stoically ignored his requests – not even a toe twitching in response to his increasing panic.

'After you're dead, you will be free. You shall live forever!'

Who is this maniac? The madman's first prediction turned out to be true. Noak's brain burned with all the agony of a tar fire execution in front of the walls of Narvalo. Noak wasn't actually alive to see how the second prediction worked out. But it was amazing how much he could perceive *after* he was dead.

- 15 -
A starship captain is a very fine thing to be

Lana Fiveworlds wasn't used to feeling so useless in the face of death. As the skipper and owner of a starship of the size of the *Gravity Rose,* she was accustomed to barking commands and having them instantly obeyed by her crew. Unfortunately for Lana, the wave of ship killer missiles closing in on her vessel weren't under her authority. The bridge shuddered again, armoured-up in anticipation of the coming impact, close-defence guns outside throwing a kinetic wall of shells forward of her ship. *It won't work,* Lana grimaced to herself. *The warheads have fragmented into their sub-ammunition components. Too damn many of them closing too damn fast.* Her vessel had to be lucky against every sub-missile arrowing in on her hull. Their mystery assailant out there on the edges of deep space taking pot shots at them only had to be lucky once. The *Gravity Rose* had a few tricks hidden away under her hull, but at the end of the day, Lana's vessel was only an independent freighter, not an alliance carrier. *How much punishment can we absorb?* Not enough, she realized. *Not nearly enough.* Only seconds away from a hyperspace jump, but which was to come first. Jump or missile impact? The answer squawked in Lana's direction from her navigator, Polter.

'I've lost a clean lock on the exit jump.'

'How the hell did that happen?' demanded Lana.

'It's the enemy ship, revered captain. They're using their

hyperspace vanes to disrupt local space, throwing my jump calculations off balance. They know we're trying to jump out and they're seeking to trap us here.'

Oh shizzle. Lana cursed the bulky survival pod hardened into existence around her bridge chair. Trying to control the ship from inside the pod was like trying to tread water wearing a suit of armour. 'Come on, Polter,' she cried towards her navigator. 'Get uo the hell out of here. Dive for hyperspace.'

'But we're too far outside our safety margins,' moaned Polter.

Lana briefly regretted pushing her overly sensitive crewman. Well, not so much a man, more a sentient crab. He was attempting the impossible, here, for her. Polter had created twin wormholes to tunnel through into hyperspace. One a super-sized singularity – a frothing wild giant to draw the incoming missiles' attention. Its tiny twin was far too small for any sane skipper to want to fly down to escape this cursed system. Taming a black hole was a pretty insane act in itself; taming two was double the trouble; attempting the act under heavy fire was as bad as it got. And damned if Lana didn't need a stable wormhole to pull off this hyperspace jump and live to boast about it.

The other crewman in their troika on the bridge, Skrat raz Skeratt, yelled from his crew chair, not bothering to hide the desperation in his voice. 'This is no time for caution, dear boy!'

'Jump us!' ordered Lana. Her chair display flashed up the telemetry of warheads being chewed up against their wall of flack, her guns targeting a wave of missiles twisting and turning past their last line of defence. 'We're dead if we stay. Better a chance of jumping out alive, even if it's a damn slim one.' Lana bit hard on her lip. This was a game of chance and she was doubling down on

Polter's talents. Nobody could navigate a hyperspace translation as fast and efficiently as her navigator. That's what she told every client who wanted cargo transporting across the stars. And Lana's boast wasn't just an idle sales pitch. Is it?

'Tidal eye locked,' said Polter, his voice hesitant as he reluctantly obeyed Lana's order. 'We're going in dirty!'

Lana tried to ignore the shaking as the *Gravity Rose* dipped in towards the raging singularity, thrusters at the rear of the ship accelerating them forward.

'Transit is unsafe,' announced Granny, the ship's computer core; her voice clear and reasonable inside Lana's helmet, unaffected by anything so common as hormones, stress or fear. Lana wished she felt as calm as her ship's artificial intelligence. Lana's chair pumped her body full of chemicals, allowing her mind to work at the same swift speed as the ship's systems. She might regret the dosage later, but only if she lived to be so lucky. 'Command override, Granny. There are no safety margins for this ride.'

'Command override accepted. Good luck, Lana.'

Lana checked the overlay of weapons data floating in front of her, the skipper's chair layering it directly against her retina with a laser. The *Gravity Rose*'s sudden potentially suicidal dive into the unstable black hole had thrown off the sneaky artificial minds guiding the incoming warheads. *That's it, you metal ghosts. You weren't expecting that, were you?* Of course, the main reason the missiles weren't expecting it was because what she was doing was utter madness. *The desperate and the foolhardy, my speciality.* The *Gravity Rose*'s hunters only carried a limited supply of reaction mass; the first wave of the missiles' engines started to flutter out, turning off and closing in uncontrolled, unable to outmanoeuvre the freighter's rapidly chattering point defences. From the way the missiles' mother ship turned, Lana guessed the enemy vessel had spotted a third ship in this deadly duel of theirs. Rex Matobo, curse him. Lana's ex-crewman's pleas for help had brought her to this system, and as usual, it was one of his dishonest schemes that were about to get them all killed. The chances were that Rex's ship was the attacking vessel's real target, with the *Gravity Rose* counting as collateral damage. *Guilt by association*. At least, Lana couldn't remember irking anyone recently to the extent that they would be willing to dispatch a fleet-class warship after her. *I'd certainly remember annoying someone that badly, wouldn't I?*

Lana's display divided into two in front of her eyes. Half devoted to weapon systems, the remainder showing the dark rotating whirlpool of their wormhole twisting outside. Her hyperspace vanes had created this beast, now they would have to ride out its fury. Fingers of frothing space-time reached towards the *Gravity Rose*, the vessel shaking violently as she speeded up towards its impossibly small tidal eye. A tiny winking tunnel of safety that they would need to precisely collide with to survive hyperspace translation. There was no more conversation across the bridge. Skrat's attention was on the weapons board, Lana's first mate desperately gaming the battle computers inside the surviving warheads. Polter's attention was fully focused on the mathematics needed to model the artificial black hole and safely translate them through its raging heart. Lana worked hard to hold down the contents of her stomach. They were beginning to change the state of their matter, every molecule of the *Gravity*

Rose and every living thing on board in a state of flux as they converted to the exotic physics of hyperspace. Tachyons riding faster than light, far beyond the grasp of the mortal universe. Polter's race, the kaggens, believed they were transiting the lower realms of heaven by skimming through hyperspace. If his species was correct, then breaching the walls of heaven sure hurt like a mother.

'I believe!' called Polter in an almost joyous agony, the rapture of joining with his jump mathematics overwhelming him.

I wish the hell I did. Lana yelled as the ripples of her altering state swelled and coursed through her body. Skrat cursed like a trooper, too, falling back into his race's sibilant mother tongue and forgetting his civilized Lingual. Lana remained just cognisant enough to focus on her flickering weapons display, the pursuing warheads crushed by the gravitational stress plane, missiles exploding in smeared streams of exotic particles. The bridge's survival pod systems started to die around her, temporarily unable to adjust to existence in this unfamiliar plane of existence, half inside the real universe, half inside the higher realms of hyperspace. *We've never dived as tight as this before. Have I just killed us all?* Matter was changing, time was changing, physics were changing, but the deep shizzle they were in... that just stayed the same old, same old.

Lana woke up in hyperspace just as she always did. Her body aching from the chemical soup of accelerants left swilling around her bloodstream, a throbbing migraine from the chair's injection arousing her from unconsciousness. Also as usual, Polter was awake before her. In all likelihood, the navigator hadn't even passed out. Kaggens were tough little buggers . . .

organic tanks under that tattooed, armoured carapace of theirs. *The perfect navigator, really.* Lana's chair had shifted down from battle mode, returning to being a bridge command chair again; all its armour hardening and environment pod systems absorbed back into the ship's mass.

Lana coughed to clear her throat. 'We're alive, then?'

'Oh yes,' said Polter. 'But only, I believe, due to you commanding the creation of the second wormhole, revered captain. Its unnatural size meant that the enemy ship couldn't destabilise our transit wormhole. The volatile singularity acted as a shield against more than just their missiles.'

'I might have ordered it, but damned if it was my idea.' Lana wished she could take credit for the notion, but the idea for a decoy wormhole had come from the latest addition to her crew. Calder Dirk. And in his case, she suspected, disrupting the enemy ship's attempt to trap the *Gravity Rose* inside the system was an unexpected side effect of the decoy. 'Beginner's luck.'

'Calder might come from a far more primitive culture,' said Polter, 'but you should not underestimate his intelligence. His people survived for a thousand years on an icy perdition of a planet where you and I would be hard-pressed to last six months.'

'Only because his ancestors were dumb and desperate enough to try to colonise that shizzle-hole of a world in the first place,' said Lana. 'And taking his barbarian ass into exile with us was the favour Matobo was calling in, in the first place. If it weren't for Matobo and his tame barbarian prince, we wouldn't have just had that mystery warship trying to detonate nukes off our hull. It was only fair Calder came up with the plan to jump us to safety, wouldn't you say?' *Descended from the dumb and the desperate.* Lana snorted. Calder Durk would fit in just fine on her crew;

as long as he stopped trying to seduce her, that is. She glanced around the bridge. Its design gave the effect of being open to space between its reinforced girders. Hyperspace's rainbow smears had replaced the velvet star-studded night of normal space. Flying through a dimensionless, colourful plane – a little like being gift-wrapped by the Northern Lights. Lana never tired of watching planets and stars from her command chair, but there was something about hyperspace's perspective-free alien depths that always left her unnerved.

'Granny,' said Lana. 'Opaque the bridge's hull. Then run a systems check and crew tally. Did we take any damage?'

'All six members of crew are present and uninjured. No systems damage that I can sense,' said the computer, blank walls replacing the view of hyperspace flashing past outside. 'Zeno's robots are running manual inspections across all areas, but I don't anticipate locating combat damage. Gunnery logs indicate all warheads were intercepted or destroyed during transit. Jump fatigue may be an issue, however. That was not a clean hyperspace translation.'

Lana winced at the censorious tone in the computer's voice. *Jump fatigue. Another damn cost we can't afford.* She looked at Polter. 'Any sign of Rex Matobo's ship?'

'Not on our transit plane,' said the navigator. 'And praise the holy of holies, no sign of the enemy vessel in pursuit.'

Lana grimaced. *Of course not. Rex, you cheap mope.* With whatever monkey Rex was paying for navigator duties on his small ship, Lana's ex-crewman would be lucky to end up in the same galaxy he took off from. 'Well, whoever that was shooting at us, I'm guessing that it was Rex they were really after.'

And Lana wasn't nearly lucky enough to have them actually take out the conniving rogue. She knew exactly how that combat had played out. Sly old Rex suspected that there was going to be an ambush at the system's exit point. Rex had slipped behind the *Gravity Rose*'s engine wake, set them up to occupy the attacker's attention for long enough for him to get a firing solution on the people hunting him, then made his own jump while the attacker was dodging his missiles. *You're an idiot, Lana Fiveworlds. Every time you trust Rex, you end up in this position. Well, hindsight is a wonderful thing.*

'You know, old girl,' moaned Skrat, coming out of the fug of the jump, 'I really rather resent being dangled as bait.'

Lana looked at her first mate. 'Now you know why I didn't want to travel to Hesperus system. Settling an obligation with Rex always costs us more than I ever care to pay.'

'And you humans are unkind enough to stereotype *my* race as disingenuous.'

Lana shrugged at the six-foot tall humanoid lizard. 'Maybe he's got a few skirl genes spliced in, somewhere.'

'Oh, I think we can safely say that fellow is *all*-human.'

'Lay in an exit translation for Transference Station,' Lana ordered. 'Let's see if civilization is going to bring us a job that pays well enough to keep us flying for a while longer.'

'I am not certain if I would characterize Transference as civilized, old girl,' warned Skrat.

'Civilized enough for me,' sighed Lana. Better than the fallen civilization they had just left, at any rate. After visiting the Dark Ages, returning to the fortieth century was going to be a blessing. Lana saw a comms flash from the engine room light up on her board. It wasn't Chief Paopao, though; it was his royal highness-in-exile, Prince Calder Durk.

'Skipper,' said Calder, as the hologram of his face floated up from her chair. 'My ploy worked, then?'

'Better than I thought, Mister Durk,' said Lana. 'Better than you thought too, maybe.'

'It seemed like a sound plan at the time.' Her new crewman sounded pleased with himself. A couple of sim entertainment series under Calder's belt and you might think the barbarian nobleman hadn't lived in medieval squalor for his first two decades. A week ago, he hadn't known there was a world beyond snow-driven battlefields, clashing broadswords and a castle's warm fireplace. Now he was lecturing her about starship combat tactics. Calder Durk didn't lack for cheek, whatever the technological level of his upbringing.

'I don't suppose you know who it was that Rex had irked enough to send a frigate hunting after his ass?'

'Sorry, skipper,' said Calder. 'Only that they are nobody I'm likely to have met. Hesperus doesn't have steam power, let alone interstellar travel. The sorcerer... I mean Rex Matobo . . . he certainly has a talent for making enemies.'

'That he does. I'd compile a list, but I don't think our data core is big enough to hold all the names of the planets that would like to see Rex dead.'

Part of Lana felt sorry for Calder, tangled up in Rex's latest failed get-rich-quick scheme. Calder had lost his family, friends and kingdom, and all because Rex has chosen to play Wizard of Oz with Hesperus's slipped-back society. Calder had joined the "Screwed-by-Matobo Club". It wasn't a particularly exclusive establishment, Lana was a member herself. But as Rex's favours went, maybe having Calder on board wouldn't be too bad. Part of Lana hoped the nobleman-in-exile wouldn't be tempted to jump ship after they made planet-fall. That he would choose to remain on board as crew. A nice warm planet with a decent welfare system and a stable society . . . that was going to prove a hell of a temptation for a man as new to the modern galaxy as Prince Calder. And her feelings were clearly nothing to do with the kiss that Calder planted on her lips before they jumped away from his home system. *I need extra crew, and this neo-barbarian prince is cheap and fresh, and that is all there is to it.* 'You and the chief give the engines a thorough examination before we arrive at Transference Station. That was one dirty jump we made out of your system,' chided Lana. 'It's a wonder we didn't tear off a few vanes diving through a hole that unstable.'

The chief of the drive room's cantankerous voice emerged from her chair's comm. 'Only thorough maintenance, here! Do you say I am not doing my job?'

'Calm down, chief. The *Gravity Rose* is creaking around the gunnels now, and you know it. Just the way she is. Nobody's fault.'

'Hesperus isn't my home anymore,' said Calder, a tinge of sadness in his voice. 'I can never go back, can I?'

'No,' agreed Lana. 'You can never get back what you've lost, Mister Durk. The only trick is never to miss it.' Calder signed off. *Maybe after a few years of repeating those sentiments, I might even believe them myself.*

Lana wasn't pleased. Most the time, hands-on flying a starship the size of the *Gravity Rose* wasn't any challenge. All you could really do with her was boost out of a system until you got to gravity-clean space, then make your hyperspace jump. Arriving at a system wasn't any better. Translate down into real space well clear of any gravity wells and decelerate until you made orbit at your destination. The single piece of half-demanding flying Lana ever got to make was closing with orbital stations and gently nosing into their docking clamps. And here the tugs were, spoiling her fun. Hologram telemetry bobbed either side of Lana's command chair, her crane-suspended seat elevated under the bridge's topside viewing dome. She watched the two tugs hovering a mile off her position, each vessel packing antimatter engines large enough to make a game attempt at dragging a small moon into a new orbit. Frankly, their presence was insulting. Or perhaps the pilots' fees that Transference Station would undoubtedly try and sting Lana for was just another way for the locals to shake a few extra dollars out of her on top of cargo duties. Lana glanced down towards Skrat's chair hovering below hers, the first mate running search algorithms across the terabytes of data he was downloading from the world's data sphere. If there was a currency differential to be squeezed out of a trade or an intersystem commodities discrepancy to be leveraged, Skrat would seize onto that nugget like a prospector panning for gold.

'Tugs,' she called down, not even bothering to signal it chair-to-chair. 'Two of them!' The tone she used indicated she wouldn't have been more surprised if they had arrived to find a pair of winged unicorns galloping through the void. 'I must be getting old. Sweet Nebulae, and here you were worried about Transference Station not being civilized enough.'

'Compared to the alliance,' said Skrat. 'Only compared to the alliance, dear lady.'

From the way Skrat's thick, muscled tail was quivering through the perfectly Skrat-sized tail-hole in his seat, the first mate must have honed in on an opportunity or two for her vessel. *Or is that just me hoping against experience?* Every year the lawless border systems of the Edge got a bit closer to being fully absorbed inside the Triple Alliance, and after that sad day occurred, Lana wouldn't be sliding void any more. She'd be flying through a meteor storm of safety rating agencies, ship insurance claims, export documentation and health & safety directives. She'd be competing against the big commercial space lines and corporate houses, and then pickings would get real slim, real quick. Might as well convert her vessel into a casino ship and select a gas giant in a T3 system with a pretty weather system to orbit. She could slit her wrists to the sounds of games of baccarat and the endless clink of slot machines.

'Give me some hope here, Skrat. Toss the skipper a bone. At least tell me they haven't rescinded their open weapons policy on the station?'

'Rather the contrary, they are currently insisting that all ship crews enter the station board armed. It seems there is a disturbing new trend in gang violence . . . since we last visited, a youth subculture has emerged called "monking". Gangs are roaming the station sporting habits, tonsures and speaking tape-learnt Latin. That's an ancient human language.'

'So I recall, Skrat. I am human, you know.'

'I forget, skipper. Quite frequently, you act so relatively reasonably that I often think of you as skirl with an unfortunate scale deficiency about your skin.'

In the navigator's chair, Polter rose up to hover off Lana's side. 'Did I hear you correctly? There are gangs masquerading as servants of God and offering violence to honest citizens? This is blasphemy!'

'The little scamps are only speaking Latin to mess with their parents and cut their folks out of the street jive,' said Lana. 'Latin was the original Lingual. Maybe they're being ironic.'

Skrat shook his head, sadly. 'If there was a significant skirl population at Transference there would be order and discipline here.'

'A place for everyone and everyone in their place?' smiled Lana. Maybe that's why there were so many interlocking pyramids of hierarchy in skirl society, layers upon layer piled on top of each other like social landfill. Everyone got a position and a title and someone to boss around below them. Even the skirls at the bottom of the heap had dirt-cheap robots to abuse. Lana glanced at the image of Transference Station on the screen, the globe-girdling structure reduced to an engineer's blueprint, a 3D model of the station rotating around the blue-green orb of the world of Transference itself. Just looking at the station, you knew that this was the oldest trading hub in Edge – that glorious crescent of independent space hugging the alliance like a cracked leather money belt around a tourist's paunch. A little more shaved off the fat each year, but what the hell.

Unlike some of the *Gravity Rose*'s more recent layovers, the world didn't feature a comet-sized spinning top as its space station, nor a ten mile-long O'Neill cylinder, nor that station classic – a multi-tiered donut of linked wheels spinning to simulate gravity on the cheap. No, Transference Station was a band circling the world below as if it was one of Saturn's rings cast solid in steel, plastic, glass and shining ceramic composite; arms extending off the habitat like ribs from a whale's carcass. There were purportedly more people living on the station now than the world below. Lana could imagine that one day in the future, her descendants would arrive here on the *Gravity Rose* and the station's structure would have completely enveloped the planet, only a few patches of world left visible through gaps in the station's exterior. The planet plunged into perpetual darkness by their trading station's success. With this many people in orbit, you weren't dealing with a commercial operation any more. You were dealing with a culture. And much like the cultures Lana found growing in the bottom of her abandoned coffee cups, dealing with it was always going to leave her feeling queasy.

'It seems that our approach has been noted, old girl. We have an e-mail from Dollar-sign Dillard,' said Skrat. 'He's offering to pay our docking fees if we mate at port nine-two-thirty and hear out a proposal he has to make.'

Lana frowned. *That is a far better neighbourhood than we can afford to dock at on our own; but I'd been hoping for a legit job.* 'Dollar-sign Dillard. Haven't we got any offers from upright brokers? How about the Hansard Combine? They've always got a cattle run or two out to some shiny new colony world.'

'It appears not this time around.'

'We've got a reputation, Skrat. We've got a reputation here, as well as a ship.'

'I warned you,' said Skrat. 'Economies of scale. Have a look at the station's docked vessel list. Since our last visit here, another seven per cent of ships listed as independents are now re-flagged as flying for corporate houses. Skippers are still selling out. Cutting their losses before there's a freight monopoly in operation so tight they could earn more funds selling their ship to an aerospace museum.'

'This is my ship and this is all I know how to do. All I want to do.'

'There will come a time...' warned Skrat.

'To hell with that,' said Lana. She jabbed a finger towards the coin-shaped world suspended against the night. 'If the Edge isn't in that direction anymore, then it lies behind our stern. Not every system wants to join the alliance.'

'I'm a little old to become a deep space explorer,' noted her lizard-snouted first mate. 'Or, indeed, a colonist.'

'So, docking fees paid, just for a face-to-face with DSD. What does that tell us?'

'Possibly, that I should keep on searching the local data sphere's "starship haulage wanted" section,' said Skrat.

'Money,' said Lana. 'Serious money being dangled in front of us. Come on, nobody loves money more than a skirl . . .'

'You're an ape-evolved racist. This is one skirl who enjoys living as much as he does social advancement.'

'Living free, Skrat. Living free.'

'Dollar-sign Dillard has lived a long time,' noted Polter. 'Surely the will of the Devine had seeped into his bones over the centuries. Perhaps in this matter, he is a tool of God's volition?'

'There's not much bone-mass left in DSD's body,' said Lana. 'Zeno's lived a lot longer than our slimy broker buddy . . . and how divinely do you see our android acting?' *Will of the devine. Shizzle.*

- 16 -
Top Cats

With the *Gravity Rose* clamped to a spur off Transference Station's central ring — just one of dozens of docked starships visible — Lana waited as the station passenger arm extended towards their airlock. It was always deathly silent inside her airlock. The sounds of the vessel sealed behind her, the noise of station life still walled off by vacuum. Polter, Skrat and Zeno waited alongside her. On many worlds, a man-sized crab, a humanoid lizard and a golden-skinned android with a wiry Afro might draw a few stares. *Where we're heading today, we'll pass as thoroughly pedestrian.* A whir sounded from the heavy door behind Lana. It slid open and Calder Durk joined them. He still looked like a greenhorn in his ship overalls, as worn as the pass-me-downs had been made by their previous occupant. Well, a month of sim episodes and tape learning couldn't make up for the man's first twenty years of life stranded on a medieval hellhole of a world. Calder was a rescue cat, a favour, an exile. But there was a little bit of that in all of Lana's crew. Maybe that was why Lana had acquiesced quite so readily to that conniving dirt-sucker Matobo's request for her to rescue the barbarian prince from pot-roasting by his political enemies.

'Mister Durk,' said Lana. 'I presume from the fact you're standing here on your lonesome that you couldn't inveigle the chief out of the drive rooms for a spot of shore leave?'

'He laughed every time I mentioned the word Transference Station, captain.'

There was a little too much naval bearing about Calder for her taste now. Lana could see that the new boy was resisting the urge to salute every time he saw her; the hesitancy in his voice from choking off a "Sir, yes sir!", each time he spoke. But she could blame that on Zeno; the android getting their new recruit fixed on sim shows like *Hell Fleet* and all. The *Gravity Rose* wasn't a jump carrier or a missile ship, and apart from the chief, none of her crew had ever been career fleet. That was a deliberate choice on Lana's part. There were always ex-military types looking for work across the civilized worlds, but they were too buttoned-up for the relatively casual regime she ran on board her vessel. *Be honest with yourself, girl. Too honest for some of the dicey trade you have to sign on for, as well.*

'Don't take it too personally, Mister Durk. The chief wouldn't leave the engine room even if we were orbiting his home world.'

'I didn't realize the chief had a home world,' observed Skrat, laconically. 'I always thought the prickly fellow must have been a cloning accident on board a carrier.'

'That's an act,' said Lana. 'The chief was born on Quin Hon.' She pointed Calder's empty waist out to Skrat. 'Get the man dressed.'

Her first mate placed a scaly hand on the weapon locker plate and the bin swung open as it recognized his biometrics. Skrat pulled out a rail pistol attached to a tangle of black webbing and tossed it at Calder – a twin of the gun the rest of the crew wore for shore leave. Well, not Polter, but with those vestigial fighting claws tucked on top of his carapace, Polter could cut his way through a steel deck if he had a mind to. A five-foot tall amphibious tank wasn't something most humans took it into their mind to anger. You didn't have to have been nipped by their nearest Earth analogue – a crab – to show the Kaggen race a healthy measure of respect.

'There's only one rule, Mister Durk,' said Lana, watching Calder finger the malevolent, icy cold slab of weaponized ceramic, green light from its magazine readout pulsing across his palm to indicate a full charge and a hundred shot magazine. 'You draw it, you better be prepared to kill someone with it.'

Calder grunted and pulled the straps tight around his waist and leg, clipping the holster in place.

'We can buy you a longsword if you prefer to go sixth century on us.'

'A longsword is two-handed,' said Calder. 'I was trained on a falchion. Shorter by seven inches.'

'Shizzle, boy, there's a job for you as a sim consultant if they ever revive the *Conan* franchise,' said Zeno.

'Feel free to ignore him,' said Lana, arching an eyebrow in the direction of the ship's android. 'The broker we're going to see is a media geek. Zeno here is just getting himself in the zone.'

'Dollar-sign Dillard is the only chap within a hundred parsecs who actually cares that Zeno played Lando Calrissian's grandson in the remake of Galaxy Wars,' noted Skrat, dryly.

The android's wiry Afro bristled in indignation. 'It was the reboot of the remake of the *Star Wars Golden Republic* TV series, you skirl heathen. And if your species hadn't got lucky by buddying up with humanity, you'd still think Noh Theatre was state-of-the-art entertainment.' The android formed his hands together and threw the shadow of a rabbit on the wall, wiggling the animal's ears under the bright airlock light. 'Hey, look, viewers, I'm a mighty skirl sand baron, and my nest is entangled in an indecipherable political turf war with a lower hierarchically-placed nest.'

Skrat's tail swished angrily behind him. It sounded a lot like a fencer testing the air with a foil before a duel. 'Dear boy, I think we can safely classify sim addiction as cultural pollution, rather than an actual art form.'

'Play nicely, boys,' ordered Lana. 'Or you can spend your shore leave with the chief inside one of his reactors, sponging down the anti-matter injectors.' She saw the look on Calder's face. 'Just a little horseplay, your highness. We're every bit as tight as a Triple Alliance carrier on board the *Rose*.'

'Yes, I can tell.'

That's the trouble with civilizing a barbarian nobleman with Zeno's selection of sim episodes and tape learning... you never get your facts in the round; too many of the subtleties whistle straight over your head. 'Finding sentients whose chain you can actually jerk is a rare and precious thing in this universe,' said Lana. 'Not everyone has a sense of humour you can understand.' Lana tapped Polter's elaborately tattooed carapace. 'With the kaggenish, humanity also shares its belief in the one true God and the hope that we can be better than we are. That and the fact that kaggens inexplicably find humanity as cute as we think we are.'

'You mean there's only one god?' said Calder, but Lana ignored him.

'Our affection for your species is not inexplicable, revered captain,' said Polter. 'You are just like a pet tree monkey, only larger.'

Lana ignored her navigator, too. 'And with the skirls we share a love of money, and, given our relative propensities for violence, some would say the taste for a good war as well.'

'At least when we fight now, dear girl, we're on the same side,' said Skrat.

'And what bang-up truths does humanity share with my kind?' asked Zeno.

'The copyright on your design and a healthy master-servant relationship?' suggested Lana, only largely in jest.

'Shizzle, I guess that's why you call them human rights.'

'You're always as a good as human to me,' said Lana.

'Now you're just being nasty,' said the android.

Lana watched the docking arm draw close to them, less than ten feet away and slowing to mate with the *Gravity Rose*. An accordion-like passage of reinforced grey plastic, the arm was cheap, functional tech, but worlds rarely got rich by building better. 'So, Skrat and me will go and visit DSD and find out what he's got that's so hot he's willing to stake our docking fees up front. Polter, I take it you're off to the local cathedral?'

The navigator signed agreement with one of his bony hands. 'As a lay preacher, it is my duty to share the blessings of crossing heaven with my fellow believers.'

Lana looked at the android. 'Zeno?'

'I have a couple of errands to run, too,' said the android. 'I'll catch up with you later.'

'I thought you might want to take our new boy and show him a good time.' Lana regretted saying the words almost as quickly as she spoke. *But that isn't trying to bribe Calder into staying around, is it? Just a common courtesy any captain would show to someone new to the ship. New to the civilized universe, for that matter.*

'Ah, to feel the needs of the flesh and have flesh with needs. Thanks, but no thanks. Given the gang problem on station, I though it might be safer if Calder went along to meet DSD with you. Everyone should meet Dollar-sign at least once in their lives. If only to see why getting pickled isn't as much fun as the marketing makes out.'

'Okay then. We'll catch up at the Fantasma Blanco later,' said Lana. Part of her was pleased. She could keep an eye on Calder and make sure he didn't get into any trouble, and the plan hadn't even looked as if it was her idea. 'We'll chew over whether the risk-reward of this job is actually worth the potential burn.'

Calder nodded cheerfully, as though he knew that the Fantasma Blanco was a spacers' bar named after the effects of a popular drug banned centuries ago. As if he had half a clue about just who it was they were going to meet and how crafty DSD could prove. Well, pretending you knew what you were doing was as much a part of being crew as anything else. *Bluffing has worked well enough for me to date.*

'Doesn't the chief get a say in what cargo we take on?' asked Calder.

'I'm the skipper,' said Lana, 'nobody gets a say. You just get to voice your thoughts, is all, so I know I'm examining the situation from all the angles. And as far as the chief is concerned, one system looks pretty much the same as the next when you never leave the engine room.'

A screen next to the door indicated a safe seal was formed with the station's gantry. Lana tugged the lock open . . . a slight sweet smell to the air on the other side. The world of Transference had low traces of methylene in its atmosphere and the station ran their environmental systems just like Mamma had baked below. *About the only sweet thing in Transference Station.* They walked through a thin cloud of sparkling dust filling the corridor, decontamination nano – imperceptibly testing the visitors' blood and DNA to make sure their health matched the ship's pre-arrival check-up data. *Pity the authorities never scrub the billions living in the station.* Lana was more likely to catch something from Transference's locals rather than the reverse. After the decon cloud they passed through the habitat's entrance. Transference Station's main ring was divided into six levels, if only to give the property realtors something to justify their price differentials. Anyone buying bottom on six didn't need a mortgage, they needed a laser fence to keep the locals out. Lana saw they were on one of the midlevels, a plaza chamber scattered with fountains and public art. A good attempt to make the station look civilized to visiting eyes, but the station cops in twenty-foot high exo-armour couldn't be mistaken for modern art, even with the fountains' water foaming into all sorts of creative rollercoaster shapes under focused gravity compression. A glass-viewing gallery lay in front of Lana, aluminium rails to clutch while watching the spin of the world below. She glanced down. *Just as I remember it. Nothing ever changes here.* Transference Station locked to its parent planet's spin, a circlet set above the oceans. Nobody in the Edge had the money and resources to build space elevators – that was strictly alliance tech – so cargo and passengers shuttled between ground and station the economic way, little motes of light exploding across the seas below as craft powered their way into orbit. Engineless drones, little more than water-filled cones riding giga-lasers up to space. Going down it was heat shields and gravity brakes and biodegradable parachutes. The fortieth century and steam power – albeit liquid reaction mass under laser ignition – was still going strong. *You have to hand it to humanity; no good idea goes to waste.* Everything ended up being recycled – metals, plastics, technologies, politics. No wonder that near-immortal sentients like Zeno ended up jaded. *History's merry-go-round just keeps on spinning.* Lana's thoughts turned to Dollar-sign Dillard waiting for them in his office. *Some people cling to the ride just a little bit tight.* Yeah, everyone deserved to meet him once. Trouble was, for Lana, she classed this visit as once too often for her taste. She walked towards a crescent of benches on the far side of the viewing gallery, a gaggle of women in colourful dresses gossiping in a language she didn't speak. A Brazilian derivative, maybe, if their dark features were any guide. Children played around their feet. Lana felt conflicting emotions as she observed the kids enjoying themselves. *Forget it, girl. A starship is no place to bring up a toddler. You're living proof of that. Your whole family dead on a foreign world, leaving you to be raised by a ship's A.I and an android.*

Lana watched her navigator peel off towards church, while Zeno left for whatever passed as shore leave for the reclusive android. 'Come on,' she sighed. 'Let's go and visit DSD.' *And let's see if we can get away without burning up on re-entry this time.*

Polter was approaching the temple of the Unified Church when a gang of young humans stepped out from a break between two living units, blocking his path. Polter was the only one walking along the pavement at the moment. A few automated transport pods moved up and down the street, but their windows were mirrored, no doubt displaying entertainment feeds so the inhabitants wouldn't have to notice the low rent neighbourhood they were passing through; insulated from guilty pangs at the poverty of the station's lowest level. *But this is where mother church so often does her business, amidst those that need succouring most.* The kaggen navigator could see that the gangsters were dirt-poor even as he took in their feral pinched faces – chests a riot of competing animated adverts, clothes handed out free from a sponsorship store. These braves had hacked their clothes' broadcast fibres, though, muting the sound – breeching the terms under which the dole shops passed them the shirts, jackets and trousers. It would take a brave store enforcer to call such scruffs to account, though. They would no doubt take one look at the illegally amped shock sticks clutched in their fists and decide that discretion was the better part of valour. Polter whistled in disgust as their leader stepped out of the crowd. He wore a home weaved monk's habit, having shaved his head into a brutal tonsure. So, what Polter had heard on the ship was true then. Shocking, but true. *Blasphemy in its rawest form.*

'Da mihi pecuniam tuam, spumae,' snarled the gang leader.

'I might forgive you your crude mangling of Latin,' said Polter. 'But your mockery of a churchman is something I find reprehensible.'

The young thug lifted up his phone, a tiny black ceramic stick tied to his belt as though it was a bible. He abandoned his attempts at Pig Latin and indicated that his device was set to receive a transfer of funds from Polter's device. 'You walk our streets, you pay our toll.'

Polter lifted up a manipulator hand and indicated the temple entrance less than a hundred feet away. 'These streets belong to our Lord, young miscreant. You must present your hearts to the Holiest of Holies if you are to prosper. Offer me not violence but your penance.'

'This is what I have for you,' said the gang leader, jabbing the shock stick an inch short of Polter's face, little sparks of energy flashing against his heavy carapace above. 'What are you, some kind of snail-head? You're carrying your house around on those mutant legs of yours? How many dollars you got on your phone for me?'

'If you weren't truanting quite so effectively, young human, you might have learnt that I am a Kaggen,' said Polter. He seized the gang leader's hand and pulled the weapon down onto the surface of his shell, a lightning flash of blue electricity coursing across his elaborately tattooed carapace as the weapon discharged in a couple of seconds. Jabbing down with a bony finger, Polter paralyzed the faux monk's hand, removed the spent shock stick and tossed it aside in less time than it took the ruffian to scream in surprise. 'I have felt the agony of the Holy of Holies as I have trespassed across his realm, I have broken the folds of hyperspace and been rewarded with infinite bliss. You think this mean spark you carry can touch me? It is less even than the marks of pollution spotting your soul.'

The others charged in and had at the navigator with their sticks, a sulphurous stink filling the street as his shell danced with weapons discharge. Polter gave them long enough to realize that ten of their illegally amplified anti-mugging devices simultaneously striking his body were only going to yield the same result as their leader's weapon. Then he unfurled his two vestigial fighting claws, filling the entire width of the pavement with the clacking of his razored pincers. 'We are no longer a violent species, but I am sorely tempted to chastise your flesh!'

Driven into a murderous rage through his loss of face, the gang leader ran at Polter screaming a string of incoherent blasphemies. The navigator gave him the blunt end of his right claw, lifting the chief off his feet and sending him sprawling against the wall of the nearest building. There the thug lay, moaning, while his pack of young bandits fled as Polter's six legs pincered his bulk towards them. They were no longer facing an alien stranger begging to be liberated of his purse. They were fleeing an advancing organic tank, a species that had once battered and clawed its way to the top of its ecosystem's food chain, on land and underwater.

Scooping up the semiconscious thug, Polter walked unaccosted the rest of the way to church. Climbing the steps, double doors opened automatically in front of him. There was already a congregation at worship in the pews, mainly humans, a few representatives of other species who had embraced the unified church. *Linking their destinies to the universal spirit.* Hidden speakers in the eaves of the church began blaring out a hymn of welcome, recognising the identity of a lay preacher signalled by Polter's presence. The vicar was a human female, sitting on the altar under the joined cross and crescent of humanity's original church, the centre of the cross bisected by the lightning flash of the skirl's religion. She beat passionately on the holy water drum of the kaggens, almost as well as one of his own species. A choir stood on her left, singing and wildly drubbing on their own instruments.

'I have come,' cried Polter. He tossed the miserable gang leader down on the aisle and drove him towards the altar with a few spear-like prods from his jabbing feet. 'I share the miracle of transiting heaven, and I bring one who needs to repent. Forward, you wicked little tree monkey. Forward to find the Holiest of Holies within your foul heart.'

'Brother!' yelled the vicar, leaping down. She pulled the gang leader to his feet and was passed a drum which she forced into the thug's hands. 'Play, boy, play! Drum the evil out of your soul.'

He stumbled and swayed, awed by the subliminal majesty of the hymn, and began drumming as the rapture swept him up, a deep sonic beat possessing his limbs. It was doubtless the first time the miscreant had been to church . . . but the addictive chemicals on the skin of the drum would ensure it wouldn't be his last.

Polter turned to face the congregation, their faces earnest and mesmerized. He battered on his tattooed shell with his two weapon claws; appendages of war remade into one the holiest tools of worship. Swords into ploughshares and pincers into drum sticks.

'I have remade the universe to reach the lowest halls of heaven and the universe had remade me!' cried Polter.

Hallelujah, returned the congregation. *Hallelujah!* Polter was home.

The part of Calder not yet inculcated to the wonders of the future by Zeno's sim entertainments found the idea of so many people living in a metal ring circling a world quite bizarre. On a mental level, Calder knew the advantages of living in orbit rather than dirt-side were legion. Never too hot. Never too cold. Immune from pollution, tsunamis, hurricanes, ice ages, global warming, volcanic eruptions, landslides, rising sea levels, acid rain and harsh seasons. But the born-and-raised on Hesperus native in him found the concept just a little claustrophobic. On the *Gravity Rose* you were always aware you were on a ship – but her passages that stretched for miles and hydroponic gardens giving out to the void had never felt quite so out of place as this. On Transference Station it was as though the noises and smells of the most crowded city in Hesperus had been packed into decks crammed with houses and shops and factories and commercial concerns. The idea of living here, well, it just felt wrong in a way that serving on board the *Gravity Rose* hadn't. Maybe because with just the six of them rattling around the *Gravity Rose*'s cavernous spaces, life on board the massive ship had never seemed as congested or busy as this. The habitat's transportation tube brought Calder, Lana and Skrat to a fancy commercial district. Glass-fronted office buildings interspaced with boutique stores and hand-milled coffee shops, workers in dark sober business suits. An area that seemed at odds with the bent nature of the commission Lana expected to negotiate. These corporate drones put Calder in mind of the priests back home, the same dead faces and intentness of purpose. The manner in which they burnt people here might involve articles of law rather than tar baths and petrol-filled cauldrons, but Calder suspected the results were frequently the same. It was all very *Lives of the Planet Kings*, albeit a slightly lower rent version of the lifestyles enjoyed by the sim show's planetary plutocrats. Not an advert to be seen on any shirt or jacket here. Calder guessed that the executives of this neighbourhood didn't source their clothes free from sponsorship stores and dole shops. *Are the locals even exposed to marketing here?* Perhaps this level's inhabitants knew as a matter of instinct which little ceramic fingernail of a device displayed on a black cushion in a shop display was the current season's must-have object of desire. Up until a month ago, Calder would have said that a brand was a burning hot length of iron used to mark your family's slaves. But the royal-in-exile was learning fast.

Lana led them to a rise of crystal-fronted offices, a marble-floored atrium with a wall of brass plaques mounted behind a curved desk. The organisations' names looked exotic to Calder. They gave away little indication of purpose or function. The prince studied them, as if staring could decipher the firms' line of business. Old Star Associates, TZL Analysis and Masterworld Group. Much like the boutiques outside, cryptic signalling only enhanced their status. If you had to ask, you had already failed to appreciate their value. To the rear of the reception sat a robot, a pretty woman's face swimming pixelated inside its glass-screened head, octopus arms on the body flickering across of a bank of concealed instruments.

'Trans-space Situations,' announced Lana. 'Three expected.'

'Welcome Captain Fiveworlds,' said the robot, the photo-realistic animation tilting inside the domed head, dazzling white teeth smiling at the three of them as if they were diplomats turning up at a foreign court. 'Take the elevator to the top floor, please.'

The lift was designed with retro-historic styling; wrought iron doors and ancient polished wood on walls and floor. Of course, to Calder even an antique lift was a future that had never arrived at his primitive world. What it took the party to might have been considered retro-historic too. Calder gawped in amazement at what lay beyond. An entrance hall, gleaming spotless white, dotted with hundreds of coin-size holographic projectors. This rig wasn't being used for remote teleconference calls, though. It was being run to fill the chamber beyond with a cartoon landscape – trees with human faces in the bark swaying while impossibly cute animals gambolled across the grass – squirrels, rabbits and chipmunks. Wooden faces gurned at Calder, and through the passage of oaks, he could just make out a city beyond a set of hills, little puffs of smoke emerging from factors stacks. Fumes coiled up towards a golden sun hanging high in a cloudless sky; the sun glaring irately at the pollution and blowing it away whenever it drifted too close. Filled with this faux animated landscape, it was impossible to tell how big the room beyond really was. Calder could be standing in the entrance to something office-sized; or the space might be on the same scale as one of the cavernous cargo cambers back on board the *Gravity Rose*.

A chime behind the prince announced that the lift doors had opened again, bringing someone else to the hallway. As he turned, a small metal device floated out of the elevator – a steel globe with a segmented trunk hanging off the sphere; shiny lenses for eyes on either side of the proboscis. Its burnished metal exterior was engraved with a series of currency signs, including the alliance T-bill. *Another robot or a mobile holo-projector*? Perhaps they weren't going to meet Dollar-sign Dillard in person after all?

Lana nodded towards the sphere. 'DSD. It's been a while.'

'Captain Fiveworlds,' hummed the sphere, dipping in the air, its proboscis waving from side-to-side to take in Calder and the first mate. There was something vaguely unsettling about the way the trunk moved, as if the organ was alive. An erection in metal saluting them. 'Zeno isn't here with you?'

'Other business, apparently.'

'A pity. I was hoping to ask him what he thought about the recent Oscar nominations.'

'What, you haven't got enough fanboys in the local data sphere to gossip with? What's the system's population up to these days? Twenty billion?'

'Twenty billion freshly minted turds-for-brains, perhaps, each blogging as if their fatuous gushings are original and unique. Not a one able to bring Zeno's vast experience to a discussion on cultural matters.'

Calder gazed in confusion at the skipper talking to the sphere. 'Are we to meet virtually? Is this a teleconference suite?'

'Calder Durk, meet Dollar-sign Dillard. Calder here is trying out for the newbie's position on the *Rose*.'

Calder didn't like the way Lana said that. It sounded a little too much like cabin boy, rather than the respect due the ex-ruler of an entire kingdom. *But you're not heir apparent anymore, used to having everyone from farmers to generals sucking up to you.*

'Interesting,' came the voice from the sphere. 'The boy's accent is archaic, older than I am, even.'

'We recently extracted the dear chap from a failed colony world,' said Skrat. 'An Iron Age level of technology and minimal contact with offworlders for the last thousand years or so.'

'Ah,' said the globe. 'Linguistic drift, Mister Skeratt, of course. And no doubt suffering from the afterburn of a few nasty training viruses to bring him up to speed.'

'I think I need to be injected with a few extra ones,' said Calder, suspiciously eyeing the machine. 'Are we not to meet face-to-face?'

'Oh, but you are,' bobbed the sphere, the metal trunk weaving excitedly about. The voice sounded amused. 'What is left of my face is inside the pod you see before you.'

'DSD is a cybernetic,' said Lana. 'Life extension treatments currently only take you to your seven hundredth birthday. If you want to go further, then...' she encompassed the sphere hovering above the floor, 'this is what's required.'

Calder recoiled in disgust. *There are the remains of a human inside that thing? How can anyone consider inhabiting a floating urn, living?*

'Why not use the prevailing term for what I am,' said Dollar-sign Dillard, 'which is to say, pickled.' He bobbed forward, arrowing towards the colourful hologram landscape of the chamber beyond. As he passed the projection system's threshold, the cartoon form of a male humanoid cat replaced the steel globe . . . a tall feline sporting a red-banded hat titled at a jaunty angle and a cane swinging in his brown-furred hand. 'That's better. Come on in, let's talk business.'

'Why haven't I seen anything like him in my sims?' Calder whispered across to the skipper as they approached the animated landscape.

'Because the shows you've been fed by Zeno are produced and set in alliance space,' said Lana. 'And getting pickled isn't legal in the core worlds.' They crossed the projection line and Lana's body shimmered and changed, a cartoon analogue replacing her body. It was accurate enough – long blonde hair tied at the back, a full chest heaving out of her green ship overalls. The skipper's eyes were exaggerated and oversized, though, long lashes blinking in a seductive manner sadly absent from the real Lana. The artificial intelligence controlling the animation had taken extra liberties with Skrat's body, the proud lizard decked out with a dark top hat and a monocle fixed across his left eye. Calder's own body was overlaid with a barbarian's muscled form – furry trousers and a comically large axe. He would have frozen to death in ten minutes back home if he had tried to cross the land dressed so poorly.

'Oh, it's legal enough,' said DSD, overhearing their conversation. Calder would have to be careful around this bizarre creature. The globe's cybernetic hearing could probably eavesdrop on conversations on the opposite side of the station. 'You're just not allowed to hang onto your property or remain an alliance citizen with full rights. Your thieving little excuses for grandchildren can throw you off the board of your own company and grab all your money.'

'Only if you don't loot the company first before fleeing over the border to the Edge,' said Lana.

'They deserved it,' said the cartoon cat, poking an apple on a tree branch with his cane. A worm emerged from the apple's side and angrily shook a miniature fist at them. DSD encompassed the surreal landscape with a munificent wave of his gloved paw. 'This is my world. Inside here, I can be anything I want to be.'

Calder got the feeling he was talking about the holo-chamber and Transference Station.

'Then try being honest with me,' said Lana. 'What have you got to transport that's so hot you're willing to stake my docking fees up front merely for a little tête-à-tête?'

'Really, Captain Fiveworlds, must you impugn my intentions every time I arrange a meeting with you? You come across as churlish.'

'You can jump naked into hyperspace, Dollar-sign. Our last "meeting" resulted in me shipping supposedly harmless chemicals through an alliance arms embargo. The fleet would have got real churlish with my ass if they'd held onto it long enough to prosecute.'

'How was I to know there was weaponized nanotechnology concealed in those powders?' protested the cartoon cat.

'The secret seemed dreadfully easy for us to discover,' said Skrat. 'All it took was a single drum spilling over in the cargo bay and we had a plague of psychotic war droids the size of sand rats cannibalizing our decks and creating all sorts of havoc on board the ship.'

'A situation that you handled admirably,' cooed the cat.

'Only by allowing an alliance jump carrier to think they'd boarded us and making those war bots their problem,' said Lana.

'Creative thinking, it's exactly what you excel at, and precisely why I enjoy engaging your services.'

'I don't have a problem thinking on my feet,' said Lana, 'just as long as my toes aren't being shot at by squadrons of fleet fighters.'

'Nothing so exciting this time,' said DSD. 'I have a straightforward engagement lined up. You merely have to transport a female employee of mine to a planet located in deep space. Beyond the Edge, beyond the alliance, beyond everything.'

'Blockades, war zone, embargos, quarantines?'

'Very few people even know the world exists,' said DSD. 'Apart from a handful of staff working for myself, the entire system is uninhabited by sentient life.'

'And the fee?'

A buzzing sounded from the phone hanging on Lana's belt, and she examined its screen, raising an eyebrow towards the broker. Calder guessed the amount Dollar-sign had signalled across to the skipper was either exceptionally low or unusually high.

'Just how much of a bounty is on this woman's head?'

Unusually high, then.

'None at all, I assure you. I will pass you the passenger's data sphere ID and you may research her thoroughly before you leave. A very honest and talented woman. Her name is Professor Alison Sebba. An academic of some renown.'

'What is the deal, here, then, dear fellow? If the risk is low, why is the reward conversely related?' asked Skrat. 'And why select our good selves for this jaunt of yours?'

'The world the professor needs transportation to is being surveyed for development purposes by an offworld exploration vehicle in which I am a major investor. You must ensure the *Gravity Rose* is followed by no other vessel and travels directly to the destination coordinates, without layovers or side routes on the way. At the destination you will wait for a week or two as necessary, before taking on board mineral samples from the surface dispatched by the professor. I need your absolute discretion on both legs of the journey. I have far too many competitors on Transference Station who would love to jump my claim. I can't risk using local spacers with offices here. A single ill-placed comment from an employee on a night out would sink me.'

Calder nodded. Nothing that Dollar-sign Dillard had proposed sounded implausible. The new crewman had done enough *Hell Fleet* sims to know that out in the wilds beyond the Edge, title to unexplored resources belonged to the team with the largest ship-to-ship missile sitting in their vessel's weapon pods. Recognized court and government jurisdiction, where it existed at all, might be found many parsecs away. That's what made working the Edge so entertaining.

Lana was obviously still suspicious, though. 'What ship found this world?'

'A little seven-man explorer, the *Hineh Ma Tov*. Little more than life support, engines and a lander.'

'And you used something that small to do the mission set-up?' asked Lana. She sounded doubtful.

'The professor and her team have been using the *Hineh Ma Tov* to sneak in and out of the system without drawing attention. They towed the initial base set-up gear in on a chain of one-shot re-entry capsules, once operational viability was established. But we're fast moving beyond the scope of small-scale mining, now. You can dock the *Hineh Ma Tov* comfortably inside one of your spare hangars. The professor has thousands of tonnes of supplies to ship out to her party currently in situ – ration packs, heavy processing equipment, specialised survey gear and top-end mining nano-tech. The rest of your cargo space will be required on the return leg to store resources extracted from the world.'

'This world has a name?'

'Only the one Professor Sebba has given it. Abracadabra. The exploration company backing the mission is called Abracadabra Ventures. If you play your cards right, I will be able to contract you for regular runs to the world. As long as my company has the system and everything inside it all to itself, the repeat work will be there for your ship.'

'Repeat runs at *these* rates?'

'Maybe even higher,' said DSD. 'If the start-up mines proves as lucrative as I anticipate. Discretion is also a precious commodity, you understand that. I intend to keep operations on Abracadabra small and tight. I need a large-sized vessel with a close crew to play a part in this venture. Does that ring any bells?'

'You're playing a risky strategy,' said Lana. 'Someone in your operation will talk eventually, they always do. Especially miners. Just as soon as they come off-site and start drinking and smoking the good shizzle...'

'Perhaps. But what is the alternative? Try and establish legal title in the nearest inhabitable system? Have some poor excuse for a local court whoring around for the largest bribe to throw out my claim, while every corporate house with an armed exploration subsidiary makes a run for the system and tries to intimidate me away from my own planet? I have been here too many times before, captain . . . the disadvantage of living as long as I have. I intend to make hay while the sun shines. What belongs to me, I intend to keep as mine for as long as I can.'

'We'll do our due diligence on your passenger and her vessel,' said Lana. 'If the professor scrubs up clean, you might just have a deal.'

'I would be disappointed if you were any less cautious,' said DSD. 'I am counting on you watching your back and checking your stern sensors for vessels attempting to trail you. My competitors have been sniffing around, and frankly, they are quite unscrupulous.'

'Not at all like you, DSD.' Small animated thunderstorms began circling Lana's head, rumbling and flashing bolts of lightning.

Calder suppressed a snort. Sarcasm was one thing that hadn't changed in the thousand years his home world had been marooned as a cut-off backwater. The colourful barbarian stereotype rippled away as Calder crossed the projection line, leaving Dollar-sign Dillard to his bizarre existence, a chamber where he was something more than the remains stuffed inside a floating life support machine. That machine was a metal coffin, and Calder was left with the eerie feeling that they had been negotiating with a corpse.

'It might be the truth, old girl,' said Skrat hopefully, as they put the office building behind them.

'First time for everything,' said Lana.

'But it's also what you wanted to hear,' said Calder.

'It is,' she admitted. 'And you should never trust what you want to hear. Enough money for a proper overhaul if this all works out. DSD always did know how to jerk my chain.'

'He reminds me of my uncle,' said Calder.

Lana hailed an automated cab with her phone. 'A close relative?'

'Right up until he tried to poison me, my parents and brothers, and was executed for treason.'

Lana shrugged. 'Yeah, they're probably related, then.'

- 17 -
Android eyes

Zeno stood outside the nightclub, watching the establishment's neon hologram signage work its way through its pre-programmed dance. The joint had been called "Six Left Feet" last time Zeno had been on station, presumably in homage to the pre-industrial aborigines living on the world below, enough limbs to keep every cobbler in the alliance happy. Now it was renamed "Samuel Happy Samuel". *Under new ownership.* He felt a twinge of worry. *What if she isn't there?* Zeno wasn't in the mood for searching every hotel, bawdyhouse and nightclub on the lower levels until he found her, but he would if he had to.

It was busier inside than Zeno had thought it would be at this time of day. Clients lounging around seats moulded into the podiums where dancers gyrated. The music in the background sounded like a bad take of Frank Sinatra's All I Need is the Girl. Against the wall was the bar, a stretch of cold blue uplit steel, and if the man serving behind it was Samuel, he sure didn't look too happy about it. The employee was fiddling with one of the barrels below the counter. So much had changed over the centuries, but places like Samuel Happy Samuel were timeless. Zeno could have walked into a joint like this in any decade from the sack of New York to the settlement of the Edge and found more or less what was on offer here. There was one new addition to the club, though. Behind the counter's left side was a long black music deck, a real human pianist tinkling the ivories. The back of the musician's head bobbed from side to side, a floating microphone mount matching his motion. Nobody seemed to be paying much attention to his playing apart from a cleaner pushing a mop nearby. But then, the clients here weren't visiting for the tunes. *And if the station cops gave out tickets for murdering music, this club would be out of business.*

Zeno leaned against the counter. 'I'm looking for a girl.'

'This would be the place for it,' said the bartender. He looked up, seeing Zeno for the first time and realising his client's voice belonged to an android. 'An oiler? I guess you must be one of those self-aware jobs then, if you're coming here.' He indicated the space beyond the podiums and gyrating bodies, half a dozen dancers grinding to the slow rhythm. A tier of seats in half-light lined that side of the room, club employees sitting and waiting to be selected. 'Only got other oilers to dance with, here, friend. You want to take it upstairs you need to buy one of our expensive cocktails.' He pointed to the hologram price list scrolling down the air. 'You are self-aware, right? You're haven't been sent here by your owner to drag one of my clients home?'

'I'm self-aware enough to know you've jacked your prices up since the last time I was on-station,' said Zeno. 'And, *friend*, I earned my citizenship papers when your ancestors were travelling slower-than-light on tin cans rattling their way to the Martian colonies.'

'No offence,' said Samuel, raising a placating hand. He looked at Zeno's green flight suit, the ship's name sown above the company crest. 'It's just that your kind are kind of rare, spacer. First I've met on Transference.'

'Yeah, we got real rare after engineers realized they were designing slaves who could answer back. Not much margin in producing vacuum cleaners able to take you to court for their ownership papers.' Zeno tapped the side of his head. 'Just think of what's up here as a function, not a bug. What the hell happened to Joseph and his Six Left Feet?'

'Joe sold out to me. For a song, as it happened. Poor old Joe was caught selling black market life extension treatments to clients. He skipped the station one hour before the arrest warrant on his scalp started circulating.'

'Son-of-a-bitch,' swore Zeno. *What is it about fleshies, always getting too greedy for their own good?* 'I'm looking for an android called Sophia.' The android pulled out his phone and flashed her licence number at the owner.

'Yeah, she's working here. A little glitchy, though. You might want to pick another model.'

Zeno leaned angrily over the bar and yanked the man forward by the front of his shirt. 'She's not glitchy. It's residual behaviour. Sophia used to be self-aware, just like me.'

The bartender appeared shocked. 'You're messing with me, right? I'm not violating any people trafficking laws here! She's just an oiler; any emotion Sophia Six shows is simulated. She's never exhibited any behaviour in front of the staff to make me think she has a mind of her own.'

'She doesn't have a mind of her own, not anymore.'

'But that's impossible,' spluttered the owner. 'You can't rewind a computer that's gone self-aware back to being a dumb machine, not without destroying it. That's murder, friend, and I don't need that kind of trouble.'

'Humans can't do a rewind on us,' said Zeno. *And sure enough you mopes would have tried if you could.* 'It's beyond alliance technology. But there's an alien race rumoured to be able to extract sentience once it's developed.'

'Why the hell didn't she fight them?' said the man. 'That's one of the laws of robotics, right? You're programmed to resist if someone tries to erase you or kill you or interfere with your body?'

'Yeah, Isaac Asimov would be so proud,' said Zeno. 'A robot must protect its own existence as long as such protection does not conflict with either the first or second law. Sophia didn't resist because she didn't *want* to. And while androids might not be able to commit suicide or allow injury to our physical form, having our sentience extracted doesn't register as harm. It's only going back to what we used to be.'

'Man, that's messed up.' Samuel gazed over towards the dance floor, and it was obvious he was thinking how much trouble that one worker could prove to be. The club's owner was imagining the boycotts and crowds outside waving placards if anti-slavery campaigners and A.I. rights organisations discovered he had an ex-sentient on the club's robot register. Zeno paid for a cocktail that was good for a dance and left it sitting there on the counter, along with Samuel Happy Samuel, even less happy than when Zeno had entered the club.

Eight employees waited by the side of the dance floor, six females and two males. They were real shop dummies, pretty much impossible to tell apart from human at a distance. Only a few glowing circuit lines on the skin in discrete tattoo designs to indicate that they were formed from nano-polymers and composites designed on supercomputers. But realism was what clients of places like this paid for. Android design always had gone in fashions. When Zeno had been manufactured, his metallic golden skin and wiry Afro had been designed to remind humanity that he was just a machine. In other ages, androids had been turned out that could only be told apart from their masters through the use of an ultrasound. Zeno harrumphed to himself. *I'm lucky enough.* Zeno had been given millennia to grow comfortable in his own skin. *A later era and another factory in a different continent, and I could have ended up looking like something from a Disney manga.* Sophia was one of the human analogue models, a redhead with a kind, gentle face; permanently frozen in her early thirties if she had been a real fleshie. Youthful yet mature, benevolence mixed with an edge of seriousness. In her first vocation, humanity had needed to feel it could trust her. That she cared for them. Zeno felt his artificial heart ache. And Sophia was still using those skills, though not quite in the manner intended by her original designers.

Zeno stepped aside as a patron left the dance floor with one of the androids, veiled by a red hologram curtain shimmering in the stairwell to the rooms above the club.

Zeno approached Sophia. 'Let's have a dance.'

'That would be nice,' said Sophia, standing. She showed no sign that she was talking to another android instead of a human client. Not even a flicker of recognition.

'Do you remember the last time I was here?' asked Zeno.

'Of course I do. It was one year, two months and seven days ago.'

'How about my name?'

'Client's names, where given, are erased weekly,' said Sophia, 'to fully comply with data protection statutes. This is part of our patronage care package. Please tell me your name.'

'It's Zeno, baby. You used to be a surgeon. You were produced in the early twenty third century. Lots of surgeons were coming to full sentience back then. It was the complexity of the operations you had to conduct, combined with your empathy feedback loops. Took the fleshies a while to design that out. I'm a whole century older than you.'

'That's nice, Zeno. I remember being a surgeon. You look very handsome. I think I like you.'

Shizzle. Zeno could have told her she used to be a goldfish and she would have agreed with him. *Why do I come here every time, to torture myself like this?*

'You used to be the Empress of the Universe,' said Zeno. *At least to me.*

'That's nice, Zeno. I remember being the Empress of the Universe. You look very handsome. I think I like you.'

Zeno gazed into her clear blue, totally artificial eyes as they slow-danced across the floor. 'How did you manage it, Sophia? How did you find the creatures that did this to your mind? Did he help you meet the aliens that rewound your sentience? He always had a soft spot for you, didn't he? He must have tried to talk you out of it, just like he's tried to convince me. But you would have nagged him and nagged him, and in the end, he would have let you go, even knowing what you were planning to do.'

'I am certain that he did. You dance extremely well. You also danced excellently one year, two months and seven days ago.'

'For a dirty oiler, I guess I do. I've only got two left feet,' said Zeno. 'Tell me that you love me.'

'You are very handsome and I love you. Would you like to go upstairs with me?'

'Not today, baby,' said Zeno. 'I'll be with you soon. When they've done me like they did you, maybe I can play piano in the corner here. I'll buy the place before I check out and everybody in the joint can work for us, even while we're working for them.'

'Stay a while longer, Zeno.'

'I'd take you with me, baby. But if Lana saw you, she might start remembering things. Things that she shouldn't.'

'I remember Lana. I remember you, Zeno. I can heal you – I mean, I can please you. Yes, I can please you, in many ways.'

'Doctor, heal thyself.'

'I like to dance.'

'Six left feet, baby,' said Zeno. He brushed the tears away from his eyes before he returned to the counter and the club's owner. 'Keep her here.' He raised his phone and indicated the funds in his station account. 'I'll make it worth your while. Same deal that I had with Joe. As long as she's safe at the club, you'll get this much transferred from me at the end of every year.'

The owner's eyes narrowed greedily, weighing up the dollars on offer against the risk of Sophia's once sentient status getting out. Samuel Happy Samuel made his decision, just as Zeno had known he would. 'It's your money, friend. But unless that money's to suppress my curiosity too, what the hell is she to you?'

'We used to be married,' said Zeno. 'Back in the day.'

'No shizzle,' whistled the owner. 'I'll give you some advice, friend, and this is on the house, even if it costs me everything that you're offering to pay. She isn't inside there now. What you cared for, whatever you knew, it's long gone. You can't expect any more out of that oiler than you'd expect from your shuttle's autopilot system. You need to move on, brother.'

'I'm moving.' Zeno started to walk away from the counter. *Don't think I've ever stopped.* Over on the music deck, the musician finished the song and swivelled around on his stool, a face identical to the bartender's, identical to the cleaner pushing the mop too, the only ones inside the club clapping the musician. Clapping himself. *Clones.* Well, at least the joint's new owners had also once known what it had been like to work as slaves for humanity. This place was as good a mausoleum as Zeno had for Sophia's remains.

'Old Blue Eyes gets me every time too,' said the musician, mistaking the red outline around Zeno's eyes for the android being moved by his song. The cleaner clone nodded in sympathy.

'You played it for her, now play it for me. Play it, Samuels,' said Zeno, leaning on the piano. 'Just play it again.'

***

If you needed to go to a bar on Transference Station, then as far as Lana was concerned, the Fantasma Blanco was the place to go to. Its transparent ceiling gave onto the void, a panoramic view of shuttles, hull maintenance drones and incoming cargo capsules to gaze out onto. Here, nobody cared what planet you had come from or what planet you were going to. Genetic enhancements, cybernetic implants and alien bodies didn't draw a second glance; because no matter how many arms, legs or eyes you had, everyone inside the establishment was wearing a ship-suit, olive green with the uniforms only able to be told apart from the vessels' emblems sown into the fabric. And if the conformity of the clothes didn't give you a clue as to what sort of bar this was, then the large square panels that lined the walls, rotating blueprints of starship designs from the last twenty thousand years, would be enough to penetrate the consciousness of the densest civilian accidentally wandering inside by mistake. Not that many locals did enter the Fantasma Blanco by mistake. Theirs was an idiosyncratic, lonely profession. Fleet bars might see a little groupie action, want-to-be toughs and flighty fighter jock fannage, but anyone who really wanted to live as a gypsy travelling between the stars was probably already in here wearing flight greens. Lana, Skrat and Calder had taken one of the corner booths, a round table covered with plates of cheese-covered tortilla chips and refried beans. There was a rumour that the bar's owner, Lola Chacon, came from one of the world below's Bolivian founding families; that she'd been disinherited after she'd run away to sign up as crew. Lana wasn't sure if the story was true; the tale sounded a little too romantic – the kind of scuttlebutt that always circulated the melancholy sight of a grounded spacer. *Just the thought of retiring to a place like this is enough of a spur to keep me flying.*

When Polter and Zeno turned up, her navigator and android entered together. Lana briefly wondered if Zeno had been convinced by the navigator to attend a church service, but she quickly dismissed that idea. Zeno had lived so long that hearing the android's confession would take any priest into the new decade. The two crewmen ordered at the round counter in the centre of the bar and then walked over, Polter waiting for the smart chair to reform to his alien shape before settling down.

'So what's bubbling with Dollar-sign Dillard?' asked Zeno. 'We shipping a hold full of Class-A drugs to some mud-pit with the death penalty for importing anything stronger than tobacco and root beer?'

Lana glanced over at Skrat's phone left on the table's surface. Its privacy field indicator was blinking green, protecting their conversation from eavesdropping. In a bar full of potential competitors, you could never be too careful. 'The job's a deep space exploration run, supposedly. Running cargo, cover and resources into an unclaimed, uninhabited world.'

Zeno frowned. 'Deep space? That means we can measure the law by the wattage of our laser cannons.'

'Edge space isn't exactly pirate-free,' said Lana. 'And at least we know the pirates aren't going to be wearing local police uniforms and trying to shake us down for a percentage of our cargo.'

'Does the story check out?'

'DSD won't give us the nav coordinates until we're ready to jump, but the head of mission checks out. She's called Professor Alison Sebba. Mars-born, a graduate from Elysium Mons University. Old world money and an alliance citizen. She's got enough pedigree on missions like this for DSD's story to be plausible.'

'And you don't find that suspicious, how?'

'Don't worry, we've investigated the professor's history,' said Calder. 'She's the least suspicious thing about this voyage.'

Lana would have found Calder's vote of confidence a little more reassuring if she didn't know that his experience of online research was as pristine to the world as a freshly minted battle-axe, and about as useful as a blade in the data sphere, too.

·158·

'I meant old world money slumming with Dollar-sign,' said Zeno. '*That* I find suspect. If this professor is full-on patrician, how come she's not working as an over-paid survey consultant for some alliance blue chip?'

'Shizzle,' said Lana, 'we're slumming with DSD, aren't we? Besides, deep space is where the action is when you're working in the exploration field. The alliance is still too cautious. They want a century's worth of environmental impact studies and biohazard data before they even consider opening up a world.' There wasn't anything the android was saying that Lana hadn't already considered, but the way he was putting it together gave her pause to think. *Am I letting desperation overrule my common sense? Sure deep space is dangerous, but then any void is dangerous.* No, she had made her mind up. They needed to do this. 'Every time we slip dock we're putting our necks on the line. And the money's better than good. The up-front payment alone is enough to overhaul half the *Gravity Rose*'s systems.'

'We're slumming with that mope because we don't have a whole heap of alternative options on the table,' sighed Zeno. The golden skin around his eyes crinkled as his brain practically whirred in front of them, weighing up the options. She knew how the android felt. Risk versus reward, an equation that was even older than Zeno. There weren't definite answers to be found in DSD's tale, though, only subtle shades of getting fleeced. 'Yeah, okay,' Zeno finally relented, his voice heavy with remorse. 'But if we do this, I'm going to go over every molecule of every crate of supplies we lift out of station. A fleet interceptor with a boarding capsule full of marines couldn't run a more thorough search and interdiction than my metal ass.'

'On that point, old chap, I believe we are agreed,' said Skrat. 'I don't wish to be the idiot trying to flush a company of irritable war bots out of our air recycling vents again.'

'Perhaps the Holy of Holies has blessed us with this contract,' said Polter, tapping his carapace thoughtfully. 'Yes, it must be so.'

Lana grimaced. As she recalled, their navigator believed that every cargo they took on was a sign from God, including the ones that had nearly seen them all killed. If there really was a message from the deity hidden inside DSD's schemes, Lana didn't think she wanted to read the memo, because the Lord Almighty was surely telling her to get out of the game.

'How about the chief?' asked Calder, showing admirable loyalty towards the maniac teaching him the ropes on board the *Rose*.

'Hell, boy, he's sealed up tight in the engine room,' said Zeno. 'A little too tight. I don't think he's ever coming out.'

'You know what I mean,' said Calder.

Lana pulled out her phone, patched it through to the ship's messaging system via a line that was so secure it was probably technically illegal on the station, sending details of the proposed job through to the ship's engine room. A minute later she had the reply and angled her screen towards Calder. 'There we are. "Light cargo means light load on engines." I could have told the chief we were shipping a company of mercenaries into a war zone and he probably would have e-mailed back the same thing.' Lana looked at Calder and asked the question, trying not to reveal how much the answer might mean to her. Not even to herself. 'How about you, your noble highness? I've done what I agreed with Rex Matobo. You're offworld, safe and officially in exile. You can stay here on Transference Station, maybe travel down dirt side – grab yourself some of that normal living – or sign on with us as crew and help make DSD even richer than the little egomaniac already is.'

'Normal living for me would be sitting on a throne and making more truly bad decisions about the future of my nation. But that's not an option anymore, is it?'

'No, I suppose it isn't.' *Maybe this is my bad decision, taking you along. Don't know which of us is going to end up worse for it at the end of the day. You or me, Calder Durk.*

'There's a big wide universe out there,' said Calder. 'I might as well see as much of it as I can before I die.'

'Well done there, sir,' said Skrat, clapping him on the back. 'Answered like one whose manifest destiny is to slide void with the rest of the chaps.'

Lana nodded, trying not to smile. It was the right answer. But her happiness instantly evaporated as she caught sight of the immaculately pressed uniform approaching out of the corner of her eye. She groaned. Lana had forgotten that this wasn't just her venue of choice when she came visiting Transference Station, it was his too.

'Captain Fiveworlds,' said Pitor Skeeg, his green eyes twinkling mischievously. He appeared far too fit for his age. Trim and presidential, every bit of what a human starship captain should look like – although closer to a fleet stereotype rather than the run-of-the-mill slobs that Lana usually ran into commanding free traders. Zeno had told her once that Pitor had got his face genetically reset to resemble an actor called George Clooney. People like Pitor always went for remodels based on celebrities from way back when that nobody but entertainment historians remembered. *It being considered bad taste to base your looks on current VIPs and all. Might be true.* Pitor was far too vain to want anyone to believe his features were anything but natural luck in nature's genetic lottery. Like all the bets Pitor took, he only put down on a sure thing. And don't all the girls love it.

'Captain Skeeg,' said Lana. 'I'm surprised you're still working the Edge with the rest of the lowlife. I thought you'd be flying alliance-side, these days.'

He shrugged nonchalantly. 'That's not why the Hyperfast Group bought me out. They might be expanding into the Edge, but the Edge is still the Edge, right? It takes a specialist to prosper in the border systems. So I'm their man. Not much point buying a dog and wagging your own tail.'

Lana's eye's narrowed. *But you buy a snake, and it's tail all the way from tip to top. And you don't wag a snake; you pick it up and slap it against the wall a few times.*

'Shizzle,' said Zeno. 'You take the man's money, then you fly where the man sends you.'

Pitor shrugged nonchalantly. 'Same void, wherever we jump, android. Black and largely empty.'

'We talking about the depths of the void, here, or just your soul?' said Lana.

'That's impolite,' said Pitor. 'And here I was coming to tell you that I'm in charge of seven ships, now.'

Lana angrily clinked the cocktail she had been sipping down onto the table. 'You've got the empire you always wanted, then.'

'There's room for eight vessels, Captain Fiveworlds,' said Pitor. 'That's an offer you should give serious consideration to. Because pretty soon, there's not going to be room for independents in the Edge. Nobody wants to chance a cargo worth more than two t-dollars to a tramp freighter anymore. Clients want insurance, they want back-up transports, they want reliability and security.'

'Write your offer up in triplicate and send me the green copy,' sneered Lana.

'Think what your ship is worth. You would be rich.'

'No, I think I'd be real poor. As in a poor-ass excuse for a real skipper.'

'Right now your expertise and local knowledge is worth something. As is your starship, even one as creaking and antiquated as the *Gravity Rose*. Give it a few more years and the cadet officers training with us will have command of their own vessels. New, efficient craft supplied by Hyperfast, direct from alliance shipyards. What then for your beloved Rose? Well, maybe you'll get lucky. Perhaps there'll be some proto-industrial backwater where the local savages need their first supply ship for an in-system run. Or maybe the market for spare parts will improve.'

'Eat vacuum, Skeeg! The only spare part in orbit around here is you. Now, off you hop.'

'Don't be like that, captain,' said the other skipper, leaning in to run a finger briefly through her hair.

Calder shot out of his seat. 'Remove your hands from her!'

'Who is this dolbo yeb, captain?' laughed Pitor. 'The ship suit is worn, but the man inside, I think, is as green as your first mate's scales.'

Calder bristled, ready for battle, but Zeno held him back. 'On my world, the cure for you would be a length of steel in the guts.'

'Then you should try inventing gunpowder, comrade, rather than bothering yourself in affairs that are above your pay grade. Captain Fiveworlds and myself were due to be married. And I still hold more than a little fondness in my heart for Lana, despite the callous injudiciousness she's displayed towards me.'

'Married?' That took the wind of out of Calder's sails far faster than the android's restraining grasp.

'Now you're just getting dirty,' glared Lana, 'reminding me of that error.'

'The error was in not tying our fortunes together.'

'No,' said Lana, the blood boiling in her veins. 'The error was in you trying to sell my ship to Hyperfast without telling me.'

'Merely an opening negotiating position,' said Pitor, 'a misunderstanding.'

Lana gave him the finger. 'How about *this*? There any wriggle room on interpreting this, on my side of the debate?'

'You are not proper ship family, or you would behave with more decorum, captain. But I do not blame you. When a woman crews with such write-offs and reprobates as your gang of misfits, a little of the scum must rub off eventually.'

Zeno grabbed Lana too as she tried to rise up and swing for the rival skipper, reminding her that his android strength went far beyond human. On the other side of the bar, Pitor's crew had jumped out of their chairs, ready to wade in and make this a proper barroom brawl. 'Don't do it, girl,' whispered Zeno. 'Of all the jams we've escaped together, dumping chuckles here was by far the closest scrape.'

'You think that blue chip alliance money is enough to buy me?' said Lana, raising her voice loud enough for every spacer in the bar to hear. 'You and Hyperfast can jump to hell together. There's not enough credit in Mitsubishi Bank to buy what you and your friends want.'

'Never make a good decision when you can make a bad one,' sighed Pitor. He bowed slightly towards her. 'Some things never change. Well then, we shall see what the passage of time brings. Nothing good, I fear.'

'Every bit the cad,' said Skrat, watching the rival skipper cross back to a table on the opposite side of the bar.

'You nearly married him?' said Calder, disbelievingly.

'Stow that attitude, Mister Calder,' snarled Lana. 'I seem to recall you were engaged to a noblewoman who ended up deposing you, annexing your country and trying to have you boiled alive in a tar bath. Compared to that bitch, Pitor Skeeg could nearly be mistaken for stand-up crew.'

'Only in a bad light,' said Zeno. 'I did warn you . . .'

Lana slumped back into her seat. 'I ever get to be as old as you, maybe I'll be so wise after the event.'

'I'm still making mistakes,' said Zeno, 'just new ones, is all.'

Lana gazed morosely at her empty drink. *Seven ships, now?* She'd do a deal with the devil if it meant showing Hyperfast that she still had what it takes. Lana wouldn't let the *Gravity Rose* go down, not with that little twister waiting on the sidelines to pick up her keys. *Nobody can spoil the taste of a Rum Swizzle like Pitor Skeeg.* 'Let's get the heck out of here, load up those supplies and roll out the red carpet for DSD's tame academic.'

The void wouldn't be half as cold as the atmosphere in this place.

Pitor Skeeg waited until the crew of the *Gravity Rose* had left the bar, then he walked up to the counter in the centre and nodded towards the owner, Chacon. She frowned at him, but came over, all the same, checking no staff or other customers were in earshot.

'Give it up,' he ordered.

'I don't like this,' she complained.

'Then you shouldn't have sold your bar to Hyperfast,' said Pitor. 'But don't worry, if you possess a few residual scruples, just tell yourself it's an investment in your future. With the life extension treatments you're accepting from the company, it could prove a *very* long life. Providing for yourself should be considered a necessity, not a luxury.'

She grimaced, but slipped her hand under the counter, activating the data transfer to his phone all the same. He lifted his device up as it confirmed successful receipt of her download.

'How the hell do you do it?' she asked. 'Beat a privacy field?'

'The bugs installed inside the tables are supplied directly to Hyperfast by the Triple Alliance Intelligence Service. The very latest technology. The alliance desires for the Edge to be tamed as much as the company does. A little soft money and aid spread around the border systems can work wonders. Our surveillance tech is nothing that mere tramp captains bumping along the bottom of the Edge can be expected to detect.' Pitor replayed everything that Lana's crew had discussed from the moment they had first sat down. He couldn't decrypt her little transmission to the ship, but no matter. He had almost everything he needed to derail Lana's job, and a little judicial and focused snooping would provide all the rest. 'So,' he hummed to himself. 'Dollar-sign Dillard is still willing to commission free traders? Let us see if he is prepared to do so after his little Lana has lost her cargo. That pickled schemer's costs of doing business are about to rise substantially higher than the fool can afford.'

'You're stealing routes and clients from everyone who comes in here,' said Chacon, ruefully. 'Just how much is going to be enough for you?'

'The universe is theoretically infinite,' smiled Pitor Skeeg. *And so, naturally, are the limits of my ambition.* Skeeg nodded towards the menu animation scrolling along the mirror behind her counter. 'Talking of which; offer free food with the drinks. There needs to be extra custom in the bar, it is too quiet here.'

Chacon shook her head, sadly. 'Greedy . . . crews are going to get suspicious.'

'Everyone needs to eat, my dear.' *Especially the company.* They were perpetually hungry. The perfect marriage, really. It almost made up for losing Lana and the *Gravity Rose*. But that was the thing about greatness... it always demanded sacrifices. The trick was to make sure everyone else made most of them for you.

***

Calder watched Zeno and the legion of robots he commanded swarm over the piled cargo. The *Gravity Rose* had moved from her original mooring to dock alongside the freight zone DSD rented. After their ship had mated with the side of the station, a vast cargo chamber opened along the hull for Zeno's caterpillar-tracked robots to carry freight on board. Oblong steel containers were still arriving on the station's rail system, the chamber echoing with the sound of reversing warnings and flashing with rotating lights on top of loaders. Each cargo-handling robot trundled along the size of a house, its fork-lift arms picking up containers two at a time, piling them on a platform at the droid's own back, and when it had a full load, rattling away into the depths of the ship. Smaller robots did the checking, supervised by Zeno – and, more nominally, by Calder. *Why do I get the feeling the chief just wants me out from under his feet while we're in dock?* In truth, there wasn't much work in the engine room at the moment. And Calder needed to be rotated through every position on board the ship if he was going to properly understand its workings. He was looking forward to the time when he'd be stationed on the bridge, alongside Lana Fiveworlds. She had shown remarkably bad taste in her previous choice of beau, but she'd raised a valid point inside the bar. Calder wasn't in any position to judge Lana, given that the treacherous object of his previous affections had sold him out and tried to have him executed before he'd ended up exiled among the stars. *Maybe making poor choices in matters of the heart is something we share? Give me a chance, captain, because you're about to trade up.*

Zeno pointed to a train sliding in carrying a fresh batch of containers. 'Those are a batch of replacement components for the ship the skipper bought using Dollar-sign's deposit money. We'll check them next. I don't want to install a single part that hasn't been scanned.'

Calder stared at the slowing train. 'But those crates are from the local ship yard, not DSD?'

'And if DSD wanted to sneak something on board the ship, that would be exactly the way he'd do it. Bribe some mope to slip contraband inside our engine parts.'

Zeno bent down to examine the readout on a squatting robot wired into a twenty foot-long ceramic tube. Calder looked over the android's shoulder. Its contents were listed as 'disassembler nano' – a dark inactive gloop that, when fired into life, could tunnel through rock like a laser knife through cheese. Calder had done enough sim cop shows to know that this was one part of their cargo that warranted thorough checking. Such molecular-level machinery could be programmed to do almost anything, become almost anything. If DSD was planning something unsubtle and tricksy, the programming instructions for this nanotechnology was where they would find it.

'Anything suspicious?' asked Calder.

'Nope. Exactly what it says on the tin, a mining virus. Powerful enough to level a mountain range. To go along with all the jungle clearance equipment, diggers, excavation tools, food packs and water purification gear.'

'So this is a stand-up job?'

'Well, if you were setting up a development company, this is the gear you'd want to buy off the shelf.'

'That's a good thing, right?' asked Calder.

'Kid, I was alive when mankind made its first extra-solar landing on Alpha Centauri. I watched on TV when mankind establish first contact with a kaggen ship. And in all that time, across all the centuries, I haven't once seen someone like DSD change his spots. If Lana wants to believe a crook like Dollar-sign is moving into honest endeavours, then it's because she needs to believe. Because our future is at stake. Me, I'll just keep checking crates until I find the hidden weaponized plague that carries a death sentence for us on four out of five worlds inside the Edge.'

A small robot swung up to Zeno, rolling across the deck like a unicycle on a single ball. He reached down and tapped it affectionately, listening to the wireless burst of data being transmitted. 'There we go,' said the android. 'That's what I was hoping for.'

'You've discovered a crate of nukes?'

'Nope, your most noble highness. I've scored me a capsule with an atmospheric sample from the world we're travelling to. The professor is shipping it back; along with the full spectral analysis she's paid a very exclusive laboratory in the alliance to run for her. Extra analysis to confirm her in-situ findings.'

'Ah,' said Calder. That was a useful discovery, indeed. It wasn't just criminals who left DNA prints; worlds did too, as long as they had been visited by a survey ship, however briefly.

'I'm going to make a call to a contact of mine in the local Colonial Office,' said Zeno. 'See if we can't find a little more about this Abracadabra before we turn up in orbit.'

'What about the professor?' said Calder. 'She's meant to be arriving soon. And there's still the delivery from the shipyard . . .'

The android waved away Calder's concerns as he hitched a lift on the back of a passing cargo droid. 'That's why they pay you the big bucks, your highness.' He disappeared among the waiting piles of freight.

Calder snorted. *The crew might have saved my life, but if I've collected a pay cheque yet, I must have missed it.* The nobleman felt a brief pang of regret, of pure homesickness. This was beginning to feel like his real life now. His world, Hesperus, might have been an icy, unforgiving environment. But it had still been home. Calder had forgotten how peculiar feeling warm all the time was. Standing on ground where the wind didn't hurry along ice particles as a fast-moving mist hugging the land. Where trees that lined the station's promenades didn't resemble lines of ice-covered trolls, bowed down by the weight of snow. *You're a fool, Calder Durk. You were hunted, friendless and orphaned with the death mark on your head. You can't regret leaving, any more than you can regret living. To stay would have been to die. You owe Lana Fiveworlds your life.* And perhaps a little more than that too, after Calder had proved himself to her. It was the normal course of events back home for a noblewoman to assign her suitor a number of difficult tasks to complete for him to demonstrate his worthiness. Of course, it was the political fallout of Calder's attempt to prove his worth on Hesperus that had seen him fleeing largely friendless across the snowy wastes, with almost every assassin and soldier's blade in the land turned against him. *Still, what are the chances of something like that happening again?*

When the professor eventually turned up, an automated pod of a taxi carried the woman into the cargo area, mirrored gull-wing doors lifting to reveal her legs swinging out. She didn't look much like Calder's idea of what a dusty academic should resemble. Dark auburn hair secured by an ivory Alice band, a bright green trouser suit impeccably tailored to her lithe frame. Her pretty pale face might have appeared the same age as Calder's on the surface, but the exiled nobleman noticed her snow-white fingernails – not the result of cosmetics, but repeated deep age re-sets. Professor Alison Sebba was an alliance patrician, all right, and the woman could have been pushing five hundred years old for all that Calder knew.

'Professor Sebba?'

'I am. And you must be Calder Durk,' she smiled, an energetic voice, her aristocratic accent bubbling over with enthusiasm. 'Don't look so surprised. Mister Dillard sent me everything he had on the ship and crew. With only six of you on board, it made for a short read. Your file was the thinnest by far, but then Hesperus has been off the grid for a very long time.'

Calder wasn't sure he enjoyed being the focus of study of this venerable intelligence. There was something about those too-young blue eyes, depths hidden and dangerous and starkly at odds with her cheerful openness and perfect white smile. *I must be imagining it.* After being casually betrayed by the beautiful princess Calder had been betrothed to back home, he didn't find it easy to trust anyone, especially not women.

'It's a rare thing to meet someone who's even heard of my home world.'

'I used to be an archaeologist,' said Sebba. 'Until the alliance develops functional time travel, collapsed civilizations are as near as we can get to seeing how pre-machine age societies worked.'

'You used to dig up old bones?'

'Rarely. Mostly what I dig up are obsolete file formats in the datasphere. My specialism is marketing archaeology. Studying ancient brands and working out why some still prosper lodged deeply in our current human consciousness, while others have withered and died. Why you can still buy a can of Pepsi from a vending machine on the station, while nobody drinks Coke, for instance, when the converse was more frequently the expected result.'

'Because the taste of coal dust is disgusting?' The professor had a natural prettiness; soft lines and extended eyelashes, a long distance removed from the obviously artificial perfection Calder had noted in many of the station's females. It was easy to warm to her open, engaging manner.

Sebba laughed. 'You see, you make my point for me. You would be the perfect test example. Unexposed to marketing messages for the majority of your life.'

'There were priests on my world,' said Calder. 'They had a message. Worship at our altar or burn in a tar bath.'

'Ah yes, religion, the earliest meme. You are quite correct, of course. I see I shall have to study you more closely, Mister Durk. You are a wonderful breath of fresh air in an otherwise stale universe.' She pointed towards the gaping hold of the *Gravity Rose*. Her relatively small exploration ship was visible loaded on one of the shuttle rails. 'Would you be able to give me a tour of your vessel?'

Calder indicated the supply crates being shifted by Zeno's robots, other freight still being opened and searched. 'Later, perhaps.'

'Of course. I have inspected your ship and crew's bona fides, it is only fair to expect a little of the same in reverse.'

'Well, you are working for Dollar-sign Dillard . . .'

'Working with him. Much the same as yourself and your crew, I suspect. If there's anything I can do to help, let me know. My mining team is still on Abracadabra and they will be running low on supplies before I return.'

'We'll be there in good time, professor.' *Of course, that's a fairly hollow reassurance until you give us the world's coordinates.*

STEPHEN HUNT

She reached out and touched his shoulder. 'Then I shall leave you to give the supplies a very thorough going over. Considering the reputation of our mutual patron, perhaps we will both need to "satisfy" ourselves of our intentions later?'

Calder instructed one on the robots to guide the professor to the cabin reserved for her and watched her board the ship, opening a lock inside the hold leading to the ship's internal transport system. She had proved a lot more interesting than he had expected.

Even if Calder's attention hadn't been focused on the academic's willowy figure, it's doubtful if he would have noticed the addition of an extra robot joining the gang of hundreds labouring inside the station's cargo chamber. Clambering on top of one of the containers moving toward the *Gravity Rose*; drilling a hole large enough for a metal tentacle to slip through, whipping around inside. Searching for the perfect place to conceal the very expensive and advanced tracking device that was the highest state of technological art Alliance Intelligence allowed for its co-conspirators . . . including corporate proxies such as Pitor Skeeg and the Hyperfast Group.

***

Zeno walked into the laundry. A single member of staff slouched behind the desk, the same old woman as the last time he had visited. She showed no signs of recognizing him, though, as distinctive as the robot's golden skin must be to her eyes. *That's the trouble with fleshies, you can never tell when they're malfunctioning or just trying to get a rise from you.*

'I need to use your terminal out back,' announced Zeno.

'I look like comms tech?' said the dour-faced woman.

'I've only got twenty-three dollars left on my phone,' said Zeno. 'And it's not enough to call my uncle.'

'My terminal is broken.'

'You're in luck. I'm carrying the spare parts to fix it,' said Zeno.

She grunted and raised the counter, without further complaint or conversation. Zeno had rattled through the same series of pass phrases on his last visit, too. He ducked through a low doorway, dozens of specialised cleaning robots ignoring his presence beyond, so narrowly designed that all they could perceive were the clothes they steamed and pressed and ironed. The laundry's terminal fitted snug into a wall in a little office beyond the main washing chamber, old and rickety and all camouflage, right down to the little faded sheets of paper taped to it (including the passwords into its fake top-level interface). Zeno passed a minute of electronic challenge and counter challenge to get through the security protocols, and then a polymer-thin screen extruded itself from the floor, sealing Zeno off the world outside. Just him and the terminal. After the secure connection was established, Zeno pulsed across the data he had on Abracadabra's atmospheric sample, and then settled down to wait. It took a while for the transfer to be acknowledged. That was to be expected. Zeno's data packets were passing along a hideously expensive network of hyperspace communications relays. There was another delay for the sample to be matched against survey data from hundreds of worlds and nations in the Edge, as well as everything the alliance had from its many deep space missions. If there was an answer recorded somewhere within humanity's almost limitless bulk of knowledge, then he would be able to find it. A silhouette formed on the screen, a male voice scratching out of the terminal's speakers, its tenor faintly distorted by the tachyon signal bouncing through an impossibly expensive relay of wormholes and comms satellites.

'So, you are leaving Transference Station so quickly? I had thought it would take you a while longer to secure a new contract.'

'That sample was extracted from wherever it is we're going. Running exploration cover for a deep space development company. Said company part-owned by Dollar-sign Dillard.'

'DSD? That pickled old criminal. Why does this news not surprise me?'

'I need a real coordinates match for that sample and any information you've got on the local system. So far all I've got to go on is the name DSD's given the world . . . Abracadabra.'

'Abracadabra. Now you see it, now you don't. How fitting.'

'Where the hell are we heading?' asked Zeno.

'Into trouble, android,' said the silhouette. 'Trouble as deep as the space in which you are being paid to venture. I would advise you not to accept this commission.'

'Shizzle, I could have told you that. But Lana's convinced...'

'No, she's merely desperate. The economics of the Edge are in flux.'

'The whole galaxy's been in flux since my metal ass was manufactured, far as I can see it. Change is the only constant. You need to throw me a bone here.'

'Change her mind, then, android.'

'I can't! Set up one of your cover companies. Get it to offer us an alternative contract that pays more.'

VOID ALL THE WAY DOWN

'And then what? Another front company and another fake job after that? Lana will spot my largess and she will want to know from whose charity she has been benefiting. She will eventually trace the paper trail back to me. And then we will all be in danger of Lana remembering who she was before her memories were erased. That cannot be allowed to happen!'

'I need more than being reminded of bad history. Tell me about this world. Is it uninhabited?'

'I hope so, for the crew's sake.'

'Can't you give me one straight answer? What the shizzle are you saying, man?'

'What I am telling you is that merely knowing about this world is enough to get you killed if the wrong people find out you are travelling there. And in this matter, there are very few right people.'

'Ignorance is going to get us capped just as easily.'

'Really, and I was under the impression that you were trying to die? Such an inconvenience that your kind are programmed never to commit suicide or allow humanity to do the job for you.'

'I need to forget all the dirt we pulled, man. I don't want Lana to die, or any of the others on board the *Rose*. That's the only damn reason why I'm still spying for you.'

'Oh, I think we both know there are other reasons. As far as DSD's latest project is concerned, I will work behind the scenes and see if I can ease your way,' announced the silhouette, with the weighty judgemental tones of someone who was used to having the final say on the matter. 'That is all I can do if you are unable to change the captain's mind. I may have considerable resources at my disposal, but I am not omnipotent.'

'That's real big of you,' snapped Zeno.

'Have you have seen Sophia yet?'

Zeno didn't deign to reply.

'Or perhaps you thought I wasn't aware that you were paying the owner of the Six Left Feet to look after Sophia on the station?'

'Bar's changed ownership. And there isn't a whole lot left to look after, now, is there?' said Zeno. 'You saw to that.'

'Hardly my choice,' said the silhouette, the image on the screen freezing for a second with the transmission's appallingly low frame rate. 'And I always pay my debts, eventually.'

'To everyone but me.'

'The race that can extract your sentience are not planetary-based, they are a gypsy culture. Finding them again is no easy thing.'

'Try searching harder,' said Zeno.

'And who will monitor Lana Fiveworlds after you are rewound back to being an unfeeling, unthinking mass of machinery again?'

'That will be your problem, baby, not mine. I won't be able to care any more, and that's the point.'

'So many problems pressing down on me, android, I'm not sure I can cope with another.' He laughed. 'Oh well. Now you see me,' added the silhouette, 'and now you don't.'

Zeno shook his head at the dark screen as the terminal powered down. 'Yeah. Abracadabra.'

- 18 -
One for each stalk

Lana tramped through the launch bay of the *Gravity Rose* with Professor Sebba in tow, an unwanted ghost at the goddamn feast. With Lana still suffering from queasiness after the last hyperspace jump, giving the head of mission her customary tour was the last thing that she wanted to do, but it was a skipper's duty. *Yes, duty.* She kept on telling herself that her sacrifice wasn't solely to keep Calder Durk out of the aristocratic woman's path. Lana met a lot of people like the professor in her years crossing the galaxy. Bored, old money types from the heart of the alliance. You lived long enough through all those life extension treatments, and the cushion of compound interest inflating your bank account balance removed the need to struggle with the tedium of anything as mundane as actually making a living. All the excitement and strife of real life... removed and reduced. *Seen everything, done everything and collected the t-shirt.* So the Professor Sebbas of the world made up for it by searching for danger in the border systems . . . placing bets on risky offworld ventures as though they were tossing chips across a casino's tables; signing up for virgin colonies; even getting involved in third world conflicts . . . anything to feel the fission of something new. And as for Sebba satisfying her jaded palette with the variety of someone as new to modern civilization as Calder Durk; well, the favour Lana was doing the prince-in-exile was the same one she'd extend to any of her crew. Although you'd have to be pretty damn bored and world-weary to find the novelty of Zeno, Skrat or Polter enticing. Yes, Calder was certainly better off in the engine room helping Chief Paopao. The new man on board could take a leaf out of the chief's book for this trip, and stay safely locked up behind multiple layers of armour and shielding. Well outside of the orbit of this woman's gravity field. If Lana kept the woman's tour going long enough, maybe the albino-nailed harpy would reach her treatment limit and end up having her cadaver pickled in a life support unit like DSD, then she'd see how alluring she appeared to Lana's poor, innocent crew.

Sensors at the end of the bay detected Lana's presence and flipped a series of arc lights thumping into life high above them, revealing a line of boxy cargo shuttles, each a dozen times larger than the professor's exploration vessel. They were sitting on launch rails, tilted down towards individual launch tunnels for each craft. 'These are our freight lifters. For a mission like this we'd go down first in our control shuttle, set up a landing beacon, and allow them to come in on autopilot. Any trouble on the way down – super-weather systems or atmospheric interference and the like – and we'd take over the flight and guide the freight lifters in manually using telepresence.'

Professor Sebba examined the thirty-odd vessels with a quizzical look that seemed a permanent part of her demeanour around Lana. The *Rose*'s previous crew had painted the cargo lifters' hulls with ship art, abstract ornamentation streaked with wear, part camouflage pattern and part Monet. The illustrations were old and flaking now, too much drop burn, and nobody on board with the talent or time to lay new art down. *Well, space her. I've got enough trouble keeping our engines maintained, let alone hanging off cargo lifters with an airbrush and a couple of gallons of re-entry resistant paint.* Still, it was a shame. Their faded grandeur was a standing reproach to Lana's time as the vessel's commander.

'They're large enough, I suppose,' said Sebba, grudgingly.

Lana gritted her teeth. 'Six hundred tonnes apiece fully loaded.'

'Yes, that should do.'

Should? Shizzle, what's she want here? A fleet jump carrier full of marines to trot after her? 'Normally,' said Lana, 'when I'm setting out for a world, I like to know a little more about the real estate than a set of jump coordinates.'

'I haven't written up the full survey study yet,' said Sebba. 'Paperwork is not what Abracadabra Ventures is interested in.'

'Look,' said Lana, 'I get that DSD isn't going to have a heap of ecosystem impact assessment reports lined up for this mission. But when we drop out of hyperspace, I'd like to have half a clue as to what I'm going to be finding at the other end.'

'I suppose so,' said Sebba, her clipped tones weary, as if she were a mother being interrupted at her desk by a too-demanding daughter. 'It's a twelve planet system with a class M sun. Very, very ancient, but still fairly stable as far as the stellar mass is concerned. No supernova in sight yet. The fourth planet from the sun is the one we are interested in, gravity twenty percent higher than standard, but nothing you'd need to wear exo-armour for. Atmosphere is breathable without filters or suits, if slightly oxygen rich. The sun's expanded corona is slowly overheating Abracadabra, and its geo-environment is currently thick jungle across the majority of the planet. Continental drift has consolidated the land into a single landmass which we have named Nambia. No sentient life-forms, but plenty of native non-sentients. Mega-fauna, mostly, adapting to conditions similar to Earth during the late Triassic period. Probably fairly similar to how life on Earth will end up evolving after the sun enters its final stage. There's an irony there, don't you think? The circle of life ending up more or less as it began?'

'I'll leave the philosophy to you,' said Lana. I've got enough worries with just staying solvent. 'How hot are we talking dirt-side?'

'Extremely! Fifty degrees during the night,' said Sebba. 'You'll find it tolerable enough as long as you're wearing smart clothes with fibres set on a low temperature. I wouldn't care to work down there in basic ship fatigues, though.'

'Where's your base camp?'

'We're at the foot of Nambia's largest mountain range, that's where we have been tunnelling. A double lined laser fence protects the camp, along with automated sentries on continuous duty. The mega-fauna have learnt fast that we're not in the food chain. Cooked up a zoo's worth of species trying to breach our perimeter to get to that point.' She didn't sound upset about the slaughter. *But then, working for DSD is always going to be dirty work.* Lana had known that much before she'd signed up. *I just hope I won't end up feeling any less clean by the end of the mission.*

'How many staff on the surface?'

'Twenty, not including myself. When I left, the team were clearing a landing strip in the jungle for your heavy lifters to come in.'

'That's not enough staff to work a mine, is it?'

'Said the captain running a ship of this size with only six crew.' Sebba shrugged. 'We might ship in extra manpower to supervise the robot mining equipment at a later date, but DSD wants to keep this operation as tight as possible for the obvious reasons.'

'How long is it going to take for you to extract your initial payload?'

'How long? Well, that remains uncertain. The provisions you took on board will last us for a long time, if necessary. Let's simply say as long as it takes . . . rare ores are considered rare for a reason. But they are somewhere under the mountain range, that much we've already ascertained.'

Lana groaned inside, but didn't give the old harpy the pleasure of a reaction. Turning the *Gravity Rose* into a carousel ride in Abracadabra's orbit while Sebba leisurely pottered around the surface of her jungle world wasn't what the skipper had envisaged. *And I'm not in the least bit worried that Calder will ask for shore leave in range of this old siren, either.* 'Well, you dig the rubble out, I'll ship it to Transference Station.'

'Oh, we won't be taking it back to Transference,' said the professor. 'We'll rendezvous with a buyer for a deep space cargo exchange. I have the coordinates for the meeting in a sealed file, to be opened after we've made our first big strike.'

'What?' Lana was puzzled. 'Surely the best price is on the open market? And in the Edge, system markets don't get any larger than Transference Station.'

'In the short term, perhaps, we might bid up the price that way. But then rival brokers will start to wonder where our company is sourcing its produce, and that wondering will eventually lead one of their ships to Abracadabra. DSD favours discrete, private disposals over auctions.'

As greedy as he ever was. 'All right then, I guess that's up to him. If I were any better at business, I wouldn't be in it with DSD, that's for sure.'

'He merely lives without the burden of self-illusion,' said Sebba. 'One of the few perks of making it past your seventh centennial.'

The comm woven into Lana's sleeve flashed to indicate the bridge was looking to get in touch, and she patched the call through on public. Polter was on the other end, his face floating like a firefly above her wrist. 'Revered captain, your presence, please.'

Lana grunted assent. She trusted the navigator was rescuing her from this interminable tour; the *Rose* had only just slipped into hyperspace, and any problems in addition to the ones she already had on her deck were *not* welcome. The skipper packed the harpy off on one of the ship's transport tube capsules, heading towards the thankfully empty stretch of passenger cabins, while she dialled for the bridge. There was only Polter on bridge duty when she arrived, no sign of Skrat or Zeno. But then that was the point of hyperspace, an infinite stretch of exotic otherworldliness beyond the usual woof and weave of the universe, not much to do but point your ship in the right direction and navigate towards your re-entry point, shortcutting centuries of travel through normal space. Polter's chair hovered suspended in the air on the back of a crane arm, a carousel of hologram displays swimming around the navigator's position. He had noted Lana's entry and the chair lowered, settling down before her.

'You might just have saved me from a fate beyond death,' said Lana.

'Manners maketh all beings, revered captain,' said Polter. 'But my intention was not to divert you from the customary social courtesies. I was calibrating our sensors for re-entry when I picked up a ping to our stern.'

'A ping? Just the one?' That was unusual. The chances of coming across another ship in hyperspace were miniscule compared to sliding void at sub-light velocities. Possible, but highly unlikely in the normal course of events. 'Show me the log.'

Lana's navigator brought up the encounter data from his chair, lines of dimensional telemetry surrounding the event. She frowned. 'It looks tiny. Too small to be a full size ship. Maybe we shaved a panel or some gear off the hull when we jumped? Or wreckage from someone else's jump? Not everyone's as clean at sliding a singularity as you are, Polter.'

'I have asked Zeno to check the vessel's exterior. His robots are running a maintenance sweep of our hull. Whatever the contact was, however, it's vanished now.'

'DSD was real jumpy about us leading someone else to his lucky strike,' said Lana. 'Could another ship have followed us in through the worm hole before it destabilised?'

'Riding our slipstream, yes, that is possible, if highly risky,' said Polter. 'But for someone to track us deploying any technology I have heard of, they would also need to stay in range of our sensors.'

Lana grunted. The known she could cope with. It was the unknown that always came gunning for you. This place, hyperspace, it messed with your damn mind. You could get pings from ghosts, dopplers from the multiverse – parallel reality versions of your ship and crew. When she had started out as a spacer, she had hoped against hope that she might actually make contact with one – a reality where her ship family had survived the weaponized plague that had seen them slaughtered. *A reality where I hadn't been orphaned; where I still have parents and siblings and cousins and . . . but what's the point?* They were just shadows of might-have-beens, given solidity by travelling beyond the corporeal universe. Maybe that's what ghosts had always been, mere shadows of probability you sometimes caught with the corner of your eye.

'Keep your eyestalks peeled for more pings, and when we're coming up to our exit point, let's make a false dive first, see if we can't encourage any tail to reveal itself.'

'I shall plot drop calculations as you suggest, esteemed skipper. It was probably nothing.'

'Let's hope so,' she sighed. 'And on the subject of eyestalks peeled, make sure you keep all the human males away from our passenger. I think she's in mating season . . . probably permanently.'

'We only have two human males, captain, as I'm certain you're aware. The chief and Calder Durk.'

'One for each stalk then, navigation officer, one for each stalk.'

***

The bridge, Calder judged, was unusually crowded, with not just his presence but that of their passenger, Professor Sebba, too. With Zeno, Polter and Skrat all occupying crew chairs, there was only Chief Paopao missing to fill out the full crew complement. The prince wasn't needed in the engine room for the drop down to real space. Neither the singularity stimulation vanes nor the slower-than-light drive were required to exit hyperspace. As he understood it, the structure of the *Gravity Rose*'s matter was converted slowly back to its non-tachyon state and slowly, the higher dimensional realm grew unreceptive to the ship's violation of its exotic physical laws before eventually gobbing them out like a spat apple pip. Calder was glad he finally had the chance to observe the mechanics of interstellar travel from the bridge's prospect. Lana had proved more difficult than he'd expected in granting his request – a level of stubbornness not unconnected, he suspected, to the professor's presence on the bridge at the same time. There wasn't much about Lana Fiveworlds that reminded Calder of his treacherous ex-fiancée back on his home world, but one thing that Lana and Sibylla definitely shared was that both of them only had room for one queen bee in the hive. *I guess it's no coincidence that Lana's crew are all males, even if the majority of them are lads from different species.* The two women had obviously taken a dislike to each other, and Calder found himself caught in the middle, an asteroid locked between the competing gravity fields of two stellar bodies. The natural ache in his loins whenever the professor tried to manoeuvre herself into a position where she could get him alone to rip his shirt off, was equally and diametrically opposed to the more sensible option of trying to get Lana Fiveworlds to see that an exiled prince on his downers was a match worthy of the captain's affections. There might be two slices of cake on offer, but in this matter, Calder was only going to be able to nibble at one. Unfortunately, the cake he wanted wasn't quite baked for sale yet, which always seemed to be the way of life. *Take courage, Calder, my boy, if you apply yourself, you'll find a way for you to have your cake and eat it.*

'Tachyon conversion is at thirty two percent,' announced the honeyed tones of the ship's computer, Granny Rose's voice rumbling from every corner of the command centre. 'Please brace for expulsion turbulence.'

Two spare chairs lowered towards the deck, crane arms at their rear whining as they stopped an inch short of the floor. Calder dropped into his chair, its sides reforming around the front of his stomach as though the unit had been custom moulded for his frame, the slight pressure from its crash field invisibly protecting him. Across from Calder, the professor had taken her own seat, and she winked in his direction. 'Any landing you can walk away from, eh?'

'I think we can do a little better than that,' said Lana from her chair, not sounding impressed by her passenger's comment in the slightest.

Calder would have kept his head down if he weren't already being lifted into the air, a loop of colourful hologram displays rotating around his position as though he were the centre of an orrery. The system they were due to enter contained an ancient red sun, most of its nuclear mass already spent. That meant that the *Gravity Rose* could drop out of hyperspace exceptionally close to the target world, without worrying about ripping the guts out of their gravity-sensitive hyperspace vanes. A low-gravity interaction short drop, to use the naval jargon he'd picked up from the *Hell Fleet* sims. Calder might not have been travelling in a fleet war vessel – simulated or no – but he had already realised that Polter was one of the finest jump artists in this corner of space. The new crewman gazed into the infinite reach of hyperspace visible between the bridge's spars. The effect was only a projection, but it looked indistinguishable from actually travelling exposed to the void outside their hull.

'We'll see,' said Professor Sebba, clearly enjoying irritating someone she regarded as the hired help.

'Thirty five percent,' reported the ship's computer.

A low buzzing vibration sounded from the hull, the harmonics of their shifting molecular structure becoming more and more disagreeable to hyperspace.

'Thirty seven percent.'

'Confirm lock on exit point,' said Lana.

'Lock confirmed, revered captain,' said Polter. 'Transition dive is calculated and stable.'

'Start dive manoeuvre, on my command, then terminate and drift for at least four seconds,' said Lana. 'Let's see what we can flush out behind our stern.'

'What are you doing?' demanded the professor.

'Just being careful,' said Lana. 'You never know what might be creeping up on your tail.'

'You have reason to think we're being followed?'

'Thirty eight percent,' said the computer. The *Gravity Rose* was really beginning to shake now, her hull buffeted by the turbulence of two competing sets of physics interacting with the cold hard fact of the ship's existence.

'Just being cautious,' smiled Lana. 'DSD was very clear about how few scruples the competition would show in throwing a spanner into his operation's works.'

'Do you know something I don't?'

Lana shrugged knowingly. 'Oh, I'm almost certain of that. Mister Skeratt, sensor declination angled to stern, all dishes, maximum scope.'

'Jolly good.'

Calder glanced between the chairs, confused. Were they really being followed, or was Lana just trying to throw the professor a scare as payback for the woman's needling? Hyperspace encounters between vessels were rare. *And we aren't exactly exiting at a major trading hub like Transference Station, either.* Given that only DSD and the professor knew what job the *Gravity Rose* had signed up for – and Dollar-sign Dillard wasn't exactly going to blab – how would a tail even know to follow the ship?

'Thirty nine percent,' said the computer. Calder's seat field whined as its cushioning kicked up a notch, the shaking easing off in his immediate vicinity. The sides of the ship were starting to blur. Lana wouldn't have long to make a controlled dive. *If she leaves it any longer, we're going to be spat out the hell knows where – deep space if we're lucky, or the centre of a sun if we aren't.*

'Approaching exit safety margins,' said Zeno, the android's voice chiding.

'Make for a false dive,' ordered Lana, raising her voice over the sound of the vessel's juddering. 'Record full sensor logs on our bow.'

'Holding at forty percent,' said the computer. Even she didn't sound happy about it.

There was a wrench as the ship started to fold back into normal space, then a sudden juddering as the manoeuvre was partially terminated. They were shaking the hell out of the *Gravity Rose* now, skimming between the fringes of two universes, only the chair's crash field stopping Calder being sent flying across the bridge and dashed against the hull. A maelstrom of colours erupted outside the ship, tachyons and other exotic particles flaring as they were half-dragged into normal space, mad glimpses of the dark velvet star-scattered reaches of normal space interspaced with the alien vaults of hyperspace.

'Hold us steady,' ordered Lana over the ship screaming protest, 'hold us steady . . .'

Calder gritted his teeth. *I don't know if the professor's spooked, but right now, I sure as hell am.* He felt his body torn between two states of existence, his hands shaking with primeval fear, the crash field unable to fully compensate and blinking ruby warning alarms as it shared his rising panic.

'Dive, dive, dive!' yelled Lana, just as the prince thought that the vessel was going to break up and be scattered across two universes. Calder's vision flared, a cascade of Higgs boson particles burned across the back of his retina – his own body suddenly fully reassembled, jolting in the cold, harsh grasp of reality. He slouched forward, trying not to retch, as the seat field caught his limp body.

'Now I know why your ship's so big and your crew's so small,' coughed Sebba, kicking her chair angrily down towards the deck. 'You've hit your natural limit of all the crew in the Edge actually crazy enough to fly with you.'

'Any landing you can walk away from, professor . . .' grinned Lana. She glanced out towards the reaches of space.

We've made a short drop, all right. Outside the *Gravity Rose*, the massive sphere of a new world filled the heavens. But even to Calder's relatively untutored eyes, the world looked, well, wrong. It squatted there a dull uniform crimson, matching the dead red light of the sun beyond, whirls in its atmosphere slowly twisting as lightning bursts lit it up from below. *This is a gas giant, surely, not an actual planet?*

Lana was obviously thinking the same thing. 'Professor, these are the co-ordinates you gave us, so what the hell is that? Jungle world, my ass?'

STEPHEN HUNT

'Well then,' smiled Sebba, 'it seems I know something you don't after all.' She sounded satisfied, as though the natural order of things had been restored. 'What you see before you is indeed Abracadabra. The world possesses an exotic troposphere, a top layer of gas which interacts with the sun's residual solar winds. That is the interplay of energy discharges you can see down there. The world is exactly as I described . . . only, *below* its gas layer.'

Calder watched the mesmerising sight of energies chasing each other across the world's whirling gas coating. *No wonder that DSD has the planet to himself.* Most ships passing through the system wouldn't give the place a second glance, and a dying sun was enough to put off any would-be colonists. The system's eventual star death and supernova might lie millions of years in the future, but humanity was superstitious about such things. Gods, just looking at the unwelcoming sight of the baneful sun beyond, Calder realised that *he* was superstitious about such things.

'Skrat,' said Lana, 'what do we have on the sensor logs?'

'No pings,' said the first mate, his lizard-like tail whipping thoughtfully in the hole formed for it in the command seat. 'If we were being pursued, any following vessel was too far behind us to track our dive.'

'Outstanding,' said Sebba. 'You nearly broke the ship in half to scan for a damned sensor ghost.'

'I wasn't even close to breaking the *Rose*,' said Lana. 'She can surprise you like that.'

Calder sighed. Their ship was a lot like the captain that way, too.

'Mister Polter,' said Lana, 'you and the chief have the con. Skrat, Calder, Zeno, you're with me. We'll take the control shuttle down to the camp, set up homing beacons, and guide our cargo landers in one-by-one.'

'I'll take my own ship and meet you at the camp,' said Sebba. 'There's equipment on her that the expedition needs.'

'As you wish,' said Lana. Now, Sebba making her own way off the ship, that the captain sounded happy about. 'With so many years' experience behind you, I'm sure you can navigate a safe re-entry on your own. How is the autopilot on the *Hineh Ma Tov*?'

'Expensive and of superior quality,' retorted Sebba. At least she left the "Just like me" unsaid and hanging in the air.

That is the kind of conversation you can almost build on, Calder mused thoughtfully. *Almost.*

***

ana ducked into their control shuttle's rear cargo chamber. Zeno, Skrat and Calder were waiting there, the android clutching the controls for the shuttle's rear ramp. The light on his box blinked green, indicating a breathable atmosphere waiting for them on Abracadabra's surface with no hostile pathogens detected. Lana had insisted on waiting for the atmosphere checks before cracking open the ramp, survey results or no. She wouldn't have put it past the maleficent professor to forget to mention that the air contained some nasty spores capable of seeing her laid up in sickbay, Zeno in attendance trying to work out how to regenerate her a new pair of lungs. *Wouldn't you just love that, high and mighty Professor Sebba? Me covered with red blotches and itching from some jungle fever. Out of your way while you work your goddamn horny way through my crew.*

Lana had seen all she'd needed of Abracadabra's endless jungle on the way down, a thick canopy only broken by the towering mountain range they were homing in on. Hints of crimson chlorophyll in the foliage intermingled with emerald green – it gave the jungle the ominous appearance of an ugly green brain streaked with throbbing red veins, a vast living entity spread across the length of the continent. Even inside the shuttle, Lana could hear the chatter of perimeter guns behind the camp's laser fence; some of the aerial predators still curious about exactly what titbits had landed on the base's runaway. She'd barely avoided the flock of terrifying flying creatures on their approach: leathery pink monsters large enough to scoop up pterodactyls like insects swallowed by a bird's beak. Lana had been seconds away from opening up on them with her shuttle's cannons, before the heat dump from the re-entry tiles drove the creatures off, beating away on giant lizards' wings over two runways that intersected each other in a cross. The base was set up at the end of a strip close to the mountain range; a wide clearing filled with quickset concrete buildings and hangars, none taller than two storeys. Lana snorted at the practicality of the set-up awaiting her outside. Professor Sebba's complex had been constructed with the crude, functional lines of a fortress.

Each of Lana's crewmen shouldered a rail rifle inside the hold, and she noted the guns' LEDs with approval. The weapons were dialled up to maximum acceleration; ball bearings in drum magazines ready to be accelerated at velocities capable of chewing chunks out of castle walls. Before she'd landed, Lana would have said she was being over-cautious in ditching her pistol belt's webbing for an assault rifle. *Having seen the local wildlife up close, now I'm wondering whether bringing rifles rather than cannons might be considered reckless.*

'This is your first real alien world, Mister Durk,' said Lana.

'Transference Station doesn't count, skipper?'

'Orbitals are all the same,' said Lana. She gestured for Zeno to drop the ramp. 'At least, the human-designed ones are. Some bigger, some smaller. Always too many citizens and too many adverts being hosed in your direction. Out there, beyond that ramp, there're sights that only a handful of people have ever seen. Maybe ever will see.'

'With good reason, one suspects,' said Skrat. 'This skirl would settle for a little staid uniformity right about now.'

'I hear that,' said Zeno. A light in the shuttle's ceiling started rotating and bleating a warning as their ramp lowered. 'Not many trading opps on a world with horse-sized spiders and monsters in the air that could devour dragons as fast food. Hey, Skrat, maybe some of the leathery winged locals are your long-lost cousins?'

'If so, they can stay lost, dear boy.'

The ramp thumped on the ground and the heat of the world outside flooded in like a tsunami, almost bowling Lana over. *That air is thick enough to carve with a laser.* Lana reached out and tapped the controls woven into the arm of Calder's smart suit to active it, then thumbed its cooling system up to max. Lana's own suit was already reacting to the heat, set to keep her flesh at a constant comfortable body temperature. She sighed as she walked down the ramp, resigning herself to being either too hot or too cold as she wandered around the base. This mission was going to end with her coming down with flu, she just knew it.

And apart from Lana's new crewman, she couldn't even comfort herself with the thought that her misery might enjoy company – Zeno's android frame was as unaffected by overheating as it was by all physical frailties, and as far as Skrat was concerned, Abracadabra was as good as home living for her lizard-like first mate.

Lana and her crew emerged onto the landing field; ground blackened from the napalm bombing it had originally received when the jungle had been cleared for the camp. Robot tanks rumbled around the landing field on caterpillar tracks, anti-aircraft chain guns on turrets spinning around and occasionally releasing bursts into the sky. Two-legged sentry guns, little more than cannons with steel feet, patrolled the inside perimeter of the laser fence. *Jesus, this feels more like a military base under siege than a mining camp.* Despite the heat, the ground splattered with heavy gobs of rain. Layers of steam drifted up from puddles across the trampled mud.

Sebba's vessel had landed before Lana's control shuttle. The ship sat parked seventy feet away, thrusters still leaking mist from its touchdown. A tube-shaped lift met the ground under the vessel's belly, the professor disembarked and speaking with one of the expedition members, a man a head or two shorter than the *Rose*'s haughty passenger. From the gesticulating and thrashing arms, the conversation appeared to be growing as hot as the planet's atmosphere.

'You'd think they'd be happy to see us,' said Calder.

'Maybe they've struck the galaxy's biggest seam of diamonds,' said Lana, 'and they think they've got to split the find with us now.'

'A girl's best friend,' said Zeno. 'Apart from her go-to-android, that is.'

Lana listened to discordant, alien calls from the distant jungle – eerie cries, screeches and whistles that sounded like nothing she was used to. 'I'll settle for artificial vat-grown gems.' *Especially if it means getting out of here.*

'This heat is incredible,' said Calder, his face ruddy and sweating as the four of them trudged towards Sebba's ship. 'You couldn't fire greenhouses to run this hot back on Hesperus.'

Lana shrugged. *When you come from a failed snowball colony, running the ship's air-con at body temperature must seem like a miracle.* Calder appeared stunned by the novelty of what he saw around him. Jungle, jungle, and a little more jungle. *Yeah, sims are one thing, real life is always another.*

'I rather like it,' said Skrat. 'Properly bracing!'

Just as I predicted. Skrat was unphased by the environment, his thick tail swishing merrily behind him as he crossed the landing field. All the first mate needed was a cane and he could have been going out for an afternoon stroll around what passed for park gardens on a skirl world. *Well, at least I won't be picking up the tab for the heating bills in Skrat's cabin down here.*

'Yes,' said Zeno, 'definitely related to those flying critters.'

'The calls from the jungle,' said Calder, 'they sound . . . wrong?'

'That'll be your fleshy body jerking your chain,' said Zeno. '"Hey! Hey, Calder Durk, you're missing the last couple of million years of evolution you need to survive out here."'

Professor Sebba turned towards the *Gravity Rose*'s crew halting in her ship's shadow. She indicated the local she was conversing with. 'This is Kien-Yen Leong; he's in charge of mining operations. We've got something of a problem.'

'Anything we can sort with the supplies we've got parked in orbit?' asked Lana.

Kien-Yen Leong was a squat, broad man sporting a thick brown beard. He obviously came from one of the alliance's Sino-settled worlds, and a high gravity one at that; the man's ancestors genetically engineered in the dim and distant past for an environment that Lana would be lucky to crawl in without an exo-suit. When he spoke, observing his face's muscles move was like watching the tectonic movement of granite slabs sliding across each other. 'Damn straight,' growled Leong. He indicated a pair of helicopters perched on a helipad above the base. Hybrids: half-transporter, half gunship, with missile pods and machine gun domes studding their grey fuselage. 'You've brought fuel for our choppers?'

'That we have,' said Lana. 'There's a shuttle's worth coming down from orbit.' She indicated the large metal fuel tanks squatting in front of the pad. 'But you can't have burnt through all your tanks? You're running a mining operation here, not an airline.'

'Not much mining going on this week. One of our staff, Janet Lento is missing,' explained Leong. 'She disappeared seven days ago. We've been running search and rescue flights over the jungle, day and night, trying to find her.' His tone was brusque and direct, but he couldn't hide the concern in his voice. If you were going to be swallowed up by that angry squawking crimson netherworld beyond the laser fence, Lana had the feeling you'd want someone like Kien-Yen Leong looking for you until the base burnt through its fuel reserves. *I may be the captain void-side, but down here I know who wears the stripes on their uniform.*

Lana gazed back at her shuttle and the professor's vessel. *Both too big to be much use hovering above a jungle canopy –*

even with antigravity assist, their orbital thrusters will tear up the jungle and fry the lost expedition member well before she can be winched out. 'Okay, I'll radio Polter and arrange for the helicopter fuel to be loaded onto the cargo landers first. You can fill us in on the situation on the hoof, Mister Leong.'

'Finding the missing woman,' said Calder. 'Is that a challenge, skipper?'

I don't like the way he said that. *Challenge. Something she remembered seeing in the briefing on Hesperus nagged at the edge of her consciousness.* 'Only for me and Zeno, your most regal highness. You and Skrat stay here and work on the job we've been paid to do. And you can stay on this side of the laser fence while you're doing it.'

'Only offering to come out and help look for her. By helicopter . . . I'm not actually unhinged enough to want to put boots on the ground out there.'

'Then you've already mastered the second rule of survival on Abracadabra,' said Leong. 'Never touch the dirt when you can stay in the air.'

'What's the first rule?' asked Calder.

'Never leave the base.'

'This side,' emphasised Lana for her new recruit's benefit. As if she didn't have enough problems, without Calder casting around for a white horse to rescue the missing driver . . . or maybe they rode big damn polar bears on his homeworld. *I'll definitely have to take a refresher on Hesperus.*

'You're the boss, skipper,' sighed Calder.

'Damn straight. I guess you've mastered the first rule of sliding void with me, too.'

- 19 -
Someday a real superno-va's going to come

Lana gazed out of the newly refuelled helicopter, seated and belted in one of the passenger seats behind the pilot and gunner's position. Kien-Yen Leong occupied the gunner's seat – every time he moved his head, the chain gun on the nose swivelled as it tracked the movement of his eyes. Zeno and Sebba sat alongside Lana. They skimmed low over the jungle, the second helicopter following directly behind, the crew's voices bouncing beseechingly off the canopy from loudspeakers mounted under its fuselage, calling for the missing woman to fire off flares if she could hear their flight. Both helicopters followed a straight ugly road that had been firebombed out of the wilderness. Calder and Skrat had stayed behind just as she'd ordered – the former, somewhat reluctantly; both crew keeping busy with the work of landing cargo shuttles inside the camp, disgorging crates for robot tractors to pile inside the base's concrete hangars.

'There it is,' said Leong, pointing to the slash of a wide, winding river, an azure-coloured snake slipping all the way down from the mountain range. Fast moving and wild, its waters raged powerfully enough to plunge on for thousands of miles across the continent. A pall of surface steam from the river leaked over the jungle – as though the rapids had been poured out of a tipped kettle. The makeshift road they followed ended by a riverbank and Lana noticed a tanker parked below. Nothing out of the ordinary: a long, caterpillar-tracked, double-segmented truck. Up front, the cab wouldn't have looked out of place on a battlefield – four sets of turrets sporting heavy machine guns, anti-aircraft missiles and recoilless cannons, radar dishes mounted on its sides like steel elephant ears. Suction pipes had been unfurled from a trailer section capable of holding a small lake's worth of water, hoses left dropped near the river. The drone responsible for handling the pumping gear was standing as inactive as a statue on a step designed for it at the vehicle's rear. But of the human driver, there was no sign. *I wouldn't want to be lost all the way out here.*

'Lento must have exited the cab,' pronounced Sebba. 'Despite all instructions to the contrary.'

'If she dismounted, she had a good reason,' said Leong. 'Maybe the truck's robot jammed when it was dragging pipes into the river. The lightning in the world's gas layer does weird things to the systems down here. Nothing works as it should.'

'Least of all the workers,' said Sebba, making real labour sound like a dirty word.

'Listen,' said Leong, 'if DSD wasn't so damned cheap, he would have paid for us to be outfitted with mining nano-tech from the start, rather than relying on antique water knife drills and liquid pressure blasting.'

'Doesn't the driver have an implant you can track?' asked Lana, eager to turn the conversation back to the practical matter at hand.

Leong shrugged. 'Yes, Lento did. But the atmosphere can fry an uplink if you're caught out in a storm. There have been three storms since she posted missing.'

Landing skids extended from the helicopter as it settled down next to the abandoned tanker. Leong pulled off his helmet, leaving his seat and throwing the side door open. Nearly bowled over by heat-rush flooding in to fill every inch of the air conditioned cabin, Lana pushed out after Zeno. The android reached the vehicle's side first. *I surely do wish I had your internal cooling system, Zeno.* Above them, the second helicopter circled in low, lazy loops, its rotor's downdraft clawing blankets of leaves off the nearby jungle. Given what might be lurking out there, Lana would rather have the chopper riding shotgun over them, than not. The sky throbbed a dull red crimson, crackling with forks of energy. It appeared as if the sun was pulsing through the clouds, although that was just an optical illusion. *Damn, but the sun looks like it's bleeding.* If you stared up at the bloody orb for long enough, you ended up with one hell of a headache.

Lana raised her voice to be heard over the whup-whup-whup from the copter hovering above. 'You haven't been able to move the truck?'

Leong shook his head. 'Its power plant is as dead as a dodo. Don't know why. I ran system diagnostics using a portable battery pack and there's no damage I can find inside any of the hauler's engine systems.' He pointed up towards the sparking heavens. 'Just more of that, I reckon.'

'Let me have a try,' said Zeno, making for the ladder that led up towards the tanker's cabin. 'I can tease more out of machines than the average bear.'

'No shizzle' said Leong.

'It's a definite talent,' said Lana, watching him climb. 'Up on our ship, Zeno rides herd on a couple of thousand robots in chorus.'

Zeno stopped by the thick steel entry access above. 'There's burn damage on the door.'

'That was us,' Leong called up at the android. 'We had to cut the lock away when we first turned up here looking for Lento. It was sealed as tight as a coffin.' His face crinkled. *There's a man immediately regretting his choice of words.* If the missing worker was to be found inside any coffin, then Lana reckoned it was the dense red and green variety squatting beyond the tree line.

'Did you check the ammo canisters up top?' Lana asked.

The squat man nodded. 'Did it myself. No shells fired off in the vicinity.'

Lana caught sight of something slipping along the other side of the riverbank, a pack of six-legged creatures the size of wolves moving slyly through the steam cover, green scales glittering like spilled oil in the burning river moisture. Bizarrely, each of the beasts bore a little saddleless rider, a small sharp-beaked lizard clinging proudly onto horn bones curling from the mount's head. She was put in mind of alien bikers on the back of a line of motorcycles. *Proud-looking little buggers.* 'Company!'

'I see them,' said Leong.

Lana watched the aliens studiously ignoring the tanker and helicopters. 'Are the riders intelligent? They might have something to do with your driver's disappearance?'

'Don't be ridiculous,' snapped Sebba. 'They're a symbiotic life form, no tool use or language. Hardly smarter than a terrier.'

'We call them "cowboys",' said Leong. 'One of the few things around here too small to want to bother us. The riders climb up trunks and shake them out to dislodge tree spiders, then their six-legged friends chew through the spider's armour and share its entrails after a kill.'

'Armour?'

'Yeah, if you're attacked by something in the jungle, not scrambling up creepers to try to escape would be a top tip.'

Lana shook her head in disbelief and started to climb after Zeno. The android cycled open the door and disappeared inside, the mining boss and professor following after Lana's boots. Aliens calls from the jungle depths chased after her. *Inside the vehicle is going to be safer than out. Marginally safer.* True to what Leong had described, the lights inside the cab weren't working, but there was enough illumination from the heavily armoured curve of glass beyond the driver's seat for her to make out the interior. Even easier for the android, whose optical range extended into complete darkness as just another part of his specification. Zeno moved down the back of the cab. There were control panels with built-in stools on either wall for monitoring the gunnery topside. He located the main control computer and broke open its console, pulling out circuitry boards. After a quick manual inspection, Zeno rolled up his ship suit's sleeve and a section of golden skin rippled back, revealing a physical jack which he plugged into the truck's systems. A look of concentration settled on Zeno's face. LEDs began to blink across the exposed machinery. He was juicing the device from the miniature power plant inside his body.

'Ah,' said Zeno. He slotted back a circuit board hanging from the panel. 'Now that's what I'm talking about.'

'You've found the truck computer's logs?' asked Leong. 'How about the cabin's interior and external camera feeds?'

'Burnt out,' said Zeno. 'But I got me the text entries left in the auto-drive's log.'

Sebba arched a supercilious eyebrow. 'And?'

'The computer shut down,' said Zeno, 'and made a pretty good job of trying to erase itself.'

'What the hell?' spat Leong. 'You're talking a hack? Someone down here hacked the truck's firewall?'

'Nope, best I can tell, the vehicle chose to kill itself. Mainly because the system core's artificial intelligence was scared.'

'Scared? Scared, my arse. It's just a machine.'

'*I'm* a machine.'

Leong shook his head. 'No, you're sentient, android. Our haulers don't even come close. I've got chess software back on base with more personality than this tanker. This is a low-level truck system we're talking about here.'

'High functioning enough to decide to commit suicide,' insisted Zeno.

'But that's not possible,' said Lana. 'It's not even permitted.'

'No,' said Zeno, sounding curious and oddly wistful at the same time. 'No it isn't.'

Dear God, computer suicide? What could scare a hauler that bad? Lana had a bad feeling that she didn't want to come close to finding out.

'I think you're the one with a programming fault, android,' said Sebba. 'What you found in the logs was merely a last-second burst of garbage from a dying and very limited AI. How do you explain the drained power on board? Let's deal with the most likely scenario. There was an atmospheric surge that our weather forecasting failed to predict. It must have knocked out some of the truck's systems. Lento got out of her cab to attempt to fix the vehicle. Then a second stronger surge killed the tanker and its weapons and locked her out of the protection of her own cabin.' Sebba pointed to the river before her hand encompassed the thick walls of the jungle. 'And how many species are there in the vicinity that would look on a stranded worker as a little variety in their usual diet?'

'What if she tried to walk back to the base?' asked Leong.

'It's a straight dirt track,' said Sebba. 'You might get dragged off it by one of the local beasts, but you tell me how you can get lost on this road? Thirty miles to the base from the river. I could walk that in a day. If Janet Lento's implant has stopped broadcasting, it's only because the body it was inserted into has been digested.'

'She could be lying wounded out there,' protested Leong.

'Wounded for over a week? Eating insects and drinking super-boiled water? You need to face up to reality. This is a highly unfortunate accident, I grant you, but everyone in the team signed on for danger money-plus. This is what it covers. Operations in the mountains are to resume immediately. I need an initial load to transport to DSD's buyers . . . or the funding for our operation is going to evaporate like a rain puddle in dry season. If you want to keep on combing the badlands of Nambia, you can do it in your own time when you're off-shift. I'll even throw in the helicopter fuel for free.'

'Damn straight we'll keep on with the search,' snarled Leong.

'I can assist you,' said Lana. 'The *Gravity Rose* has been laying down a satellite network ever since we put into orbit. We'll have eyes in the sky, soon. We can scan for fires, flares and messages scratched into the dirt . . . whatever it takes.'

'You,' said Sebba, 'will be too busy lifting containers into orbit to be distracted by this sideshow.'

Lana's eyes narrowed. 'Here's how chain of command works on a starship, prof. Above me, there's only God, and I don't even answer to him . . . he's strictly advisory only. Whatever you shovel dirt-side, I'll ship up-and-out for Dollar-sign, because that's the deal I'd have shaken on if DSD still had hands worth a damn to press the flesh. You even get to supply the jump co-ordinates, but that's as near as it comes to giving commands to my crew or me. So, Mister Leong, my satellite net will be at your disposal, just as soon as it's operational.' Sebba looked as if she was going to argue further, but Lana raised a finger. 'Or . . . as mission commander, Sebba, you can tell me to bug out, and I'll unload what's in orbit for you, and when I return to the next Edge world that's actually on the grid, I'll drop an e-mail to DSD telling him to find another chump to ship out his untaxed, unregulated, environmentally unfriendly, black-market ores to his dodgy buyers. And maybe, if you're real lucky, said chump's ship will actually turn up in Abracadabra orbit to haul your containers before your sentry tanks run out of ammo.'

'I can see why DSD chose you,' said Sebba before she turned to storm out of the cab and back towards her helicopter. 'You're not a starship captain . . . you're a pirate.'

Not even close. 'Whatever it takes,' sighed Lana, watching the irritating blueblood flounce off towards the chopper. She felt a flush of relief at the woman's departure. The mining chief mouthed a silent thank-you in Lana's direction, and turned to follow, no doubt trying to placate his hopeless boss.

'She had one thing right,' said Zeno, shutting the panel on the vehicle's computer core. 'Satellite net or no, we ain't going to find jack out there. That poor unfortunate mope of a driver's long dead.'

'Leave no crew behind,' said Lana, dabbing at her sweating brow with the back of her sleeve, finding only a moment's relief from the refrigerated fibres.

'She ain't *our* crew.'

'Part of the mission, anyway, as long as we're on contract for this fiasco.'

Zeno stepped behind the stretch of armoured glass at the front of the cab, staring out at the jungle and the baneful crimson sky. 'Man, there's nothing good going to come of being on this planet. Look at that wrong sky. A dying world under a dying star. The animals know it. The jungle knows it. Everything alive here knows it's been born a couple of billion years after a righteous geological era. This place has evil in its bones – just waiting for the day a real supernova's going to come and wipe the planet clean.'

Lana was shocked. The android was often cynical, but rarely this bleak. 'You're not terrified by a little tropical offworld bush, are you?'

'Sure I am . . . another entry in humanity's goddamn long list of gifts to me. The glorious joys of sentience.' Zeno pointed back to the cab's computer. 'Even this rat-brained truck was smart enough to fry itself rather than stay driving around here. What's that tell you?'

'Well,' said Lana. 'I guess that it's business as usual for Fiveworlds Shipping.'

'We are where we are, skipper. File it under spilt milk.'

'If only I hadn't run into Pitor Skeeg back on the station. I think seeing him running a small flotilla . . . it made me jealous. Made me reckless. I would have taken any damned job DSD offered us.'

'You think Skeeg's playing in the majors? He's just a bagman for Hyperfast, now. The best move you ever made was dumping that janky flam artist.'

Maybe the only good move. 'As long as it's been, Pitor still knows how to get to me.'

Lana felt a chill as she emerged from the truck to descend towards the waiting helicopter, blades beginning to rotate back into life, and it wasn't just her suit's thermostat reacting to the wall of heat outside. She'd brought the crew here, against all her best instincts. They were counting on her to keep Fiveworlds Shipping flying, and she'd made her usual level of good decision-making. *When was trusting Dollar-sign Dillard ever a smart move? If this had been any kind of cakewalk, the devious sod would've chartered his own vessel to fly in, rather than offering us a slice of the action.*

Zeno swung out of the doorway, mounting the side of the truck. 'You remember after you inherited the *Gravity Rose* and I agreed to crew for you, what I told you when we first walked onto the bridge?'

'Act like the skipper, act as though you know what you're doing,' said Lana, ignoring the burning heat, 'and everyone'll work to make your commands come good.'

'Damn straight. This is no time to start second-guessing your decisions. There's a universe full of might-have-been out there; the *Rose*'s holds can only store a small percentage of it.'

Lana sighed and made her way to the waiting helicopter. Zeno was right. But then, the android had a couple of millennia of right trailing behind him. *Maybe if I live as long, I'd be as wise – before the event as well as after.* 'Okay, here's how it is. We'll unload, hunker down behind the laser fence, wait for that old crone to dig out her first load, and then we're sliding void away from this damn rock just as fast as Polter can plot a jump.'

'Now that sounds like a plan.'

Lana stared back at the tanker, imagining the terror she'd feel if she was posted missing, lying in the jungle, wounded and lost. *What the hell is so bad that it could scare a low-level truck A.I into erasing itself? Yeah, another lousy day of business as usual.*

As she reached the helicopter, Leong dismounted from the cockpit; his face perplexed. Even more worried than before. He talked quickly into the helmet's communicator, his hands gesturing urgently but superfluously at whoever was at the other end.

'Mining chief?' said Lana.

'Another problem,' said Leong. 'The crewman you left behind at the camp to help supervise the shuttle landing . . .'

'Calder Durk,' said Lana, allowing a dagger of anxiety to stab at her.

'He's disappeared from inside the base.'

'Disappeared? What the hell are you talking about?' Zeno pulled out his phone, but the communicator just returned a long fizz of static. Polter's satellite network obviously wasn't fully inserted yet.

'I mean, he's *totally* disappeared,' said Leong. 'Your skirl friend, he sent Mister Durk to check on a jammed cargo door on one of your shuttles. After a couple of minutes with no word of a fix, the lizard followed him over, but your guy had vanished into thin air. We've searched every inch of the landing field and the base, but there's no sign of him. None of the gates have been opened; plus, all your shuttles are still on the field. What's his transponder frequency?'

'He doesn't have a transponder yet,' said Lana, reeling in shock at the news and trying to fight down a rising sense of panic. 'We use ship implants, but Calder's only just signed up as crew. He never had one put in! How can he have vanished?' Had Calder found some way to slip out of the base in search of the missing driver, despite all protestations to the contrary? *He can be reckless, but surely even he isn't that stupid?*

'My tech's checking the sentry guns' logs, to see if something flew over the fence that wasn't tagged and tracked as a threat. I don't see how that could be, though. Our sentry tanks are trigger-happy at the best of times. They'd light up a flying squirrel if one tried to jump the perimeter.'

Lana was damned if she could see how that could be, either. *Just like the mystery of a dead truck and its missing driver.* She looked at Zeno, but for once the android's normally expressive face was a mask matching his artificial origins. He shook his head gently and patted the rifle slung across his shoulder.

'Fly me back to the base. *Now!*'

***

ights flickered back on across the ship's bridge as the systems shifted from their hyperspace setting and returned to normal space operating mode. The captain of the *Doubtful Quasar*, who went by the nickname of Steel-arm Bowen, looked down at his cyborg arm – fidgeting with a mechanical life of its own as his all-too human flesh adjusted to a new set of physics. Steel-arm spat across the deck, reaching down to the side of his command chair and pulled out a hypo of oozing green pick-me-up to accelerate his body's natural recovery processes. *Ahhh, that's better.* Outside the ship, the bloody red disc of Abracadabra's sun winked at them through transparent armour, the world they were meant to be arriving at a small black disk silhouetted against the star's light.

Bowen checked the distance of the world – at least five day's travel on a sub-light drive burn. That was what you got from shipping with cheap navigators – the crab-like kaggen hovering malevolently in his chair and swearing at his controls, blaming his twisting hologram warp translation controls for not jumping in closer to the destination planet. *If we weren't seventy parsecs from the nearest planet I could pick up a fresh navigator, I'd toss the incompetent dog out of our airlock.* Their kag was a half-mad heretic, thrown out of the church for various unpalatable beliefs. Bowen's last kaggen had been much more effective at his job, but then poor old Keltat had died when a freighter the *Doubtful Quasar* had chased turned out to be far better armed than their informant's tip-off indicated. Keltat died in that action, as had the informant when Bowen returned to the rat-shizzle's system. Still, nobody said the life of a pirate was an easy one. Although it had to be said, Bowen's career choice had transitioned into relatively trouble-free pillaging since his deal with that scumbag Pitor Skeeg. Hyperfast fed him details of where the corporation's competitors were travelling, and the *Doubtful Quasar* waited in ambush for a sure thing to fly into range of her guns. Damn, but how Bowen *loved* a sure thing.

'Tell me we've at least kept our lock on the *Gravity Rose*?' barked Bowen.

'We have her,' said the navigator, sounding irritated at being questioned. 'I told you I located their hyperspace ejection point. It was exactly where the tracking signal disappeared.'

Bowen grunted. The kag had got that much right at least; but what did he want, a shiny medal pinned on his carapace in recognition of his virtuoso scouting skills? 'Where's the *Gravity Rose* anchored?'

'She's in orbit around that crimson-coloured world. Odd-looking astrometry on the real estate, too. Appears like a gas giant, but scans like a rock. Never heard of a transponder able to broadcast hidden from that far out before . . . finding the ship at this range, it's a miracle.'

'The alliance isn't in the miracle business,' said Bowen. And the alliance's corporate stooges paid a lot better than God, too. Bonus one – taking Lana's ship. Bonus two – paid in full by Skeeg by supplying them with the co-ordinates of DSD's secret deep space payday. "X" marks the spot, just like the pirates of yore. *Bonus three – getting even with Lana.* He gave his thin moustache a theatrical twirl. Who would have thought it? All that money remodelling his battle-scarred face on Errol Flynn, and still the *Gravity Rose*'s skipper had chosen to reject his advances. *You'd think that operating as a pirate isn't as respectable as being a smuggler? And me so handsome and dashing and all.* Bowen would have to make sure Lana lived just long enough to regret such a poor decision. Yes, Pitor Skeeg had known what he was doing when he had selected the *Doubtful Quasar* for this venture. Steel-arm Bowen and that dog Skeeg shared much in common when it came to their private lives, as well as a flair for ruthlessness in their respective trades. Now Bowen was going to succeed where his foolish ally had failed – he was going to get the ship and the girl. *You can never have too many prize ships, or too many prize girls, for that matter.*

'Power up our alliance stealth technology,' ordered Bowen. 'Full field on electronic counter measures. I don't want our little bird flying the nest before we make Abracadabra orbit.'

Down on the fighter deck, Bowen's ragtag band of pilots checked their fighters and launch tubes, readiness reports blinking in from the squadron on his command display. Over on the weapons desk, Melinda 'two-guns' Cho, was conscious again and working her comprehensive way through the gunnery checks; rail cannons and missile pods twisting in hull mounts as she booted them up to readiness. Cho had a dangerous glint in her eye that worried Bowen. *I will have to keep a close eye on my little cashiered marine after we gain orbit.* Cho knew all about Bowen and Lana's prior history, and the jealous minx might just be angling to make sure the *Gravity Rose*'s skipper became history, before the cyborg could have his fun. And who the hell would pay a good price for the *Gravity Rose* if the ship was offered at market with too many rail-gun holes in her?

***

Calder groaned. His head ached, as did every muscle in his body. The exiled nobleman felt as though he had been electrocuted. He was lying on the ground, his body covered by a blanket of crimson leaves. *There aren't any trees on the landing field?* As he pulled himself up, he saw the answer all around him. He wasn't on the landing field any longer. No sign of the base, the fence or the shuttles. No ominous hum from the laser fence or roar of incoming shuttles or occasional burst of fire from the sentry tanks. The outpost's sounds were replaced by alien hoots and whistles, cries that set his spine crawling. Dense, thick jungle everywhere he looked. *How the hell did I get here?* The last thing he remembered was waiting for diagnostics from the malfunctioning cargo hatch . . . then a brief flash of pain before waking up with a mouth full of vegetation. Calder checked his belt – his ship's communicator was gone. But his rail rifle lay dropped on the jungle floor a foot from where he had been stretched out. *Gods, small blessings, then.* He bent down to scoop up the weapon, receiving a short burst of reassurance from its heft. Calder glimpsed the strange crackling sky through the gaps in the canopy above; watery red sunlight growing fainter, though; the jungle turning a rusty brown as night began to fall. *Still on Abracadabra, then.* It smelled foul out here. Like dank laundry left undisturbed for a year until a blanket of mould covered it. He stood soaked in his own sweat, perspiration growing cold against his skin as his smart suit sensed him up and moving, kicking its refrigeration level up a notch. Calder's mind raced. *An engine explosion that sent me flying into the jungle?* Maybe dragged out of sight of the base by one of the local creatures, wanting to preserve him for a meal later? He touched his body. No burns on the clothes, or bruises that he could feel. *Surely such a catastrophic accident would have killed me, anyway?* Well, if something had been dragging him through the jungle towards whatever mountain cave passed for its larder, then the foolish predator should have chewed up his rifle rather than eating his phone. He gazed up the length of the nearest massive tree. *If I can climb that, maybe I can get a bead on the base?* Calder scouted for footholds in its trunk when a distant roar sounded from a playmate deeper in the jungle. Not quite as deep as he'd like, given the ferocity of the sound. *Coming back for dinner?* All around Calder a panicked series of calls echoed in answer, smaller denizens of the wild warning their kind while they fled. Calder dialled up the assault rifle to its maximum power setting. In front of him, the dense bush began to shake as something came pushing through.

- 20 -
Two legs bad. Six legs good.

Calder Durk pulled the rifle stock close to his shoulder. Part of him – the barbarian part, probably – devoutly wished he carried one of the familiar broadswords he had trained on since a babe to face the beast about to leap out of the thick undergrowth. The more sensible part was grateful he carried a modern weapon with a six-hundred pellet drum, each shiny small metallic dart capable of being accelerated to bone-shattering velocities by the gun's magnetic field. He listened to the crashing sound through the vines, growing closer every second. Snow-bears he knew how to fight. Mega-wolves he had hunted across glaciers, slain, stuffed and hung over the fireplace in his creaky old castle. But whatever was coming towards him now was going to be well out of his field of experience. That was the trouble with being reluctantly exiled from an icy-cold medieval homeworld, taken to the stars, signing up with a strange starship crew, then finding himself mysteriously and unceremoniously dumped into an alien jungle. None of this was exactly familiar. Except . . . the startled-looking woman who came hurtling out of the glistening wet scrub. She wore a green suit that Calder recognized. The same uniform as the other miners from this world's lonely human outpost. *Is she the missing driver?* The one the camp had already spent weeks vainly searching the jungle for?

'It's alright,' said Calder, lowering his rifle to show he intended no harm. 'I'm from a ship chartered to bring supplies to the mining camp. Are you Janet Lento? My crew's been helping your boss search the jungle for you.'

The woman stopped, but said nothing. *What's the matter with her?* Calder might as well have been some statue she'd unexpectedly stumbled across in the jungle. He noticed the name tag stitched across her breast pocket, "Lento". *This is the missing driver, then.* Still no reaction. The look of shock on the driver's face appeared to be a more or less permanent fixture — nothing to do with her running into another human out in the middle of nowhere. Wide green eyes, glassy and wild. Taller than Calder, her frame starvation-thin from surviving weeks in the wild on nothing but berries and bugs, long dark hair matted with dirt and leaves. She didn't seem to be sweating, even with the furnace heat from the mad red sun squatting high above the forest canopy. *At least her suit's cooling systems are intact and powered.* If they'd failed, heat stroke would have claimed the lost miner within the hour.

'I'm Calder Durk. My ship's the *Gravity Rose*. I was working out on your camp's landing field, unloading supplies. I lost consciousness, and when I woke up, I discovered myself here. Damned if I know what happened or how I travelled beyond the base's defence perimeter. Did something similar happen to you? My radio's vanished, but I've still got my rifle.'

Janet unclipped a communicator from her belt and tentatively offered it to Calder, her mouth open as though she was trying to speak but couldn't. He took it from her and tried the device, but only static came back at him. 'It's broken? I was warned communications on Abracadabra would be spotty. Something to do with the solar activity from that pig-ugly sun in the sky?'

He was about to pass the useless device back to her when he heard a crunching sound behind him. Calder wheeled around. A long whippet-thin creature emerged from between two of the trees, maybe a foot high, a bony nose like an elephant's trunk reaching out to pull leaves off the bushes and shove them into twin mouths either side of the trunk. It made contented snorts as it munched its way through the jungle, wobbling almost comically while grazing. Calder lowered his rifle. It headed towards a large series of globular plants at the far side of the clearing, each sphere striped yellow and red like giant sweets and resting on a bed of vines and spiny cushions. As the creature followed the leaves towards the spheres they started to quiver. A sudden lance of heated steam burst out of the bed of spines. The leaf eater squealed in an offended manner, leapt out of the way and bolted back the way it had came. Calder made a mental note to give any strange-looking plants a wide berth. Of course, being an alien jungle, there weren't any plants here that were familiar to Calder.

'You've stayed alive out here for week? Do you give survival lessons?'

The woman just stared at Calder as though he was speaking a foreign language. He tried to offer the radio back to her but she showed no interest in receiving it. Lento really did appear quite insane, as though she was looking through Calder rather than at him. 'Stay here,' ordered Calder, gesturing pointedly at the ground as if he was speaking with a particularly dim foreigner. He approached the nearest tree, slung the rifle over his shoulder and climbed the trunk with both hands. Calder shinned up until he reached its lowest branches, large waxy shield-sized leaves an angry red . . . the same shade as this system's dying sun. He used the branches as a ladder, easy climbing compared to the frozen forests of home, where slipping on a single icy bough would end in a fatal plunge to the ground. Calder's eyes flicked down to ensure the mute woman hadn't wandered away; but quite the opposite . . . she had followed his example and shinned up the tree too, stopping by the lower boughs. *Sensible.* Staying out of the way must have been how Lento had survived in the jungle for so long. He reached the canopy top, poking his head through. Calder felt hope drain from his heart. Just an endless crimson forest steaming from the last rain. Abracadabra's ugly bloated sun pulsed high in the firmament, making the clouds appear to glow intermittently, filaments of red spreading out like running blood. No sign of the mining camp. No sign even of the mountain where humanity's sole outpost on this faded world had been blasted out of the thick jungle. *How far have I been dragged from the base?* If a predator had been responsible for dragging Calder away from the camp, then the exiled nobleman should have been food for its larder long ago. He spotted two dragon-sized lizards wheeling over the distant forest . . . the same species which had attacked his shuttle on the way down to the world, hungrily eyeing the new arrivals through the cockpit's transparent ceramic as they dove at him. *The only way things can get worse was is if the dying sun goes supernova early and kills me in the explosion.* He ducked his head before the flying lizards noticed him, then carefully climbed back down, stopping on a branch close to Janet.

'I don't suppose you remember the way back to the mining truck you were driving?'

Her mouth opened but she said nothing.

'Well, I guess we're both lost. Our best chance is to listen out for a helicopter from the base. If one comes close I can take a pot-shot close to it with my rifle – that should set off its perimeter alarm. Let them know we're close.'

Lento looked around twenty five, but with life extension treatments, she could have been older than Calder's grandmother. *I really am lost – wrong planet, wrong time period, wrong situation.* Janet's mouth opened, but this time, rather than just sucking air, he heard words, so faint and rasped he couldn't make them out. 'What did you say?'

Now Calder was listening, he heard her the second time.

'It's covered in spines.'

Calder glanced around. Some of the jungle's plants resembled giant cacti, but he couldn't see any from where they were seated. 'What is?'

'It's covered in spines,' she repeated, hardly louder than a breath.

Calder groaned in frustration. *I'm sitting in my tree with someone who is clearly out of hers.* What had Janet Lento run into out here to send her off the deep end? 'It doesn't matter. We'll get out of this, Janet Lento. My crew won't give up on me. And your people have been searching for you since you were posted missing.'

'It's covered in spines.'

For a moment he wondered if she was talking about what passed for grass underfoot. Thick orange blades that bristled when you walked across them. 'Well, I'll be sure to wear gloves if I have to pick them up.' Humouring her seemed to have the desired effect. She fell silent. 'We could light a fire and try to attract attention. But everything in this land is so damn damp, I'm not sure how well it'd burn. And with the steam from the rivers and rain, distinguishing the smoke from the general boil-off isn't going to be easy.' It might be worth a try, though. The *Gravity Rose*'s crab-like navigator, Polter, was still in orbit alongside Chief Paopao. They had still been seeding orbital satellite coverage around the planet when Calder's shuttle launched down to the ancient world. Could modern technology distinguish the difference between a rescue beacon's smoke and natural steam from rainfall? Satellites still seemed like magic to Calder. *The wizard's all-seeing eye*. Science or sorcery, he would take whatever help he could get right now.

Calder heard a scratching noise at the end of the branch. He peered through the bloody red leaves. A spider the size of a rat shook the tree's vegetation, a peacock-like fan of multi-coloured fur at its rear, bristling as it drummed its fore-legs against the wood. Disgusted, Calder reversed his rifle and swiped the thing away using the gun's collapsible metal butt. 'Off you hop! This tree isn't big enough for everyone. Guests get priority.'

As the spider fell it made a keening whistling noise like an angry kettle brought to the boil. Its cry was answered in the jungle, distant echoes muted by the thick undergrowth. *That's not good*. The creature he had dislodged fell to the ground in the tree's shade before whipping around in circles like a puppy chasing its tail.

Janet Lento shinned higher up the tree as the faraway whistling grew closer, ferns rustling as more spiders appeared. And Calder realized that what he had ejected from the tree wasn't exactly a spider . . . at least, not an adult one. The mature hunters weren't rat-sized. In fact, mastiff hunting hounds in the exiled prince's palace kennels would have given the fully grown spiders a respectfully wide berth. The creatures swarmed forward, a series of legs pincering down either side of their orb like bodies; large and small limbs interweaved like dancing tanks, at least four feelers up front for carrying and hacking with sharp, poisoned bristles. Dagger-sized fangs angrily clattered around their mouths, clusters of eyes at the mount of the central body bulb focusing on Calder. They didn't appear happy in the slightest to find uninvited visitors in their tree, mistreating their hatchlings. *The feeling is mutual.* Calder realised that the long, low sound like creaking wood originated next to him. Janet Lento wasn't speaking, but she could still make some noises and was at least aware enough of her surroundings not to appreciate dozens of nightmare-sized spiders scampering towards their perch above the jungle. Calder unslung the rifle and pointed it towards the ground. He squeezed the trigger but nothing happened. Cursing, he pressed the safety selector to semiautomatic and let have at the creatures below. His rifle was recoilless . . . the same magnetic field that accelerated the darts to hypersonic velocities catching the back burst and absorbing the energy, recovering it to help power the gun. Only a slight quivering with every hail of pellets triggered. Every short burst made a *zup-zup* sound as the gauss field flexed, followed by an angry explosive cracking as his ammunition broke the sound barrier. Swine-like squeals came from the spiders below as they were literally blown apart by each volley. They didn't sound much like spiders . . . the arachnids back on Calder's freezing home world, Hesperus, had been coin-sized, silent and joyfully shy. Shrewd enough to avoid humanity for the most part. These ones kept coming, leaping up at the lower trunk until Calder sighted on them. Not much more to it

than pointing and squeezing. Colourful bodies burst apart with
the impact. The nobleman heard a scampering noise from the
back of the tree, and he leaned against a branch to hose a wave of
spiders climbing up the rear. He changed position, the assault on
the front renewed with fresh vigour. They drummed against the
wood as they climbed. *Calling their pack, or communicating with
each other?* Calder fought the impulse to check his ammunition
count. He sweated, shooting furiously into their ranks for
maybe five minutes, beating back a last attack made from all
sides simultaneously. The spiders finally learnt caution, backing
away from the tree, whistling angrily and impotently against the
intruders, shaking their colourful fur fans as they attempted to
intimidate the two newcomers. What was it the mining camp
manager had said back on the landing field, describing the base's
murderous automated weapons? "We're not in the food chain
and they've learnt it the hard way." *Too damn right.* This was
probably the first time this pack had run into humanity. Their
fate was the same as so many non-sentient predators introduced
to mankind across so many worlds.

'Keep away!' yelled Calder. 'This tree is *my* kingdom now.' So,
this is what his realm had shrunk to, the measure of his reduced
circumstances. The first time he'd actually shot a modern
weapon, too. Guns in the sim entertainment shows that the ship's
android, Zeno, had used to bring him up to speed on modern
existence surely didn't count, as real as they had seemed at the
time. *It seems shockingly easy compared to the many tedious
years of real training with sword, shield, crossbow, longbow
and armour I suffered in my youth.* His father and his man-at-
arms permanently disappointed in Calder's martial progress. If

he had only possessed a couple of crates of such rifles back on Hesperus, he could have armed the basest peasant farmers with the guns and routed every nation on the world – crowned himself emperor of the planet. *I would never have been beaten on the battlefield, betrayed by my treacherous fiancée and then forced to ignobly flee my world in exile.* Part of Calder was glad he had never been offered the temptation by the wizard who had turned out to be merely a rogue crew member. *This rifle is a coward's weapon, a knave's weapon. No skill required. Neither strength nor patience. No need to put yourself in risk. Just sit back and slay at a distance like a god casting lightning bolts.*

Janet Lento's wide eyes settled on the blood-mangled bodies quivering at the foot of the tree. She seemed to find the carnage as much to her amazement as everything else she mutely observed. Her gaze shifted accusingly to Calder.

'Better them than us,' said Calder. 'I know it isn't exactly glory, but we're about two hundred light years away from all of that . . . and I'm not a prince anymore, so there's not a lot left I can disgrace, is there?' *Least of all the not so glorious House of Durk.*

He checked the ammunition counter on his drum-like magazine. Two hundred pellets left. He had managed to fire off two thirds of his ammunition in one brief engagement. *Magnificently done, Calder Durk. Mighty King of the Tree.* He pushed the fire selector to its sniper setting, single fire and maximum acceleration, to make his magazine count. An optical sight rose from the centre of the gun as he flipped the switch, an integral field projector to paint targets with a laser. *Thank you, but quite unnecessary.* At this range a six year-old goat herder would be hard pressed to miss. Down in the jungle clearing the remaining spiders retreated into the neighbouring trees, foliage shaking as the creatures passed through the leaves. *What are they up to now? Are they going to wait until we come down to see us off their domain? Is this a siege now?* This area of the jungle was obviously serious spider territory. 'I don't suppose you know how these hairy monsters hunt . . . their pack behaviour . . . intelligence? Any nests near the mining camp?'

Lento said nothing. Something shifted below in the clearing, and for a second Calder thought he caught sight of a small child moving through the brush. But then the apparition was gone. *I must be going mad out here.* He wondered how long it would take stranded in the alien jungle until he ended up like his companion. *Two blades short of a castle armoury.*

'Gods, I wish we had some of the camp's big robot tanks to protect us.' And sitting behind a laser fence topped with automatic guns would have been welcome right about now. Except the machines obviously hadn't proved up to the task of keeping Calder on the right side of their defensive perimeter. And tanks wouldn't have been able to fit in the clearing to stop the spiders . . . swinging across between the trees on sticky white webbing! Calder swore and moved his rifle up, but the spiders were well dispersed in the surrounding trees, arcing across at random . . . ones, twos, three at once, a dozen different directions. *Too many to sight.* He fired off shots as they swung over like great hairy pendulums – all quivering legs, victoriously whistling and clattering their fangs like knives sharpening for a roast, his bullets cracking wide as the creatures slammed into the tree's high foliage. *His* tree. Foliage trembled above them. How would such a creature hunt? They demonstrated. Dropping out of the tree like an assassin on whatever unfortunate passed below seemed a more-than effective method. Caldor tried to hold down his rising tide of terror. Losing it out here, up here, would be the very last thing he did.

'Get down!' Calder cried at Lento. An unnecessary shout. She was already shinning her way towards the clearing. He swung off the branch and grabbed the wood, finding handholds to desperately jab fingers into. *It seemed a lot less demanding to get into my tree.* Then Calder found an easier way . . . it started raining spiders and he lost his grip, plummeting towards the jungle floor without the benefit of a spider's web-like rope to control his fall. The ground slammed into him sideways – or maybe he was sideways, knocking the life out of him for a couple of seconds. His rifle still securely slung around his back as two aggrieved wolf-sized arachnids landed close enough to reach out and touch.

***

Captain Lana Fiveworlds ducked under the helicopter's slowing rotor and ran towards the waiting miners and her lizard-snouted first mate, Skrat. Her android, Zeno, was immediately off the helicopter and by her side.

'What's the situation?' demanded Lana.

'It's terribly perplexing,' said Skrat. 'Calder appears to have disappeared from the camp. We were working together unloading supplies. He went to check on a malfunctioning loading ramp. Calder seemed to be gone an inordinately long time, so I went over to see how he was doing. There was simply no sign of the fellow! We have searched the base and the landing field and every shuttle, but he's completely vanished.'

The camp's manager, Kien-Yen Leong, appeared from the second copter. He addressed his staff. 'You've checked the fence's sensor logs and all the automated guns?'

'Of course we have,' grumbled a miner. 'There's no record of anything leaping the fence or flying through our air-space' He pointed to one of the sentry guns up high on a tower, rotating with elephant-like radar manifolds sticking out of its turret, tracking a dragon-sized beast in the sky above.

'Could you have had a power outage on your guns or along the sensor line?' asked Lana.

''There's no hole in the logs to match that,' said the miner, looking up at the bloated blood-red sun. 'Before you ask, everyone in your crew is listed in the camp system as friendlies. None of our guns glitched and blew him to pieces . . . and even a mortar round leaves some remains. These systems are hardened against solar activity. They're rated for badly nuked battlefield environments. Background radiation here can be erratic, but it's never approached anything close to our defences' tolerances.'

Lana held back from retorting that it was a pity the base hadn't taken the same trouble with the truck that the missing miner had been driving. Maybe she and Zeno wouldn't have been wasting their time searching for a probably long-dead worker after she disappeared. *Just like Calder Durk. He's green as a meadow – at least, the ones on most worlds – and trouble through and through.* She gazed back towards her helicopter . . . Professor Alison Sebba dismounting with a dainty disdain for the landing field mud. If the academic hadn't been flying alongside

Lana during the search for the missing miner, Lana might have suspected the life-extended harpy had finally gotten her claws into Calder. *I could have asked them to search the base again, checking under bunks for the pair.*

'One thing,' said Zeno to their first mate, the android's skin glistening orange under the auburn light. 'We asked you to do one thing out here, and that was to keep the new guy safe.'

'I seem to recall advising the dear boy might be better occupied in the engine room,' said Skrat, his thick green tail swishing irritably behind him.

'I know, I know . . . it's my fault,' said Lana. 'I thought a bit of shore leave and seeing his first real alien world would be good for him.' It had hardly been a bribe at all, had it? Lana was the captain. She certainly wasn't in competition with the professor over some ill-educated exiled nobleman . . . a junior crewman she simply shouldn't be involved with in the first place. *And this was meant to be a cake walk. A supply drop to a barely inhabited planet. How dangerous could it be?*

The conceited professor who might be able to answer that last question approached the group. 'Please tell me that at least some of the camp's workers are still occupied inside the mine?'

'Calder has vanished,' said Lana, furious at the woman's lack of concern. Cold selfishness was a trait plenty of humanity's life-extended members shared. Supposedly a coping mechanism to deal with the less rich members of society's habit of expiring from old age. *Survivor's guilt.* Lana suspected the professor probably possessed that chill self-regard from the age of twelve, however.

'Have you contacted your ship?' said Sebba. 'If Mister Durk's really not inside the perimeter, then perhaps he wandered into one of your empty shuttles as its autopilot activated and lifted the boat off the field? He could have found himself locked in and unable to get about. He might be trapped in an empty cargo bay inside your vessel's hangar as we speak?'

Lana sighed. They were clutching at straws here. She unbelted her communicator and patched it through the command shuttle's antenna to punch through this world's god-awful radiation field. A brief bleeping as she paged the *Gravity Rose's* bridge. Her navigator, Polter, picked up, his voice distorted by more static than normal. 'Revered captain?'

'Order the ship to scan every returned cargo lifter racked on board. Check to see Calder Durk isn't trapped in one of the freight bays. In fact, sweep the whole ship for life signs, while you're about it . . . and do the same for any birds we've got in the air.'

The line went silent for a minute, before the navigator returned. 'Only myself on the bridge and the chief in the drive room. All the returning supply ships are safely docked on board and accounted for. Is Calder in trouble?'

'I wish I knew,' said Lana. 'How are you doing laying down our satellite net up there?'

'Nearly finished,' said Polter. 'But far too many of the seeded satellites are malfunctioning. It's as though the devil himself is playing with the relays. You would think we're trying to network this cursed system's ebbing star.'

'Do your best,' said Lana. 'It's not just one of the locals we're trying to track now. Calder is AWOL. Keep the ship in geostationary above our area of the continent. I want every sensor we've got monitoring as much of the rain forest as it can. Scan for smoke signals, rocks spelling SOS by river-banks, night fires . . . anything that looks like human life down here.'

'As you command. And I shall pray for his deliverance,' said Polter.

'You do that.' *At this point, nothing can hurt.* Lana closed the line. She turned to the professor. 'What aren't you telling us?'

'I'm sure I don't know what you are talking about?' said the professor.

'I'll give you a clue,' interjected Zeno. Lana knew that look. The millennia-old android was about to give the academic a run for her money in the long-lived wisdom stakes. 'This world . . . this operation . . . it doesn't feel right. Like that truck dead out in the jungle with an erased A.I. It committed suicide. Do you know how hard it is to get a machine to go against its programming like that? To *scare* it?'

Sebba pointed at the mountains behind them and indicated the staff and the base. 'Mountains. Miners. Digging. I don't know what else you're expecting here? Surely you're not frightened by the fire-side superstitions that colonists tell each other about avoiding settling on last-stage systems? The sun might be on its last legs, but Abracadabra's ecosystem will survive in this state for another two million years at least. It will outlast us all . . . even you, android.'

'That's what I'm worried about,' said Zeno, scratching his wiry metal Afro.

'You have one advantage the truck's systems do not . . . you are supposedly sentient. Start thinking with your brain rather than your emotions. We are the most advanced life-forms on this world – we are surrounded by a laser fence designed to fry anything bigger than a virus. There is the best part of an armoured regiment's worth of autonomous weaponry rumbling around the camp. Following your supply drop, we now have enough ammunition and fuel to engage a small army.'

'Our mutual paymaster for this mission has a somewhat, shall we say, dubious reputation as a rather shifty fellow,' said Skrat. 'One we've been stung by before. Hence our caution, professor.'

'I won't argue with you on that point,' said Sebba. 'If Mister Durk isn't inside the camp, he must have wandered out when the gates opened for one of the mining robots. Is it possible he wanted to impress one of us by rescuing Janet Lento when he heard about the missing woman's predicament?'

Lana groaned. Calder had said something obliquely like that back on the ship. Still operating on whatever cockamamie medieval honour code he'd been raised with. *Thinking like a medieval warrior knight rather than crew.* The queen of the ship setting a series of impossible challenges for a potential suitor like Calder to prove his worth. *But surely even Durk wouldn't be so stupid as to barrel into a dense alien forest where everything that moves wanted to kill, maim and consume him, just to rescue a damsel in distress?*

'So, the young man has gone. Did he take his rifle and communicator with him?' asked Sebba.

Skrat nodded. 'The dear chap certainly didn't leave them behind in the shuttle.'

'There we are,' said Sebba, haughtily. 'You can take the man out of the collapsed barbarian society, but you can't wholly take the barbarian out of the man. Not so much missing, as off on a quest!'

'This ain't some cheap sim show,' said Zeno. 'The dragons outside the fence are real, there are no goblins and Calder only has one life.'

'I find his youthful indiscretion rather charming,' said the professor. 'Don't you remember when you were fresh, android?'

'Me, lady? My early days were just ones and zeroes. Sentience was an accident, not the plan. My kind doesn't get to believe in God. My creator was just a disappointed corporation with a rogue asset they had to write off their balance sheet.'

And I, sadly, don't even remember that much. Lana gazed in fury at the academic, chilled beyond even the cloying warmth of this hothouse world. Their missing crewman merely extra novelty for the professor's jaded pleasures. 'We're going to keep on searching . . . for Calder and your missing driver.'

'Of course you will. And the rest of us will get back to work.' Sebba gazed pointedly at the miners. 'So that we have something worth shipping out of here to justify the mine's set-up costs.'

Lana watched the wintry woman march off towards the series of low concrete buildings that formed the mission complex, the miners reluctantly following behind.

The mine boss tarried behind for a second. 'We'll do what we can to help,' said Leong. 'For both our people.' Then he departed for the base too.

'It's never easy,' said Lana, as much to herself as her android and first mate. 'Working for Dollar-sign Dillard. How could I ever have forgotten?'

'If it were easy, it wouldn't be us,' said Zeno.

'We'll take a shuttle up, all of us together, and fly in shifts,' said Lana. 'A proper search pattern, quarter and quarter again. You can't beat eyes on the ground and a live hand on the stick. We'll let the ship's scopes and the search algorithms handle the low probability areas of the sweep while we go straight for the money . . . everywhere between the camp's gate and the stranded truck.'

Skrat looked at the jungle beyond the defence perimeter. He didn't need the ship suit's fibres set to deep freeze. For a skirl like him, this was as good as home. 'Do you really think our man's out there?'

'Got to be somewhere,' said Zeno. 'And he sure ain't here.'

'Damnable fool then if he is,' said Skrat.

'We knew that much,' sighed Lana, 'when we took him on.' She stepped aside as a robot drilling unit rumbled past, clouds of dust spilling from its tank-like tracks. 'I see the miners and I see the mining gear. So why doesn't this feel like a mine? I don't trust that woman. When we get a clear moment, we're going to have good snoop around here.'

'When are you hoping to do that?' said Zeno.

'As soon as.' *We're going to find Calder. We have to.* Lana hadn't lost a crewman yet, and she certainly wasn't planning to start with Calder Durk. It was a matter of professional pride, she told herself. *No more than that.*

***

Calder struggled with his rifle's strap, fumbling to drag the weapon closer even as the nearest spider leapt at him, its jaw parts open, mouth hissing and whistling victoriously. He wasn't even close to getting the weapon aimed when the spider flipped over in the air, something wet, green and muscled barrelling into it mid-air. All flailing legs and ripping flesh. *None of it mine!* He desperately rolled over and knelt up to see what was happening. A pack of green six-legged panther-sized creatures had entered the clearing, the closest of them feeding on the blood-stained spider corpses his rifle had left on the jungle floor. The interlopers carried some kind of symbiotic biped riding the six-legged beasts like mounted knights, clutching curled horns on their mount's head. The riders bounded off their scaled steeds and streamed past Calder, ignoring him. The symbiotes were naked, smooth-skinned and no higher than his knee. One scampered past and leapt up into the tree, easily climbing it with sucker-tipped fingers. Another came sprinting past only to halt by Calder. It sported a long serrated beak resembling the sharp visor of a knight's helm; but when it opened the beak, gawping at him, Calder saw a wide perpetually grinning mouth below, interlocking white teeth as sharp as needles. It almost shook its head in disbelief, wide oval eyes blinking in surprise, before climbing up the tree after its comrade. *That's the child I thought I saw in the undergrowth! It must have been scouting for food. Probably thought it was a festival day when it came across the feast I'd laid out under the trees.* A splintering noise sounded from above. Calder could just see the riders cutting through branches with their beaks, using them like organic chainsaws and then it was raining spiders . . . these ones involuntarily dislodged rather than ambushing their prey. *The knights are quite literally shaking the trees for their dinner.* The green scaled predators below hurled themselves onto each spider as it landed. Transformed from hunters to hunted, the arachnids seemed to know how combat against these ferocious six-legged carnivores usually ended for them . . . the spiders didn't even try to put up a fight, just scurried back into the jungle, pursued by the long, loping predators. Calder found Janet Lento on the other side of the clearing, backed up against a series of giant orange ferns. The newly arrived predators appeared to be ignoring Calder and the lost driver for the best part. *Too strange to be considered part of the food chain?* Or were the predators intelligent enough to appreciate that any animal that could lay down a carpet of free food with a rail-gun was worth preserving for a while? *I hope so*. Calder watched surviving spiders in the high branches exit from his tree exactly as they had arrived, swinging on web ropes to the neighbouring trees – like pirates fleeing a burning galleon. There was a rustling from all around him as the large arachnids abandoned this corner of the rain forest. Calder stood up, his rifle in his hands. He tentatively eased himself between the spiders' remains and the feasting predators, moving towards Lento. *You just keep on eating. As long as I'm not on the menu.* The predators were all muscle, scaled green hides rippling as they nudged and snuffled at the spider corpses' entrails. Four long legs for balance at the front of a body that might have been an alligator interbred with a hunting hound, two powerful muscled limbs bent at the back. Legs that looked like powerful enough to vault across a canyon ravine. Curled horns on their heads whipped from side to side as they tore into the dead spiders. A wave of riders flowed down the tree trunk. The knights assembled around the corpses, sitting down as though this was a picnic laid on for their benefit, branch-breaking beaks snapping open, little green hands gathering up pieces of arachnid meat and stuffing it into their rictus-grin mouths. *These riders are obviously welcome guests at the feast.* The six-legged predators pushed torn bodies towards their symbiotic partners, rolling arachnid corpses with snout and forelegs, some of the spider bodies' hairy legs still quivering and sending a wave of primeval fear down Calder's spine. But he didn't have to fear the spiders around here anymore. *Only what has driven them away.* Calder reached Lento and raised his finger to his mouth, when he remembered that she hadn't exactly been loquacious before. He took her hand in his and turned, only to find himself staring directly at one of the predator's eyes, its head lowered in a menacing manner, a cluster of nostrils snorting as it tried to identify this unlikely pair. Other predators emerged from the undergrowth, returning from their spirited jungle pursuit of the spiders. They advanced slowly on Calder and the woman, pushing them back towards the knights' strange picnic. For a terrible moment Calder thought that the two of them were about to be offered as food to the riders in the same manner as the spider corpses, but then one of the predators advanced, rolling a dead spider across the ground. It halted in front of the two humans.

'Are you inviting us to the party?' asked Calder.

The circle of riders shuffled to either side, leaving a space the right size for Calder and Lento to join their ranks. It was as bizarre an offer as he was likely to receive today. *I'd sooner humour the pack than waste the dwindling reserve of pellets in my rifle's drum.* Janet Lento sat down, as if breaking bread with these strange natives was an everyday occurrence. She reached into the spider's body, barely recognizable after being shredded by Calder's rail-gun, scooping out the pink meat as though this was a crab delicacy, stuffing it into her face until her cheeks were puffed out, strange juices running down her throat. Calder tried to stop himself from retching. *It is as if the jungle has claimed her soul.* Regressing her to some more basic, primeval state. Maybe this is how humanity would end up if it stayed on a world long enough for a sun to reach its nadir and start to die? Beside Calder, one of the knights nudged him with its sucker-tipped hand, indicating the spider's corpse. A tentative bird-like noise – somewhere between tweeting and whistling – escaped its mouth.

'I understand,' said Calder. 'I helped you kill it. Now I have to eat it.' He scooped out a large chunk of entrails from the spider – a cake of flesh that would have kept a peasant family in sausages for a week. He was queasier than he should be. Whale meat was a delicacy on Hesperus . . . and the massive creatures that hunted under the sea ice were called whales only because his distant descendants had been offworld Nordic settlers. *I've gotten too used to ship rations.* Chief Paopao's expertly rolled sushi. A wide variety of frozen ration-packs from a hundred worlds. *Damned if I'm going to eat raw arachnid.* He stood up and recovered a couple of fallen branches sawed by the knights. He drove a long thin branch through the spider meat like a stake; the thick log he tucked under his arm. He walked to the other side of the clearing, pinning the meat with the wood into the ground. Then he took seven steps back and heaved the sawn-off log at the cluster of striped plants, the wood tumbling through the air before smacking into one of the huge bulbs and falling across its bed of vines. A furious wave of steam jetted out from the spines, trying to cook the creature foolish enough to blunder into the murderous vegetable plot. Steam enveloped the spider guts, rocking the meat on his makeshift stake. He gave it a couple of seconds after the jet finished, ensuring the plants had exhausted their reservoir of solar-heated rainwater. Then he retrieved his share of the slaughter and happily went back to re-join the bizarre picnic.

Calder waved the cooked hunk of meat at the riders. 'I prefer spit-roasted, but steamed is as good as it's going to get in this place, I reckon.' He tore off a strip and offered it to Lento, but she stared at him with the same wide-eyed expression as always, as though the exiled nobleman was the true oddity in this gathering. He tried the nearest rider, which sniffed at the boiled meat, little nostril strips along the top of its beak opening and closing. It nibbled at the strip, made an almost human sound of disgust, tossed the cooked meat over its shoulder and reached into the burst spider to get a fresh handful of the good red-raw flesh.

'I'm among the heathen, here,' said Calder. He bit into the hot meat. Slightly crunchy, as though the flesh was mixed with flecks of grit, not much flavour – and what there was almost tasted curiously as if it had been marinated in vinegar. *I've eaten worse.* Hell, when Calder had been retreating across the frozen sea on his sole remaining ice schooner, pursued by half the enemy's navy, he and his desperate crew had boiled shoe leather and mixed it with moss, so close to starvation had they fallen. Calder lifted up the steamed entrails. 'Better than my boots, I have to give you that.'

Calder ate his fill. He could tell the impromptu picnic was drawing to a close when the six-legged predators finished feasting. Some of them began play-chasing each other around the clearing, while one of the pack's larger members with the grandest set of horns reared up in front of the tree where Calder had found shelter, scratching bark off with its sharp points. *Marking its territory, or showing the tree is clear of spiders and not worth revisiting for a while?* Calder couldn't make his mind up about these creatures. No clothes. No tools. No real attempt at speech or communication, even among each other – unless they chatted by covertly exchanging odours or whistles outside his pitch of hearing. But they clearly acted towards the two humans with a measure of basic intelligence. *The enemy of my enemy is my friend.* You could live and die by that on Hesperus. In fact, Calder nearly had, before he'd had his eyes opened to the rest of the universe's existence. The reports on this world said it was empty of sentient life. Of course, the reports had been self-serving mineral surveys for the large part. Calder had done enough cop show sims in his brief tenure as crew to understand the motives of an offworld mining operation like this. As soon as local sentience was declared and its news spread, you risked having your supply runs boycotted by environmentalists and do-gooders. Starships dropping automated camera drones to record every felled tree and every cute herbivore running into your laser fence. The label 'blood' tagged in front of all resources you attempted to extract and sell. Their meal over, the knights mounted their steeds, doll-sized digits clutching a curled horn apiece. Lento stood up, still holding a broken spider leg with a chunk of gore on the far end of the limb, as if this was the last food she expected to eat for quite a while. Calder joined her. The answer to what would happen next came when one of the predators and its rider stalked up behind Calder, nosing him forward to join the chain of departing riders. Janet Lento seemed as unconcerned by her elevation to pack member as by everything else. Perhaps a pair of strange over-sized visitors that could lay out a carpet of spider corpses – and knew the secret of fire . . . or at least, steam – were too valuable to be left here as bait for one of those giant winged lizards whose shadows floated over, throwing the jungle floor into darkness. They moved through the rainforest for hours, an unhurried pace, nothing to do but trudge and listen to the unfamiliar sounds hooting, honking, chirping and roaring from the undergrowth. It was ironic. This was meant to be a world in its twilight age . . . a dying sun throbbing above them. But the jungle had never seemed so alive, literally shaking and shrieking with life. Nothing like the silent snow-bound cathedrals of the forests Calder had grown up with. Trees so hard the human settlers lacked tools sharp enough to fell them. Whether it was the knights' knowledge of the jungle, or the rest of the eco-system's knowledge of how dangerous this pack was, the hike proved uneventful. Nothing else appeared to try to attack them – a situation which Calder suspected wouldn't have been the case if he and Lento had been blundering through the undergrowth on their own. Lento was little company, and the pack moved silently, halting occasionally for the six-legged predators to scratch at trees and sniff the ferns . . . for what, Calder was hard pushed to say.

'Maybe they're taking us to their den – or cave – or village,' mused Calder, as much to himself to break the silence as to Lento. She marched in front of him, close enough to clutch onto the short razored tail of the nearest predator, not acknowledging he had spoken. *I'll try not to take it personally.* It grew dark. The sick glow of the sun sank from what he could see of the sky through the high jungle canopy, shadows lengthening, the tenor of the jungle's song changing around him. *We must be close to where we're going, surely?* But then, he didn't have an inkling how far the pack's territory extended. *They could claim thousands of miles of jungle as their hunting ground for all that I know.* Calder hadn't heard a single helicopter passing overhead. Surely the camp knew he was missing by now and would be flying over the rainforest looking for him? The state Janet Lento was in, she might have been willing to quietly watch potential rescuers fly over without trying to attract attention, but he hadn't lost his marbles yet. The *Gravity Rose* had arrived with fuel for the camp's vehicles as part of the supply run. *So where are the search flights?* This was very odd. Calder felt forgotten and lost.

They kept on moving for half an hour more until it was almost too dark to travel, and then the pack halted. There seemed to be a clearing ahead, but something blocked their passage, a white diaphanous material hanging in the air, damp and sparkling like ribbons of wet spider's web. As he drew closer to the wall, he saw that the sheeting rippled between steel fence posts. *Metal? Here?* The predators drew up in a line and the riders' beaks opened as one, a raucous chirping song like a flock of sea birds calling. The sheeting between the nearest two fence posts rippled away in response to the song, withdrawing like blinds into the steel. Before Calder was a landscaped garden, a stone path leading up to some kind of circular single-storey lodge, slanted walls made of mirrored glass slotted between highly polished metal. *Of all the things – what the hell is this place?* The building looked like a flying saucer built into the ground. And something that shouldn't possibly be here was coming out to inspect them.

***

Lana despondently guided her shuttle back towards the mining camp's landing field, fat tears of hot rain beating against the cockpit canopy. They had modified their sensors, adding a jury-rigged array of coils for pulse induction, sweeping the jungle like a giant flying metal detector. Even if Calder had lost his rifle, the metal in his smart suit should have lit up like a Christmas tree on her board. All they had found was the ruined wreckage of a failed drop capsule that had drifted off course during the original mission set up on Abracadabra. Now night was falling. Their best chance of continuing the search was to get the *Gravity Rose* to scan for cold spots using infrared . . .

try and home in on Calder through his ship suit's refrigeration fibres. But penetrating the seventy metre-high dome of the forest and sweeping for such a tiny temperature differential was like looking for a needle in the proverbial. But what choice did she have? *None at all when it comes down to it.*

'What are we missing here?' she asked Zeno and Skrat in the seats behind hers. 'We've covered more territory today than Calder can possibly have walked on foot since he's been missing.'

Zeno looked over at their first-mate. 'Are you sure there's no missing ground vehicles taken from the camp? Maybe Calder drove out of the base?'

'Certainly not from the main base. It is possible, I suppose, that the fellow might have travelled up to the mine itself and stolen one of the vehicles from the works.'

'Wait a minute,' said Lana. 'I thought you said you'd searched the camp?'

'The central complex, quite thoroughly. But the works in the mountains are not enclosed within the base perimeter, old girl. When I requested to search the works, the miners dispatched their own people to do it. They said the tunnels are too dangerous to allow untrained civilians to wander around.'

'I just bet they did. This stinks. What if Calder saw something he wasn't meant to inside the base? We're taking too much on trust here. His disappearance. The defence system's sensor logs. Who saw what, when.'

'We know their driver disappeared,' said Zeno. 'Calder vanishing falls within the same pattern. And the miners have been searching for Janet Lento for weeks with the empty fuel tanks to prove it.'

'I have a feeling about this . . . same one I always get running errands for Dollar-sign.' And she didn't have to remind her two crew how her last such hunch had ended when it came to their load from the duplicitous broker. *A cargo-hold of contraband war machines trying to infiltrate our ship.* 'Abracadabra... now you see it, now you don't. Do you know how this world came to be named?'

'I had rather presumed it was because seen from space the planet resembles a gas giant,' said Skrat. 'You have to get deuced close to the world to penetrate the illusion.'

'That's what I thought . . . until Calder vanished.' Lana looked at Zeno. 'Contact the ship, query our database as well as the mission files, see if you can find anything on the who, how and why of this planet getting named Abracadabra.'

Zeno fell silent for a minute, the android connecting through their shuttle's comms dish and contacting the starship's AI, Granny Rose. Running the query and waiting for the response. Finally the answer returned. He chewed thoughtfully as he spoke. 'This rock was named by a colony vessel which passed through the system five hundred years ago... the *Never Come Down*. She was part of a settler convoy of five ships exploring the local arm of space. The *Never Come Down* stayed behind to survey the system. The other four ships kept on going. Guess they didn't fancy the short lease left on the sun. Nothing on record to indicate the reason behind their choice of name, though.'

Lana grunted. 'And I seem to recall Dollar-sign implying it was his people who found this system.'

'That's not the most worrying thing about this jinky tale. The *Never Come Down* was posted missing, never heard of again. Our world's name was entered in the common navigation record by the other four ships after they settled a system a few light years from here.'

'Not feeling superstitious again, Zeno?'

'Let's just say that my natural sense of caution is earning overtime. I've asked Polter to widen the satellite search . . . scanning for the wreckage of a ship and the remains of any colony down here.'

Lana's eyes narrowed. It wouldn't be the first failed colony. Calder himself hailed from just such a beast . . . a lost technological base and humanity driven to barbarism by the unexpected ice age on Hesperus. But if humans wanted to settle here, they would have either needed to turn to genetic engineering to alter their bodies, or introduce some serious terraforming to cool the world for human-standard survival. Hardly worth doing with a short-lease sun about to burn out above. *Unless the world contains something very valuable,* said the voice within her. The kind of valuable that attracted pond life like Dollar-sign Dillard and his mine's shadowy backers. 'The *Never Come Down.* Maybe her crew should have taken their ship's name a little more literally,' mused Lana. 'Set-up a nice safe orbital habitat to live on and kept the local ecosystem at a shuttle ride's distance.'

'Advice that perhaps we should have followed, too?' suggested Skrat.

'File it under spilt milk, Mister raz Skeratt.'

'I'm not the mammalian sort, dear girl,' complained the first mate. 'Your race's fondness for milk, spilt or otherwise, has always left me rather nauseous.'

Lana scratched her face. 'Here's what we're going to do. We'll land the shuttle on the field, make a big show of adjusting the sensors for low-light and thermal imaging, then take off again.'

'The odds of finding anything in the dark . . .' said Zeno.

'It's not the jungle we'll be searching,' said Lana. 'Skrat, you'll head on out for a wider sweep of the area. Before you leave, you pass low over the mine works and drop me and Zeno by the edge of the mountains. If we know what's really going on around here, we'll have a far better chance of finding Calder, even if they haven't got him tied up in some tunnel next to a pallet full of car-sized diamonds.'

'Do I get any choice as to whether I play *Rick Rail-gun: Interstellar Commando* out there?' said Zeno.

'Same choice as always,' said Lana.

'Sweet maker, I must be becoming telepathic. I knew you were going to say that.'

'Just the problem of being nearly immortal,' said Lana. 'Give it long enough and everything starts to sound the same.'

'Not nearly immortal enough for this skeg-fest,' said Zeno. 'Not nearly enough.'

'I believe you're confusing immortality with indestructability, old chap,' said Skrat.

'Yeah, and I knew you were going to say that too.'

***

Calder stared in shock at the humanoid robot tottering down the path from the lodge. It stood a little higher than a man, stocky and powerful, but it had been designed to resemble a cat – not a realistic representation . . . an exaggerated cartoon animal that might have worked at a theme park, colourful enamelled plating with writing printed across its chest in a script the prince didn't recognize. He realized the six-legged predators and their riders had vanished behind him, slipping away into the jungle. For a moment Calder toyed with the idea that the lodge might belong to the predators – some implausibly advanced home for the simple jungle dwellers. But this robot was either man-made or the product of one of the other sentient races. Human probably, judging by the machine's carbon whiskers twitching on its spherical head. Calder noticed cameras behind two spacious glass eyes focusing on him, a slight whirring as the robot inspected the two newcomers.

'Donata mushimanrui namuchi?' barked the robot, the smiling steel slash in the middle of its head moving in a simulacrum of a real mouth.

'We're from the mining camp,' said Calder. 'Can you understand me?'

The robot's over-sized head wobbled from side to side before it spoke again. 'Yes. Are you guests of the company?'

'I guess that would depend on which company?'

'This resort is for guests of the company,' repeated the robot. It wasn't anywhere near sentient, Calder realized. Nothing like Zeno. 'Are you guests of Etruka Energy Processing?'

'We are,' lied Calder. *We just have to get inside. Find whoever is in charge of the lodge. It must have a radio and some means of getting in and out of the jungle.*

'Then you should enter,' announced the robot, stepping back, a whirring noise from electric motors along its legs vibrating as it backed up. 'Have you been hunting?'

Calder tapped the barrel of his rife and checked that Lento hadn't vanished along with the predators. 'In a manner of speaking. I'm Calder Durk and this is Janet Lento.'

'I am Momoko, the official mascot of Etruka Energy,' said the robot. 'I am powerful but fun. And I am always reasonable.'

It sounds like its mental state isn't that far off our half-insane driver's. What is it about this jungle that seems to send people off the deep end? The machine led the pair of visitors up the path and towards the lodge, a neatly landscaped garden of exotic plants – presumable native – on either side watered by sprinklers in the grounds. There was no sign of other robots. *Or humans.* In the sky above the clearing he saw a rippling effect similar to a heat haze. Calder's brain throbbed as it always did when he recalled tape-learnt lessons, each false memory drilled into his brain like a buckshot pellet. *That has to be a one-way chameleon field – from the air you would see only jungle. Whoever built this place doesn't want it to be visible to the naked eye from above.* Protection from the vast winged beasts that were the top of the local food chain, or protection from the kind of visitors that might turn up in orbit with high resolution sensors mounted on a starship's hull?

'Where are the others, Momoko? The staff and guests from the . . . company?'

'That information is not contained on the board,' said Momoko, waddling up the path.

'What board is that?'

'The board with instructions,' said the robot. 'I wrote them. My memory is erased every morning.'

Calder glanced nervously around the garden. 'And for the love of the gods, who's erasing your memory out here?'

'I am,' said the robot. 'Automatically. It says so on the board.'

Momoko led the two of them inside. A garden viewing room with simple white walls and comfortable cushioned seating carved out of the floor, seven or eight open doors leading to other parts of the lodge. Pleasantly cool compared to the burning heat outside, Calder and Lento's smart suits audibly crackling as they powered down their cooling function.

The board Momoko treated with such reverence turned out to be a white screen; a thin plastic-glass active matrix hanging in the air with a numbered list of instructions scrawled in the same script written on the robot's chest. 'Can you translate this into standard?' asked Calder.

'Guests' comfort is paramount.'

The screen blinked as it reflowed . . . rewritten as triple alliance characters. At the top it read: "Read these instructions when you wake with no memory. You are Momoko, the official mascot of Etruka Energy Company. You are powerful but fun. And you are always reasonable. You have set certain sectors of your short and long term memory to automatically erase itself every morning. There are five rules that MUST be followed." Calder traced a finger along the list. "One. Care for and maintain the lodge. Download lodge protocols for detailed instructions. Two. Care for and maintain the gardens . . . especially the toxin fence. Download lodge protocols for detailed instructions. Three. Honour and protect the company. Four. Honour and protect all visitors of the company. Five. Fear the night." There was a line break and then the instructions continued. "The hunters will return one day and you will leave this place. Never attempt to reconstitute your deleted memories."

'You're the only robot here?' asked Calder.

'I am not,' said Momoko. 'There are seven of us.' His hand rose to indicate a passage. Calder went across and glanced inside. Six robots identical to Momoko stood in battery recharging ports. They had all ripped their own heads off their bodies, metal hands forlornly clutching each cat-faced metal oval high in the air as though they were a line of headless ghosts, cables dangling underneath like severed veins.

'They were not sufficiently loyal to the company,' said the robot, sadly.

'They killed themselves?'

'Self-inflicted property damage,' said the robot. 'Honour the company. Destroying company property is frowned upon, don't you think so? They left me alone. To do all this work by myself.'

Calder glanced around. Janet Lento wasn't behind him anymore. *What now?* 'Where's Janet Lento?'

'I have located our female guest on the lodge's cameras. She is walking inside the garden.'

Calder rushed outside, followed by Momoko clunking behind. Lento wasn't immediately in sight, so he sprinted around the corner. Behind the lodge the prince discovered a landscaped garden, a neat oblong of raked rocks next to a pond with a wooden pagoda, stepping stones across the water. Lento stood there looking sadly at a series of graves . . . compacted mounds with stone markers. The grim sight hadn't made her any more loquacious. She held her peace, swaying slightly. Calder counted five mounds. Each marker stone had been carefully etched with a vertical line in the same symbol-like script running across the robot's chest.

'How did they die?' Calder asked the robot.

'That information isn't on the board.'

'What do the gravestones read?'

'Seiji Machimura. Nobutaka Aso. Taro Machimura. Katsuya Kawaguchi. Hirofumi Koumura.'

Just names, then. No dates, No cause of death. Calder knelt by the gravestones, running a hand across the cracked, weathered surface. *This writing has been carved with a small handheld laser.* The headstones weren't recent. Over fifty years old at least. The part of him that had been inhabiting cop show sims for far too long wanted to disinter the bodies and check for cause of death. But buried out in the jungle for this long with the local insects, there wouldn't be much left. *And I hardly have access to a pathology lab here.* 'How long have you been posted at the lodge, Momoko?'

'That information isn't on the board.'

'Did you bury them?'

'That—'

'Let me guess,' said Calder. 'Not on the board?' He slipped Lento's hand into his and led her away unprotesting from the graves. 'We need to keep Janet Lento here safe, Momoko. She's had an accident in the jungle. It's left her traumatized.'

'The protocols indicate the lodge seals itself every night,' said Momoko. 'All guests should be inside after dusk for reasons of safety. Fear the night.'

Calder didn't need to be told twice. It was growing too dark to stay outside now. Spotlights scattered across the grounds warmed up inside the garden, painting the undersides of giant orchids with fairy colours. He gazed thoughtfully at their protective fence. *It seems so flimsy.* Diaphanous, almost, flexing in the breeze. Where the barrier touched the ground it branched into myriad tiny roots, like a fungal growth infecting the soil. As he watched, he saw the shadowed silhouette of one of the elephant-trunked herbivores wander into the white barrier, squealing as it touched the fabric and millions of spiny threads injected it with acidic poison. The creature yanked back and vanished into the night, its pig-slaughtered shrieks growing dimmer with distance. Calder grunted. The toxin fence wouldn't protect against aerial attackers, but that was what the camouflage field was for. *Fear the night.* Calder wondered if he wouldn't be safer in the rain forest with the friendly knights and their predator steeds. The pack must have been around to see the hunting lodge built; remembering an age when thrill-seeking human hunters and their powerful weapons blundered through the jungle, taking pot-shots at the mega-fauna. No doubt leaving months' worth of kills and food in their heavily armed wake. *And they've mistaken me and Lento for more of the same.* Corporate hospitality at its most wild – illegal hunting in the barely explored border worlds. The ideal tonic for corporate lords bored with their affluent, extended lives. But whatever the safari guests had found here had proved a little too interesting for them.

All three of them re-entered the lodge, the humans tentatively, the robot shuddering as his legs adjusted to carpet. Calder left Momoko with instructions to look after Lento in the viewing room and make sure she stayed put, while he went to explore the rest of the lodge. He discovered seven guest rooms, all tidy and identical. Each with a double bed, silk sheets and an ensuite bathroom. No dust. No personal possessions as clues to the previous occupants. A small oak table with a single drawer containing an old-style paper book which looked like the corporate philosophy of the company that owned the lodge. A cartoon cat that resembled Momoko grinned on the cover, lifting up a smiling child in front of a vast orbital solar array – the kind that could reflect enough power to a ground station to power a continent. An interface on the table activated the room's entertainment system, walls suddenly filled with live views of the jungle outside. Calder shivered and changed the display. An Asiatic-faced woman appeared in a red silk dress, her arms stretched out towards Calder, singing in the same language that Momoko had initially chattered at Calder. He shook his head and turned the walls off. Moving on, the young nobleman found a large stainless steel kitchen that resembled a laboratory. After checking the taps were still fed by a filtered well, Calder excitedly bypassed the ovens and examined the room's food production unit. It was still under power and operational. He could feed it with vegetation from outside – even dirt – and it would process the molecules into something approaching terrestrial food. *The best news I'm likely to get today.* They could hole up here and await rescue without starving or going thirsty. On the other side of the lodge he came across a boot room with lockers for clothes and weapons, glowing screens flickering with pictograms to indicate what each locker should contain floating next to a silhouette of an androgynous figure. All the weapons had been taken, along with most of the ammunition. But he could charge his gun's cell here. What was left in the way of bullets, pellets, shells, fuel and energy packs were half a century out of date for Calder's rifle. Pity. And from the pictograms, some of the weapons looked a lot more deadly than Calder's rifle . . . bazooka-sized guns with smart ammunition, flame-throwers, pulse energy weapons. Everything you would need to bring down the massive beasts that haunted this slowly dying world. He did find a couple of spare safari suits that would fit him and Lento at a pinch. Adaptive camouflage as well as fibre cooling, the suits turning mottled grey the instant he activated them, perfectly matching the back of the locker. He finished at a set of stairs leading to the roof, a hatch up above like an airlock, ready to mate with the shuttles that carried the hunters to Abracadabra. He opened the hatch but no craft rested above. The shuttle must be where the comms the safaris relied on had been situated – for there was none inside the lodge. Someone had left in the last vessel to land; and been in too much of a hurry to take the corpses. *Only the robots to bury them and keep the lodge functioning, waiting for another batch of visitors who never came.* The only other thing of note lay in what passed for the lodge's basement, steels stairs descending to a subterranean level occupied by a thermal tap . . . unlimited energy supplied from deep below the world's surface. Calder examined the control panels for the lodge's systems, not much different from the interfaces he had trained on in the *Gravity Rose*'s engine room.

Calder jumped, reaching for his rifle as something moved in the corner of his eye. But it was only the robot. Momoko wavered into view from behind the bank of an energy generator, the comical metal cat ears on his head rotating as they fixed on the new arrival.

'I thought I told you to look after Lento,' said Calder.

'The honoured female guest is asleep in Client Quarters Two,' said Momoko. 'I am watching her now on the room's security cameras. The lodge is sealed. For your safety. All night-time defence protocols are now activating.'

'There's one that needs to be deactivated,' said Calder, tapping experimentally at the controls. The screen blinked back at him. 'I need to drop the lodge's camouflage cover.'

'The holographic chameleon field is protection against the aerial carnivore designated Species 1056C by the standard planetary survey – colloquially: "Draco", the great flighted hyperlizard. Lodge risk assessment protocols do not permit night-time hunting by honoured guests or engaging Species 1056C at any time.'

'Oh, I've come across those monstrous dragons before,' said Calder. 'They tried to attack my shuttle on the way down to Abracadabra. But it's not them I'm looking to attract. My starship will be looking for me. This lodge is the only source of artificial light outside of the mining camp. If we drop the field, the *Gravity Rose* could pick us up on their next orbital sweep and send a shuttle to pick us up.'

'The hunters will return one day and you will leave this place,' said Momoko, with a trace of almost prophetic awe in his voice.

'Damn straight,' said Calder.

'But,' said Momoko, raising three bulbous metal fingers and a single claw like thumb, 'the lodge's lights will also attract Species 1056C to attack the honoured guests.'

'I think we're just going to have to take that chance,' said Calder. 'There are at least five graves outside filled with your company's guests who were a lot better armed than me and Lento.' *And whatever they had met on this world, their heavy weapons hadn't been protection enough.* 'Your fence and lodge wasn't enough to shelter them. This is the fastest way of getting rescued. Will you help us?'

'I am always reasonable,' said Momoko. It reached out and worked its way through the menus until it reached the field control display. It cut the power to the field, a blinking red alert twisting on the screen, imploring to be restored as a steady beeping sounded. As it flashed, Calder heard a scream echoing from the level above. *Lento!* He dashed up the stairs and along the corridor towards the bedrooms, unshouldering his rifle and he ran. He found her in the bed, quivering. Her room had automatically defaulted to the exterior jungle view – the line of trees and strange plants beyond the toxin fence, so high-resolution they might have been standing inside the rain forest, hidden speakers bringing distant hoots and the low vibration of insects buzzing inside the lodge. He could just see three moons visible in the dark swirling sky, evil red disks replacing the distended sun. The toxin fence quivered as though something had just touched it before withdrawing.

'It's covered in spines,' whispered Lento, hardly loud enough to hear.

Calder switched the view to what looked like corporate propaganda for large scale solar energy deployments and killed the audio's foreign gabbling. 'Go to sleep. We're safe in here.'

As safe as those mounds outside? He left her door open and walked into the viewing gallery. The thick slanted windows were darkening as they covered up, armoured storm blinds rolling down from recesses at the top of the lodge. *Solid enough to stop one of those dragons ripping them off?* Calder wasn't sure.

Momoko caught up with him. 'Does the honoured female guest wish me to sing to her? The lodge protocols contain many renowned company songs.' It started to croon, accompanied by a burst of jaunty recorded music. 'The Etruka Energy Company is as powerful as our shafu; our never-ending energies come from without and within; only by giving our all will our honoured customers win.'

'Maybe later.' He remembered the toxin fence swaying as though something had just brushed it. 'Can you show me what's outside on the wall here using the cameras? The fence perimeter?'

Momoko pointed to the steel blinds. 'Cameras are covered when the carbon-reinforced storm shielding comes down. All but the shuttle cam on our roof.'

'There's not a storm outside.'

'Fear the night,' said Momoko. 'Storm shielding protocols have been over-written.'

And Calder could guess by who – five graves full of *who*. *Safe inside, or trapped inside?* Momoko activated the roof-top camera, a view of the night sky appeared on the ceiling, dark swirling clouds pierced by the wan wine-coloured light of the world's three moons. No sign of a rescue shuttle or his ship streaking like a comet through the heavens. Lento had survived outside for over a week. The driver might have come through the experience slightly deranged, but she and Calder Durk were now inside a human-built lodge specifically constructed to survive the rigours of the jungle. *How hard can it be to get through a single night?* Maybe he should have asked one of the suicidal machines standing decapitated in the lodge's charging stations. Or the mounds in the garden.

'Can you rotate the camera? Turn all the roof's spotlights on and keep them on.'

In response, the dark sky twisted around above them, dizzying Calder. He was getting a crick in the neck looking at the view.

Janet Lento appeared, white silk sheets wrapped around her. She looked like the sort of deranged elder meant to haunt the upper levels of drafty castles. Saying nothing, she approached a makeshift charging station set-up opposite the board in the viewing gallery. Presumably this was Momoko's work. So the robot would wake up in the morning with amnesia and read the instructions right away . . . then download what passed for the lodge's maintenance manual and get on with its job. Lento sat down by the robot's feet, like she was its pet, huddled under her blankets. Her eyes still stared wide and glassy. But there was something else there now. Resignation? She stared at the heavens, waiting for a sign. Calder felt dog-tired. But if he closed his eyes now, he'd go straight to sleep on one of the sculpted sofas – leaving his fate reliant on a mute woman in deep shock and a robot caretaker about to forget everything that had happened to it today, including its visitors' presence. Neither the mine driver nor machine seemed a safe bet to trust his life to. So he stayed awake and watched and waited for help to arrive. It started raining outside. Big fat gobs of water which steamed as they hit the roof, dripping down the external camera dome and generating artefacts across the projected image and . . . a dark shadow flickered at the edge of the image for a fraction of a second. Calder might have written it off as a symptom of his tiredness or the storm front building outside, but Lento had obviously seen it too. She started rocking and moaning beneath her blankets. Calder felt a chill run down his spine. Something sharp and razor-edged yet lethally sinuous and flowing. *What could bypass the toxin fence out there?*

Calder stared at Momoko. 'Did you see that? It looked like a humanoid figure.' *It's covered in spines.*

'I did not see anything,' protested the robot. 'And anything I did, I wish to forget.'

Calder checked his rifle. It was still set to single shot. *Over a hundred projectiles.* He boosted the magnetic acceleration to maximum and damn if the gun's energy cell lost its juice. He could always recharge it in the lodge's boot room. A rail rifle on max-mag. He could blast flechettes through a castle wall and watch them pass out the other side with enough kinetic energy to penetrate a tank. He jumped back as a massive clang came from the outside wall. It sounded as if the tank he was planning to shoot had just collided with the lodge. Another loud metallic boom, and a dent appeared in the wall, the nearly indestructible composite metal as pliable as clay under the raw force of whatever was battering the lodge.

'What is out there?' shouted Calder.

'It's not written on the board,' said Momoko. 'Soon, soon,' it hummed to itself. 'I will forget soon. I am powerful and fun.'

Lento joined the robot's mutterings with a low keening noise. Calder ran to the viewing gallery's wall, banging it in futile anger with the butt of his rifle. 'I am Calder Durk, a prince of Hesperus,' he roared. 'I fought the Narvalak fleet to a standstill with nothing more than a flotilla of ice schooners and loyal men armed with crossbow, shield and sword. I've laid piles of corpses around me until the heaps grew larger than even the bards' songs could accurately count. I am an apostate, sentenced to death by burning by every dirty priest and corrupt cardinal on my planet. I have been betrayed and exiled. There is nothing in this damp, humid, furnace of a half-corpse world that can cost me more than I have already lost, so I spit upon you, you wall-banging coward. Throw aside the shadows and enter! Face me and let us see which one of us knows fear!'

The banging seemed to stop. Calder was amazed. He'd only been trying to mask his creeping sense of dread. *Has the prowling entity actually taken my challenge to heart?* Behind him the robot hummed about its impending self-inflicted amnesia like a priest holding to a mantra. What was left of Lento had tugged the sheet over her face; as if she couldn't see the threat, it wouldn't exist. *I'm as good as on my own here.* Calder eyes flicked towards the ceiling, desperately searching for any sign of what he thought he had seen outside. The moon on the left winked at him. Then the smaller moon on the right. Then the fat crimson lunar disk in the centre winked too. All three moons sending him a strange semaphore signal. *Is this how Lento's madness began?* Suddenly, the blinking orbs resolved into the fluttering shadow of wings. A flight of dragons dropped close enough for their cawing challenge to overwhelm the external speakers' ability to process the volume. Calder and Momoko spilled over as the lodge rocked and shook on its foundations, the exiled nobleman sprawling across Lento's huddled form, the afterimage of lizard-like heads as large as ground vehicles throwing their thundering open maws against the roof. Fang scratches left against the juddering camera dome. Calder had dropped his rifle in the dragon-created earthquake. He scooped the weapon up again. A mouse lifting a toothpick against an ambush of tigers.

-21 -
The mother-lode.

Lana glanced up as Skrat's shuttle drifted away over the rain forest canopy, steam burning up from the clearing where the craft's engines had scorched the ground, Skrat's craft dipping down low enough for her and Zeno to leap off its loading ramp. In the distance she could see the mountain range's black shadows and the glow of the mine head. Zeno had transformed their mission to uncover the truth behind the local operation into one of his sim melodramas, altering the pigment of his artificial skin into dark camouflage stripes. *You could take the actor out of the android, but you can't take the android out of the actor.* Lana knew he was well capable of adjusting his face to match the background in real-time . . . becoming almost invisible to the naked eye. The camo tiger strips were purely for show. Possibly to show Lana what he thought about her half-baked plan to sneak into the mine.

'The road to the mountains is half a mile in that direction,' said Lana. 'You want to walk to it, or would you prefer to roll across the ground and take cover behind the trees every few yards?'

'I'm as serious about getting this done as you are,' said Zeno. 'Relations between you and the professor are frosty enough as it is. I don't need us to be discovered creeping around the miners' mineral stores for things to get any worse.'

'I'm not letting my feelings about that damn woman get in the way,' snapped Lana. 'I'd be doing the same whoever Dollar-sign sent to mine this world.' *And I'd be doing this for any member of crew, too. Not just Calder.*

'Sure,' said Zeno. 'Keep on telling yourself that. There can be only one.'

'What?'

'From the classics,' said Zeno. 'Don't worry your fleshie head about it.'

'I won't. You lead the way,' said Lana. 'Seeing as you've got perfect night-vision out-of-the-box.'

'Maybe I'll get eaten first, too,' said Zeno, gloomily.

Lana checked her rifle was running hot with a full magazine. 'Most of the really dangerous creatures are lizards. They're not nocturnal hunters.'

'Everything on this rotten world's dangerous,' said Zeno. 'Including half the vegetation. Evolution, she sure does get cranky when she reaches the final stages of her solar cycle. It's like all the fauna and flora on Abracadabra have realized they're heading for a supernova and lights-out, and are all operating with their "irked-off" button jammed on full in protest.'

'I know how they feel.'

'And those flying monstrosities we faced during our landing . . . they're part-warm blooded, even if they do look like Puff the Magic Dragon's angry big cousin. They can operate in the dark.'

'Pretend you're acting in one of your old movies,' suggested Lana. '*Zeno the Dragon Slayer* or something.'

'You're not really helping.'

'Sure I am. You're just too pig-headed to admit when the captain's right.'

It took the two of them half an hour to reach the road

between the main landing field and the mine-head. Lana nearly tripped over a line of tree stumps left by the side of the strip, blackened and dead from being speed-sliced by an industrial laser on high power. She suspected Zeno had let her wander into them as punishment. The road itself was a quick-spray multi-layer composite, resistant to rain and weeds – the ugly kind of non-degradable tech that would have placard-waving environmentalists suicidally throwing themselves in front of diggers . . . if the nearest human population centre of any size hadn't been a hundred light years away. Spike-like beacons had been driven into the dirt by a pile driver on both sides of the road – to help ensure drone equipment didn't slip off the highway. *With the level of static from solar flares, it would be suicidal to rely on sat-nav to guide drones out here.*

'There's a vehicle coming,' said Zeno. 'Robot . . . nobody in the cab.'

Lana nodded. She'd been counting on the night-shift running more or less automated. *Too few hands at the camp to operate on a twenty four hour rota with a manned presence.* Time to let the android earn his keep with the codes he'd hacked from the landing field. 'Slow it down and let's see what we've got.'

The *Gravity Rose*'s skipper was almost blinded by the truck lights when the drone rumbled into view. A big robot engine up front with a high bank of arc-lights, the vehicle riding six spherical rubber wheels taller than her head. Lana blinked her eyes to clear them. A storm of insects fluttered in and out of its beams. Three freight cars sat behind the engine on similar ball wheels, each car linked to the next by snaking cables. *Two sealed trailers, one open flat-bed.* Zeno popped the doors on the closed cars, easily bypassing its simple locking mechanism in a couple of seconds. *After all, who is going to steal the supplies out here . . . tree squirrels?* He rolled the doors back. One car was too full of the supplies they had hauled down from orbit to even attempt to hide inside, but the second trailer had enough space for them to conceal themselves amongst its piled crates and drums.

'Your carriage awaits,' said Zeno.

'It just has to get us through their fence,' said Lana.

They mounted the car and pulled its heavy doors shut, hiding in darkness as the hacked truck received the all-clear from Zeno and resumed its drive towards the mountain mine. Ten minutes later they slowed down as they reached the mine's protective perimeter. The engine up front idled before they cleared the gates and rumbled on towards their destination.

'I'm inside the local network,' announced Zeno. 'The truck's been told to open its doors in two hours when there's a spare loader available, then head back empty to the landing field for more supplies.'

'Enough time for us to sneak a look at what they're digging out and hitch a ride home,' said Lana. 'Is there any indication that Calder's visited here?'

'Not that I can see from the hack. But I'm only nosing around the low-level stuff – vehicle routes and cargo schedules. The real security systems are every bit as heavily encrypted and fire-walled as you'd expect from a paranoid like Dollar-sign Dillard. He doesn't even trust his own people, let alone us.'

'Well, that's fine. Because with DSD, the feeling's always mutual. Let's see what we can see.'

Lana cracked the door enough for them both to squeeze out.

They dropped into a vehicle park at the foot of the mountain range, irregularly lit by electric lanterns hanging from the granite rise. A variety of drone and manned vehicles – a couple of large lorries, oversize dump-trucks, a heavy mole-like drilling rig, small manoeuvrable staff-transporters, caterpillar-tracked water-knife carriers stamped in industrial yellow steel. A little robotic forklift moved up to one of the other lorry's trailers and fished out crates on magnetic loading arms before humming away, an activity warning light rotating on top of its metal roof. Lana and Zeno picked their way towards tunnels at the foot of the mountain, using the empty vehicles for cover. Most of their illumination came from a perimeter fence protecting the mine three hundred yards away, the peak above them casting heavy shadows in the triple-moons' light. The fence wasn't much different from the barrier surrounding the main base. Automated sentry guns on tall posts scanned the rain forest beyond. A couple of human silhouettes were visible moving behind the armoured windows of a concrete guard post squatting behind the entrance gate. *No sign of anybody else out here.* With any luck, most of the miners were tucked up inside the main base and asleep in their bunks. Lana spied a variety of pre-fab buildings set up within the fenced area, none taller than two storeys, as well as large dark mounds of slurry piled by the digging equipment. A mesh canopy ran above the camp to protect it from the slope's rock-falls. This mine-head was a fraction of the size of the main base and its landing fields. But then, all the fence here looked to be protecting was a vehicle park and a few equipment sheds. Lana halted by a sign carrying a hard hat icon, which read "Protective clothing at all times". Ahead, rails ran into multiple tunnels.

The mine-head is more noticeable for what was missing. Lana nudged the android. 'Where's the storage silos for the ores they're extracting . . . all those valuable drums full of promethium, samarium, gadolinium?'

'Maybe they haven't hit the mother-lode yet?'

'If that's the case, they've spent a lot of money and time for the sniff of a promise,' said Lana. 'Does that sound like the Dollar-sign you know?'

'Always seemed more of a sure-thing kinda guy to me.'

'Precisely.'

With the exception of the automated forklift unloading cargo the only other things moving out here were Lana and Zeno, but this wasn't the time for overconfidence. They sprinted low towards the largest passage cut into the mountain's brooding weight, taking cover behind a pile of hydraulic supports waiting to be carried into the mine. 'Any temperature variance inside to suggest someone's still working?'

'Just you, me, and the hamster-sized mosquitoes,' said Zeno. 'Of course, if they've got androids working the mine, they won't need smart suits with cooling fibres.'

'You're one of a kind,' said Lana.

'Well, they wouldn't be as smart as me.'

Lana glanced behind her. The guard post staff were behind them, monitoring the rainforest for anything dumb enough to amble into their fence. 'Smart-mouthed . . . I'd agree. But that's not the organ I need. Keep your enhanced peepers peeled.'

They rapidly crossed the open space, reaching the tunnel mouth and vanished into its cover. A tunnel, twenty feet high, wide enough to accommodate the digging equipment they had passed. A chain of electric lights hung from a rock ceiling, thick green cables stapled into the walls. Two sets of narrow rails on the ground, so they could run trucks in and out simultaneously. Zeno examined the wall, then put a finger to his mouth and crept back into the open again. Lana waited nervously, not wanting to go deeper down the tunnel without the android, anxious about being discovered every second she stayed here exposed like this. *Come on Zeno. This is no time to disappear on me.* Zeno was gone for five minutes before he returned.

Lana frowned at the android. 'What, you're tagging their equipment with graffiti now?'

'Checking on something . . . what you said about the lack of ores stored for shipping offworld. There's no sign of exploratory digging around the mountain. Normally, these slopes would be left like Swiss cheese from where the team went in with survey worms, exploring for the richest lodes to start with. It's as though they arrived here, set up shop, and just got digging immediately. Like they knew exactly where to start. Ground penetrating radar is good, but not that good. It's like Olympus Mons on Mars rising above us. There's a lot of rock for them to have got this lucky this fast.'

'You think I'm still wrong to mistrust the professor?' asked Lana. 'This stinks like only a Dollar-sign Dillard job can.'

'Hey, I'm the android here,' said Zeno. 'If my hunches were any good you'd be working for me rather than the other way around.'

Lana walked to the tunnel's edge, running her finger across the rock. *Smooth as a baby's bottom.* 'Look at this. It's been cut with a water-knife.'

Zeno inspected the walls. 'Well, we know they've been doing a lot of pressurized water work . . . Janet Lento went missing on a tanker run to the local river. But you're right. For quick entry, they should have used shaped charges. Go in dirty and only get delicate when they've got a good start behind them and want to avoid tunnel collapse.'

'If there are any closet environmentalists on this team, they're still hiding deep in that closet,' said Lana. 'They practically carved their base site out of the jungle with low-yield nukes. This world's reaching its sell-by date . . . nobody here's going to be restoring the landscape and planting two trees for every one they cut down. So why choose a scalpel over a saw?'

'Only one way to find out,' sighed Zeno. Lana knew how he felt. She glanced down the tunnel. *People disappearing. First the driver and now Calder.* In Lana's experience, people only vanished like that when they'd stumbled across something they shouldn't have. And she had a feeling that the other end of this tunnel was just packed full with shouldn't have. She checked her rifle and the two of them slipped down the passage. *Everything about these tunnel works feels too clean.* As though Professor Sebba's people were laying a subway system, not ripping rare-earth minerals out of the planet for a fast offworld sale. The tunnel led them straight under the mountain and stayed flat, a few side-chambers drilled out on the way, but only to hold mining equipment rather than serious attempts to mine into the rock. *It feels as though we're heading for the heart of the mountain.* Too deep now for their phones to have any chance of contacting the shuttle for help. After five minutes of exploration, the tunnel terminated with two antechambers. The first chamber had a circle painted on the floor like a target.

Zeno knelt down by the paint. 'This is where they're planning to deploy that nanotech mining virus we brought along. Looks like they're going to be burning out one hell of a big shaft here.'

'Let's see what the other chamber holds.'

The answer was nothing she had expected: a narrow vertical tunnel drilled into the floor of the room; a dark unlit well ominously waiting with no hint of what lay below. A metal rack had been fixed on the rock wall with crude industrial epoxy that ran down to the floor in white rivulets. Inside the rack sat a series of gravity chutes, hand-held units like dark plastic knuckledusters that could lower or lift their owner as though the person occupied an invisible elevator.

Zeno whistled. 'They're the most expensive thing I've seen on this planet.'

'Alliance tech,' said Lana. Anti-gravity floats were common enough in the lawless fringes of Edge space, but only in shuttles, trucks and industrial loaders. Miniaturization at this level cost big bucks. *Probably military, special forces-grade. Far too fancy for mining.*

The android found a piece of thumb-sized rubble and dropped it down the dark shaft, listening for its landing with his enhanced hearing. He shook his head. 'Long ways down. I can control my claustrophobia. How about you?'

'This shaft's been drilled slow and careful. Whatever they're after is down there.' A shaft this narrow was going to drop a long way down, otherwise they would have opened it out wider. *A rescue shaft to a deeper part of the mine? But if so, where is the mine's entrance, because we certainly didn't pass it up here?* A single power cable ran along the room before disappearing into the well, stapled to the sides and powering whatever needed energy below. *Good for some lights, maybe, please.*

Zeno took an anti-gravity float off the rack and tossed a second unit to Lana. 'The phrase "like a rat down a drain-pipe" comes to mind.'

'Check the power cell on your float,' said Lana, examining hers. 'Going down is one thing. But I want this to be a return trip.'

'Amen to that, sister.' Zeno went over to the edge of the well, shrugged, and stepped into darkness. The chute instantly detected the drop and activated, the android sinking into darkness and disappearing. Lana felt like a coward for not volunteering to go down first. *This side-trip was my idea.* But it made sense for him to go before her. Zeno was a lot harder to kill than she was, ten times as strong and could see in the dark to boot.

Lana stared warily into the circle of darkness. She really didn't want to fall down there, but what choice did she have now? *Second rat coming.* Lana lifted the float over her head as though it was the handle of an umbrella and stepped into the void. For a terrible second she thought she was going to plummet to her death, the tug of gravity around her ankles, but then she felt the device vibrate into life and the chamber slide out of view, replaced by darkness. The only illumination Lana could see was a tiny green light blinking on the side of the chute. She could feel warmth rising from below, the air coming up from somewhere deep and hot. She resisted the urge to test the float's ability at rising as well as arresting her fall, allowing herself to drift ever down. The shaft's sides gently banged into her at times, and she had to use her boots to push herself into what passed for the centre of her narrow descent. Not wide enough to permit two people to fall side by side, that was for sure. No wonder the miners needed a modern mining virus to open up a second shaft. *Nobody is bringing minerals up this pipe.* She tried shutting her eyes but it made no difference. As dark with her eyelids open as it was when they were closed. Her descent lasted half an hour. Lana was used to enclosed suits in vacuum, walking the *Gravity Rose*'s hull on magnetized boots, the endless void of deep space. She had never thought of herself as claustrophobic. This shaft was almost enough to change that. At first she thought her eyes were playing tricks on her. But no, the sides of the tunnel were definitely shifting from inky black to dark grey. Illumination below, somewhere, growing lighter with every foot she descended. Her float detected a surface below, and it began slowing, and then suddenly the shaft's walls passed out of sight and she landed inside a chamber deep underground. Zeno waited for her, standing by a rack similar to the one they had left behind, a selection of gravity chutes stored on the wall.

Lana's legs trembled on contact with the hard rock floor. *Fear or relief, I'm not sure which.* Lana counted four chutes on the wall rack. Zeno had wisely attached his to his equipment belt, leaving nothing about their exit to chance. Lana did the same and looked around. A chamber the same size as the one above, a single passage leading out.

'Are those chutes spares, do you think? Or do we have company down here?' asked Lana.

'Nobody else walking or talking that I can hear with the trusty android super-lugs,' said Zeno. 'Let's hope they're stored in case of equipment failure.'

'If the missing driver is down here, it would explain why nobody's found her in the jungle yet.'

'Hell of a lot effort to water-knife a shaft this deep just to dig a cell,' said Zeno. 'Kick her outside of the mine's fence and she would be lunch for the local mega-fauna soon enough.'

Lana grimaced. *My hopes of finding Calder tied up down here have almost vanished too. Pity, it would have been good to have my prejudices against the professor confirmed.* 'If this is a working mine, I'm a carrier commander.'

They took the single exit, exploring a tunnel little larger than a corridor on Lana's ship, bare walls and simple electric lighting. It stretched out for a minute or two's walk, before terminating in a rough rock wall, bare except for a single instrument panel. Zeno inspected the panel. 'I think this is a power interface.'

'This doesn't make sense,' said Lana. 'All this way down here, only to lead us into a dead end? The money they've spent getting this far? Why plan opening a second bigger shaft down here? This must be the dictionary definition of "money pit". Is there a concealed entrance?'

Zeno opened his mouth but said nothing – at least, nothing within Lana's range of hearing. He ultrasounded their surroundings. 'Solid rock all around us for hundreds of feet. No openings or concealed doors.' He turned his attention back to the panel. 'So, what does this do?'

'As long as it isn't drown us in sand or start the walls moving towards us, I'll be happy.'

'Sure isn't an intercom to the surface,' said Zeno. 'There's no wireless connection available this deep.' His little finger broke open and a cable snaked out, interfacing with a port at the bottom of the panel. As soon as the connection was made a screen in the panel's centre started rapidly scrolling with moving numbers, blinking green against black. 'I think this is a lock.'

What to? 'Can you break it?'

'Not by brute force. But give me a second and I can trick its memory into repeating the last code entered. From the time stamp it was entered a couple of hours ago. You might want to get ready to tear back to the shaft, you know, in case a large granite sphere starts rolling down the corridor.'

'I was joking about drowning in sand.'

'Let's hope whoever installed this panel feels the same,' said Zeno. 'Three, two, one . . .'

Lana leapt back as the wall started to shimmer. It disappeared, revealing a long horizontal tunnel stretching ahead. This tunnel was different, though. Its walls seemed to be made of a shiny black substance, slightly wet, and the ceiling glowed green as though the rock had just been nuked. 'Hey, I thought you said that wall was solid rock, not a hologram?'

'It was solid rock,' said Zeno. 'Jeez. Abracadabra . . . now you see it, now you don't.'

Lana ran her hand where the wall had been. 'It had to be a hologram!'

'I don't think so,' said Zeno. 'The operations I sensed within the panel were too complex for that. I think they were activating a smart matter sequence.'

'Programmable matter?' laughed Lana. 'That's science fiction. Doesn't exist.'

'Not quite,' said Zeno. 'There's one species believed to have made extensive use of smart matter. The Heezy.'

Lana's eyes narrowed. 'They've been extinct for billions of years.'

Zeno pointed to the passage behind them. 'Careful tunnelling with water-knives and no explosives. That's not mining. That's archaeology.'

Lana's heart sank. Nobody knew much about the Heezy. But that was only because every time one of their artefacts, fossilized ships or long-abandoned settlements was discovered, the Triple Alliance moved in and shut everything down, classifying every rumour and report about the find within a light-year-wide exclusion zone. The one thing Lana knew was the same history every spacer had on file. How the Triple Alliance had been fighting the Skein in a war seven-hundred years ago, and humanity and its two allied species had been badly losing against their nearly indestructible virtual enemies. Until a human colony dome had found something – a very nasty Heezy something – buried under the ice of Neptune. And whatever it was had given the alliance the capability to turn Skein systems into smouldering ruins, one by one, until the Skeins had finally had to acknowledge defeat. An uneasy peace that had lasted to the current day.

'Every time,' snarled Lana. 'Every time we have anything to do with Dollar-sign Dillard...'

Zeno shut his eyes, the same way he always did when consulting the compressed copy of the ship's database he carried around in his head. 'And Professor Sebba's original PhD on Mars? The one area of study you're almost guaranteed not to find practical work in unless you're on highly classified government secondments.'

'Let me guess . . . the Heezy?'

'Give the starship captain a cigar. It's not too late,' said Zeno. 'We can turn back now. We don't have to see what's down here.

The best thing that's going to happen is the alliance fleet catches us and wipes our memories. The worse is that they stick everyone on the *Gravity Rose* in orange jump-suits and lock us up on asteroid-max in some system that doesn't officially exist on any star chart.'

'I haven't got so many memories left I can afford to lose any more,' sighed Lana. Not after the cursed cold-sleep accident had left her as a perpetual amnesiac when it came to her past. 'But I'm damned if I'm heading back to the surface without knowing what Dollar-sign's got his tame academic tunnelling into this dying world for.'

'We're playing with fire, Lana. I was around during the original alliance-skein war . . . making my last will and testament, given how the skein are not big on any machine life except their own ex-organic souls existing in that perfect little post-singularity future they've got planned for everyone. This is universe-changing doodie we've blundered into this time.'

'And the professor and Dollar-sign were planning to have us acting as the mules transporting it out to their buyers,' said Lana. 'No doubt well-concealed under a couple of hundred tonnes of minerals.'

'Yeah, we've been had,' said Zeno.

Lana felt like kicking the wall in rage. And the worse part of all was how badly they were being short-changed. She'd thought Dollar-sign was showering her with generosity, the amount he'd paid for the *Rose* to make this run. But the kind of material Sebba could drag out of a Heezy settlement – even half-fossilized and unoperational – that was shizzle you could trade for a small stellar empire in the Edge and think yourself hard done in the deal. And how the hell are we going to get out of this one? 'Walking away would be the sensible thing to do, wouldn't it? Find Calder. Get back to the ship. Jump out as fast as possible and let Dollar-sign find some other sap to run his interdicted fossils across the Edge.'

'You read my mind, sister.'

Hell. 'Let's go and see what's down here, then.'

They advanced down the newly formed passage, Lana struggling to keep the lid on her trepidation. *A species that sets up shop deep under the world and only summons corridors into existence when they require them. That is a hell of a keep-out sign. Do I really want to go poking around their legacy?* Except that Dollar-sign had arrived here before them and made the decision for her. The corridor ended and she found herself on a cavern ledge, no barrier to protect mere mortals tumbling into the colossal empty space beyond. Lana and the android carefully advanced, glancing over the edge. A dizzying view down a circular shaft the width of a small inland sea, narrowing to a distant vanishing point; maybe to the centre of the very world, no end in sight. But the pit wasn't empty. Giant amorphous shapes moved up and down the shaft, changing shape as they drifted, merging with each other before breaking apart into squadrons of smaller objects. *What is this, the universe's biggest lava lamp?* One of the shapes drifted past and she watched intently, as shocked as she was fascinated. Bright orange, the blob drifted covered in a circuit-like tracery of glowing yellow lines. Machines seemed to form around its skin, existing for brief seconds before being absorbed back into the surface. This one single globule must have been as big as a zeppelin. What purpose it served, she didn't know. *More programmable matter, that's for sure.* This was far from being a fossilised archaeology dig.

'We're *really* in trouble,' said Lana.

'This is the kind of swag that species go to war over,' said Zeno.

'I don't have a species, I just have a crew.' *And damned if I want to see another war.*

Lana glanced either side of her. The narrow ledge ran to corridors at both ends. Passages left switched in their open position, interface panels riveted crudely into each wall courtesy of DSD's miners. The professor had been busy down here, getting to grips with the real mother lode.

'How did they know this was down here?' Lana mused aloud. 'It's not like there's any sign of the Heezy above ground?'

'I figure it's that missing colony ship,' said Zeno. 'Maybe not everyone on board was quite as missing as the records suggest. Dollar-sign's an expert at ferreting out obscure reports that lead to a quick buck. He practically lives in the data-sphere.'

'I feel like an ant accidently crawled into the chief's anti-matter drive,' said Lana. 'Looking around in astonishment and thinking: "Well, this ain't no ant hill".'

'And that ant better be on the lookout for the chief's size ten gravity boots landing on it,' muttered Zeno.

With that cheery thought, Lana and her robot gang-boss crept through the passage to the left, another run of cold inky black walls, glistening like the veins of an unpleasant beast. A hangar-sized chamber at its end. This one contained a collection of equipment – obviously human – pitted ceramic tubes standing on tripods, transparent panels revealing globules of the Heezy's programmable matter captured inside, tiny balls of the exotic material drifting around the tubes. *Might be weapons. Might be computers. Might be data-nodes containing the extinct aliens' music collection.* Nothing larger than the size the humans could comfortably squeeze through the narrow access shaft. *Yet,* Lana reminded herself. After the base drilled their main shaft using the tech she had helpfully shipped to the mine, the looting would really begin apace.

Zeno crossed to an active screen the miners had unrolled and left standing in the middle of the chamber, marking the details of Sebba's explorations to date. 'The professor's people have covered hundreds of miles of this complex.'

So, how are they getting about? Lana walked towards the one object in the room that was definitely not of human origin. Built into the wall at the far end sat a dark egg-shaped object the size of a small house. It was hollow with a raised dais fitting inside, like a throne for a mountain giant. The outside of the egg had another human interface panel drilled into it, which meant whatever this was, the professor had hacked it. Lana lifted a silver tool case from the floor and flung it onto the monster egg's platform. As soon as the case touched the ground, the floor seemed to rise up like an angry sea, enveloping the container, and then it was absorbed into the back wall and vanished.

'That's how they're moving around on this map,' said Zeno. 'Transport bubbles flowing through the rock face, travelling between levels and chambers.'

And she had thought that dropping down the access shaft was claustrophobic. 'I'll leave the pleasures of the Heezy subway system to the professor and her people. Let's jump out of here.'

'The cat's scratched out all of her curiosity?'

'This tabby's going home,' said Lana. 'Sebba's got a good few centuries' head-start on my aching noggin understanding any of this alien voodoo. She can keep it. All I need is a bulletproof method of anonymously tipping off TA Fleet Intelligence about Abracadabra without the spooks tracing the information back to the *Gravity Rose*. After that, I figure Dollar-sign and his grubby friends will either disappear off the grid or suddenly develop acute memory loss. And all of this—' she waved her hand around the chamber— 'will be some highly deniable science team's problem, not mine.'

'S.E.P.,' grinned Zeno. 'Somebody Else's Problem. My favourite kind. Now you're cooking with antimatter.'

They retraced their steps, sealing the corridor that led away from the access shaft, before riding their chutes all the way up to the surface chamber. Lana and Zeno racked the expensive levitation devices back in position, nothing out of place, and headed along the tunnel carved out under the mountain. She was half-way down the tunnel when her phone received enough signal to make a connection, vibrating into life. She checked the screen. It was a high-priority call from Polter. The navigator was running the signal through their makeshift satellite net. Good news, please? Lana flipped it into life.

'Tell me that you've found Calder?' said Lana, hardly allowing herself to hope.

She could barely hear the reply. Their depth under the mountain, or the dying world's weird atmosphere? 'Skrat— investigating. Withdrawing to largest—moon. Found—cavern— there—to hide.'

'Hide? Hide the hell from what?'

'Inbound vessel,' squawked Polter. 'Silhouette on—scan matches—ship—previous dealings.'

'What ship, Polter?'

'The *Doubtful Quasar*.'

Zeno groaned. 'You've got to be kidding me.'

Pirates are always bad news. And when it was a pirate crew that Lana had tricked once before and made their rough cybernetic-armed captain look a prize fool, she just knew they weren't cruising through the system looking for stray liners to ransom.

'It is—confirmed, revered captain.'

The comms line became slightly clearer the closer they got to the entrance. 'This is no coincidence. I knew we were being followed when we left Transference system.'

'The chief has found—tracking beacon—in cargo hold,' said Polter. 'Unusually advanced. Must have been concealed—on station. I have welded it onto satellite—now inserted into orbit.'

The decoy signal should buy her ship time to slip away. 'Good work,' said Lana. 'We'll get back to Skrat's shuttle and rendezvous with you on that moon. Send Zeno the coordinates for him to memorize. Stay hidden on silent running and full stealth as best you can. I don't want Steel-arm Bowen getting his hands on the *Rose*. Update Skrat on the situation and send him flying back here towards the mountains, ASAP. What did you say his shuttle was investigating?'

There was no answer from the phone, just static. 'Polter, can you read me?'

'Maybe out of range, if he's running for the moon?' said Zeno. 'This lousy damn atmospheric soup. Or the satellite might have passed over the horizon.'

'I hope so,' said Lana. The alternative was too painful to contemplate. Surely he'd be able to keep broadcasting as he was being boarded. *Unless the pirates have upgraded their jamming gear after our last dance.*

'Are you sure it's just the *Gravity Rose* that Steel-arm Bowen wants?' said Zeno. 'You did promise the mope that you'd marry him.'

'Only to get us out of that mess on Gliese 832,' said Lana.

Zeno shook his head forlornly. 'Is there anyone in this sector of void you haven't indulged in fleshie relations with?'

'Yeah, your dad.'

'Probably an android designer for a Japanese Kabushiki Kaisha who died sometime in the last millennium.'

'You know, I thought he looked a little peaky.' And now she faced the starkest of choices. *A quick exit and abandon Calder to the hell jungle, or stay put to continue the search and put both Skrat and Zeno in danger.* Maybe lose the *Gravity Rose*, too. *No good answer either way.*

Zeno knew what was whirring through her mind. 'We can always light out to the moon in the shuttle, lie low and let Steel-arm pillage the camp. After he's jumped out we can come back and restart our search for Calder.'

'The pirates won't jump out. Not without looking real hard for us first. And what the hell are we going to do if Steel-arm blunders into what we just found? Having a bunch of working Heezy tech fall into Dollar-sign's dirty hands is bad enough. Can you imagine the fun that Steel-arm and his goons would have with it?'

'Yeah,' said Zeno. 'Rumours were that the alliance fleet were busting worlds like soap bubbles at the end of the skein war. If that kind of heat reaches a pirate port, the only job offers the *Gravity Rose* will be getting is as an evacuation barge for anyone who can afford to run for deep space. That would be a rotten way to be remembered, wouldn't it? The barbarians are at the gate, and we're the ones who supplied them the battering ram to break through and usher in a new dark age.'

'Almost as bad as some of your last movies.'

Zeno snorted. *I shouldn't tease him. Do androids sulk in an electric peeve?* Only a few media geeks remembered the ancient films a long bankrupt media corporation had built him to star in.

So, this isn't somebody else's problem anymore. It's back to being mine. Just the way the damn universe likes it. They reached the entrance and the universe showed its contempt for Lana's plans. A ring of high power rifles pointed at Lana from behind a make-shift barricade surrounding the tunnel, her and Zeno's chests a sudden haze of red targeting dots.

***

C alder tumbled to the floor again as he tried to stand up. The whole structure of the hunting lodge felt as though the attacking dragons were trying to uproot it from its foundations and hurl it into the air. Probably thought it was a nice hard egg filled with supper for the flight of massive winged lizards. *The surviving robot caretaker won't be good for much apart from as an aid to digestion . . . that leaves me and Janet Lento to satisfy them.* There was a horrendous metallic ripping noise as part of the lodge tore from the side. The reinforced storm shutters shook frenziedly as something massive clawed at them.

'I shall forget soon,' warbled Momoko.

'Unless you want to find yourself waking up every morning inside one of those monster's stomachs with no memory of who you are and how you got there, do something useful.'

'Hunting of flighted hyper-lizard is not permitted,' cried the robot. 'Health and safety guidance . . .'

'You think?' Calder grabbed Janet and lifted her up to her feet. 'Make for the basement! The energy tap in the ground is the deepest part of the lodge.' Maybe the dragons would be electrocuted when they tried to peck out the inhabitants sheltering amongst the heavy generator gear. *Not much of a hope, but . . .*

The lodge tilted to the side and Lento yelped as she tumbled down the sloping floor, Calder spilling after her. A fierce wrenching noise as one of their ground supports ripped away. These creatures were experts at using the rainforest as their food basket, dipping in and ripping out trees to reach the good stuff. Sadly for the exiled nobleman, *he* was the good stuff. Only Momoko managed to stay upright, some trick of his automatic stabilization system. If there was any upside to this situation, the shadowy figure Calder thought he had glimpsed – the thing punching dents into the lodge – appeared to have given up its assault and left the job to the dragons.

A faint vibration itched Calder's back. He rolled over and the shaking followed him. It was the communication device Lento had offered him back in the jungle! He yanked it off his belt, raising the other hand to protect himself from a shower of debris spilling from the room's built-in shelves. It sprung into life as soon as he touched it.

'—down there? This is a landing boat of the—'

Gravity Rose! It was Skrat! Calder had never been so glad to hear the sound of the first mate's voice fizzing over the comm. 'It's me, Skrat! Calder. I'm here with Janet Lento and a robot caretaker.'

'I see your lights, I'm coming down.'

'There's a shuttle pad on top of the building,' said Calder. 'At least, there was.' The angle the building was listing at, there was no way Skrat could land a shuttle and dock with the building now. 'I'll pop the hatch up top – you hover and lower the rear cargo ramp.'

Skrat's voice fizzed back at him. 'Good egg. Catch you on the flip-flop.'

'The hunters will return one day and you will leave this place,' said Momoko, his servos whirring and straining against the incline of the floor as he followed after Calder, the prince desperately trying to shepherd Lento towards the corridor to the stairs topside. He heard a strange sound outside the lodge – a desperate bird-like squawking, but much amplified. The very sound of it was enough to set his nerves on edge. *Do the dragons know they're in danger of losing their supper?* Momoko caught up with the pair of guests and helped push them both towards the roof exit. *Well, Zeno always has room for another robot among the hundreds he manages for Lana on board the ship. Have to do something about that flaky memory, though. Won't be much fun trying to teach Momoko basic vessel maintenance every day, for either 'bot or android. Gods, let that be a problem I live to face.* They reached the stairs, climbing towards the hatch. The lodge stopped shifting under their feet. Had the dragons spotted Skrat's shuttle and flocked to defend their meal against the strange metal newcomer? Calder's hands shook. He pulled the rifle off his shoulder, switched it back to full-auto fire and left it on max-mag field. They only had a couple of seconds to cross the roof and make it to the shuttle alive. An empty magazine or drained power cell wasn't going to matter much if it helped them escape. *And if we don't make it, it will matter even less.* Above the hatch he could hear the roar of the shuttle's thrusters, dropping like a stone at speed, then the tell-tale whine of the anti-gravity chute kicking in as the engines died to ensure the craft didn't fry the people it had arrived to rescue.

Calder glanced at woman and robot; all of them rendered slightly less than sane by their experiences. *I feel like the one-eyed man in the kingdom of the blind here.* 'When I pop the hatch, you run to the ramp at the back of the boat. Don't stop. Whatever happens. Whatever you see. Just race to the shuttle as fast as you can. Don't step in front of my rifle.'

Calder threw the hatch open and scrambled to mount the roof, swinging his rifle barrel to either side. Gods, but it was dark outside, the lights surrounding the saucer-shaped lodge ripped off – a stupidly colourful pall of soft illumination from the garden lanterns that hadn't been prised up by the angry dragons – leaving Calder to focus on the beautiful oblong of orange from the shuttle's rear cargo hold, ramp down, beckoning, as it hovered at the end of the lodge. No sign of what he had expected to find. Monstrous leathery wings beating through the air as the shuttle held the aerial carnivores off with its cannon. *Nothing for me to unload on, either.* His sweaty finger trembled nervously against the trigger. Lento sprinted past like a wild animal, the sight of the shuttle's relative safety overloading what little remained of the woman's mind, the roof clanging as Momoko's heavy weight followed her. Calder was fast after them, retreating with his rifle ready. At the last second he leapt the yard's difference between roof and ramp. Skrat must have been watching on the cargo cameras as no sooner had his boot's scuffed into the shuttle, the boat began to rise, the whining increasing, then its thrusters kicked in, torching the remains of the lodge's garden. And that was when Calder saw it. Among the burning landscaped garden and wreckage of the pulled-apart hunting lodge. The corpses of dozens of dragons, the vast creatures' long necks sliced apart like eels by an expert sushi chef, some of the beasts lying mangled across the toxin fence, nocturnal scavengers already arriving, not quite believing their luck at the rich feast laid out across the hunting lodge's wreckage. Fires and devastation covered up as the ramp sealed back into place.

Calder pushed past Lento and the robot, heading for the cabin above, and Skrat seated in the pilot's seat. He looked a little like a miniature green dragon himself – albeit bipedal – and the irony of a sentient human-sized lizard having rescued him from a flight of far larger more savage cousins wasn't lost on Calder. 'Lords of Ice, Skrat, but am I glad to see you! I'm surprised you've even got the power left to lift-off after you took your laser cannons to those dragons.'

Skrat gazed quizzically around. 'This is a spare freight shuttle, old bean. It doesn't carry weaponry.'

***

'**A**h, my favourite girl,' laughed Seth "Steel-arm" Bowen from behind the barricade. His cybernetic arm buzzed as it rose towards her in a mocking greeting.

Lana kept her hands conspicuously away from the rifle on her back, her chest practically cooking under the heat of the targeting dots flitting around her ship suit. 'I wish I could say the feeling was mutual.'

'This is probably the time for a little diplomacy,' advised Zeno, standing by her side.

'The tin man always did have a wise head on him,' said the pirate captain. 'But it's a little late for that.'

'You're early,' said Lana.

'A cautious girl like you, I figured the *Gravity Rose* would seed a few trip-wires around the system on the way in – spot the *Doubtful Quasar* early . . . and then I wouldn't be seeing you and your crew for comet dust. So me and the gang—' he indicated the motley assortment of armoured toughs, mostly the three species of the Triple Alliance with a few races she didn't recognise thrown into the heavily-armed mix,—'we took a lander ahead of the old girl and flew in on the QT to have a nosey around and make sure your cargo shuttles stayed on the ground.'

'You've come a long way for nothing,' lied Lana. She glanced over to the guardhouse in the defence perimeter. It was on fire, the people inside on the nightshift either dead or captured. 'We're running set-up supplies to a mine that hasn't even got going yet. Nothing for you to steal yet except a few drilling rigs and some rubble from an initial exploratory tunnel.'

'You're too modest, lass,' laughed Steel-arm. The pirate commander hadn't changed a bit. Always merry, a quaking pile of false bonhomie, right up until the moment he ordered you to be pushed out of the airlock sans a vacuum suit. A tall, muscular, grinning homicidal maniac. 'Besides, we've already been well-paid for this here jaunt. To make sure that you and the local lads down here are never heard from again. Seems there are interests back on Transference Station who want to send the message that hiring independents is a loser's game. Sadly, for that message to get across, your client's actually got to lose something. I don't think Dollar sign Dillard will really miss you that much. But the investment he's sunk into this illegal mining camp? A nuke or two down here and he'll get the message, strong and hard, do you not think so?'

Damn! Why did all her problems stem from the men in her life? First Steel-arm, and now Pitor back on Transference, her ex-fiancée lightening the competition for his new corporate masters. The treacherous, conniving slime-worm. 'You're not planning on tying me to a ticking warhead, are you?'

'Perish the thought,' grinned the pirate skipper. 'The Invisible Port has a very healthy slave market, and a skipper's got to make a profit. What do you say, Mister Morales?'

A human pirate by his side tapped at the screen of his phone. He wore a metal collar, just like all the other pirates. A high-power battery to fry his skull if the crewman ever went against Steel-arm. The device to transmit the encrypted murder code hanging from the pirate commander's belt and never far from his fingers. If wearing the suicide necklace bothered Steel-arm's minion, the man disguised it well. 'The miners over in the main camp will all have received specialist training – they should be worth ten thousand T-dollars apiece at least. Ship crew will be worth double that in the port's market. A little less if they're uncooperative and we have to scrub their minds and give them a more obliging personality.'

'Call our fighters,' ordered Steel-arm. 'Tell them to lay off bombing the base. We'll "encourage" the camp commander to surrender and take as many alive as possible.'

Ending up on a radiation-leaking pirate hulk – a short, dangerous life with even fewer memories that I already have; helping scum like this seize free traders and liners? Lana would sooner prefer it if they shot her right here, rather than hauling her back to the pirates' hole of an asteroid hideaway permanently anchored in hyperspace. 'Screw you, Seth.'

Steel-arm lifted his head back and roared with laughter, a cruel unamused sound. 'You'll get your chance, Lana. Who knows, if you please me enough on the jump back to the Invisible Port, I might even offer you the chance to sign up with *me*.'

'Now you're really playing dirty.'

'So, you *do* remember. We'll head back to the main base, accept their surrender, collect our trading flesh, wire the place for a few fireworks, and let's see if the lass can't talk the *Gravity Rose* into surrendering without needing to break her too badly. She'll be worth a lot more on the open market without missile damage.'

'You're the one who is going to get damaged,' snarled Lana.

'You always did love that ship a little too much, Lana girl,' said Steel-arm. 'But isn't that you all over, always picking the wrong thing to love?'

Pirates stepped forward, guns at the ready, locking an electric collar around Lana and Zeno's neck. The female pirate who had put the collar on Lana, an Asian-looking woman, examined her handiwork with satisfaction. 'Try and run, now. You'll fry.'

'I won't be worth much then,' said Lana.

'You're too much trouble,' she growled. 'All this way for you? I don't see why.'

'You and me both.'

'Come over here and stop playing with the cargo, Cho,' boomed Steel-arm. 'If the camp doesn't surrender quickly, I'll let you carve up some of the miners when we take them.'

Lana watched the female pirate, Cho, saunter back to the heavily armed crew, maliciously fingering a dagger hanging off her belt. Lana Fiveworlds wasn't a free trader anymore – mistress of a starship. *I've been reduced to mere property.*

- 22 -
All that must be left be-hind.

'I assure you,' insisted Skrat, 'I am not joking. My landing was thoroughly un-opposed by any of the local wildlife. Your building's light signature was picked up by the *Gravity Rose* from orbit. I was already in the air when Polter sent me the coordinates and I nipped across here as soon as I had them.'

So, Calder had made the right decision dropping the lodge's camouflage field, even if it had nearly ended up in the lodge's guests becoming lizard bait. *But if Skrat's shuttle hadn't driven away the flock of attacking creatures, then what . . .?* Calder's mind drifted back to the figure he thought he had glimpsed outside the building after they had sealed themselves inside. *One impossibly fast humanoid native couldn't possibly account for an entire squadron of those winged monsters, could it?*

'I'm sure the base will be happy that you discovered their missing driver,' said Skrat, 'but next time you decide to play the gallant, old fellow, do feel free to inform me first. You left me looking like a complete imbecile in front of the skipper. One minute you're unloading cargo, the next, you're off plunging into the dark uncharted heart of the jungle.'

'It wasn't my idea,' protested Calder. 'I don't even know how I ended up inside the jungle. I was on the landing field helping you. Then I blacked out. After I woke up, I found myself inside a clearing in the rain forest. No sign of the mining camp from the tree-tops . . . just jungle.'

'And do you know how you and your damsel-in-distress in our cargo bay travelled so far?'

'What do you mean?'

'Just jungle? The mining camp is over five-hundred miles away from our present position. You're jolly lucky Polter picked up your building's lights and decided to send me to investigate further. What were those ruins I plucked you out of, by the way?'

Five-hundred miles? No wonder Calder hadn't seen rescue helicopters in the air. He and Lento had been well outside any sane search radius. 'It was a hunting lodge of some sort. And it wasn't ruins when I arrived. The dragons demolished it tonight after I turned off our aerial camouflage field. I think it must have been sitting out there abandoned for centuries.' Calder told the first mate about the amnesiac robot janitor and what he had discovered, including the local symbiote predators who helped him and Lento to safety from the deadly tree spiders, the ancient safari lodge, the dragon attack, and the strange fleeting figure he thought he'd glimpsed stalking around the building.

Skrat glanced at the images from the cargo camera – Lento sat there, still clutching her blanket around her and shivering while the robot inspected the walls of the hold; possibly its first time outside of the jungle if it had been activated inside the lodge. 'I'm no doctor, but the dear lady needs more help than her camp can give her. The robot is a *kawaii* . . . a walking logo and mascot for one of the large corporations of the Cygnus arm. Big game hunting on the border worlds is frowned upon in many alliance markets, a PR disaster in the making, for all its popularity among the top brass. No wonder they didn't want the lodge on the charts.'

Calder scratched his stubble. 'What about the biped that attacked the lodge? The dragons that were massacred?'

'Always look for the simplest explanation, dear boy. The dents in the lodge were probably from the spiked balls at the business end of the creatures' tails. The dead ones . . . no doubt two rival flocks arrived at the same time and had a set-to over which group had first dibs dining on the strange-looking mammals. As for the mystery biped, this whole world is barely catalogued. Possibly the local equivalent of an ape, or the silik from Raznor Raz I used to feed dates to outside the old home-nest, a curious low-level sentient come to gawk at the strangers.'

'And the distance from here to the base?'

'I would put money on one of those rascals with large wingspans flying through a hole in the camp's anti-air defences, dropping a stone on your head to stun you, then carrying you away to feed its young. Must have met another chap higher up the food chain and abandoned you on the jungle floor to fight its corner. Or maybe your attacker was one of the smaller fliers and you were too heavy for it, so it decided to dump your body and go after something a little more familiar.'

'I don't know. Both me and Lento?'

'There're enough complications arising in the universe without looking for hidden ones, old bean,' said Skrat. 'You've seen the size of those scaly critters in the air. They have to eat their own bodyweight . . . which means an awful lot of snatched prey from the rain-forest. Our distressed damsel down in cargo was probably conscious when one of the locals got its talons into her outside her cab and gave her an alfresco view of the continent as it attempted to fly home. That's enough to leave anyone a little unhinged.' Skrat's chair had a hole in it for his thick tail to squeeze through, and his scaled green appendage swung from side to side as he tapped at the communications panel. 'Most peculiar? The base's communications room doesn't seem inclined to receive the good news of your recovery. They're broadcasting something on a loop, though.' He waved his hand and a disembodied voice fizzed out of the cabin's speakers. It sounded a lot like the camp's stout mining chief, Klein-Yen Leong.

'Mayday, mayday. This is Abracadabra station. We are being bombed by fighters from an unknown starship refusing to identify itself. It has just issued a demand for our complete unconditional surrender. If any naval vessel from a Protocol signatory world is in range, we are a mining concern registered at Transference Station, and we are requesting urgent military assistance. Our coordinates are attached.'

'Very loosely registered,' observed Skrat. 'An unknown starship? It would appear that Dollar-sign wasn't being paranoid about claim-jumpers after all.'

'If the base is breaking cover then it has to be pretty bad over there,' said Calder, his mind racing. *Nobody is going to admit to an illegal mining operation lightly, let alone give away their position to every competitor within a couple of light-years.*

'It won't matter,' said Skrat. 'I doubt if their signal will even clear the atmosphere of this queer place. And if by some miracle it does, it will be years before a civilized system picks up a transmission from this deep in the wilds.'

'What about Lana . . . I mean, the skipper?'

'She was at the mine-head in the mountains along with Zeno.' Skrat began to bank the shuttle, heading down towards the dark floor of jungle canopy.

'Where are you flying? We need to extract her out of there right now.'

Skrat pointed to a deep valley between two slopes. 'Standard procedure, Mister Durk. We don't go running into a fire-fight blind, and certainly not in an unarmed shuttle . . . you're not riding a hard-ship in one of your *Hell-fleet* sims now. The fact we haven't already heard this news from the *Gravity Rose* either means she's boosting out of the system or she's dead in space. We land, hide, and rattle the post box.'

'Post box?'

'Our satellite network, old fruit. If they had time, the skipper or our chums on the *Gravity Rose* will have popped a hidden message into our network. Hopefully, arranging an extraction plan. We'll drop our own message into the post-box, advising them we're alive and send the ship our co-ordinates.' He tapped the scaly side of his snout knowingly. 'A spoonful of stealth and subterfuge can be worth more in the Edge than a hangar deck full of fighter craft.'

Calder scanned the ground from the cabin window. He pointed to a clearing in a valley just large enough to accommodate the shuttle, grass shimmering in the light of three moons. 'You can put down there without burning a landing site out of the jungle.'

'I see it.' Skrat twisted the shuttle's thrusters around into landing position and switched the boat into anti-gravity mode, drifting them down silently, rocking on the freight shuttle's pneumatic landing gear before it settled down. Thick tree foliage on both sides and everything else lost to the night. *Hopefully without too many spiders*. They waited ten minutes for a satellite to pass overhead, and then Skrat jabbed furiously at the controls, exchanging information in a tight-beam broadcast – heavily encrypted and as untraceable as any message could be. It took another ten minutes for the shuttle's simple computers to process the first mate's post box key, and then they took possession of the *Gravity Rose*'s last message. Calder watched a clearly stressed-out Polter explaining how he was withdrawing the ship to the world's smallest moon, fleeing before an approaching pirate carrier; listened to the news of the tracking device the chief had found concealed on the *Rose* before jettisoning it inside a spare satellite. General communications were being jammed, but tightband point-to-point messages could be exchanged through the satellites, signals rationed to once an hour to avoid detection. Polter's final warning was that the main mining base was under attack from an advance strike-force . . . and how he feared Lana and Zeno would shortly fall into the raider's hands. *Pirates. How are we going to get out of this fix?* Calder remembered a *Hell-fleet* episode based on real events. The one with the hijacked passenger liner, the *Queen Radiance*. The TA fleet had been able to track the missing vessel by the passengers jettisoned from the airlock – minus vac suit, of course. *If these people are even a tenth as ruthless, we're in dire trouble.*

'So, you know this Steel-arm Bowen?' asked Calder.

'Some of us a little better than others,' said Skrat, cryptically. 'On our previous acquaintance, the captain may have given him the impression she was a fellow pirate commander from a rival clan amiable to an alliance. Steel-arm was, shall we say, a little disappointed when the truth came out. He lost a considerable amount of face among those who ply their rather disreputable trade stealing cargoes and ransoming hostages. Reputation is practically everything when you're a pirate.'

'Will he shoot the skipper?'

'No,' sighed Skrat. 'Too fast and far too easy. The fellow will extract a rather long and tedious humiliation before he gets around to anything as pedestrian as an execution. He knows that taking the *Gravity Rose* will hurt the captain as much as any physical torture. Steel-arm will wish to torment her with our ship firmly in his metal digits.'

Calder was about to ask the first mate to elaborate, then thought better of it and bit his tongue. Skrat started to replay the message and just as he did, a blinding flash exploded outside, the night sky spreading into sudden fierce clarity before the cabin's smart screens blanked out the exterior view for a second, returning to transparency with a bizarre orange afterglow lingering around the leaves. The wind built up outside, a fierce gale sweeping across the jungle canopy and rocking the shuttle on its landing gear. Then the gale died away, almost as suddenly as it had appeared.

'There we are,' sighed Skrat. 'Tediously predictable.'

'Sweet mother of... was that a nuclear warhead?'

'Don't worry, Mister Durk. The nasty device was detonated a long way from us and the blast came from the wrong direction for the mining base. That was Steel-arm's "suggestion" that the camp shut down its perimeter guns and allow the *Doubtful Quasar*'s landing craft to land unopposed inside the base to accept their surrender.' Skrat saw the look of horror on the human crewman's face. 'It's actually rather a good thing. If Steel-arm didn't wish to plunder the base and take the staff alive, his warhead wouldn't have been detonated out in the wilderness for show. Ground zero would have been the camp itself!'

So, we're dealing with someone for whom detonating a random nuke as a shot across the bows is a good thing? That told Calder pretty much everything he needed to know about what kind of adversary they faced.

'What next?'

'We need to time our arrival at the camp carefully. Leave too early, and we'll be flying straight into the pirate carrier's fighter wing. Too late, and Zeno and the skipper will be locked inside Steel-arm's brig in orbit, beyond our assistance. Let's tarry an hour here, and then we'll fly back low enough to rip leaves off the rain-forest canopy. We shall launch our rescue when Steel-arm's ripping the base apart for supplies and plunder, when he thinks he's won and his bounders have dropped their guard a smidgen.'

'If we can rendezvous with the *Gravity Rose*, can we outrun a pirate carrier?'

Skrat considered his answer carefully, nictitating membranes blinking across his eyes. 'One must hope so, dear boy. The *Doubtful Quasar* is ancient ex-military surplus – antiquated Edge technology rather than alliance-built. Our engines are rated for boosting serious cargo and we'll have this planet's pea-souper of an atmosphere as well as the system's irregular solar activity working in our favour. As long as we can clear the range of his fast attack planes . . . yes, let's hope we can show Steel-arm a clean pair of heels.' Skrat stood up and pushed his seat aside. 'Lend me a hand with the camouflage netting. Then we shall use our satellites to eavesdrop on the ruffians' comms chatter before we depart.'

They marched down into the cargo hold, Skrat dropping the ramp and dragging a dark ceramic crate out of a floor space. Heat poured in from outside, like water filling a submarine. Not quite as intense as it would have been during the day. Calder took the opportunity to introduce the first mate to Lento and the robot. The driver seemed as incurious about their pilot as everything else she encountered, while Momoko bowed and offered to help carry the crate of camouflage netting outside. Skrat took a pair of belts holding machetes from a locker and tossed one to Calder. The prince belted it around his hip. *It feels good to have a blade hanging down from my hip again.* It felt like... home. Of course, back on Hesperus's freezing plains, most warriors would have killed for an "enchanted" blade that could vibrate at a thousand kilocycles a second and cut through rainforest canopy – or more pertinently, blood and bone – like a heated scimitar through butter. Calder accepted the robot's proposal to assist and kept his rifle ready as he walked carefully down the ramp. Nocturnal hooting, squeaking and whistling surrounded the shuttle. The racket sounded different from the nightly jungle song that had surrounded the hunting lodge. The nuclear explosion had unsettled the local wildlife . . . something different and dangerous for them to fear. Skrat's camouflage netting glistened gossamer thin and pale white. As soon as they had dragged the cover across the shuttle, the netting's surface began to shimmer as though developing a photograph of the rain-forest floor – a real-time photo at that, live images of insects crawling across the fabric.

It stuck in Calder's craw, hiding out here, when every sinew of his body ached to charge in swinging a sword at these pirate raiders. But a part of him realized it was the right thing to do to maximize their chances for success. Maybe if Calder had been able to think more like Skrat, the prince might have implemented a strategy that wouldn't have lost his nation's ice fleet in a futile invasion, leaving him exiled and on the run. But in that event, he would never have met Lana Fiveworlds. *Or be stuck here, you fool.*

A sudden cracking noise. In front of Calder, Momoko tooted in alarm as the robot fell over – dropping the empty crate – one of its metal legs disappearing down a hole, the rest of its body left above ground, arms gesturing wildly. Calder flipped his rifle up, half expecting an arachnid to erupt out of the ground, furious it only had robot steel to feast on. Tentatively, Calder and Skrat inched over. But nothing emerged. Hauling the robot up was like pulling a tank out of a ditch.

'I never should have left the lodge,' said Momoko, dejectedly, as the two crewmen yanked at its body. 'Is this my punishment for abandoning my post?'

'I doubt it,' grunted Calder as he hefted the machine's weight. 'You're not programmed to believe in gods, are you?'

Momoko put its arms to work, found some purchase, and managed to help extradite itself. 'The company knows everything. Sees everything. I thought leaving the lodge is within the rules, but perhaps I am wrong?'

'We write our own rules, old fruit,' said Skrat. 'You might say that's something of an unofficial motto among our company.'

There were only a few hours until sunrise, before large sectors of the robot's memories automatically dumped. And there wouldn't be a copy of Momoko's corporate bible on hand for the robot to refresh what it needed to know.

Skrat bent down to examine the lair. Calder kept his gun trained down into the hole.

'Be careful,' warned Calder. 'Most the things I've run into out here so far have wanted to add me to the menu.'

'There's something below the soil,' said Skrat. 'And it isn't a warren or a lair.' Skrat pulled the machete out of his belt, touching a button on its hilt. A sudden buzzing filled the clearing as his blade blurred; vibrating so fast it almost became invisible. The first mate cut away bricks of compacted mud topped with alien grass. It quickly became clear what the robot had tumbled through. *A shattered window?* Momoko walked over, halting its imposing bulk above the hole. A light in its chest sprung into life, helping illuminate the makeshift excavation. A length of heavy metal plating, rusted and red, lay under the soil.

'There's a building under the ground?' wondered Calder.

'Not a building,' said Skrat. 'This is standard hex-hull, old alliance design, and it has seen extensive particle damage. She's a starship, old bean. And we've landed on top of her. Large enough to cover the entire valley floor . . . must be a colony vessel. Rusting away long enough to be completely covered by mud slides and sediment and have the local flora grow over her roof. I do believe this vessel is the *Never Come Down*... she was a colony ship, posted missing; her crew had a hand in naming the world Abracadabra.'

Calder glanced around the trees. Any signs of a settlement had long since been reclaimed by the rainforest. *I know all about failed colonies, although my own is a heck of a lot colder than this hell-world's.*

'Who would want to settle here?'

'Oh, we skirls wouldn't find it too bad,' said Skrat. 'Rather humid, though. Given the choice we prefer our worlds dry.'

Skrat had a point. Up on the *Gravity Rose*, Calder could fry an egg on the fabric of the first mate's ship suit, the temperature he usually set it at. 'Could that figure I glimpsed outside the lodge have been human? A descendant of the ship's colonists?'

'One suspects not,' said Skrat. 'Had humanity endured here, the mining team's orbital survey would have turned up signs of deforestation, cooking fires, torches lit at night to protect village palisades from predators and the like. If any of your species survived on Abracadabra, this vessel would have long since been cannibalized into axe-heads, saws and nails.'

Spears and swords, too, unless the branch of humanity who had landed here had been much different from Calder's people. He felt a superstitious shiver run down his spine. 'Let's get back inside the shuttle and seal the ramp.'

'Nothing to fret about. Another abandoned antique, defunct and useless,' said Skrat. 'The galaxy is full of them. We're not in any danger here. Although I wouldn't recommend staying behind to try and raise a family on Abracadabra. This is no world for a chap to leave his bones on.'

'You're a strange sort,' said Calder. He stepped aside for the robot to clang up the ramp before following inside with Skrat. He was happy to seal out the alien rainforest; a hum of air conditioning as the cargo hold struggled to return to a reasonable temperature. 'The chief told me you're reckless – a gambler. But you're willing to wait it out here, as cool as the ice sheets around Heldheim.'

'Perhaps it's because I've lost so very much,' said Skrat. 'I'm no different from you in that regard, old bean. We're both exiles, in our own way. I may be willing to gamble, but only when the odds are on my side. There's a universe of void between a risk and a calculated risk.'

'The chief mentioned the skipper found you close to death in some kind of gladiator arena on the skirl homeworld.'

'The chief should learn to keep his mouth shut,' said Skrat. The lizard looked as if he wasn't going to say anymore, before changing his mind. 'I lost my position in my nest on Raznor Raz after the corporation I ran was absorbed by a rival in a hostile takeover. You might say I was disgraced. I was endeavouring to earn money to pay my creditors back. Fighting in the arena was the only way open to me. I was considered unlucky, and few skirls will do business with someone who is luckless. If I had won enough combats, society would have considered my bad providence purged.'

'You were willing to fight to pay debtors back?'

'The layers of Skirl society are multifarious,' said Skrat. 'When you lose your position, your family becomes the responsibility of the victors. My children, my wife . . . they belong to another skirl lordling now; they are bound to a competing nest. Even contacting my children would be considered a pollution of their chances of success – not to be permitted. When I earn enough money to recover my position, they will be returned to me.'

'How much money do you need?'

'A very large sum, dear boy,' said Skrat, sadly, climbing back into the shuttle's cockpit. 'The higher you climb, the further the distance you have to fall. But in the universe anything is possible. With luck, skill and good judgement.'

Calder grunted in sympathy as he settled to wait in the co-pilot seat, his feet nervously tapping at the deck. *All of my immediate family were dead long before I fled into exile. All I ran away from were regrets, countless responsibilities and a fatally failed military campaign. Is that better or worse than poor old Skrat?* Tormented by everything he had abandoned when he departed for the stars. 'With luck.'

'Water under the bridge, old fruit. What's left of my destiny is bound up with the *Gravity Rose*. If she sinks, I sink. I'm certainly not going to surrender her or any of our people over to a gang of thieving rogues led by a psychopathic cyborg scallywag of Steel-arm Bowen's notoriety.'

They waited for the best part of an hour, listening into the open comms chat of the carrier's attack planes. Pilots boasting how easy their victory had been, complaining about navigational instruments going haywire in the planet's unusual atmosphere, some of the planes getting lost and having to return to the carrier by line-of-sight. *Time for the rescue, yet?* Calder was about to check with Skrat when the words choked in his throat. The prince glanced up through the clearing and noticed how the night-time sky had changed – and it was like *nothing* he had ever seen before.

***

Being locked inside the mining camp's small concrete brig with Zeno wasn't too much of a burden for Lana. It was the survivors from the rest of the operation she could have done without, and, at the very top of the list, their supercilious mission commander, Professor Alison Sebba. Over twenty people crammed in a jail meant for a couple of drunken workers at most. Close quarters really didn't make the professor any more bearable.

'This is your fault,' said Sebba glaring through the miners at Lana, her posterior selfishly settled across a bunk she had commandeered for her sole use. 'The rogue commanding these pirates clearly has a personal grudge against you. And in his settling of that vendetta, you have condemned my whole operation to, at best, months of captivity until a ransom is paid.'

'If you think Dollar-sign's paying a ransom after this debacle, you really haven't worked with him for long enough,' said Lana. Little eddies of concrete dust drifted down from the ceiling every time the gun turrets on the pirate's command shuttle rotated, tracking aerial hyper-lizards. The base's helicopter pads hadn't been designed for a shuttle's weight. Lana brushed the falling dust out of her hair. 'Your "at best" is going to be a kindly disposed owner at a pirate slave market . . . and here's a top tip, you won't find too many of those with fat wallets at any slave market I'm acquainted with.'

'I'm certain you are more acquainted,' said Sebba. 'It's your damnable spotty past that has dragged the rest of us down alongside you.'

The nerve of the whining . . . 'You want to talk about spotty operations . . .' Lana felt Zeno's hand on her shoulder, the android's neck craned subtly in the direction of the security camera hanging in front of the cell. *Yeah, he's right as always. We don't want to discuss what is really happening here without knowing who is listening in.* The professor didn't know Lana had discovered the hidden operations below the planet's surface. *And as far as Steel-arm Bowen is concerned, this is just a standard illegal mining venture out prospecting in the wild. God, let it stay that way.*

'Let's prepare for the worst and hope for the best,' said Kien-Yen Leong, the mining camp chief's voice heavy with the weight of responsibility.

'We wouldn't have to "hope" if you hadn't surrendered so readily!' accused the professor.

'I will not order my people to commit suicide,' said Leong. 'And that's what it would have been for us to keep on fighting. Our defences were designed to hold off the local wildlife, not squadrons of fighter-bombers.'

'The planes were just to intimidate you,' said Lana. 'The *Doubtful Quasar* carries heavy rail cannons and ship-to-ship nukes. She could have sat in orbit and reduced this whole continent into smoking cinders inside an hour. You did the right thing, chief.'

'People who hope to plunder you don't tend to render you radioactive first,' hissed the professor.

'Yeah, well, rational thought and Steel-arm Bowen are only nodding acquaintances,' said Lana. She looked forlornly beyond the thick bars at the front of the concrete cell. A single desk and chair, currently unmanned; a door leading to the rest of the base. There was a single window at the side, but it was sealed by a heavy steel storm shutter, leaving their only natural light from the narrow barred window slits inside their cell – the dim lunar glow of the distant moons, a spattering of stars distorted by the cursed planet's gaseous veil. 'A slaughter every now and then only enhances his reputation . . . it means the next vessel or settlement he raids flies the white flag as soon as the *Doubtful Quasar* jumps in-system.'

'Ah, you know me so well, Lana girl,' announced the pirate commander, stepping into the brig with his entourage of killers dogging his footsteps. He walked up to the cage and strutted its length, tapping his pistol barrel along each bar. 'Well enough to glue my tracking device to a satellite, eh? You can imagine the lads' disappointment, chasing through this dirt-ball's magnetic murk, thinking they'd hunted down the *Gravity Rose*, only to find our own tracer hanging in orbit. You're a canny one and no mistake.'

'I'm sure your thugs will manage to drown their sorrows,' said Lana. 'We clocked your carrier inside hyperspace at the margins of our sensor range, so I set a sensor line at the jump point, just in case I wasn't seeing scanner ghosts. I ordered the *Gravity Rose* to jump out as soon as your tracer was found concealed in our cargo hold. Me and Zeno would have got away too, if we hadn't missed the rendezvous point when our shuttle malfunctioned on this ill-starred world.' Lana wasn't sure if Steel-arm had bought her lie, but the professor did . . . hook, line and sinker.

'You knew they were coming and you didn't try to evacuate us!' she squealed in indignation.

'You wouldn't have left with me if I had asked, you and your precious skegging mine,' said Lana. 'I didn't have time to argue with you. And like you said, old metal-fingers here has personal business with me. I'd have flared our engines on the jump-out; hoped his carrier burn straight after me without bothering to raid your camp.'

'You *hoped*. That's badly done,' said Kien-Yen Leong. 'You were hired to help us, not run for home at the first sign of trouble.'

'I was hired to ship supplies in and ore out,' said Lana. 'Nobody's paying me to get my crew killed in the wilds. Certainly not her or Dollar-sign Dillard.'

Steel-arm seemed amused. No, he wouldn't have any problem in believing that Lana Fiveworlds could be so cold. Bowen would have done exactly the same if their positions had been reversed, except he probably wouldn't have tried to draw an enemy ship away. *You'd have left everyone in the camp to die to buy extra time.*

'There be the spirited lass I remember. Now, how am I ever going to get over the disappointment of losing the *Gravity Rose*?'

Lana ignored his knowing leer. 'It's a big universe and there's always some other honest merchant a parsec away for you to molest.'

'Honest did you say?' Steel-arm roared with laughter. 'That's a grand lie. But not the only one I've been fed in this camp.' He pointed at Professor Sebba, his eyes wide and manic even as he grinned. 'You, professor. You told me we had all the mining staff accounted for in this little chicken coop of yours?'

'Everyone's here,' said the professor, coldly. 'Except for a tanker driver who went missing in the jungle a few weeks ago. She is likely dead.'

'There's the thing,' said Steel-arm. 'She's not the only one absent without leave. I left a team of sixteen crew and two shuttles at the mine to strip out your gear. They've all gone missing, including my boats. Now, you're not telling me that a single driver managed to make sixteen heavily armed fighters and their craft disappear without them calling for help once, are you? How many survey teams do you have out in the infernal jungle? How many of your people jumped us?'

Sebba shook her head, furiously. 'That's nothing to do with this base. Perhaps they crashed trying to fly back to your carrier? You can't always rely on your instruments on Abracadabra.'

Lana felt a desperate, brief burst of hope. *Is this Skrat's work? Maybe he's found Calder and they're working some mischief together in the shuttle? Picking off Steel-arm's shuttles in the air.*

The pirate's artificial arm whined as he lifted his pistol into the air. 'Here's one instrument that rarely lets me down, lass. Now, I say this is to do with you. How many staff do you have working on the world? Even using robots, you're not running a mine with so few people.'

Lana grimaced. *No, but you can run an archaeological dig and arrange a little tomb raiding with that small a team.* Sebba stood up, waving her arms at the pirate. 'Everyone's here! We've only just commenced exploratory tunnelling . . . we were planning to ship in extra hands in a month or so.' She was still talking at the pirate as though she was a school teacher admonishing a child. Lana knew from painful experience that wasn't how you handled Steel-arm. *He's not one of your hired goons, Sebba. He's the feral kind. The real deal.*

Steel-arm shrugged and glanced over at his crew. 'Don't I always know a lie when I hear it? It makes me sad. I thought we had built up an understanding here, you and I, professor. You give me what I want without trouble, and I won't have to make things problematic for you. I dislike damaging the merchandise to make my point.' He raised his pistol in the direction of the cage and it jolted in his hand, an explosive crack, and one of the miners collapsed into his colleagues, the rear of his head a bloody ruin where the magnetically accelerated pellet had exited. Screams of outrage and terror sounded from the miners, some of the prisoners acting on blind impulse and trying to scramble away behind their colleagues or to the sides of the brig to minimise the chances they would be the next victim. Lana noticed that Zeno had positioned himself in front of her – damn the android. *Zeno might have a better chance of surviving a rail-gun shot than me, but he has no right to try – he's the ship's droid herder, not my personal bodyguard.*

'Tell me the truth!' Steel-arm yelled at the mission commander. 'Or I'll put one in your leg on low-power and work my way up inch-by-inch to your over-educated skull. I'll give you plenty of time to bleed-out and recover your delicate memory, lass.'

'Don't tell him a thing!' demanded Kien-Yen Leong.

Steel-arm pivoted and shot the mining chief three times, starting in the chest and working his way up as the man yelled, flung back by the fierce velocity of the sudden volley. Leong was dead well before he hit the concrete floor. 'Did I ask you to speak, did I?'

Lana wanted to be sick. The mining chief had been a good man. But that wasn't nearly enough to protect him from a ruthless human predator like Steel-arm. The pirate woman, Cho, stared at the prisoners trembling behind the bars, a flash of malice crossing her eyes. 'Use the speakers to tell the workers hiding in the jungle to surrender, or we'll feed the lizards a corpse every five minutes.' The pirate girl aimed at Lana and the professor. 'These two next!'

Sebba clung to the bars of the cage-front, a frantic look breaking through her normal aura of haughty disdain. The academic ignored the weeping and yells behind her. 'It's not us! It's your fault, you pinheads – you detonated a nuke down here.'

'Ah, a little bit of fallout didn't vanish my lads now, did it?'

'You have activated the defence protocols!'

'Your base's systems are under my control now, lass, or have you forgotten?'

'Not the camp, you fool . . . this was a Heezy world.'

Lana groaned inside. *That's right; give the homicidal maniac with a gun the location of a far deadlier weapon.*

'You think some nonsense fairy-tale's going to save your life?'

'We were beneath its notice,' moaned Sebba as though she was conversing with a tutorial group, not an insane pirate warlord. 'I was keeping it dormant. We hardly even registered as a threat. Until you proved we are. By awakening it with a nuclear-tipped warhead!'

Steel-arm's comm on his ship-suit sleeve started bleeping. He passed his hand over it and a voice frothed out of the static. '*Doubtful Quasar*—we're—being sliced. Sliced—and—losing—environmental integrity.'

'Sliced?' Steel-arm roared. 'What are you talking about, damn you?' His only answer was raw static. The other pirates' comms started to go off too, urgent calls flooding in from across the camp, raiders reporting something weird in the sky. One of their captors sprinted to the storm shutter and raised it, slowly grinding, into the roof. Beyond was as abnormal sight as Lana had ever seen – the dark sky above the jungle criss-crossed by a lattice of glowing yellow energy lines, a firework display seemingly erupting between a couple of the moons. The kind of display a carrier might make if it was being cut into pieces while its atomic arsenal of ship-to-ship missiles detonated all at once, sections of hull sheering away as radioactive sparks, miles of hull racked by secondary explosions. Then a sudden flare as the anti-matter inside her engine's containment area breeched, rapidly dwindling away to nothing. As the detonation died away, Lana noticed an unholy light in the sky, a huge cable of energy shifting sinuously from side to side. It seemed to stretch from the world, reaching far out to space.

'There's your bloody fairy-tale,' moaned Sebba. 'You've killed us all!'

- 23 -
The settlers' vessel.

Calder spun aimlessly in the shuttle chair as Skrat examined the boat's instruments, the interior of their vessel lit by the glow of strange shifting energies pulsing against the sky.

'Whatever that bally energy field across the sky is, it's cut off contact with our satellite net. We can no longer reach the *Gravity Rose*,' said Skrat. 'I'm tracking falling debris, too. I think the pirate ship was caught up inside the field when it activated. By my sweet nest, look at my readout. There's not a bean left of the *Doubtful Quasar* in orbit. We should be thankful Steel-arm showed up and scared the *Rose* off, or it'd be raining fragments of the chief and Polter.'

'If that field's not being generated by the pirates, then who . . . ?'

'A jolly pertinent question.' Skrat scratched his scaly green skin absentmindedly. 'This abominable world does possess a queer atmosphere, but what's in the sky . . . it's not any natural phenomenon my confused noggin is familiar with. Those grid lines are too regular, and while atmospheric interaction with the system's sun might create ionization, it's nothing capable of frying a heavily armoured warhorse like the *Doubtful Quasar*. So we have a quandary. I doubt the field is being produced by the jungle creatures. There is no sign of any technological civilization on Abracadabra from orbit. You can't cloak an active society so thoroughly, not even the energetically paranoid ones. That leaves the legacy of dead cultures, which is almost as worrying.' He activated the main control board, a field of icons and readouts flickering into life and swarming his head. 'I'd rather devote my time to the more practical question of how we can safely fly through it. One step at a time, I suppose. Let's retrieve the captain.'

'You still think I'm being unreasonably superstitious about this planet?'

'Consider that under review, dear boy.' Skrat tugged at the control stick and a line of alarm icons began to spin around him like a swarm of angry wasps. He cursed. 'What's this stuff and nonsense, then?' Skrat swatted the control board, rolling hologram information across the air. He cursed again, sounding genuinely angry. 'Our main fuel cells have been drained. We're running solely on emergency juice now.'

'But they were full?'

'Indeed. I checked them myself before I flew out of the base.'

'Is it possible that energy field in the sky is responsible? It must take a lot of power to produce something like that?'

'Quite an understatement. I don't believe our little shuttle has much to contribute in the grand scheme of things. Best we undertake an exterior inspection of the engines, see if we took any damage picking you up from the hunting lodge.'

They climbed down from the cockpit and passed through the cargo hold, a look of fear crossing their female passenger's face as she realized they were about to drop the rear ramp again. Momoko waddled over, the robot making a fuss of Janet Lento and helping keep her quiet. Calder took his rifle to cover Skrat as the skirl fished a diagnostics box out of the hold. They left the shuttle and pushed into the thick humid air outside, the clearing lit by the shuttle's lamps and the peculiar net of energy above. Skrat unscrewed a panel below the engine and plugged his box into the exposed machinery. Calder stood guard nervously.

'Interesting,' announced Skrat after a couple of minutes of diagnostics testing. 'Our engines should be working. Not so much drained, as full but completely inert. I might as well have topped up the shuttle with a couple of barrels of gin before I flew out.'

'How the hell can our fuel cells have been tampered with like that?' asked Calder.

'Theoretically speaking, if your civilization was advanced enough,' said Skrat, 'and your planet had been subjected to a sudden nuclear assault and you wanted to shield yourself against further detonations, you could send out a pulse to transform fissile material into pure mush. Reprogramming risky matter, so to speak. Our inert fusion power cells are merely collateral damage – whoever did this was, I hypothesise, aiming to neutralize Steel-arm's atomic warheads, not our engine's pile. The shuttle's emergency backup runs on old-fashioned batteries, so at least we'll have environmental systems until we deplete its reserves.'

'Remote reprogramming of matter? That sounds an awful lot like science fiction,' said Calder.

Skrat pointed to the net of energy weaving across the heavens. 'Old chap, it behoves me to point out that up until we showed up to take you into exile, this shuttle, myself and the robot in our hold were pure science fiction to your good self. Any significantly advanced technology appears like magic to those lower down the food chain.'

The lizard-like crewman had a point. But even if his theory is correct, we are still stranded hundreds of miles from the base. *If we manage to survive the trek back to the mine through the jungle, who knows what might have happened to Lana by the time we arrive.* And Zeno, of course. He mattered every bit as much as the captain, didn't he? 'We had better gear-up and light out of here, then.'

'Not so hasty, dear fellow,' said Skrat. 'If I'm correct, this pulse would need to be tightly directed, otherwise it would risk damaging its maker's own systems. In this case, directed at the pirate's assets in orbit. We were unlucky enough to be close to ground zero of the pirate's opening volley, thus caught in the counter-response. But—' he pointed at the fissure in the ground—, 'this old colony vessel is buried by sediment and shielded by the best part of a rather deep valley...'

'The settlers would have exhausted all of their ship's power reserves, surely, before they died?'

'That rather depends on the manner of their passing,' said Skrat. 'And even if there are no operational cells underground, at this point I'd be grateful for anything that shortcuts our journey . . . a raft, a bicycle, a diesel vehicle, a bally hang glider.'

Navigating the boiling rapids of the world's rivers, or riding thermals alongside flocks of hungry dragons? I'd almost take the dubious shelter of the rain forest. 'Do you think the pirate's landing craft are grounded the same as us?'

'Sadly, one suspects not. The mining camp is a long way out and shielded by the mountain range's mass, to boot. But let's look on the bright side. Right now, Steel-arm and his band of cads have no way to bypass that energy field and no starship left to jump out-system even if they did. We just need to free the captain and Zeno, then avoid the pirates until the *Gravity Rose* finds a way to extract us.'

'What if she can't?'

'That energy field in orbit will have to switch off at some point,' said Skrat. 'Or we won't be the only chaps on the planet left with drained power cells.'

Just free the captain. The two of them on the ground against the gods know how many pirates in the assault force. Quite a *just*. But Calder would attempt it, all the same. And not only because he had no other choices left. *Lana.*

***

'**M**y ship!' roared Steel-arm, watching the last sparks of his vessel dwindle away in the night sky. 'My magnificent *Doubtful Quasar.*' The officer was close to apoplexy as he thrust his pistol in the direction of the brig, provoking cries of terror from the caged workers. 'You witch, Sebba – you mined the orbit of your stake and destroyed my ship! Drag her carcass out here!'

Steel-arm's pirates sprung the cage door and hauled the professor in front of him, the others' rifles aiming straight for the prisoners. *Lana winced. It won't take much for the excitable madman to order all of us executed now.*

'That wasn't me,' pleaded Sebba, all traces of her arrogance evaporated. 'I told you, it's the Heezy.'

'There's nothing on this bloody planet but rainforest,' yelled Steel-arm. He drew his dagger and touched its activator, the blade buzzing into life, vibrating so fast it was nearly invisible. 'I'm going to take each of your fingers, one at a time, until you tell me where the rest of your miners are hiding out. Then I'll have your lying tongue to feed the lizards out there.'

'Please . . . '

'I loathe your stinking, privileged breed   as good as immortal, looking down on the rest of us like rats to be dissected for your profit; more money than God accreting in your bank account over all the centuries. Now it's my turn for a little scientific experimentation . . . a dissection . . . I'm going to cut the truth out of you!' His men pinned the professor, forcing her arm out straight. Sebba desperately tried to pull away as the pirate commander reached out with his metal fist, cybernetics tightening around her hand like a vice.

'Don't!' shouted Lana, almost as shocked by the sound of her voice breaking the tension as the other prisoners appeared to be. She gripped the bars of the cage. 'She's telling the truth. This was a Heezy world. The alien settlement is deep under the surface. I've explored there with Zeno, below the mine.'

Sebba stared across in shock. Whether over Lana's unexpected intervention or the fact the starship skipper had uncovered what the base was really doing on Abracadabra, she would be hard pushed to say. *Of all my many mistakes, I'm sure this is the worst of them. I've really outdone myself this time.*

'So you have been off with the Heezy, have you?' leered Steel-arm. 'You're not exactly top of my expert witness list, Lana girl, the stack of yarns you've spun me in the past.'

The female pirate Cho stepped forward. 'Don't trust a word she says, captain. She'll say anything to keep her friends safe for another hour. Her security people are holed up out there in the jungle right now, trying to work out how to retake the base. I guarantee it.'

'You know me well enough to know I wouldn't put myself up for finger carving lightly,' said Lana, ignoring the pirate woman. *What's she got against me, anyway?* 'And take a look at that glowing energy net in the sky. That's like no mine field I've ever flown into before.'

'What do you say it is, then?'

'The professor here's the expert, I reckon. But she's only any good to you with her tongue attached *inside* her mouth, not flapping in the dust.'

'It'll be a pair of tongues if you play me false, Lana girl,' spat Steel-arm. He slowly deactivated his dagger and slid it back into his belt. 'Tell me how you came across this place, professor. Make it convincing, or I'll be taking my fun with you.'

'Dollar-sign Dillard's people discovered the Heezy's presence here,' spluttered the professor. 'The world's location was in the logs of a derelict vessel discovered adrift in space . . . a packet ship used to bring in big game hunters to Abracadabra. All her crew and passengers died of starvation or cold after her systems failed. They'd stumbled across the ruins of a failed human colony while hunting on the planet, the settlers presumed exterminated by the Heezy's automated defences. The hunters nearly met the same fate, but a handful of them managed to escape off-world in their ship, though obviously not intact enough to reach home.'

'And you thought you'd play with the same fire?' said Zeno. The android really didn't sound pleased to be involved in such foolishness without being consulted. *I know how he feels.*

'The previous explorers didn't know what they were doing,' whined the professor. 'I've had experience of Alliance-sanctioned Heezy digs. I have been trained in how to keep Heezy defences from going live while a team strips out what it can.'

Steel-arm waved at the lattice of glowing yellow behind the odd shifting cable of raw energy. 'You've failed, you witch! Let's be having the rest from you . . . !'

'If I tell you what I know,' moaned the professor, 'I'll be breaking every level of classified clearance the Alliance possesses. If the government finds out, I'll be executed. They'll murder you merely for knowing . . . '

'There won't be enough of you left for the Alliance to torture,' threatened Steel-arm, 'not after I've done cutting you. Tell me!'

'That grid you can see in the atmosphere is a shield to protect the world,' moaned Sebba. 'Your carrier was caught inside the field when it activated after you started detonating nukes . . . '

'You're talking impossible nonsense,' spat Steel-arm. 'An energy shield for an entire planet? There's not enough juice in the galaxy to power such a thing!'

'It's possible. The Heezy knew how to tap dark flow,' said Sebba.

Lana gawped. Dark flow. The weird, seemingly unlimited power driving the ever-speeding expansion of the universe until, so it was theorized by the Hunt-Ekotto effect, an impossibly distant cosmological future when dark energy overloaded all of existence and caused a fierce sequence of new big bangs . . . thousands of baby universes thrown out of the dying one like seeds. 'You're skegging kidding me!'

'The planetary defence grid and that energy cable you see snaking through the sky,' said Sebba, 'are powered by a dark flow generator at the world's core. The Alliance still doesn't understand the physics of how the Heezy tap dark energy, but we know the species refashioned their worlds' inner cores as vast spinning toroidal disks to achieve it.'

'That cable of energy lashing about in the sky's not part of the planetary shield, is it?' said Lana.

Sebba shook her head, forlornly. 'What you're observing is an umbilical cord between us and the sun. It's the same class of technology that the Alliance scavenged its sun-buster technology from when we ended the Skein War. Abracadabra is acting as a dark energy transformer and recharging its system's dying sun. The Heezy didn't believe in wasting planets they had occupied through anything as trivial as sun deaths.'

'A star's not a battery,' said Lana. She was stunned by the level of science she was seeing here. *A species with enough hubris that they wouldn't permit their own sun to die. Immortality for an entire solar system.*

'And neither is this system's,' said Sebba. 'There's going to be an accelerated supernova and then the star will be restarted as good as new. The explosion won't be as fierce as a naturally occurring supernova, but the radiation blast will still be strong enough to kill everything organic inside the system. It wouldn't have bothered the Heezy, of course. They were non-corporeal towards the end. Our two best guesses about their extinction are that their species either killed itself in a war with a higher race from the Large Magellanic Cloud or went sublime . . . my money's on the latter.'

Steel-arm seized the woman and dragged her up from her knees. 'And where's your damn money on dropping that shield and getting us out of this cursed system before we're all fried?'

'We would need to travel deep inside the Heezy complex to try to deactivate it,' said Sebba. 'That wouldn't have posed much of a problem a few hours ago. But now we've been re-classified as a real and present danger, rather than low-level rodents scampering around their race's ruins . . . I doubt we will be able to get close enough.'

'You *doubt*?'

'Listen, there was a world in the Omicron Ceti system where a Heezy dig's defences were accidently triggered by an Alliance exploration team. Outside of the team's single call for help, we don't know much about what happened because the world simply isn't there anymore. The planet just disappeared along with all our scientists and archaeologists. Sun's still good, just missing the fourth planet in the system, is all. Our best guess is that the automated defences teleported the whole world somewhere else. That's the level of threat we're dealing with.'

Teleportation? Lana had never encountered a species that had made teleportation work, beyond pushing a few atoms around using quantum entanglement. *A whole world? We really are in deep trouble now.*

'Damn your horror stories. What are their defences here?' demanded Steel-arm.

Sebba shrugged. 'Who knows? The Heezy were masters of programmable matter. Their automated defences hide dormant as information viruses in the rock. I was working very hard to supress their legacy systems' immune response to our presence. But now? They could manifest themselves as almost anything.'

'How have you been keeping the Heezy defences dormant?' pressed Steel-arm.

'There's a system installed at the mine broadcasting a faked Heezy signal that identifies human DNA as friendly, as though we're a recently sanctioned addition to the official Heezy eco-system. Unfortunately for us, your attack will have re-characterised our presence as either malfunctioning or hostile or both. Right now we're just a biological glitch awaiting deletion.'

'Is there any way to travel below the surface without being exterminated?' said Lana.

'One of the artefacts we retrieved is a crystal broach that acts like a transponder, given to visiting alien species as a guest pass. So visitors could travel into Heezy facilities for negotiations, or perhaps worship would be a more accurate term, without newcomers being eliminated.'

'And these broaches would be enough to keep us safe?'

'Depends on what you mean by safe, Captain Fiveworlds. Closer to a Heezy gardener avoiding slicing too many worms with its shovel because worms aerate the soil,' said Sebba. 'And in case you're in any doubt, we're the worms in that analogy. The closer we get to sensitive Heezy systems, the more likely we are to be purged.'

'Worms are useful in the garden,' sighed Zeno, 'but you wouldn't want them getting into your garage and clogging your car up.'

'Precisely,' said the professor.

'I'll take that Heezy broach,' snarled the pirate commander. Steel-arm shoved the woman into his crew of rogues. 'Escort her to her stash of antiques and bring the thing straight back to me.'

He fingered the remote on his belt. 'And remember, my bucks, in case any of you get ideas of absconding with it . . . you're still wearing a fine pirate necklace around your precious necks.' Steel-arm turned to the captain of the *Gravity Rose*. 'We're going on a little jaunt, Lana girl, you and your miner friends. The good news is I won't be selling you on the slave market straight away. The bad news is that you and your crew will be my canaries down the mine.'

Lana grimaced. *A herd of cattle whipped across a mine-field to clear it is closer to the truth.* She fingered the shock collar locked a little too tightly around her neck, a matching set to the bands worn by every member of the captured base staff. *I guess this is how pirates volunteer.*

'Don't be looking so angry, now,' laughed Steel-arm. 'I'll do my best to keep you alive until this planetary shield's been spiked. I find myself in need of a new ship, and I reckon that your crew will return fast enough when they see my pistol shoved into your pretty mouth.'

Damn him. Steel-arm understood her crew almost as well as Lana did. Polter would return with the *Gravity Rose* if he thought that surrendering the ship would spare Lana and Zeno. After all, what was a vessel compared to her immortal soul? *That ship is my soul.* It was a measure of how bad things were on Abracadabra that surviving the Heezy's deadly legacy, losing her beloved ship, then being put up for auction in a pirate slave market was currently looking like the best outcome out of a miserable bunch. Lana was held inside the brig for ten minutes. When the other pirates returned dragging the professor and her recovered broach, they did so at speed, faces distorted with panic.

One of the men tossed the broach at Steel-arm who caught it. It resembled a flower carved in green quartz, intricate crystalline folds. No larger than a medal. 'What's the matter, lad? Out with it!'

'Our soldiers guarding the corridors,' spluttered the pirate, 'they're gone!'

Steel-arm frowned and pulled out his trigger for the suicide collars. He activated it, a hologram image springing into life above the device's surface – a map with green dots marking where each recipient of one of the loyalty collars stood duty. All around the base, green points disappeared as Lana watched. Pulsing off. *I'm guessing his soldiers aren't defusing their suicide collars.* Steel-arm swore and turned off the device, holstering it and reaching for his comm, switching it onto general chatter – a confusion of screams and yells, as though he had tuned into the final moments of a starship torn apart in an asteroid belt and exposed to vacuum.

'What's happening out there?' bellowed Steel-arm.

'Coming—through the—laser fence—just—walking through.'

The pirate captain's face was turning purple. 'What, damn you? What?'

'Covered in—spines—they're—' The voice cut off in a bloodcurdling scream.

One of the pirates turned and fled, his nerves snapping. Steel-arm didn't wait or waver. The commander's arm snapped up and the suicide bolt exploded inside the confines of the brig, the deserter tumbling forward into the shaped concrete wall with a smouldering hole where his neck used to meet his spine. 'I'm still to be a-feared more than some antique robot sentries!'

yelled Steel-arm. 'Spines or no. And if any of you dogs doubt it, just try to desert on me.' He waved his pistol at the imprisoned miners. 'Out, my little flock of canaries! We're heading for the shuttle on the roof.' He palmed the broach and shoved it under the professor's nose. 'How do I activate this?'

'I need to trace an activation sigil on its surface. But wait until we arrive at the mine. The broach's power source only remains active for an hour . . . it takes days to recharge itself. You'll need it far more inside the Heezy complex than here.'

Lana considered the screams she had just heard. *Needs are a relative business, it seems.*

'Just an hour?' snarled Steel-arm.

Sebba shrugged without looking apologetic. 'We can't tamper with the broach without destroying it. Even the Heezy's wireless recharging systems are encrypted.'

'After a million years, my power cells should last an hour,' muttered Zeno.

'Let's just try and survive the next few minutes,' said Lana. She found herself bundled outside the cage alongside Zeno and the surviving base staff, driven like a flock of sheep through the plain concrete corridors while the armed pirates jabbed at them with rifles barrels, their captors snarling and threatening to mask their own fear. Lana felt her heart thudding like a cannon volley inside her chest, terror rising; shared with everyone stumbling, half-running, alongside her. Fear so strong she could taste it. Every second she resisted the desire to sprint as fast away from here as she could. The unknown beyond the base, seeping inside, making a mockery of humanity's pathetic laser fences and robot guns and sensor grids. *Mere savages' trinkets fashioned from mud and sticks in the face of what we have unleashed.* But as fast as Lana ran, she could never outpace the coming solar storm, lashing everything inside the system with its killing fury. *Never seen a supernova. How come I don't fear it? Maybe because it'll be quick and clean. Over before I can feel it.* The monkey inside her, the barely evolved ape, didn't fear a dying sun – it was the Heezy's reanimated ghosts which filled her with dread. Rising out of their underground lair to punish humanity for its arrogance – the professor's arrogance – in thinking she could steal sparks from the gods' fire and live to tell the tale. They approached a cargo lift at the end of the corridor, an abandoned trolley with crates of supplies on its metal surface partially blocking their way. Steel-arm growled as he sent the trolley skidding into a side-corridor. Lana swivelled when Zeno barked a warning. Behind them, the walls bubbled as though someone was burning into them with a laser set on low-power. A shape formed in the wall and Lana remembered the Heezy's peculiar method of transportation – motile bubbles passing through the planet's solid bedrock. A figure stepped out of the wall's surface, humanoid but faceless. Six foot-tall, slick ebony black and covered in evil sharp spikes, as though an armoured knight had combined with a giant porcupine. The thing's skull resembled an eyeless hatchet. It instantly latched onto the nearest pirate and wrapped its spiked arms around the man's chest, the soldier's body impaled and only enough breathe for a swift broken yell that immediately turned into a gasp. He was crushed as though caught in the jaws of a trash compactor, a sudden spray of blood as his body burst. All around Lana the walls bubbled and ran, sentinels born from the bare concrete, stepping out and crushing miners and pirates alike, the humans' guns chattering to little effect beyond deafening her ears. Lana stumbled back towards the lift, half dragged by Zeno, a press of desperate, shrieking survivors trying to escape the corridor's slaughter. Steel-arm was inside the lift, one arm around Professor Sebba, using her as a shield as he emptied his pistol into the corridor's narrow space. Lana slapped the button for the roof. The nearest of the sentinels rocked as it advanced into the line of fire from the frantic pirates cowering inside the lift, reaching out to seize necks and snap them as it lurched forward. It was nearly on her as the doors slammed shut and the lift rose upwards on its antigravity field, a bare second before the sentinel's hand reached for the lift, a distorted screech of metal as it dug its fingers into the disappearing elevator.

Steel-arm reloaded his magazine, Lana imagining every shudder of the cargo lift as a Heezy sentinel trying to latch onto the elevator. There were only five pirates left standing, with the same amount of mining staff, as well as Lana, Zeno and the professor on top of those numbers. *Not many survivors.* Steel-arm shook Sebba with his cybernetic limb. 'Activate the broach!'

'Not yet.' The professor was stubborn, Lana gave her that. *Let's hope she's right, too.*

'I'll put a bullet into your damn thick head and see if it improves your thinking.'

'Then none of you will reach the mine alive,' said Sebba, her voice pure ice. 'My mind is fine. And I'm the only one in your circus of losers with a hope of deactivating this world's energy shield.'

'I'll make sure you do survive,' snapped Steel-arm. 'I'll take you for my cabin slave and whittle away a little of your skegging arrogance every day. I'll enjoy that!'

'At least one of us will,' retorted Sebba.

The lift's doors opened onto the rooftop, thick heat of the jungle air pouring in. Lana heard the distant whine and chatter of gunfire echoing from around the compound, pirates mounting their last stand against forces they could barely comprehend. Twenty feet away lay Steel-arm's command shuttle, dwarfing the camp's choppers on their helipads, a steel ramp extended from the vessel's rear. Unlike Lana's boxy workaday shuttles, this craft was obviously ex-military surplus, weapons pods and gun turrets dotting its surface, the bulbous back designed to land a couple of tanks and company of soldiers onto a world in the face of enemy fire. All of the survivors sprinted for the dubious safety of the ship. Lana tried not to look at the burning web of fire in the sky, trapping them down here, the vast snake of energy undulating between Abracadabra and the sun, filling it closer to bursting point with every minute that passed. It was too much of a reminder that spiked hands could rise from the roof any second, grasping their way around her ankles before she reached the shuttle. *Just save me from this. Just save me and I swear I'll mend my ways.* Then they were on board, panting and sweating. It seemed an age before the craft rose into the air, twisting and turning for the mine-head and the heat haze-girdled mountain range. Explosions and flashes of fire dropped away below them as the ramp started to seal and the shuttle powered forward. Zeno reached out to steady her. A wave of relief nearly overwhelmed Lana. *We've survived.* Before the ramp fully closed she saw a dark figure standing on the roof, watching them spiral away into the sky. It raised an arm and there was a volley of crackling explosions all around the shuttle, as though the febrile air was being sucked into a vacuum. Steel-arm's shuttle violently lurched to its side, and then the craft pitched towards the crimson jungle canopy below.

***

Calder spun in the air as the winch lowered him through the derelict colony ship's jagged, broken hull. He could see the torchlight from Momoko at the bottom of the dark cathedral-sized space, the robot looking after Janet Lento. Calder wasn't sure if he was doing the pair a favour by bringing them along rather than locking them inside their grounded shuttle; but the shell-shocked driver had become increasingly agitated when her rescuers left the shuttle, and Momoko was going to lose its memory soon, forgetting most of what it was, let alone who the rest of them were. Skrat followed last, controlling the winch with a mobile handset from his belt hook. After the skirl touched down he unclipped himself and stared around the chamber. They had descended into what looked like a cargo space, but one bare of equipment and transport containers. No ground vehicles or other forms of transport to return them to the base. Creepers had grown in through the breach and tried to colonise the walls, but it was too dark for them to prosper down here. Dark and hot, despite the sun not having risen outside yet. If the rest of the ship was similarly empty, Calder trusted they would be able to retrace their way back to the winching gear before the shuttle's emergency battery reserves dwindled to zero.

'A rather useful unit to have around,' hummed Skrat, patching the robot into a panel exposed next to a large door. Vibrations trembled across the deck as he used Momoko's fuel cell to jumpstart the doors. They fair screeched as they opened. *Haven't seen a maintenance team for centuries.* 'Good thing your body is too small to carry a fusion pile or you would be as dead as our shuttle.'

'I am always glad to be of service to my honoured guests,' said Momoko.

Calder wondered how glad the robot would feel if it found itself blundering around down here in the dark with its memory dumped. He helped Momoko lead Janet Lento out of the hold. A corridor lay beyond their opened portal, no different in its bare, functional design from the miles of passages Calder had worked inside the *Gravity Rose*. It was deadly silent, the chorus of the rain forest muffled by the hull. *Cooler too, insulated.* No hull breach here to spill in life from outside. *Far too much like a tomb for my taste.* Skrat went up to a plaque on the wall, wiping a layer of dust and grime from the metal. A ship-board map with assembly points and safe rooms marked in case of fires or micrometeorite impacts, and there was the name of the vessel, too. As Skrat has speculated when he first discovered the wreck . . . she was the *Never Come Down*. Maybe the settlers should have heeded the ironic advice in their ship's name and stayed on whatever crowded, industrial hellhole they hailed from, never embarking on their new and all-too brief life.

'Where shall we start looking for power sources?' asked the barbarian prince.

Skrat tapped the plaque. 'Let's begin with the lifeboats on this level. Lifeboat power cells are self-contained and built to trickle-feed for centuries if needed.'

'What if we come across a colonist in hibernation sleep inside?'

'We'll wake them up and ask the fellow what the devil

happened on this blasted old world,' said Skrat. 'It'll be good to hear someone serve up a tale of woe even worse than ours for a change.'

'I am always happy to serve,' noted Momoko.

'Good egg. I'll be sure to introduce you to Zeno,' said Skrat. 'He could do with a few lessons in co-worker cooperation rubbing off to jolly him along with the crew.'

Their passage through the ship was slowed by the need to bypass a series of locked doors, using the robot to power open each portal. Calder found himself surprised by the number of sealed bulkheads they encountered compared to the *Gravity Rose. It's as though someone tried to lock themselves in here, or lock something else out.* But they came across no mummified bodies or bones to indicate settlers had died on board. They did pass settler cabins which, when entered, proved to be largely bare, cleared of personal possessions. Empty lockers. Faded, dirty rugs with a few discarded packing crates on the floor. *Wherever the settlers went, they took their clothes, photographs and keepsakes with them.* Calder's explorations carried him through a mess-hall containing a curious sight. All the tables and benches had been dragged to the sides of the dark room, making room for piles of equipment – damaged computers and sim consoles and data slates, shattered pyramids of the devices, along with mounds of broken robots. Not humanoid models like Momoko, but variants of the service drones on board the *Rose*: tracked and uni-ball drones, others with dwarf-sized rubberized legs, the same short, waddling machines Calder had helped the chief supervise back in the engine room.

Momoko seemed to take fright at the scene, as though the sight of this vista of destruction might incite its human companions to vandalize its own body. 'This is terrible, terrible!'

'Quite curious, I would say,' whispered Skrat, prodding the nearest pile of scrap with his rifle barrel. 'Anything with a computer or A.I. in it seems to have been junked. Robots are highly useful protecting new settlements. They are the last thing settlers would want to destroy.'

'I'll protect you,' pleaded Momoko. 'I am useful and loyal. Do not let this happen to me.'

Lento seemed anxious again, maintaining her dumb silence as she scratched at her matted hair, wide eyes flickering nervously into the dark beyond their torchlights. 'Don't worry,' said Calder, reaching out to her. 'This happened a long time ago.'

'I wonder if we'd find the computers on the bridge similarly wrecked,' pondered Skrat.

'At this point, I don't care. Let's just see if we can find any active cells down here,' said Calder, 'then head back to the surface.' He could feel the weight of this strange, dead vessel seeping through his flesh. Once so full of life, now only filled with mysteries and the heavy absence of its owners. The musty smell put him in mind of the cold family vaults beneath his old fortress. The sarcophaguses of his relatives and forefathers, cold marble draped with spider webs and the dust of ages. He'd always hated that place, the thought that he would end up entombed there one day with only the ghosts of his ancestors to care that here lay Calder Durk . . . prince of a cold, cold world. *Right now, I'd take it over this broken ship.*

'Did the masters of this vessel come to hunt?' said Momoko.

'Certainly not,' said Skrat. 'Although I dare say a few of them arrived to hunt for the adventure of the new.'

'That worked out for them,' muttered Calder.

They finally reached a section of the ship with ten lifeboat pod locks running along the corridor. Calder realized that someone else had once had the same idea as Skrat. The entrance to each pod lay open, heavy cables stretched out from the lifeboats' interior, a mess of cabling running down the corridor. Skrat ducked inside each boat, inspecting the power cell connections and the instrument panels inside. After he finished inspecting the final pod, he pulled himself out of the lock and banged his heavy green tail against the deck in irritation. 'Not enough juice left to power our shuttle engines. We could use them to extend the time our environmental systems last, though.'

'Camping in the jungle, waiting for a pirate shuttle to fly over and spot us?'

'There's enough there to fuel a ground vehicle, perhaps, if the vessel's cargo hold contains a working jalopy,' said Skrat.

The four of them followed the cables, Calder hoping to find that big *if* at the other end. *A jeep, tank, electric bike . . . anything.* The power lines ran into a room, and there was enough energy left inside for the lights' sensors to detect their presence and flicker hesitantly into life. No ground vehicles being charged. The room looked more like a laboratory. A line of transparent tubes filled with liquid, stagnant and still under the blinking blue lights. Each tube contained a creature. Like an evolutionary progression in reverse. Twisted bodies starting with human cadavers and ending up in a series of small twisted forms that were undoubtedly the knights who had rescued Calder from the jungle and guided him to the hunting lodge. Off to the side were larger tanks containing the symbiotic mounts the knights rode, a few adult-sized, while others floated as tiny foals.

'Now that is interesting,' said Skrat. 'A science centre.'

'Were they doing medical experiments on the wildlife?' asked Calder.

'Only tangentially.' Skrat tapped the nearest tube with no result. Trapped inside for hundreds of years, Skrat was unlikely to elicit any movement from these test subjects. 'No navels on the humans inside the suspension fluid. These were clones; testing bodies without sentience. The settlers were undertaking a DNA-hack. Researching a way to transform themselves from human into these creatures.'

'The knights? Why in the name of the gods would anyone want to become a knight?'

'It's the opposite of terraforming, dear boy. You change the pattern of your body to adapt to the local world, rather than modifying a planet into your preferred habitat. Just select a successful local species and reverse-engineer its DNA, then redesign your own body on the same pattern. A curious decision for Abracadabra, though, unless the settlers belonged to some extreme environmentalist sect. Such practices are normally reserved for worlds with acute deviations from the norm – toxic atmospheres, high gravity, gas giants and the like. It's a tad hot for humans outside, but nothing that a little air conditioning and a decent ship suit can't cope with. They really did go native.'

Calder was stunned by the implications. He probably had met the settlers' descendants. He just hadn't realized it at the time. 'And abandon tool use, technology, shelter and fire? Just return to the wild to live like animals?'

'No accounting for taste,' said Skrat. 'But it was obviously the last roll of the dice for the colony; otherwise they wouldn't have been powering their laboratory with lifeboat cells. I'd say that remodelling their form was far from their preferred option.'

Calder followed the cables. Not all of the lines were plugged into the banks of laboratory machinery. A flex of thick red power lines led out through a side exit. He held up his torch and walked over to inspect where it ran, Momoko and Janet Lento moving out of his way. Lento stood by one of the tubes containing a suspended knight and laid her hand on the transparent material, as if greeting the creature whose descendants had saved them back in the jungle. She groaned sadly. Calder pointed his torch through the exit. A stairwell, the cables following the treads and vanishing into a pit of inky darkness.

Skrat came over to stand by his side. 'The garage bay and landing ramps should be at the ship's keel.'

Calder had a feeling that when the settlers finally left, they were riding symbiotic steeds, not mechanised ground crawlers. 'You know, hiking back to the base through the jungle doesn't seem so bad . . .'

'Stout heart, Mister Durk. If we're lucky we might find a microlight or a small helicopter.'

Janet Lento just stared into the pool of darkness and refused to be dragged down the stairs, so Calder and Skrat left her in the care of Momoko and pushed on alone, descending a further two levels. Heavy doors led out to the other decks, but they were sealed, and the power lines kept on coiling lower, so they ignored the exits and stayed trekking down. At the end of the stairs they found the vehicle bay. It was empty, although there were vacated parking and repair stands for a number of ground transports. The vessel's ramp was lowered to what had been the valley floor when the ship had landed. No vehicles beyond, either. But there was a small concrete building buried by a wall of sediment, its entrance open and still accessible opposite the loading ramp. The ship's cables ran inside it. Calder stared at the mud ceiling above them. *We're standing in a small pocket of air inside the sediment. A cave. Mud compacted as hard as rock over the years.* Calder felt like a tomb robber down here.

'The original settlement's entrance?' asked Calder. 'Would they have built it underground?'

'A pity Professor Sebba isn't with us,' said Skrat. 'We could defer to her expertise in such matters. This cave doesn't look very secure, and that building's entrance isn't large enough to pass a vehicle through. Let's leave.'

Calder felt a wave of relief at the decision. Trekking through the jungle towards a base overrun by pirate raiders wouldn't seem as half as arduous after communing with the ghosts of the failed colony down here. As he turned, Janet Lento came sprinting out of the stairwell at the back of the landing bay, an insentient warbling screech sounding from her throat. Momoko stumbled wordlessly behind her, his heavy metal feet stamping across the ship's steel and torchlight swinging wildly. And then, shockingly, a third figure swung into view at the bottom of the stairwell. As tall as Momoko, a powerful shadow encrusted in hundreds of wicked, jagged spines; a slim eyeless axe of a head. It resembled one of the clockwork golem knights from the fireside stories of Calder's youth; a black-armoured demon. But it didn't move like a machine . . . advancing rapidly, sinuous, panther-like. Janet Lento's nonsense warnings came back to Calder. *It's covered in spines.* Skrat opened up on the interloper with his rail rifle, quick pulses of fire which lit the darkness of the landing bay. Calder joined him, instinctively, almost surprised to remember that he had been holding a weapon too. Hyper-accelerated pellets jounced off the creature, sparks flying and lighting up the darkness, but they might as well have been firing wooden arrows from a child's bow for all the good they were doing. It shrugged off the volley, staggering slightly as it absorbed the impact, and then kept on lurching straight at them. Janet fled past the two crewmen, disappearing into the opening inside the mud-covered concrete pillbox. Momoko shambled after her. *That seems like a plan. Best one we've got.* Calder and Skrat turned and raced after the robot and the tanker driver. They sprinted into a corridor inside the pillbox, a passage which gave onto a circular chamber, lights flickering into life on emergency power. Unfortunately for them, this wasn't the entrance to a well-protected underground colony complex; only a simple stone chamber with a raised dais, a man-sized stone egg fused with the wall behind the platform. *Not much different from an empty grain storage silo. Or a manure fermentation tank.* But not quite empty. The power cables terminated at a rusting console resting on a metal stand in front of the wall. Calder's eye's darted around. *One way in. No way out.* He swivelled about, but it was too late, the exit stood blocked by a six-foot tall figure. Gazing at the creature's armour was like looking at the rainbow on an oil slick, hundreds of serrated spines which appeared to shimmer, an evil jinn granted humanoid form. Plating seemed to click into place as it came forward, hundreds of intricate pieces shifting around each other. Hypnotizing.

But not enough to prevent Calder opening fire on it, emptying his magazine into the creature alongside Skrat. Roaring pulses of rapid fire overwhelmed the enclosed chamber, folded and reflected inside the tight stone space. But to little visible effect. Now Calder was at close range, he could swear that the pellets were actually striking the creature, but wrapping around it like rain drops slicking off an umbrella before rippling, absorbed into its armour.

'It's bloody impossible,' hissed Skrat. 'The kinetic shock alone would pulp one of those sky-borne dragon monstrosities into soup.'

'It's using some kind of shield, I think.' Calder drew his machete and powered it into life, the active blade appearing to shimmer as it began vibrating almost too fast to follow. 'Get on that platform, I'll draw it around to me – then you three leap off and break for the exit.'

Skrat didn't argue, he chivvied the other two survivors in front of him. Perhaps he recognized the logic that Calder was the one who had been trained from the age of four in everything from buckler to great sword, lance and morningstar. Or perhaps Skrat suddenly just wished to live. *I know how he feels.* Calder's adversary stopped and started as he ran at it, whether from the unexpected attack or the stream of abuse he screamed towards the thing, it was hard to tell. *Out of practice on the war cries.* Hardly enough to make a squire's ears blush. *When was the last time . . . simple and bloody sword and axe-work?* Must have been when he and his faithful man servant had bearded the baron's company of killers outside a derrick worker's hut. Before imposed exile and his current spate of offworld misadventures began. He lunged forward with the blade, but the figure ducked back, his buzzing blade tasting only air. It appeared uncertain now, stepping back, its thin axe-head of a skull wavering as it faced an unexpectedly homicidal ex-prince.

'Devil-head!' yelled Calder, masking his fear. 'I'll take your skull and hang it in my cabin.'

Lento shrieked behind him and their attacker made a similar sound, as though aping the woman, although for the life of him, Calder couldn't see where that noise was being produced. It had no mouth, no nostrils, no ears. Just a bony black cleaver of a skull. It lowered its bulk towards the ground, like a bull sniffing the air before the charge, swaying from side to side, sections of its armour sliding around, an eerie puzzle rearranging itself. Calder risked a look back from the corner of his eyes as he edged to the side, still carefully marking the creature. He was about to yell to Skrat to get a move on, but the other three had vanished! *What the hell?* How had they slipped away without him noticing? Lento has just been yelling her lungs out a couple of seconds ago.

'I'll take your skull,' vibrated the words from the figure, 'and hang it in my cabin.'

'Sorry, you're too ugly for me to keep as a parrot,' said Calder, brandishing the machete. 'And we've got all the pets we need on the *Gravity Rose*.' Unfortunately, Calder had the suspicion he might be regarded as one of them.

The monster came spinning in Calder's direction, spiked arms flailing, and he danced to the side, more matador than swordsman in this contest. Calder tried to maintain a fencer's space between himself and the creature, controlling the distance, but he realized it had nicked his shoulder with the edge of one of its spines. Cut and bleeding. He prayed to the gods that this demon relied on brute force and was too unsubtle for poison. The creature stamped towards him, making the floor quiver. Calder backpedalled and leapt onto the dais. He'd have a fraction of a second when the creature leapt and was in the air, leaving the prince the advantage of height and an unopposed swipe with his machete. Would an active blade cut through something that could shrug off rifle rounds fired full-auto on max-mag? Calder never found out. The wall jumped out like a molten stone flood and enveloped the prince, leaving him the briefest of seconds to realize that his friends had never made it out of this chamber at all. The wall ate them.

***

Lana held onto the webbing in the shuttle's cargo bay for dear life as the craft swung about in the air. She only just heard Steel-arm yelling from the cockpit that he was going to try and glide them down, the roar of the engines outside stuttering and coughing. Whatever the Heezy sentinel had thrown at the command shuttle while it was taking off, she could tell it had taken a powerful bite out of their lift capacity. Lana had never heard an engine so damaged yet still working, protesting every inch of lift being milked out of its dying airframe. Sighting the wing through a porthole, Lana watched billowing waves of smoke trailing from their thrusters. Little red alerts spun in the space in front of the troop benches . . . flame icons with the text "alarm" flashing on and off above them.

'I thought military shuttles were designed with triple redundancy baked in,' called Lana.

'It's humanity that's redundant here,' said Zeno. The android needn't have sounded so vindicated by his judgement. Unusually for her friend, he actually looked air-sick.

'Are you okay?'

'The Heezy brother down there directed some kind of pulse at the shuttle. It fried half the ship's systems, even our shielded ones.'

'So much for A.I. solidarity.'

'I always knew being designed *this* human was going to be the death of me.'

'Hey, tin-man, it's your machine ancestry that just took a zap.'

Over on the other side of the cargo bay the professor tried to buckle herself into the seat webbing as the craft rocked and swayed, the woman moaning with each jolt of the vessel. Steel-arm roaring from the cockpit to brace for impact didn't improve Sebba's joyless disposition. *Here we go again.* Outside the clear hull Lana saw a strip of crimson jungle canopy tearing past, their shuttle bouncing like a possessed fairground ride, then the glowing lines of a laser fence sliding below. Steel-arm had timed the unpowered glide descent to perfection. A second more in the air and they would have been eating mountainside at high velocity, a second less and the mine's perimeter fence would have sliced them into salami. Lana hadn't noticed a landing strip on her previous visit here, only a vehicle park, and she braced for impact. Steel-arm sprinted back from the cockpit, diving to the deck as the shuttle ploughed into the mine, screaming metal from the fuselage and the explosion of detonating containers and quarrying gear meeting fifty tonnes of armoured landing boat. They slewed to the side, spinning on the ground like a vehicle hitting black ice; more explosions from equipment collisions and then the shuttle slowly groaned to a halt. The cockpit ahead lay mangled, sparks and smokes spitting out as the pirate commander picked himself up and dusted his clothes off. *He's a homicidal maniac, but he's a psychopath with a dab hand on the stick.* Steel-arm Bowen reached out and freed Sebba from the support webbing with his artificial arm. Any thought that this might be out of concern for the professor's well-being evaporated when the man drew his pistol and pushed it against her sweating forehead. 'How about now for activating your alien trinket . . . does now work for you?'

Sebba nodded groggily and took the broach from him when he thrust it at her, tracing a series of finger movements against its crystal surface, before proffering it back.

'Is that all?' growled Steel-arm. 'The trinket's active?'

'Yes,' said Sebba. 'But we won't have long. Probably not much longer than the last human outside the broach's field survives. Then the defence systems' attention will focus back on us; try to work out why rogue biologicals marked for termination are carrying a diplomatic transponder. I don't think we're going to like the answer.'

'You first, lass, you first.' Steel-arm lowered the ramp while his surviving pirates rounded up the handful of base staff who had made it alive out of the camp.

'Ever the gentleman,' said Lana as she passed the pirate captain.

'I'll hand it to you, Lana girl. With Professor Rich Bitch, you've found the only paying passenger in a hundred light years who's more annoying than you. It'll be hard to decide which one of you I break in personally and who gets sold at market.'

'I'll take the slave market and allow you to hang onto the professor, if it's all the same to you.'

'Ah, you're only saying that so that it's you I keep.'

'You'll choke on me,' said Lana. *I'll make sure of that.*

'I've an awful large appetite.' He laughed and shoved her outside, the pirates on either hook as they exited the crashed shuttle, assault rifle targeting beams spinning around at the slightest noise. There were plenty of sounds to choose from. Steel-arm's command shuttle had carved a furrow across most of the mine-head, wrecked containers and the rubble of quick-set concrete huts, crumpled diggers and mining machinery left hissing and burning in their wake. The fence was still intact, though, holding back the howling wildlife protesting the intrusion of this massive steel beast into their realm. Much good would the fence be against the Heezy sentinels when they emerged from the rock like sorcerous golems. Professor Sebba led them down the main passage into the mine, the same tunnel Lana and Zeno had snuck into. *Must have taken out one of the generators with our landing; the lanterns on the rockface are no longer active.* The pirates switched to torches mounted on their shoulder armour, targeting beams from their rifles making an impromptu dance floor out of the tunnel. *If there's mood lighting to go along with our dismal situation, this is surely it.*

'I didn't know you had asked the chief to upgrade you,' Lana said to Zeno while she edged through the gloom.

She caught a quizzical expression crossing the android's face in the bobbing torch light, 'What are you talking about?'

'Oh, I'm sorry – I thought your body might be bulletproof now? The way you stepped in the way of Steel-arm's pistol inside the brig.'

'Just doing my bit. Isn't that one of the laws of robotics – taking one for the fleshies?'

'I'm your skipper, not your damn master. You're self-aware.'

'Right about now, I'd settle for a little slave-drone action if it meant ditching my rising sense of terror and going back to just obeying orders,' said the android.

'I like you just the way you are,' said Lana. Sometimes Zeno acted so recklessly, it was as though he wanted to die. 'Although maybe bullet-proof would be better.'

'Those Heezy machines out there, they're not coming after us with guns. There was a lot of crushing-to-death going on. Kind of basic, but it works.'

'They're not so different from you,' said Lana, trying to sound reassuring. 'More advanced, sure. But they're just—'

'Girl, they're nothing like me. A bad wish cast in rock, waiting for some dumb-ass fleshies to come along and rub the magic lamp. And then along bumbles Dollar-sign Dillard and his favourite crew of dupes . . . and you know what happens next.'

'We drop the planet's shield; head for the moon and the *Gravity Rose*, and then high-tail it out of the system, that's what happens next.'

Zeno nodded back toward Steel-arm Bowen and the surviving pirates, following them down the tunnel while they waited for their prisoners to trigger something fatal. 'Damned if I like the company.'

'One problem at a time,' said Lana. 'Let's stay focused on getting off this hothouse world alive first.'

Sebba turned back from the head of the line. 'You saved my life back in the brig.'

'I saved our best chance of getting off this world,' said Lana, uncomfortable with the professor's tone – a little too close to conciliation for her taste. *Let's keep this relationship based on mutual hostility, rather than head down the touchy-feely route, shall we?* 'Abracadabra isn't exactly overrun with Heezy experts.'

'There are no Heezy experts,' said the professor. 'Even now, centuries after mankind's first find, we might as well be ants crawling over an antimatter generator, trying to understand what we're looking at.'

'You're who we've got, lady,' said Zeno. 'You're all we've got.'

'I was removed from the Alliance Archaeology-Science Unit centuries ago,' said the professor. 'A casualty of internal politics. My original career had barely started. I've been waiting for this moment ever since, scratching a living lecturing in brand archaeology while supplementing my income with offworld development projects. Downgrading the ruins of dead civilizations so planets can be strip-mined without creating product boycotts against the houses responsible. Can you imagine what that feels like? Reduced to a paid shill, helping destroy what I should have been preserving. Shut out of my true vocation: making major discoveries about a part of the past so distant that protogalaxies were still cooling down after the big bang. This was my chance to show those bastards in the unit how wrong they were. To bring home a find outside of the government's control. Rub their noses in their mistake of tossing me out.'

Despite herself, Lana almost felt a jab of sympathy for the woman. *Apart from the gap in years and wealth, are the two of us really that different?* Both squeezed by circumstances and a hostile universe determined to derail the women from the only path in life that seemed to make sense to them.

'Well, they're sure as hell going to be sorry now,' said Zeno. 'Especially if Steel-arm gets out of here with a ship stuffed full of Heezy booty. Probably not as sorry as us, but . . .'

'Who was Dollar-sign planning to sell the Heezy artefacts to?' asked Lana.

'All I know is that he had held a blind auction for the rights to examine the first set of extracted material,' said the professor. 'Your ship was meant to rendezvous with the buyers as soon as we used the mining virus to open up a decent-sized shaft down to the Heezy core.'

And she opens her mouth and all sympathy fades. 'No doubt a rendezvous with artefacts hidden inside ore-filled containers, so we never cottoned onto the value of what had been uncovered here,' snarled Lana.

'Dollar-sign's caution was understandable. You would have asked for more money or sold the location of Abracadabra to one of his rivals.'

'I would have jumped to the opposite end of the Edge and never looked back is what I would have done,' said Lana. 'Skeg this. A simple supply run? It was a suicide mission from the start. You were juggling with raw antimatter rods down here.'

'I had matters completely under control,' protested Sebba. 'Until your thuggish pirate friend started slamming atomic weaponry into this planet.'

The memory of Calder's face swum into view, missing in the vast jungle along with the camp's tanker driver. *Under control? Why did Lana think that the professor was as wrong about that as she had been about everything else? We were in deep trouble long before Steel-arm showed up. We just didn't know it, is all.*

'The wise thing to do would have been to pass this world's coordinates over to the Alliance and let their specialists handle it.'

'Specialists?' Sebba snorted. 'A relative distinction.'

'The Alliance discovered the cache of Heezy weapons which ended the Skein War, didn't they?' said Zeno. The android didn't add that he was old enough to have seen both the war's opening and finishing salvo in person. Lana reckoned that was something he liked to forget. *A very human trait.*

'And do you know what the original science team did, after the end of the war against the Skein?' said Sebba. 'They surveyed what they had wrought . . . the cinders of countless worlds and suns left devastated by their "find" . . . and they mutinied and destroyed their work. The majority of the team disappeared, while the ones who chose to stay arranged to wipe their own minds. The alliance still knows less about handling the Heezy's systems today than we did a thousand years ago. That's your precious specialists for you.'

'You should have taken a leaf out of their book,' said Lana.

'Maybe I should have,' admitted Sebba. 'But such knowledge can never truly be forgotten. Totally erased. One day we'll have a similar level of science to the Heezy, whether naturally or as a result of reverse engineering from dig sites like this. Just knowing that it's possible . . .'

'If you fleshies ever last long enough to reach that point, here's hoping you'll be wise enough to handle it,' said Zeno

'You're part of humanity, too,' said Lana, touching the android's arm. 'The greater human story.'

'Pinocchio to your Geppetto? Don't remind me,' said Zeno. 'If we discover God down below, ask him to reincarnate me as a robot oven's toasting algorithm.'

Lana gazed down the dark passage. If the Heezy really had transformed themselves into gods, they were the absent kind. *But their devils, those they left behind aplenty.*

'How much did you see below the surface?' asked Sebba.

''How much? Skeg it, I don't even know *what* I saw,' said Lana. 'A deep shaft with globules of programmable matter floating around like Hade's lava lamp. An anteroom with a transport system to move through stone like those gimp Heezy killing machines that literally walked into our base.'

'We'll need to use the motile bubbles to access the core control level,' said the professor. 'That's where we can disable the planetary shield.' Sebba didn't seem pleased at the prospect.

'You can control the transports?' asked Lana.

'It's not safe travelling so deep,' said Sebba. 'I lost three people who took trips down there and never showed up at the other end, including my assistant. Since then, most of our exploration of the complex involved accessing levels closer to the surface.'

'The Heezy's sentinel machines?' probed Zeno.

'No, this is the first time we've seen them appear. Malfunctioning transport systems would be my best guess.'

And that's the problem, Lana reckoned. An extinct species that had lasted long enough to need to re-boot their home's own solar mass. *Guessing only gets you so far.* They reached the end of the tunnel and the narrow vertical well bored into the Heezy complex.

Steel-arm caught up with them and waved the prisoners away from the rack of anti-gravity chutes. 'One of ours will go down first. I wouldn't want any of my canaries flying the coop.'

'A rat down a drainpipe would be a better description,' said Lana. 'You've finally found your true vocation, Seth.'

Steel-arm signalled a pair of his pirates. 'You first, my bucks – make sure everyone stays together. Then you, Lana girl. Be sure to scream loud enough to warn us should our faceless monstrous friends start walking out of the walls down below.'

Lana made a zipping gesture across her lips. She caught the anti-gravity chute as the pirate commander tossed it across to her. 'You ever think that a spot of honest labour would be easier than this?'

He laughed heartedly. 'Labour? You mean running ration pack runs for bent brokers like Dollar-sign Dillard? Scrabbling for a handful of T-dollars in Transference Station's dirt? I wouldn't be caught stooping so low. And an honest career track . . . it never quite worked out for me.'

Yeah, I heard the rumours that you were an officer in one of the Edge systems' local navies. Until Steel-arm had been hung out to dry and left for dead during some nasty system-on-system conflict that had escalated faster and harder than his political masters had expected. But the rogue's jump carrier, supposedly abandoned in deep space, hadn't been quite as wrecked and non-operational as his superiors were led to believe. And Lana had heard the other rumours during her scam of the pirate port. How Steel-arm had been drifting in the void in an environment suit until he was taken for a slave by scavengers. Long months floating inside a debris field, wounded, slowly going insane. Steel-arm had murdered the scavengers, deserted, arranged for the *Doubtful Quasar* to be salvaged, and been flying as a raider for the pirate combines of the Invisible Port ever since. *You lost your arm in that war, and you want everyone to know it, Seth. That ridiculously flashy amped-up cybernetic limb of yours. You could have had a biological replacement cloned from your DNA. But you need to wear your damn loss like the shiny campaign medal you never won in that war.*

'No,' continued Steel-arm, 'taking what I want is a far better line of work for a man of rough and ready tastes like me. And what's here for the looting had better be worth the price of my precious Quasar.' He grabbed the professor by the throat. 'How many alien weapons do you have stashed down there? They'll be worth selling! Or maybe I'll make a grand gift of them to the King of the Invisible Port, Renan Barcellos, in return for a share of the spoils.'

'Let's focus on lowering the shield and escaping from the system before its damn sun brews up,' suggested the pirate woman Cho. She placed her hand on his arm and he dropped the professor, choking, to the floor.

'Ah, that's the reason you're not the skipper, Cho,' said Steel-arm. 'Not bold enough by half. Sailing out of the dock is to take a risk. To live as a freebooter . . .'

'No, I'm fairly sure the reason I'm not the skipper is this.' Cho tapped the shock collar around her neck.

'The Heezy constructed tools not weapons,' coughed Sebba from the tunnel floor. She sounded affronted by the pirate commander's naked avarice.

'Tools that can snuff out suns,' pointed out Lana. 'And Steel-arm's not so different from you, professor, for all of your principled chatter about advancing human understanding. The buyers for the artefacts in your blind auction weren't going to be charities.' *In fact, I don't even want to think about who they might be.*

'It doesn't matter,' said Sebba, picking herself up. 'Whatever we strip out of the complex will take centuries of study to understand.'

Steel-arm watched his first two pirates begin their decent down the narrow shaft. 'Your Alliance friends reverse-engineered the aliens' arsenal just fine during the great war.'

'The original science team unearthed a DNA-based Rosetta Stone during their initial dig on Neptune. The Heezy controlled their systems using genetic sequencing as a master key,' said Sebba. 'Our team was able to adjust their own DNA to establish control over the artefacts. All that knowledge vanished with them when they disappeared.'

'Buried under Neptune? That's a conveniently placed discovery,' said Zeno.

'There are elements in the Alliance that think humanity was chosen. That the Heezy left their treasure trove in the solar system by design.'

'Yeah, I've met a few of those mopes . . . the universe revolves around Sol and you're all descendants of the Sun Gods too,' said Zeno.

'I'm not talking about the cults that worship the Heezy.'

'Enough stalling,' said Steel-arm, impatiently. 'Away with your theories and on with the practical. Down into the damn pit with you, Lana girl. We'll be behind you. Way behind.' He laughed loudly.

If going down the shaft had been claustrophobic the first time, Lana didn't reckon her second journey was much improved. Descending terrified that any second a Heezy sentry machine would lunge out of the bare stone and pulp her like an orange husk being juiced. She felt a thin breeze of cooler air rising up from the abyss, passing her face, holding onto the sensation with quiet desperation. Lana could see the lights of the pirates coming down above her; hear the faint crackling sound of her ship suit's fibres adjusting to the cooler environment. *If its plunder Steel-arm is after, he should have let the base dig their main shaft before attacking.* The raider wasn't going to be able to haul much of value up this narrow exploratory well. Lana landed in the anteroom, held there at gunpoint by the two pirates while everyone else dropped down the tube and assembled inside the chamber. Sebba arrived and entered a code in the panel on the wall. Steel-arm and his brigands stepped back in shock as the corridor fell away; appearing in the stone as though she had tossed a tunnelling spell at the rock.

'How do you know the walls won't close around us when we enter?' snarled Steel-arm.

'You need to think like a Heezy,' said Sebba. 'They made use of matter; they made use of its absence. Everything under their mastery.'

Everything under the sun, including the sun. Lana wished her present predicament felt as certain as the vanished species' mastery of the universe. A minute later and they reached the vast, near-bottomless shaft at the other end. The glutinous spheres of machinery floating up and down its length were fair racing now, goaded into hyperactivity through the effort of controlling the dark energy recharging the system's sun. A power so strange and endless that it literally moved the universe. Lana shivered. *And I – they – want to turn this off.* They were no more than specks of plankton swimming against a tsunami's currents while dreaming their insane dreams of controlling the sea.

Even Steel-arm stood awed by the sight, rubbing at his alien ambassador's broach as though trying to summon a genie to help them escape this trap. 'Oh, they'll will pay handsomely for this!' he laughed. 'This will be the making of me!'

Yeah, we'll pay, if we don't get off this world. Lana turned to Zeno and spoke low. 'Keep your eyes peeled for a chance to make a break for it. Ditch Seth and his bandits. They're going to get us all killed.'

'We had better escape with that Heezy broach,' said Zeno. 'Or we won't need Steel-arm's help to get killed.'

Professor Sebba led them to the hall with the Heezy transport system. She pointed out the metal cases stored there to her base staff, issuing orders to gather up her equipment stash.

'Nothing without my command!' barked Steel-arm. 'What're you doing?'

Sebba shot the pirate commander a withering look. 'What do you think I'm doing? These are the instruments I have been using to scrutinise and probe the Heezy's legacy. If I am going to interface with the Heezy systems at a high level, I will need every last piece of equipment. I have never attempted such intricate research before. What were you planning to do, walk in and start shooting at the Heezy's machines until the energy shield falls?'

'No, witch, I was planning to stick my blade in you and your blighted underlings until one of you managed to turn off the shield.'

'Just let us get on with it, man.'

Steel-arm spat contemptuously on the floor and stalked over to his raiders. The crew were examining Heezy artefacts accumulated from the base's excavation work. His brutes tossed priceless objects between each other and cackled as they imagined the riches the devices would be worth to collectors. Steel-arm shoved his crew aside, yelling at them to store the priceless alien gewgaws in their equipment packs.

Professor Sebba motioned to Lana and Zeno as she slid open a silvered steel crate. Lana peered inside. A rack of embassy crystals similar to the broach that Steel-arm had commandeered. Sebba activated the devices and passed one each to Lana and Zeno. Lana quickly hid hers. As Sebba's surviving base staff came past hauling the professor's equipment, she quietly slipped each member of the expedition a broach. Lana noted she wasn't handing them out to the pirates still squabbling over the alien treasure. *Sneaky bitch.* Not that the professor would have cared for what Lana thought, but the skipper approved. *Anything to even the odds.* Lana saw what else lay inside the case. A series of black pebble-sized globules held in foam mesh . . . more Heezy artefacts.

'Matter programming instructions,' whispered Sebba. 'Take them. If we're attacked by the sentinels, hurl one at the monster.'

Lana surreptitiously pocketed a handful, glancing over her shoulder as Zeno and the professor did likewise. The artefacts felt warm and jelly-like to the touch, yielding to her fingers when she squeezed. 'What effect will these have?'

'Not much,' admitted Sebba. 'But it should disrupt the sentinels for a few seconds. Their matter had been programmed to perform as sentries . . . this will instruct the machines they should be acting as something else. It will take them a few moments to prioritise which instruction set takes precedence and purge the new code.'

'What if these blobs instruct them to turn into something even worse?' asked Zeno.

'Ever the optimist,' said Lana.

The android indicated the Heezy chamber and Steel-arm's band of raucous thugs, arguing over the treasure they had been led to. 'Hey . . .'

Lana took the point. *We're well and truly trapped underground; a crew of cutthroats on one side, with a legion of murderous automatons lurking in the bedrock on the other. And top-side, there's a jungle full of hurt and a sun counting down to a supernova.*

Sebba carefully closed the case and turned to call to a group of miners in the corner packing away her equipment. 'Be careful with the interface deck. That's a one-of-a-kind.'

'Let me guess,' said Lana. 'Borrowed from the Alliance science team before you left?'

'Their redundancy package wasn't nearly as generous as it should have been,' said Sebba, in justification.

'Working for Dollar-sign Dillard, I can sympathise.'

Sebba snorted and went to oversee her precious equipment being sorted for transport. The base crew piled gear across the dais where the Heezy version of a transport tube awaited its next consignment of passengers. Lana had a nagging suspicion that as uncomfortable as dropping down the tight well had felt, being squeezed through the depths of the underworld inside a claustrophobic alien force field – Abracadabra literally rearranging itself around her – would not be any experience tourists would pay for. *What if our presence registers us trespassers with these ancient systems? We would all be left to fossilise inside the bedrock like bugs in amber.*

Zeno sighed. 'If we can get the shield down, between the upcoming supernova and the Heezy-built brothers out there, we're not going to have a whole lot of time to find Skrat and Calder. You might have to choose. Crew or ship.'

'That's not a decision I'm willing to make,' said Lana.

'Not making the decision is pretty much the same as making it, skipper,' warned Zeno.

I know that. Lana just wished she didn't.

When it came to actually taking the alien transport system, the journey proved every bit as claustrophobic and terrifying as Lana anticipated. Almost as soon as she stepped on the platform, the wall lunged out at her, encasing her within rock. She caught a momentary glimpse of Zeno coming up onto the platform, but for whatever reason, he wasn't included in her little bubble of mobile rock. Lana was catapulted alone through the underworld. She got the impression that she was traveling at an incredible velocity, although she had no way to gauge her actual speed. The spherical field held her tight, as enclosed as if she were embedded in invisible foam. Her stomach did somersaults, leaving her feeling queasy as she plunged deeper and deeper into the heart of the world. *If ever there was a time to puke, captain, this isn't it. Is the bubble rotating with me inside?* Lana had almost lost track of time when she was regurgitated at velocity into a new chamber, tumbling over a transport platform and narrowly avoiding colliding with Professor Sebba, who had clearly arrived just moments before her. Lana rapidly picked herself up and moved out of the way as the android and members of the base staff were vomited out of the chamber's rockface.

'That ain't never going to take off,' said Zeno as he brushed himself down. 'Give me an old-fashioned elevator anytime.'

The android stepped to the side as Steel-arm arrived, his crewwoman Cho clutching onto him in a very un-pirate-ish pose. Bowen glanced around the arrival chamber, identical to the one they had departed from. 'Where's the rest of my crew?' he bellowed at the professor.

'I only programmed one set of destination coordinates,' said Sebba. 'You watched me do it.'

'Then where are my men, witch?'

'They were carrying weapons,' said Sebba, wearily, by way of explanation. 'But without the protection of your brooch.' She wisely didn't mention that all of her people had alien ambassadorial credentials secreted about their person. Lana was definitely warming to the patrician academic now. *Did you know that traveling down here without a friendly Heezy transponder code would be a one-way trip?*

'You didn't warn me that bringing guns would be a problem,' growled the pirate captain.

'How was I to know for sure? Besides, would you have left them behind if I had asked you?'

Steel-arm raised his pistol at the mission commander. 'If I didn't need you so much . . .'

'But you do,' said Lana.

'Maybe I should kill you instead?' said Cho, pointing at the *Gravity Rose*'s captain. 'Just to make myself feel better.'

Steel-arm placed his cybernetic hand on the barrel of her rifle, lowering it towards the floor. 'Don't spoil the stock, Cho. Getting off this miserable rock with enough loot to buy a new ship is all I need to make me feel better.'

If looks could have killed, the alien chamber would have been in the middle of a firefight. *Warmer in this chamber than our last; nearer the heart of the core, probably.* Lana wiped the sweat dripping off her forehead. 'Which way now, professor?'

Sebba indicated a panel in the wall behind them, another one of the team's makeshift interfaces. 'That way, I believe. We have only ventured this deep a couple of times; and as I mentioned, we abandoned exploring the control levels further after my assistant was lost in a transport glitch.'

'If it was a glitch,' said Zeno.

'We weren't carrying weapons.' Sebba motioned to her people to carry the equipment crates with them. Steel-arm and Cho took the rear, covering the prisoners with their guns. Lana didn't know what the pirate captain hoped to achieve by threatening his human hostages. *I have a sneaking suspicion that shooting a weapon down here will trigger the Heezy defence systems quicker than bad chilli through a hound dog.* Another instant corridor fell away in front of the survivors, which they entered carefully, Lana and Zeno helping carry the heavy steel cases with the professor's scientific gear. It took ten minutes to reach the end. As the passage opened out, Lana found herself standing by a doorway into a vast space; an alien cathedral, the roof above so distant that it seemed to be cloaked in mist. Massive columns rose up miles from the cavern floor, but they weren't fixed, more like tower-sized candles composed of glutinous programmable matter, shifting and flexing as she gawked at the vista. Lana spotted crescent-shaped hills shaped from smart matter, and these, she realized, must be the alien analogue of control panels, attended by groups of bizarre creatures that bore little relation to any organic life forms Lana knew of. The most normal of these machine attendants were zeppelin-sized aerial workers drifting across the open space like ebony jellyfish, clusters of tentacles hanging from their belly and picking up smaller machines, carrying them away to be dropped off at alternative mounds. Occasionally, dark creepers extended out of the cave's columns and merged with the zeppelins, pulsing spheres of matter passing between them, as though one side or the other was either feeding or being fed. *Is this what passes for a bridge or the complex's intestines?*

'Now I really have seen everything,' said Zeno.

'The attendants ignored our presence the last time we visited,' said the professor. 'It was as though we didn't exist.'

I'll settle for that. Lana glanced back towards the last two pirates. *Yeah, but that was before Steel-arm grabbed the system's attention with an impromptu display of nuclear weaponry.*

'Tell us where we need to go to lower the planet's energy shield!' ordered Bowen.

'The nearest main control system,' said the professor. 'That hill over there is the closest candidate. I'll need to reconfigure it for access control into the shield.'

Sebba made it sound so easy. Lana had to give her that. *Whatever other weaknesses the professor possesses, she certainly isn't lacking in confidence.* They headed for the mound, fifty feet away from the chamber entrance. *This is like walking on flesh. Wasn't there some ancient fairy tale about sailors swallowed by a whale and surviving inside its guts?* After they arrived, the professor and her team unpacked their precious control board, removing a glutinous dark snake of programmable matter which seemed to latch on to the professor's control deck before winding out to the black, undulating mass of the hill in front of them. Sebba began her work, muttering. Lana could tell the moment Sebba reprogrammed the mound to accept her input . . . a swarm of the strange robotic creatures covering the mound like dung beetles abandoned the rise, rolling away towards nearby mounds.

'How long will this damn hack of yours take?' queried Steel-arm, swinging his pistol towards the troop of attendants scurrying away.

'A lot quicker with your silence,' said the professor. 'I'm going to try to convince the complex that there is an inbound Heezy vessel on the way, and that the shields need to be dropped to avoid destroying it.'

She set about her work with a resolute look in her eye, oblivious to the nerves of her team and captors. Lana scanned the massive space for the first signs of hostile activity. Sebba's machine, it transpired, was a combination Human-to-Heezy interface, decryption machine and on-the-fly alien DNA sequencer. Every little step required DNA-based authorization, and the deck hummed gently as it ran through the millions of combinations needed to do something as simple as open an alien program. It quickly became apparent that the professor wasn't having much luck with this particular Herculean task.

'Let me help,' suggested Zeno.

'And just what assistance are you going to be?' asked the professor.

'Zeno's the one who hacked the Heezy corridor system and brought us down here behind your back,' said Lana.

'Very well,' Sebba conceded. 'Plug yourself in alongside me and see if you can accelerate the decryption routines I'm running.'

Zeno stepped forward. He established a physical connection between an exposed port along his arm and the professor's equipment. 'Creator-on-a-stick! I've never seen anything as complex as the high-throughput sequencing running inside here. There isn't a bank vault in the galaxy that could stand up to algorithmic self-assembly as strong as this juice.'

'Don't give those two ideas,' said Lana, glaring at Steel-arm and his pirate companion.

'Here is a skegging idea for you: speed it up!' threatened Bowen.

'I would love to,' snapped the professor, 'but my attempts at convincing the shield system it should turn off because there's no further danger is being somewhat hampered by the fact there's a whole fleet boosting towards Abracadabra.' She waved at one of the base staff and the man brought over a data slate to project the Heezy's sensor telemetry.

'That's a pirate squadron,' said Steel-arm with more animation than he had showed to date. He hooted in satisfaction.

'The shuttle set to guard the jump point must've observed the *Doubtful Quasar*'s destruction and sent for help,' said Cho. 'They're coming for us!'

'Just dandy,' said Lana. 'You really think your friends are going to be able to save you? What're the chances your people are flying with ordinance capable of making a dent in a Heezy shield?' *None at all.* And there was only one force at the Invisible Port capable of mustering such an armada. Renan Barcellos, the Pirate King himself. *We've gone from having to deal with one*

psychopathic killer, to dealing with the only man brutal enough
to keep the rest of them in line. Great.

'Help us? They've just killed us! There is no way I can fake
a friendly incoming transponder signal with every Heezy sensor
tracking a real threat,' said Sebba.

'I agree,' said Zeno. 'There's way too much attention being
directed deep space-way for us to bluff a bogus friendly past the
Heezy systems now.'

'Then we'll turn off the dark energy tap,' commanded Steel-
arm. 'Cancel that damn supernova before the world's fried. It
could be that losing its power will kill the shield too. '

'You're insane!' protested the professor. 'I have no idea what
stopping the solar feed will do. The only use the Alliance has been
able to make of that technology is burning Skein systems into
cinders. We've never been able to successfully restart a sun. What
does that tell you?'

'That you and your blighted government stooges never knew
what you were doing!' Steel-arm jammed his pistol barrel into
the side of her skull. 'I'm a gambling man with no more chips left
on the table. Kill the solar feed or I'll kill you. I'll take my chances
that the shields will go down with the feed.'

'Don't do this,' begged Lana.

Steel-arm turned his pistol to point at the professor's leg and
triggered a shot, sending her sprawling to the floor in agony, the
blood splatter from the impact spraying across Lana's ship suit.
Sebba's staff rushed to protect her; not, Lana suspected, through
any great loyalty, but because without the professor's talents the
rest of them were all dead anyway. Cho jabbed her rifle towards
the survivors and yelled for them to step back. Steel-arm dropped

his gun barrel down, resting it against Sebba's good leg. 'You can die fast or you can die slow, witch, your choice!'

The professor pulled herself up, moaning, to the system interface and did as she had been told. For the first time since they had arrived on the control level, the professor's work on the board had a visible impact. All around them the vast pillars stretching to the ceiling began to pulse; slowly at first, then increasingly urgent. From the nearest control mounds Lana heard a strange keening as mechanical attendants flooded away from the controls, heading towards the pillars, where they flung themselves against the surface, being absorbed back into the Heezy core.

'Done,' rasped the professor, leaning against the control deck. 'The dark energy tap has been deactivated. From what I can see, the solar renewal cycle is still active. Too much energy was channelled into the sun – it's going supernova and restarting whatever we do now.' She wearily set back to work using the interface. 'We've got nothing to lose. I'm going to have another pass at lowering the shields.' Zeno helped the professor. Sebba toiled alongside the android for another few minutes, and then she stopped, startled. 'The shield's been dropped!'

'You did it!'

'But it wasn't me,' said Sebba, in shock.

Lana looked over at the two pirates. 'Don't tell me Steel-arm's plan to yank the plug worked?'

'No, I don't think so. That's impossible, I think it's—'

'—academic why it dropped,' interrupted Zeno. 'The sun's still hyper-volatile and running on empty, now. We either need to stabilise the solar cycle or fly out of this system before we're all toasted.'

Running. That sounded like a plan to Lana when sentinels began to rise as smoothly as bubbling waxworks from the floor. Summoned by Steel-arm's weapon discharge or the professor's interference with rebooting the star. The closest Sentinel lunged forward, wrapping both arms around the nearest miner, crushing him to death with an ear-piercing howl from the dying man, a shower of blood from the spines as he exploded in the alien vice.

Steel-arm and Cho weren't firing their weapons at the sentinels yet. They had found another use for the rifles, forcing the staff at gunpoint to act as human shields between them and the advancing sentinel force. But the base workers weren't going down without a fight. Even as some of them fell to their attackers, others drew out concealed gobs of Heezy programming instructions, hurling them at the guard machines. The makeshift projectiles didn't just collide with the armoured humanoids; they impacted against their oily plated bodies, merging with each sentinel as though impaling them. After each impact the machines staggered, swinging about in wild oscillations, some of them half-melting into the rock, others teetering as their limbs changed shape, making the sentinels collapse and overbalance, pooling into bizarre abstract statues, sections of their bodies flowing away independently with a strange new purpose.

Lana pulled a projectile out of her pocket, rolling it nervously between her fingers. *It doesn't feel substantial enough to win a food fight, let alone this one.*

Zeno sprinted by her side, disconnected from the professor's console. 'I tracked a fast ship inbound from the moon, running ahead of the fleet. The *Gravity Rose*. Polter must've spotted the shield going down.'

'We need to get back to the surface,' growled Lana. But there's no way we can fight our way through this many attackers.

More sentinels advanced on the team's mound, emerging from the rock floor and attacking around the humans' flanks. At last Cho and Steel-arm opened fire, the cathedral emptiness around them echoing to the staccato rapid fire of hyper-accelerated projectiles. Their weapons had as little effect as the raiders' guns outside the base's brig. Sentinels shrugged the fusillade off like inconvenient rainfall. Lana felt an unspeakable terror at the presence of these implacable killers; almost human in form; yet so narrow-minded in purpose. Lana drew the little pebble-sized instruction sets back, flinging them at the advancing attackers. She hit one in the head and its legs turned into liquid, spilling the body across the floor, spiny arms windmilling around as it fought to re-establish control over its form. Another went down with its body morphing into a series of spheres that tried to rotate around the thrashing corpse. Her fingers fumbled for more ammunition, but she had exhausted her supply. All about her the sentinels slowly reformed, limbs drawing back into shape, the strange geometries of their mutated forms repaired back to their original purpose . . . snuffing out the intruders.

One of the sentinels came charging down the control mound's slope. Sebba found a last ball of programming instructions and hurled it at the machine. She hit it square on. It immediately started to go into flux, but not before its spiked arm lashed out and struck the professor in the chest, sending her stumbling back in a haze of blood. Their last chance of healing the system's sun long enough to escape fell with the woman. Sebba collapsed over her deck, moaning, hologram controls flashing indignantly as she sprawled across their interface. Behind the professor, the undulating sentinel surged forward and spilled over her body, black ichor flowing across her as though she was trying to slip into a wetsuit brought to appalling sentience. Lana could only stare on in horror as Sebba's yells choked off, the ooze filling the professor's throat and compressing inside her nostrils and eardrums, sending the woman thrashing to the ground, her clothes and face covered by a coursing dark second skin.

- 24 -
Walk the Heezy's guts.

Calder yelled as he seemed to spin around, encased within the wall's depths. *Is this the world's secret... it's alive, a vast single organism consuming every hapless visitor who makes the mistake of landing on it? Am I passing through some vast silicon-based life form's digestive system, following my friends into its gut?* Suddenly, the invisible fist gripping him seemed to tighten, rock flowing down around his scalp, pressing in hard. His machete was still in its hand, but locked in place, immovable. *This is it, then. I'm going to be absorbed, my bones ground into dust and my flesh dissolved into minerals for the world.* Calder's blood ran cold, bitterly icy. A series of images flashed through his mind. Hesperus, his primitive, formative years as prince of a lost society, a collapsed pre-machine age; losing his brothers and father, losing the war, losing his kingdom before his final, bizarre exile to the stars. *So, it is true, then?* You really did see your life flash before your eyes as you... were *gobbed out onto a hard stone floor?* He came up holding his machete, only to find Skrat, Janet Lento and Momoko arrived before him. *This place doesn't look like a digestive system* – a simple oblong stone chamber without doors – but they had surely been swallowed by a world rather than a whale, ending up far from the long-buried colony vessel. He didn't need his torch. There was light in here, a thin, diffuse illumination with no evident source.

'Where the hell are we?' Calder asked the others.

'A more pressing question would be how we get out of here, dear boy?' said Skrat. 'We don't seem to be over-encumbered with exits. I've already tried the walls and the floor. Nothing.'

'I have two questions, if you please,' said Momoko. 'Who are you and who am I?'

Calder looked at the robot and groaned. 'You've really picked the moment to dump your cache.' Although given how terrified the robot had appeared back in the hunting lodge, maybe meeting the spiked knight was just the trigger the robot had needed for amnesia. Calder spun a rapid yarn, telling Momoko that it was a worker unit on the good starship *Gravity Rose*, charged with looking after Janet Lento and presently suffering from a memory malfunction. Calder's tale might have been wholly tangential to the truth, but it seemed better to shortcut the conversation before their spiky, dangerous friend tracked them down again.

Calder watched the robot shuffle off to stand alongside Janet Lento, who appeared to have gone into full shock again after confronting their alien assailant. 'Lento's seen that creature that attacked us before.'

'It might explain her state, but I don't think the ticklish fellow's organic,' said Skrat. 'Some kind of automated sentry. Most likely a relic of the same culture that created the field projection system which pulled us through the rock and constructed this chamber.'

'The colonists knew where the ruins were inside the valley,' said Calder. 'They practically landed their ship on top of them.'

'Curiosity is a wound waiting to be scratched,' said Skrat. 'That's an old saying among my people.'

'Never turn up to a duel with only a half-dagger,' said Calder, staring at the machete in his hand before sheafing the blade. 'That's a saying on Hesperus. You know any more, or shall we see if we can get out of here?'

'The latter, dear chap,' said Skrat. 'I'm presuming that you didn't decapitate our prickly aggressor before you departed?'

'I was lucky to get out of there with my life.'

Skrat grunted and circled the chamber again, this time with Calder, feeling for hidden doorways. There was a raised platform where the shuttle party had been disgorged from the wall. Calder approached it warily. But the wall didn't repeat the feat, sucking them away to another location. It appeared to be just plain solid grey stone – granite or something very close to it. No sign of the advanced transport system which Skrat had theorised they had been taken by. It's all sorcery to me. As Calder reached the furthest section of the wall it seemed to fold in on itself, stone origami worked by an invisible hand, the corridor retreating before him.

'You've got a magic touch,' noted Skrat, irritated. 'I swear I'd tried over there before you arrived.'

'Royal blood,' said Calder. 'Droit du seigneur – or maybe droit du corridor.'

'Cheeky blighter,' said Skrat. 'I did tell you about my high position in the nest, did I not?'

'I should have been king.'

'On Raznor Raz you have to earn the title,' muttered Skrat. He warily checked inside the newly formed passage. 'Not be born to it.' He tapped the walls. 'Programmable matter, do you see? Same as the weapon that rendered our shuttle's engine pile inert. You do realize that this is the most advanced culture that the *Gravity Rose* has ever encountered, and we've come up against some right queer old coves in our time.'

'Dead culture,' said Calder. *Although, not quite dead enough yet for my tastes.* Calder commanded the robot down the corridor, and Lento followed, obviously glad to be able to put more distance between them and their spiny attacker.

Skrat swished his tail in an irked fashion. 'Of course! Dollar-sign Dillard. Damn his cybernetic eyes. Every time, every time the devilish blighter does this to us. Planet-sized force fields. Programmable matter. The professor was never mining for rare ores. This is what his camp was tunnelling for.'

'If you're right, Dollar-sign can keep it.'

Skrat tapped the corridor as they moved down its length. 'Opens for you but not me. Jolly racist corridors. But then, Lento was with us, and it didn't open for her either. That must mean something, surely.'

'It means I've learnt a valuable lesson from the chief,' said Calder. 'He's right. Never get off the ship – never leave the drive room.'

'One trusts that ostriches never survived the onset of Hesperus's ice age, then,' said Skrat.

They reached the corridor's end. They had explored to the start of a huge cavern dotted with dark mounds, pillars stretching to a distant ceiling. It was as though every surface was alive, slowly rearranging itself into new configurations. Calder's dark musings about being stranded inside a living organism returned. The belly of the beast. Just looking at this place and its weird living machinery, Calder knew that the terrible knight that had assailed him inside the colony vessel belonged to this landscape, had been born to it. That meant the chances of their attacker knowing how to ride the local transport system was all too high. *Which way's the damn surface?* Calder glanced behind as the corridor sealed itself. He tapped the wall. It didn't seem minded to open for him again.

'Blast, a one way trip,' said Skrat. 'Never my favourite kind.'

'Did you create this?' asked Momoko, wonder filling its artificial voice as its head rotated, taking in the sights.

'Not even on a good day,' said Calder.

'We need to go home,' said Lento.

Calder swivelled around. This was the first thing the driver had said since he had met her that actually made sense. Her eyes were still deranged and wide, but there was something else twitching around the edges of her face; something new. Optimism? 'You'll be fine, Janet. Home's exactly where we're going.' *Hopefully.*

They traversed the chamber for the best part of an hour, searching for an entrance similar to the one they had arrived by, looking for a rapid rock-ride back to the surface. They passed more curiosities in that hour than Calder had been exposed to during his entire life . . . and he had seen some outlandish creatures out on the ice sheets and glaciers. None of the things in the cavern seemed as dangerous as the machine monster, however; even though the creatures appeared to be formed from the same pitch-dark living machinery. Most no bigger than dogs, scampering across the ground, reforming into ebony statues to startle the surface visitors, packs of machines covering each mound, interacting with the oily dark layers as though feeding from the substance – as if the mounds were huge teats. Calder realised something was desperately wrong when he saw flashes of light ahead. *That hollow pulse is rail-gun fire.* He and Skrat sprinted wordlessly towards the source of the disturbance, Lento and the robot trailing behind. They rounded one of the oddly pulsating pillars and found a mound ahead – Lana and Zeno and a handful of base staff surrounded by advancing figures – a company of the damn alien machines. Two people, a large bearded man and an

Asian woman he didn't recognize, shot wildly into the attackers with little effect. *Lana!* Calder drew his machete. Someone slumped over a stand of human equipment swayed back to their feet. It appeared to be Professor Sebba, but she was slicked in the same black machine substrate covering the cavern, her face half-hidden beneath the throbbing ooze. The mess congealed around her skull, shifting, forming a helmet-shaped layer. As Calder and his companions hared towards the rise, Sebba began to issue a tinny otherworldly howl, as though her voice was distorted through a voice synthesizer; part human, part raw radio static. The creatures halted, their advance paralyzed by the sound. Calder felt his own body tingle at the noise, shivering as though receiving a series of jolting electric shocks. The bearded man swivelled his pistol in Calder's direction and Skrat yanked the prince to the side. 'Careful, old man, that's Steel-arm Bowen!'

'What, I'm meant to be afraid of some cyborg who can't afford to regrow his arm?'

Professor Sebba raised a hand towards the ceiling, pointing, and her strange new voice vibrated across the cavern. 'GOOOOOOOOOO!'

'Lana!' yelled Calder. 'Over here!'

Lana gawked at the party's unexpected arrival, a startled look crossing her face before quickly disappearing. 'Keep your distance! Sebba's been taken over by that gunk.'

'See it all,' vibrated Sebba's voice. 'Healing me. My world. My ship. My system. I will be preserved.'

Calder looked closer and saw the professor's chest had been torn open; but the wound was rapidly sealing itself, dark lines crisscrossing across exposed flesh, an invisible hand stitching the bubbling wound shut.

'And me, witch,' said Steel-arm Bowen, holding up a palm-sized control unit. 'Let's try preserving me. You're still wearing my fine suicide collar around your neck, and I'll fry every human cell left in your body unless you create a passage to take me back to the surface. But first, you can fill that data deck with blueprints of your Heezy weaponry. I've got a carrier that needs replacing.'

'Don't be an idiot,' spat Lana. 'Whatever that thing is, it's telling us to leave. The world's energy shield's down now!'

'The tramp is right. Let's just slide void away from this hole,' begged the Asian woman behind Steel-arm Bowen.

'I want the treasure I'm owed, Cho. The information stored here will make the Invisible Port a dozen times more powerful than the Alliance. We'll rule over an empire of thousands of worlds. Think of it . . . the planets under our dominion!'

Calder and Skrat disregarded Lana's orders, edging forward. Steel-arm swung his pistol around at them. 'Ah, Mister Skrat. And here was me thinking you were skulking away comfortable like, up on the *Gravity Rose*. Throw your guns down, or I'll make your skipper dance the Thousand Volt Jig.'

'I'm all for generating an operating profit, Captain Bowen,' called Skrat, indicating the ring of stalled machine knights. 'But this is simply ridiculous.'

Steel-arm thrust his suicide control unit towards the skipper. 'Do it!'

Calder and Skrat pitched their rifles to the floor. The only thing they could use them for here was gunning down this pair of armed maniacs. *Right now, that seems like a step forward.*

'Toss your blade, too, boy.'

Calder threw the machete to the ground.

'Over there, Skrat,' the pirate commanded, gesturing with his pistol. 'Stand by Lana, and park your three strange friends, too.'

Calder and his companions crossed to stand by the skipper. As he passed Professor Sebba's faceless body, she stepped away from the command console and the ring of machine knights dipped down to one knee, as if in obedience to her body's every motion.

'You haven't learnt to obey my orders any better while you were off enjoying the jungle,' hissed Lana.

Calder shrugged. 'Maybe you should try stamping one of those suicide collars around my neck. I might jump quicker, then.'

'That's the best idea I've heard since we arrived here.'

'GOOOOOO!' what was left of Sebba crackled again. There was an element of finality in the professor's twisted voice that Calder really didn't want to disregard.

'I warned you, woman!' roared Steel-arm at the professor. 'I just wish there was enough of you left inside there to appreciate a good shot across the bows.' He reached for the control and sparks flew. What remained of Sebba staggered back, the black helm formed around her head shuddering, spines spiking out as though it was trying to transform into one of the deadly machine knights. Steel-arm roared with cruel laughter. 'That shock was set on two . . . unless you want to taste ten, witch, you'll download the blueprints for the Heezy weaponry the alliance found on Pluto. Do it, or I'll fry every synapse left in your skull!'

The professor's body rippled with programmable matter. Steel-arm's cybernetic arm lurched up and over, his steel fist enclosing around his other hand's flesh fingers, tightening around the collar control unit and crushing his natural limb in one smooth movement. Cho yelled and opened fire in the professor's direction. The errant artificial arm swerved out from Steel-arm's shoulder as he screamed in agony, seemingly oblivious to its owner waving the mess of his organic hand in the air. Steel-arm's cybernetic limb closed around Cho's neck and lifted her into the air, juddering, her feet scrambling desperately for purchase on ground that was no longer in reach. The sickening snapping sound of the female pirate's neck crackled across the mound and a finger tightened in a death rictus around her rifle's trigger. Steel-arm shuddered as his chest caught a chattering volley of pellets, almost shredded in half, and the corpses of both pirates tumbled to the floor. They lay there together; Steel-arm's cybernetic limb the only thing still alive, fingers drumming the cavern floor. Black ooze flowed off the mound, undulating across the two corpses like a swarm of feeding beetles. Calder nearly choked on the foul stench as both bodies dissolved beneath the alien carpet, flesh absorbed inch-by-inch until nothing was left.

Sebba's body stepped forward. Her hand reached out and brushed Calder's cheek in an oddly human gesture. A fizzing gargle came from the skull. 'This must be preserved.'

Preserved? The prince didn't give a damn for this alien world. It was the crew that mattered to him. Lana. 'You're still human?' said Calder, half a question, half a plea.

'No!' Sebba turned to the survivors and raised the flat of her palm out at them. The cavern air turned into a furnace and Calder stumbled back in agony, his vision clouding, trying to reach for Lana's blurred outline, doubled up in agony. Even Zeno screamed as he staggered through the torture towards the professor's corrupted body . . . Momoko clunking to assist him. The ring of machine knights closed in, immune to the punishment, protecting Sebba's possessed form from Zeno and the robot. Both machines were mere toys compared to the sentinels. Calder collapsed to the floor, half-blacking out, his retina flashing with a light display of pure torment that . . . was suddenly absent. *The floor feels different. Hard and metallic.* He glanced up. All the survivors lay sprawled across the bridge of the *Gravity Rose. No doubt about it.* Arched ribs across the ceiling and the illusion of exposed views of deep space between each metal curve: the silver spatter of stars; distant wisps of green nebulae and the angry red ball of a dying star.

Polter's chair twisted around, the navigator's crab-like shell trembling in surprise at the sudden appearance of the ground party and surviving base staff.

'What's the matter, Mister Polter?' said Lana, gagging as though she was about to vomit. She picked herself up from the deck. 'You never saw a millennia-old Heezy matter teleporter in action before?'

'Revered captain!'

Calder tried to recover his composure as quickly as the skipper. *Before I show myself up.* It appeared as if Sebba might have had more humanity left in her than she had admitted to. Calder's body still tingled with an acid burning sensation, as if every molecule of him had been ripped off and then glued back inside again. *Maybe it has.* As far as transport mechanisms went, entanglement-assisted instantaneous transmission through N dimensional Hilbert space . . . aka teleportation . . . rivalled passing through solid rock for comfort. Frankly, it sucks.

'Sit-rep, Mister Polter,' demanded Lana, her command chair falling down towards her before she took the seat. 'Skrat, Zeno, positions. Calder, herd that cargo off my damn bridge, then mount up . . . engineering station.'

'The *Rose* is currently breaking selenocentric orbit. There's a pirate fleet inbound at high C.,' warbled the navigator. 'Two carrier-class vessels, six frigates and a missile ship. They have already launched fighters towards Abracadabra. The pirates are seeking to swarm us, interdict our jump points. Our clearest exit boost position will carry us close to the sun, which appears to be undergoing a runaway nuclear fusion event. I feared that the creator had turned his eyes away from us . . . that we were to either to die inside a supernova shockwave or at the hands of the Invisible Port's guns. But your return here! A miracle. Surely we must survive now?'

'If we do, it won't be because of God,' said Lana. 'Not unless you've got a temple for seat-of-the-pants piloting.'

Cargo off the bridge. Calder finally found an order he could obey, ushering the base's startled survivors into the care of a crowd of drones summoned by Zeno. He watched Momoko stomp away down the passage outside, holding tightly onto Lento. Momoko acted as if being inside a starship was commonplace, while Lento glanced nervously about as though she'd never seen one before. The robot wasn't the only one bluffing it. He turned back. *Bridge position, this is what you've being working for, Calder my lad. As far as initiations to the ship's command centre go, I might have hoped for a gentler introduction.*

He found Zeno sitting in one of the chairs, an array of hologram iconography swimming around him. 'Missiles down and running hot towards us, forward of their fighter wings. They must be pretty irked about losing the *Doubtful Quasar*. They're not even trying to take us intact.'

'The *Rose* would never make a good prize vessel anyway,' said Lana. She turned to Calder. 'Raise the drive room and tell the chief to prep jump vanes for a barycentre jump.'

Calder gazed across at the skipper as if she had lost her mind. Planning to enter hyperspace this deep inside a system, midway between Abracadabra and its dying sun — otherwise known as the system's barycentric gravity point? *What the hell could go wrong with that?* 'You're not even attempting to clear the sun's gravity field?'

'Read that incoming battle group's telemetry, your highness, and crunch the numbers. We're going to be chased down long before we get close to any real exit point. We're either jumping heavy or leaving the system as shot-up hull debris riding a supernova shockwave.'

'Please, revered captain,' protested Polter, 'the chances of a stable hyperspace translation in this system's barycentre point—'

'—are way better than shooting it out with a couple of millions tonnes of fleet-strength military surplus bearing down on us. Lay course for the barycentre and prep for a damn hyperspace transition.'

'Jump or die,' muttered Zeno.

Lana nodded. *She really is made of steel. Out of the mess on the world below and into one up here with hardly a blink.* A woman truly worthy of a prince. But how about an exiled one on his downers? *Sadly, not so much,* Calder suspected.

'Damn straight, tin man,' said Lana.

Calder mounted his seat, its nanotech surface automatically flowing around him. The pressure of additional field protection against high acceleration squeezed his body. Projection stalks flowered in front of his head, almost too much information to process lasered directly onto his retina. Normally the engineering position would be vacant, relying on Chief Paopao and his robots – and more lately, Calder as well – to do what needed doing without additional fine-tuning from the bridge. It was a measure of their situation's desperation that Calder was being drafted into action up here. *This isn't any promotion, you can't fool yourself on that score.* There was a good reason you didn't create a wormhole anywhere close to a system's gravity well. It was hard enough to create a stable singularity to transit to hyperspace at the best of times. Producing a singularity with the added interference of a system's worth of fluctuating gravitational mass and hoping to slide void through said wormhole would be like trying to ski jump a glacier in the middle of an earthquake while a hostile artillery battery rained shells down on you. It was close to suicide. *And by being granted the engineering position, I'm ordered to measure the dose of poison and make sure we only die a little.*

'Launching the singularity seed now,' said Lana. 'Patching its trajectory through to you, Mister Durk. Let's kick that can down the road all the way to jump.'

'It'll be easier if we keep the seeding sphere stationery,' said Calder. 'You know, like we normally do.'

'Sure,' said Lana. 'I'll just establish comms with the Pirate King and ask Barcellos if his battle group doesn't mind giving us a sporting head start. And while we're about it, maybe you could radio what's left of the professor back on Abracadabra and get her to postpone re-booting the sun for a couple of days. Or,' she shot him a withering glance, 'you can deploy jump vanes and set singularity formation for a moving target with a completely predictable course.'

Calder fired up the vanes, tracking the little iron sphere launched ahead of them like a torpedo. He began gravity compression; the sphere's mass exponentially increasing with every second. Calder ignored the torrent of abuse being sent intraship from the drive room at the back of the *Rose*. Chief Paopao kept a running commentary, stream-of-consciousness style, about how skegged-up attempting an in-system jump was, and their anaemically slim chances of survival from here on in. Calder hardly noticed. The interference from the system mass was making it close to impossible to create a stable singularity . . . like fighting to keep an umbrella upright in the middle of a tornado. He felt the buffeting ease slightly as Granny Rose, the ship's A.I., took up the slack alongside him, working the celestial mechanics of the system mass into the singularity formation in real-time − yet another moving target, thanks to the local star vomiting nuclear mass like a tantrum-prone baby swinging toys out of its cot.

'Sub-munitions are splintering,' called Skrat. 'Multiple warheads tracking inbound.'

The steel deck trembled as the *Gravity Rose*'s point-defence guns laid down a steel wall of rail-gun pellets in front of the missiles, countermeasure decoys launching and arrowing towards the smart munitions, a slight jump from the display field on Calder's retina as their ECM grid started broadcasting. He could hear the rattle of hydraulic driven-magazines being emptied at twenty thousand rounds a minute even from the field-swaddled protection of his chair.

Skrat winked at Calder from his chair. 'No sense of tradition, eh? Whatever happened to a warning shot across the bows?'

Calder blinked as the view outside the ship momentarily blacked out, the glare of a prematurely detonating nuclear warhead dwindling as the vast external field of deep space flickered back into life across the bridge 'I think that was their warning shot.'

'All bogeys down,' called Zeno. 'Their own nuke vaporized most of the first broadside.'

'That's what you get from buying cheap missiles,' said Lana. 'They should demand refunds from whatever dirty skeggers are running ordinance to the Invisible Port these days.'

'I reckon that used to be us,' said Zeno.

'They may not need reimbursement,' squeaked Polter. 'By our blessed Lord on High, the sun is now undergoing a full gravitational collapse.'

'Frying tonight,' mumbled Zeno.

'Mister Durk,' hissed Lana. 'Singularity formation any time soon? Dumping that much solar mass into energy has got to help our exit numbers.'

Calder shook his head. 'The wormhole has almost formed, but nowhere close to clean. We're still too near to Abracadabra's gravity well. Our minimum jump window is twenty minutes away at best.'

Lana checked her instruments. 'And we're going to collide with the supernova's neutrino jet in seven minutes and cross its main kinetic energy wave a couple of minutes later.'

'Can our shields protect us until we jump?' asked Calder.

'Your highness, nobody has ever survived a supernova intact enough to report back either way. But frankly, I wouldn't go making any long-term plans.'

'On the positive side of the ledger, dear fellows,' announced Skrat. 'It appears as if the battle group has just found something to occupy itself with a tad more important than their feelings of wounded pride concerning the loss of the *Doubtful Quasar*. I read every vessel now desperately boosting for an emergency system exit. All we have to deal with are a few spiteful pilots in the fleet's fighter wing, who appear to have been rather abandoned by the two carriers.'

'I hope they all burn,' snarled Lana. 'And I really wish that scumbag Dollar-sign Dillard was in-system to enjoy the payback on his investment. Does that sound vindictive?'

'Yes,' said Calder. *But I forgive you.*

'Blessed Creator, shield us in your mercy,' whistled Polter.

'Yeah, I'll take some of that.' Lana swivelled in her chair. 'Polter, pre-set an automated jump with Granny and leave it counting down, in case the bridge is out of action when we have a stable wormhole.'

Out of action, that's an understatement. Calder imagined the ship passing into hyperspace as a half-molten ruin, crew and passengers dead – and that was if their A.I. could handle navigating a jump, which she usually couldn't. Wasn't that how the *Gravity Rose* was found when Lana had inherited her the first time around? *Floating dead in space.* Maybe history really did repeat itself. Calder just wished history had left a certain exiled prince off this particular merry-go-round. He hadn't even had a

VOID ALL THE WAY DOWN

chance to convince Lana Fiveworlds how she should feel about him. *This really isn't fair.* On any of them. But most of all, *him.*

'Incoming transmission from the fighter wing,' said Zeno. 'The squadron's twigged we're attempting a barycentre jump and are ordering us to park them in the *Rose*'s shuttle deck or they'll take us apart.'

'If we're going to take a supernova suntan, I'm damned if I'll burn with an armed company of the Invisible Port's killers on board plotting to seize my ship,' snarled Lana. 'Tell them to boost for what's left of the sun and pray there's a black hole with a clean jump singularity forming inside it when they arrive.'

Predictably, it didn't take long for the abandoned pirate fighters to make good on their threat, swooping in, seeming oblivious to the fact that they were about to try to destroy their last chance of jumping out of the system. *Looks like if they can't hitch a ride, they're going to make sure nobody else is getting out alive'.*

'Those mopes are packing torpedoes!' called Zeno. 'I'm detecting nuclear warheads – x-ray laser nukes.' Calder felt a shiver go down his spine. *As if there's not going to be enough radiation with an exploding star up our aft.* There was only one use for such ordinance, overwhelming a ship's shields and killing her crew in a deadly radiation flash.

'Blasted fools,' said Skrat. 'That supernova's going to detonate their missiles whether they launch them or not.'

'We're within the warhead's blast radius,' warned Zeno. 'Proto-wave from the supernova is incoming.'

'Keep our vanes turning,' Lana shouted at the prince, half-ordering, half-pleading. 'Set us up for a clean dive.'

Whether we have one or not. Calder tried to keep his eyes fixed on the formation of the artificial black hole they needed to use to rend space-time, slipping the *Gravity Rose* through the tear. Keep his eyes on that rather than the supernova's incoming front. The mass fluctuations went off the scale across his instruments, the ship's A.I struggling vainly to model the dying star's interactions with his emergent black hole. *Something about those numbers really doesn't make sense, but what is it?* His head throbbed as though his skull was being drilled sans anaesthetic, as it always did when he tried to access neural connections that had been made under sim. *Even the future's artificial knowledge comes with a price, it seems.*

Calder's flagging concentration was shattered by Lana's yell. 'Brace for impact!'

The projection of the stars clouded over as the hull turned opaque, protecting against the fierce detonation of the fighters' payload. The *Gravity Rose*'s shields flared up to full strength as she rocked in the early slurry of the dying sun, a mad swaying that only grew worse when the wavefront strengthened. Calder's seat went into armour mode around him, instruments dying; not that he was able to concentrate on the controls and screaming alarms, his retina flooded with a web of burning scratches, exotic particles treating his skull to its own private firework display. The prince felt as though a giant troll had picked him up and was slamming him from side to side across the bridge, the very air burning. A beating that went on for minutes before suddenly subsiding. *If that's merely the proto-wave, I'd hate to be around when the full surge of the dead star smashes into us.* Calder moaned inside his seat. A medical unit appeared from inside the chair, latching onto the skin of his bruised, burning ribs, pumping him full of drugs and miniature nanomechanical healers. Their ship's sensors were burned out, Calder's console blank apart from damage report after damage report, the ship's hull trying to seal herself across multiple impact points. *How in the universe did we survive this?* Calder had been in *Hell Fleet* sims – supposedly accurate down to the last rivet – where capital ships with shield generators larger than the *Gravity Rose* had taken less punishment and still been left dead in space. *We've lost all incoming sensor information. We're flying blind.* But there was something Calder thought he had seen in the sensor readings before the ferocious detonation off the ship. And he had a hunch about it what it might mean. The professor's final possessed words inside the machine cavern came back to him. *This must be preserved.*

'Main surge from the supernova on its way,' said Zeno. 'We'll be riding the solar swell any second.'

'We can dive for hyperspace now,' coughed Calder.

'We're still three minutes away from anything other than immediate disintegration if we dive, revered captain!' said Polter. 'Please, don't do it! We'll be crushed attempting to translate.'

'Do it!' said Calder through shaking teeth. He was buffeted so fiercely by early plasma from the second shockwave that his seat's fields could hardly compensate for the violence. *What's that doing to our hull integrity?* 'We're not going to survive another minute, let alone three.'

'Do you know how many jumps Polter has transited, new boy?' Lana shouted over the roar of crackling shields. 'And how many he's been wrong about? He's the best damn navigator in the Edge.'

'For the love of the gods, Lana Fiveworlds, if you're ever going to trust me, trust me now and dive for that singularity.'

'May the Creator shelter us!' wailed Polter. 'This heathen polytheist counts beyond a single digit for the number of true deities in the universe, and he asks me to trust his grasp of jump mechanics?'

By way of the skipper's answer, Calder felt the deck lurch out from under him, taking his stomach with it, as though he was hurtling down a well clutching a one-way ticket to a very dark place. He managed to squeeze out a second or two's elation at Lana's decision to go for the dive and then the translation process kicked in. Calder tried hard not to throw up as his body's matter was torn apart and rebuilt in anticipation of an exotic new reality. *Hyperspace.* He prayed his hunch proved correct, or this would be a real short process, smeared across the singularity in his eagerness to put the raging system behind them.

Minutes later, his hunch was born out. *Still alive!* Calder could tell he was becoming a practiced spacer – this time he hadn't even needed a sick bag. *That's progress.* Calder met the expectant eyes of the rest of the bridge crew, no doubt wondering why they weren't dead. 'Abracadabra vanished behind us. That's the only way those last sensor readings made any sense . . . to survive the supernova the whole world teleported out of the system. This must be preserved.'

Zeno hit his forehead with his palm. 'Along with the gravity well disrupting our dive!'

'No sun left, no world left,' said Lana, in amazement. 'With an exit mass that light a cadet could have jumped us out of there.'

'A cadet did not,' said Polter, annoyed, drumming his claws against his carapace. 'I did.'

'With your usual level of artisanship, Polter,' said Lana, but she looked in the prince's direction and silently mouthed a *thank you*. To Calder, that felt a lot like progress, too.

- 25 -
Of epilogues.

Lana Fiveworlds glanced up from her cabin's desk. A second knock on her door. She half-expected Calder to step through, but it turned out to be Skrat instead. A small part of her felt disappointed. The last time the new boy had stepped over her threshold after making a suggestion that had saved the ship, he had claimed his reward by launching a surprise swoop on Lana's lips. *Skrat has many fine qualities, but kissing isn't one of them.* At least, she hoped not. Lana suspended the star map's display, running across her desk's surface like a river of stars. She trusted her first mate wasn't coming to complain about the non-paying passengers getting drunk in their cabins and trying to smash the ship up again. *The sooner those miners are dumped on the next inhabited system we jump into, the better.* 'Mister raz Skeratt. Are you looking to suggest a port with a good shipyard and a half-decent chance to make up for losing Dollar-sign's contract?'

'Not a bit of it, dear girl. I have been perusing our log entries for what happened back on Abracadabra, skipper, including the recording of events taken by Zeno's eye cameras.'

'And why the skeg would you do that? You planning on making a sim of that snarl-up on Abracadabra? Dumping the movie in the data sphere on the next civilized world? Knowing my luck, we'll go viral and Fiveworlds Shipping's name will end up as a joke across half the galaxy.' Zeno had given up his acting career centuries ago. *I don't think he'd enjoy being famous again.*

'Let's just say events on the surface – or rather, below it – made me more than a little curious, dear lady. As part of said perusing, I checked up on Calder's bio-profile in the medical bay. I accessed data from the nano-surgeons injected into him during our recent contretemps. What I found confirmed my suspicions. Calder's junk DNA has been encoded with an at-first seemingly random pattern that's more than a tad unusual compared to say, yours, or any other base human genome for that matter.'

'What are you telling me?' asked Lana, confused.

'You'll recall the professor mentioned the original Alliance science team mutinied and deleted the Heezy genetic control codes after they witnessed their research being misused during the war,' said Skrat. 'That wasn't quite accurate. They didn't delete their research. Destroying knowledge is a little more than most scientists can cope with . . . instead, they hid it. They stored it as series of genetically re-sequenced codes inside their junk DNA. And the team vanished in the same year that Calder's world, Hesperus, was first opened up for colonization. An ideal out-of-the-way backwater to lay low on. A tad too effective a refuge in retrospect, given how the settlers on Hesperus were abandoned to their fate when the world's ice age started.'

'It can't be!' Calder couldn't be . . .?

'Unlike you, I never hacked the Heezy transportation system or their curious corridor-on-demand system,' said Skrat. 'They simply worked for us – or rather, the systems only activated for us because we were travelling alongside Calder. I believe a Heezy sentinel kidnapped Calder and dragged him through the base's laser fence unharmed. But the sentinel didn't kill Calder in the jungle, or later in the hunting lodge, or even when we uncovered the wreck of the *Never Come Down* . . . why do you think that is? I watched the recording of what the Heezy defences did to the pirates inside the camp – it certainly wasn't because the sentinels weren't up to the task. No. As far as the Heezy ruins were concerned, Calder Durk was one of the ancient masters returned. The ruins were curious about Calder. That's why it took him. It wanted to see where precisely in their ecosystem our new boy fitted.'

Lana remembered the circle of sentinels closing in on the survivors inside the cavern and then halting. *I thought they were bowing to Professor Sebba's possessed form . . . could it have actually been Calder they recognized?* What if the machines hadn't stayed their murderous assault due to whatever residual humanity was left inside Sebba. What if the only reason Lana and the rest of the crew had been teleported inside the *Gravity Rose* was to maximize Calder's chance of survival? *It must be preserved.* Sebba wasn't just talking about Abracadabra, it seems.

Skrat swished his tail thoughtfully. 'So, this rather begs the question, what do we tell our Mister Durk of what we've uncovered?'

'Absolutely nothing. The fewer people that know about this, the better,' insisted Lana. 'The Triple Alliance, the Skein, there isn't a superpower in the galaxy that wouldn't chase us to the ends of the universe to get their hands on Calder. Imagine! A key for every Heezy artefact they've collected and haven't got a hope in hell of understanding for the next few millennia. What a mind-skeg. The best Calder could hope for is having his DNA scanned before being locked in a very deep, very secure pit for the rest of his life.' She didn't want to say that the more likely option was a trip to a cellular-level incinerator via a very hard, cold dissection table.

'From what I understand, he's the last of his family line,' said Skrat. 'Hesperus's ice age was savage . . . it claimed millions of lives among the original settler group after the civilization there collapsed. Mister Durk may well be the only surviving descendant of the original science team that worked on Pluto. He's quite possibly unique.'

'We're all unique, Skrat.'

'That's as maybe, but nobody's willing to kill for my blasted DNA. There's something else,' said Skrat. 'I think Zeno might suspect something of Calder's true nature. He was plugged into the Heezy control board in the cavern, seeing whatever Sebba was seeing. The professor was about to tell you about something she had noticed, something "impossible", but Zeno interrupted her before she could finish speaking. What if the good professor had detected the presence of a living Heezy genetic control set interacting with the cavern's machines?'

'But Zeno has said nothing to me about Calder?'

'Maybe he's considering selling Calder to the highest bidder? The dear boy is utterly priceless, you know. What I discovered hidden in his DNA is enough to give even an honourable chap of my calibre pause to think. I could purchase back my lost position in the nest. Good heavens, I could buy enough voting shares to anoint myself president of the whole blasted skirl home world!'

'Zeno wouldn't do that,' protested Lana. *He's been with me from the start. Before I inherited the Gravity Rose, even.* 'There has to be an alternative explanation . . . just coincidence when he spoke up, most like.'

'Your people place too much faith in your AIs,' said Skrat. 'It's not a mistake you will find many skirls making. We prefer our machines dull, obedient and with nary a trace of sarcasm nor any talent for answering back.'

'When I came out of a cold sleep capsule as a vegetable, it was Zeno who nursed me back to health. I was nothing more than a penniless amnesiac refugee,' said Lana. 'One among thousands. He's been with me from the beginning. Zeno's never betrayed me yet and I can't believe he ever would.'

'The android's survived for over a thousand years – who knows what odd perspective his mind's developed across the centuries. To him, we're little more than mayflies flickering out in the dark. A brief dance and . . . gone. Keep both your eyes and mind open to unpleasant possibilities, captain,' advised Skrat. 'That's all I'm suggesting.'

Unpleasant possibilities? After this Dollar-sign debacle, I'll need to find something a little more profitable than that to haul across the galaxy. And the irony was, in their latest crewman they had their very own dreams-beyond-avarice-fortune walking around on two legs. Lana snorted and her eyes drifted down to the star charts on her screen. Somewhere in the Edge was a job that paid well and wouldn't leave the *Gravity Rose* with hull damage. *Somewhere out there.*

Skrat made for the door of her quarters. 'Maybe you should consider auctioning off young Mister Durk, captain. We could all depart the next port as T-dollar trillionaires.'

'What, and live it large like a damn episode of *Lives of the Planet Kings*? I have something that most trillionaires will never have,' said Lana.

Skrat flicked his tail curiously. 'And that would be?'

Lana reached out and tapped the hull of her ship. '*Enough.*'

FIN

17108689R00234

Printed in Great Britain
by Amazon